MINDSURGE

HEATHER SUNSERI

Sun Publishing
VERSAILLES, KENTUCKY

Heather Sunseri/Sun Publishing
PO Box 1264
Versailles, Kentucky 40383
www.heathersunseri.com

Book Layout ©2014 BookDesignTemplates.com
Cover design by Heather Plunkett
Edited by David Gatewood

Ordering Information:
Quantity sales. Special discounts are available on quantity purchases by corporations, associations, and others. For details, contact the "Special Sales Department" at the address above.

MINDSURGE/ Heather Sunseri. -- 1st ed.
ISBN 978-0-9887153-7-0

To Maggie and Robert:
Together you remind me of what matters in this world. You are the best of what God created through me. You make me proud every single day with your amazing accomplishments and with the caring and thoughtful way you approach life. I couldn't love you more.

ONE

Two weeks, two days.

A whopping sixteen days of normalcy before that raging psycho Sandra wedged herself back into my life. I stared at her note in disbelief.

"Hi." Jack touched a finger to my chin. I hadn't even heard him approach.

I quickly folded the note and tucked it into the small back pocket of my running shorts, along with the thumb drive that had accompanied it. When my eyes met the blue of Jack's, I managed a smile that I knew couldn't hide my worry.

Jack quirked a brow and leaned his head to the side as if to see whatever it was I hid. "What was that?"

We stood in the middle of Wellington's campus post office, in the student center. My evil DNA donor had actually used snail mail to send me a package.

"Oh... just some files I needed for an English Lit project."

"They were mailed to you?" Then he shrugged it off and gave his head a little shake. "Never mind, it doesn't matter. I'm just glad you texted me."

I had invited him on a jog as a sort of peace offering, after barely speaking to him the past two weeks—since the day he'd led me into a trap and forced me to face the one person who had deceived me more than any other—my mom, Alyson Roslin.

"Are we running or not?" I swallowed hard. The thumb drive felt heavy in my pocket, throwing me off balance.

As we left the post office, Jonas nodded at us from a table just inside the coffee shop across the way. His dark hair lay haphazardly across his forehead. His slightly cocked head and smart-aleck smirk told me he hadn't missed what had just happened.

Jack saw him, too, but only lifted his head in acknowledgement, then reached down and laced his fingers with mine. "Where do you want to jog?"

"In the woods behind the stable, I guess?" The warmth of his hand threatened to burn through my skin at the same time that Sandra's words chilled my very core. I pulled my fingers from his, then attempted to play it off by stretching my arms and shoulders out.

His side-glance told me I hadn't succeeded.

Ten minutes later, I was sprinting through the woods behind Wellington Boarding School, leaping over tree roots and dodging low-hanging branches. The fall breeze smelled of apples and of the horses living nearby. Cool air hit the back of my throat while the contrasting heat of the sun occasionally broke through the changing leaves to warm my face. The filtered light played with my vision, making it difficult to keep steady footing as I sped up.

Jack was behind me somewhere. He had let me run ahead. I knew this because he could run twice as fast as me on any given day. But I was determined. Determined to outrun Sandra's ongoing mischief, and determined to outrun the emotions my mother's reappearance had stirred.

As I ran, I thought back to my recent encounter with her. I still remembered the feel of the wood on my knuckles as I knocked on the door to the safe house—a house I had known as a very young child, but had few memories of. I knew that Dad still owned the house before he died, but I had refused to visit for fear that the longing for a life and a mother I never got to know would surface and burn—the way my father's and my best friend's deaths now simmered in my heart.

My mom smiled when she saw me. I did not.

She opened the door wider, inviting me in. I recognized her from the many pictures I had seen over the years. Her blond hair was styled differently, short and just above her shoulders, and her eyes showed a few additional years in the creases, but she was still the attractive woman I'd longed for ever since I was old enough to understand she was missing.

Jack's hand had pressed into the small of my back, encouraging me to enter, but my feet were cemented to the brick porch, my eyes glued to my mother's.

"Why are you here?" My voice was a choked whisper. Before coming here, I had assumed the house would be home to nothing but old furniture covered in white sheets, brass light fixtures draped in cobwebs. But as we'd driven up the drive, I'd somehow known—but didn't believe—whom I would find inside.

I continued. "I thought you were dead."

More like hoped. The only thought that had gotten me through years and years of missing a mother I never knew was the assumption that she had died—that she couldn't get back to her one and only daughter. Finding out that she *chose* not to be a part of my life... it just made me resent her even more.

"I'm here to help you," she said.

"Help?" A laugh escaped my throat in a hysterical sound that was foreign to me. "I don't want or need your help."

"Lexi," Jack said, a warning in his voice. "Don't you want to hear what she has to say?"

I turned on him so fast that he dropped his hand and backed up a step. "No, Jack, I don't." I stepped past him, knocking him with my shoulder. At the motorcycle, I pushed the helmet back on my head, climbed on, and waited.

It didn't take Jack long to admit defeat. From the corner of my eye, I saw him offer some sort of apology, which only added more ice to the blood running through my veins.

And that was that; we left. Five words from my mother, and it was already too much.

Now, barely two weeks later, I was still angry with Jack for keeping my mother's reappearance a secret, but I owed him the chance to explain and apologize.

And I missed him.

Besides, most of my anger wasn't directed toward Jack. No, it was Alyson—the mother who'd stripped me of the opportunity to live any semblance of the normal life I had craved for so long—who'd earned the brunt of my fury.

Of course, nothing went according to plan these days.

It had been sixteen days since Sandra Whitmeyer murdered my best friend, Danielle Gray. And as if mourning the death of my father and now my best friend wasn't enough, I now had to deal with these packages from Sandra, taunting me with evidence of who killed my father.

I ran harder. I was almost to the edge of the woods, a hundred yards from Wellington's horse stable. I couldn't keep up this pace forever. I couldn't keep running, dodging obstacles, both on the trail and in my heart.

As soon as that thought entered my mind, my foot hit a small dip in the path, and my knee buckled. Pain shot through my leg as the world around me tilted off kilter. Unable to stop my forward momentum, I hit the ground with a thud and a grunt. My leg and right arm broke my fall, but not without significant pain.

Rolling over, gasping for breath, and attempting to recover before Jack reached me, I discovered blood dripping from my elbow, through dirt that caked the skin.

I heard his footsteps before I saw his face. He stopped, towering over me. Not an ounce of humor showed in the hard line of his jaw or in his eyes. "Are you okay?" His voice was uneven as he tried to slow his breathing.

Did I *look* okay? I pushed myself to my feet, wincing from the pain in my knee. "I'm fine." I tried to brush some of the dirt off my leg, only to discover more blood from another scrape there. Jack just stood, staring, as if wondering whether he should help me or not.

I turned and walked slowly in the direction of campus, trying with everything in me to hide my limp.

Dried leaves crunched beneath his feet as he followed closely. He reached out and wrapped his fingers around my uninjured arm. "Just stop, all right?"

I stared down at his hand, and as I did, he loosened his grip, but didn't break contact. It was the third time he had touched me—that I'd *allowed* him to touch me—in two weeks. I savored every touch, because, based on Sandra's message, I never knew when one touch might be the last.

"I thought we were finally getting somewhere when you asked me to run with you today. But you won't even look at me." He glanced behind him. "And what was that? You were running like a maniac. That wasn't a friendly workout."

I studied his eyes. There was no anger there, only concern. Sweat dripped from his earlobe. His long-sleeved shirt was soaked and clinging to his body. I placed my unharmed hand on my hip, letting my fingers graze over the lump where the thumb drive was safely tucked into the pocket in my shorts.

"We *are* getting somewhere." It was a step forward, I argued inside my head. Could I make my anger be about my mother? Was that fair? He had known my mother was in town, but kept it from me. He'd said nothing when he found me inside The Farm on the University of Kentucky's campus. He'd said nothing after we'd fled the burning lab. And he'd said nothing for two days after that. He'd said nothing, and I'd had to discover my mother with my own eyes.

But that wasn't what this was about.

Now, I was the hypocrite. I had received a package—a lone thumb drive—and a message from Sandra, and I couldn't tell Jack. The message from Sandra, a handwritten note, still echoed in my head:

Sarah, On this thumb drive is the evidence you need to prove John DeWeese murdered your father. Only Jonas can give you the password to unlock the video. The password is tied to the gift you'll receive tonight. Just in time for your special day. ~S

P.S. I wouldn't show Jack. I don't imagine he would take the news that his father killed your dad very well. And, to be honest, I don't like you hanging around Jack. Break up with him. Or the next gift I send will be aimed at Jack.

I could easily imagine the evil smile that came with this note. My "special day." Somehow that monster knew it was my birthday. Not even Jack realized that today was my birthday.

"How many times do I have to apologize?"

Jack's voice brought me back to the present. He released my arm and, leaning his head into his shoulder, wiped dripping sweat from his brow. The hurt in his eyes made my heart constrict. I blamed and hated Sandra for always inserting herself into our lives. I decided that I wouldn't hurt Jack with Sandra's note until I confirmed that whatever "evidence" she sent me on the thumb drive was real.

When I didn't respond, Jack asked again, "How many times, Lexi?"

"You don't," I whispered. My heart ached at the thought that I would hurt him further.

"What? I didn't hear you. Because it sounded like you said I don't have to apologize again."

"You don't." I risked another look at him. I had to find a way to be with him and hide this new information at the same time. But could I? "*I'm* the one that's sorry. I'm just worked up about this party tonight." And about whatever was on this thumb drive that I couldn't access without Jonas. And the bonus gift Sandra promised to send later.

Jack sucked in a deep breath, then let it out slowly. Then another, as if he was ordering himself to calm. "Are we still going to the party together?"

I cocked my head. "I assumed so."

"Well, I hadn't. You've barely spoken to me the past two weeks, and you still refuse to discuss what's at the heart of our feud." He touched a cool finger to my chin and lifted. "Are you not even going to mention your moth—"

I held up a hand to stop him. "Don't. Can we just go to this party and not discuss my mother?" She was becoming the least of my concerns.

"I thought that was what this run was about." He raised his hands to the side in frustration before he dropped them, and his face softened. His eyes narrowed in on mine. The warmth behind them about did me in. "I'm on your side. I'm always on your side. You know this."

I averted my eyes and watched some squirrels playing in the fallen leaves behind Jack. How could I look at him, knowing that I was now the one not being honest? That I could very well be the one who would hurt *him*? This run was supposed to have been about forgiving him.

I squeezed my eyes tight, pushing back the pain of tears that I knew wouldn't come. Sandra would pay for what she'd done to us—for constantly screwing up our lives, for Dani's death, for my dad's death. Even if her gift proved she wasn't directly responsible, I couldn't accept that she wasn't involved at all. One way or another, I would repay her.

And I couldn't forget that I'd watched her kill Dani with my own eyes. All the evidence in the world wouldn't change that.

"I know. I'm trying."

"We'll keep trying together."

I nodded—though I didn't believe we'd get that chance—then turned my arm to see the thick and now dried blood on my elbow. "I guess I better get myself cleaned up."

Jack stepped in close to me. He lifted my wrist and studied my arm. "I can fix this. And your knee."

"I know you can, but I'm still not convinced we should be using these powers that came from such evil." It felt wrong to let him heal me when I could feel myself throwing up barricades to distance us. "Besides, I'm pretty sure I can suffer through a couple of scrapes."

"It's me, Lexi. You don't have to be tough with me." Jack's thumb rubbed against my forearm. His touch was warm and addictive. "Just because our abilities rose out of Sandra's evil intentions, we can still find ways to use them for good. And I think keeping you from bleeding all over your dress or from limping in high heels on our date tonight qualifies as a good deed for the day."

"I don't want you to be sick for the party," I said. "Briana would never let me hear the end of it if I was the reason any one of us didn't show up. And on time."

Jack shook his head. "I don't think these small injuries will make me sick. Nothing's broken or dislocated. Besides, I'm getting better at controlling the nausea."

It was true. I was making a lot of headway with the nosebleeds, too. Many of us had been working hard to improve how we used our minds while minimizing the side effects. Jonas had been working with me daily. I mindspoke to a teacher earlier in the week—when I'd failed to turn in some homework—and my upper lip had remained one-hundred-percent dry. Sandra had fooled us into thinking we needed *her* to cure our side effects. But we were starting to discover that our own minds held the keys to controlling the repercussions of using our abilities.

"Are you sure?" I glanced down at my swollen knee.

"Just a strained ligament." He had already examined my injuries.

Jack brushed loose hair off of my face. "Let me do this for you. I want tonight to be good for us, and I can't have my girlfriend limping around with an open wound on her arm."

Girlfriend. I still wanted that title.

Finally, I nodded.

TWO

Holding my masquerade mask to my face with one hand, while clenching the other into a fist, I backed up against the far wall. As I scanned the room for Jack, I saw her again—a girl with a certain familiarity, dressed in black from head to toe. Her hair was pulled away from her face, and strands of brunette with streaks of cherry hung over her shoulders and down to her chest. Her skin was pale, her lips were blood red, and an intricate lace formed a mask that covered her eyes and nose.

The ballroom had been transformed. Layers of dark fabric had been draped across the ceiling to a point in the center where a chandelier hung, dimmed to romantic perfection. Twinkle lights were strung around the outer perimeters, providing enough light to make out most faces, but dark enough for me—dressed in black and deep green—to fade into the background.

Briana had been instrumental in planning the Halloween gala, including the decorations and the music. She even took it upon herself to pick out the gown and mask I wore. She wasn't convinced I'd show up if she didn't plan my ensemble. I wasn't either.

I was dressed chest to ankles in black silk. Emerald-green rhinestones and black lace accented the strapless bodice, showing a little more skin than I would have liked. Feathers and the same emerald stones and lace decorated my hand-held mask and the wristlet that hung on my gloved arm.

Students danced. Some hung out by the punch. By the looks on some of the lowerclassmen's faces, the punch was spiked. Not surprising, since many of the adults had been so preoccupied as of late.

I continued to scan the crowd as I skirted the outer edge of the party, holding my mask to my face. I spotted Briana over by the band. Though the room was rather dark, it was easy to make out Briana, dressed in cardinal red. Feathers adorned the bodice of both her dress and her mask, which was also red—a bold statement for someone with hair the color of shimmering copper.

To her right and by the windows were Georgia, Fred, Lin, and Dia. Seth had talked each of them into attending Wellington's Halloween masquerade in the hope that they would reconsider enrolling at the school. But at the moment, they didn't appear happy to be there.

Georgia stood with her arms crossed like a protective shield. Instead of wearing a mask, paint decorated her cheeks and swirled around her eyes in shades of white and canary yellow, a stark contrast to her dark skin. Her eyes were accented with gold metallic shadow so thick that I could see it from across the ballroom.

Dia had straightened her red hair—setting her apart from her twin clone, Briana—and was dressed in a tightly fitted, silver dress. Both Fred and Lin wore simple tuxes, but in true Fred fashion, his bow tie and accessories matched Georgia's canary yellow, as did his gold, shimmery eyes.

Lin angled toward Dia. He leaned in and whispered something in her ear. He looked so much like Jack that my heart suddenly felt too big for my chest as I watched the intimacy between them. Dia nodded as he kissed her temple.

I gave my head a little shake. I had to focus on what was important. Dia and Lin were still recovering from what Sandra and Dr. John DeWeese did to them. And I planned to use their anger to learn more about Sandra's operation.

School would officially be different on Monday, and I needed as many of the clones as possible to stay at Wellington. Seth Whitmeyer, Sandra's brother, would be teaching the students here when he wasn't fulfilling his obligations as a neurologist at the University of Kentucky Hospital. He planned to help each of us come to terms with who and what we were, and he hoped to fill in many of the blanks we all had.

I was pretty certain I needed the other clones more than I needed Seth. Dia and Lin were sure to have knowledge Seth didn't possess. I had Dad's journals, which I hoped would clue us in to what he had discovered before he was killed. And every day I was more and more amazed at the amount of knowledge that Jonas and Jack had hidden from me. My objective, currently, was to discover where Sandra's operation was now located, and I would do whatever I had to do to find out where Sandra Whitmeyer and John DeWeese were hiding.

I craned my neck as I again spotted the familiar girl masked in lace. She glided through a crowd of dancers with grace and maturity, leading me to believe she was an upperclassman, yet I couldn't figure out who she was. Her short height made it difficult to keep her in my sight. I took a step forward, determined to identify her, when an arm circled my waist and pulled me backward.

"Why are you hiding back here?" Jonas's voice came out in a breathy whisper. The muscles in my waist and back tensed. He slithered in and around my mind.

"You can poke around inside my head all you want. You'll find nothing." I turned in his arms, attempting to wriggle from his hold, but he just gripped me tighter. "And I wasn't hiding, I was scoping out the party. People-watching." I shrugged, while glancing over my shoulder for the mystery girl.

Jonas loosened his grasp, but remained close, and to prove I wasn't affected by him, I didn't move. The band was loud, and he leaned into my ear to speak. "Okay, then. Tell me this. Why are you avoiding Jack?"

"Why do you care?" I wasn't avoiding Jack. I had called him to tell him I would meet him at the party. He hadn't answered.

Jonas pulled back and looked into my eyes, but kept his face close enough that I could feel the heat of his breath and smell spearmint. "Don't play games with me, Lexi. We've all been through too much for you to close up like this and shut everybody out."

"I'm not shutting—"

"Save it. Want to tell me about the package you got in the mail today?"

I stood straighter and took a step backward, fiddling with my gloves. "I don't know what you're talking about." I was planning to tell him before the night was out, but I was waiting to see what else Sandra threw at me first—what other "gift" she was sending.

I glanced across the room. As I did, I spotted Addison standing by herself and staring out the windows at something below.

Addison was one of our newest students. Like a sister to Jack and fresh out of a coma, Addison seemed to know more about her supernatural ability to disappear than any of the rest of us knew about our own powers.

"I saw you." He placed a hand on my shoulder and tugged, forcing me to look at him. "You opened a large envelope and pulled a small object and a note from it. I kept my promise not to invade your thoughts, but I sensed every one of your emotions while you processed what you read. And some of those thoughts were aimed at me. I felt fear; and an anger I hadn't seen from you since the day you came back from your hot date with Jack two weeks ago. You know, after seeing your mom."

I stared into his pleading brown eyes. There was an unmistakable attraction there. I shifted on my feet, but I didn't dare look away. "Your *mother* sent me a present—a thumb drive."

Jonas's jaw hardened and he rolled his shoulders. "What was on it?"

"I don't know." Not exactly, anyway. "Said you would know the password once I received the second part of my gift."

"What gift?" He made a quick scan of the room while unbuttoning the top button of his shirt. I'd hit a nerve.

"Don't know that either. Said I'd get it tonight."

"Why didn't you tell me sooner?"

"Because I didn't. Why does this make you jittery?"

Jonas's gaze narrowed as we continued our staring battle. He looked away first and released his hold on me. He rubbed both hands across his face. A low growl erupted from somewhere deep inside his chest. "You are so frustrating, you know that?"

"I do." But I didn't care.

"What do you think this 'gift' is?" Jonas seemed to accept my careless shrug that was anything but careless. "Then we'll just have to be patient. Something tells me Sandra won't make us wait long." He backed up slightly. "Where is Jack, anyway?"

"I haven't seen him." Though I was surprised he hadn't found me yet. A twinge of worry sparked in the pit of my stomach. After lifting my mask to my face again, I turned and stood beside Jonas so that I could watch the crowd. The loud, fast-paced music had slowed.

"Well, his loss. Let's dance." Jonas grabbed my free hand and pulled me toward the dance floor. With the slightest resistance from me, Jonas entered my head. *Please don't pull away.*

There's more, I said.

He stopped and faced me. I reached into my wristlet and pulled out the note from Sandra. After he read it, he raised his head, and for a minute, I thought I witnessed an ounce of sympathy in the way his cheeks fell. "What are you going to do?"

"I'm going to dance with you."

He led me into the middle of the crowd of slow dancers and spun me into him. His hand slid to the small of my back, burning through the thin fabric of my dress. I stared into his eyes through my Venetian mask. Reaching up, he took my hand that held the mask and guided it around his neck, then linked his fingers with my other hand.

"This doesn't feel very brother-sisterly." I tried to lighten the mood. Jonas had once tried to convince me that he would try to see me as a sister, seeing as he was born from Sandra's womb and I was born of Sandra's DNA.

Grinning, he leaned in, his mouth right next to my ear. "Like I've explained before, there isn't an ounce of relation in our genetic code, and I don't consider your witch of a DNA donor my mother. So we're safe."

We most definitely were *not* safe. "What about Jack? Your best friend." I countered. "And Briana? What's going on between the two of you?"

The muscles in his neck and shoulders tightened. He suddenly guided me in a twirl. When I came back to him, not even a molecule of air separated us. He didn't answer my questions, but I saw the regret in his hardened jaw.

There was no question that my relationship with Jonas had always had a strange edge. I wondered if we would have dated if I had met him first. A relationship between Jonas and me would have been riddled with epic fights, I had no doubt. And it would have ended soon after I'd met Jack.

And now, a woman filled with so much ugliness and hate, who had caused so much suffering to the people I loved, was threatening the bond between Jack and me. The hate in my heart for her was too much at times. Pushing back from Jonas, I reached my hand to massage the spot on my chest, willing the pressure on my heart to release.

Jonas cupped my cheek. "Hey... you okay?"

I managed a nod.

"I'm sorry I pushed. I go too far with you sometimes." He went too far *most* times. I didn't know if it had to do with Sandra's past manipulation—when Sandra controlled Jonas through the tracker at the base of his skull—or if it was simply Jonas's personality. "But maybe you should listen to Sandra and break up with Jack."

I stiffened in his arms.

"Just distance yourself from him until we know what she has planned. Or what's on the video. Do you think Jack's going to be excited that the man who raised him—with whom he shares identical DNA—was the one to murder your dad?"

A big part of me knew Jonas was right. But I couldn't hurt Jack. And until I knew what Sandra meant by her threat, I would continue to fear what she could do.

"Hi, Jonas, Lexi."

Jonas's head lifted slightly at the sound of Briana's voice behind me. He stared over my shoulder, and the taut muscles in his cheeks seemed to relax.

I turned. "Hi, Bree." Unlike mine, her mask was attached to her head with a satin ribbon, but there was no mistaking her red, wavy locks. "You've done an amazing job with the party," I told her. "And now, you should enjoy yourself. Here..." I pulled Jonas's hand forward and forced it to link with hers. "...dance with Jonas."

We aren't done here, Jonas mindspoke.

We never are.

Don't go far, he warned. *I've got a bad feeling about whatever it is Sandra's got planned.*

"Thanks, Lexi." Briana smiled, oblivious to our mental conversation. "Oh, and happy birthday."

My eyes widened, then darted to Jonas's. I had kept my birthday a secret, and Briana knew I didn't want others to know.

"It's your birthday?" *Why didn't you tell me?*

"It's just another day."

THREE

"What are you staring at?" I asked Addison as I approached her from behind. She wore a short sapphire dress with a glittery and sequined bodice and full mesh skirt. Her black hair hung in loose strands down her back. From behind, she looked like any other Wellington student, tall for her young age of eight. But when she twirled around in ballet flats and faced me, I was reminded by her youthful face that she wasn't even old enough to attend Wellington.

"Jack. He's in the courtyard."

"By himself?"

She shook her head, fear in her eyes. I took two hesitant steps closer to the window and peered down. Sure enough, Jack was there. With the same mysterious girl with scarlet lips and red-streaked hair that I saw earlier but didn't recognize.

They were standing close together; Jack's back was to me. Lace still covered half the girl's face. "Do you know who she is?"

"I've never met her."

"That's not what I asked." When Addison said nothing, I turned slowly to find her hands shaking, tears in her eyes. "Addi? What is it? Who is she?"

"Jack has been having me track your whereabouts lately. I'm sorry—it's just that he's been worried. Anyway, he asked me to find you about ten minutes ago. I told him you were walking toward the courtyard, coming from the dorms. And then I saw you dancing with Jonas."

"What are you saying?" I grabbed both of Addison's shoulders, the realization dawning on me. "Who is that down there with Jack?"

Her eyes looked frightened. "I thought it was you."

I released her. Stumbling back, I pressed a hand to my stomach, the taste of bile rising to my throat. "Me? Why would you think that was me?"

But I already knew the answer. This was my present from Sandra.

"I should have predicted this," I said. We'd already seen duplicates of Jack, Briana, and Jonas. Why not me? I turned back to the window, trying to get a better look at a second human clone of the infamous Sandra Whitmeyer.

A thousand thoughts ran through my head. Where had this girl been living? Did Jonas know she existed? Did Jack think he was staring at *me*?

I swallowed hard against the burning sensation at the back of my throat, then faced Addison again. "Tell no one. You hear me? Not even Jack. I will take care of this." If he didn't already know.

~~~~~

I nearly fell as I ran down the stairs and flew out the door. High heels were not my thing, but they went with the costume.

The temperature had fallen over the last hour. Cool air pinched my cheeks, and I could see my breath. Steam rose from the fountain I stumbled toward.
~~~~~

I slowed at the entrance to the courtyard and looked up at the windows where the Halloween party continued. Addison no longer stood there. The muffled sound of music drowned out all other sounds.

Jack was at the opposite side of the courtyard with his back to me. A large stone fountain separated us, and between the fountain and his tall frame, I was blocked from seeing the mystery clone in front of him.

One by one, I slipped my heels off and threw them into the dormant rose bushes to my right. I padded quietly across the brick sidewalk and ducked behind a line of tall boxwoods. I hoped the dark color of my gown and the barrier of the shrubs would hide me from Jack and my clone.

As I got closer, Jack's voice rose above the music of the dance.

"You've shut me out completely for two weeks. I thought we had finally gotten somewhere after our run today, but now you're back to avoiding me. Enough's enough, Lex."

My heart thudded in my chest. For a moment, I forgot it wasn't me he was speaking to. The clone was standing with her back to Jack. If she faced him, surely he would recognize her for the fraud she was. I directed a thought to only her. *Turn around. Face Jack.*

She did as I ordered. But when she did, a smile stretched across her face. A genuine smile. Anyone else looking at the two of them would think it was Jack and me, taking a romantic moment alone, away from the party. I had to stop this. My mind raced with how to confront this stranger.

"I'm sorry I've avoided you," she said. "You just made me so angry. But I'm ready to put it all behind us. Let's start over, okay?"

She sounded exactly like me. She *looked* exactly like me, except for the dark red streaks painted through her hair. Of course she did. I wanted to scream in frustration. Did Jack think I had just magically colored my hair in the three hours since he last saw me? I wanted to march over and jerk that lace mask off her face. Surely *something* was different about her. Jack knew me better than anyone. He would figure out that this fraud was just *pretending* to be me.

I tried to move, but couldn't. A part of me wanted to just storm forward and confront her, but another, calmer part of me realized that I needed to know more about this clone before exposing her. So I watched. I watched in horror as Jack moved closer to her—close enough to smell her scent. Didn't he know my scent?

"I would love that." He brushed his fingers along the side of her face; she leaned into his touch. "We can fix this," he said. "I know we can. I didn't keep your mom's reappearance a secret to hurt you. You know that now, right?"

The girl nodded. Jack stroked her cheek with his thumb. Was her skin the same texture as mine? I would know the feel of Jack's face with my eyes closed. The way his brows furrowed when I ran my fingers along his forehead. The way a dimple formed when he smiled, but only on the right side.

I focused hard on the girl's head, bringing the image of her brain before me. I could see that her brain was firing at a rapid pace, in small golden bursts, and most of the activity seemed to be originating from one place. I squinted my eyes, zooming in.

That's when I found it. This girl had a tracker.

I dropped the image and focused once again on the couple before me. Was this clone being controlled? Had she been sent to hurt Jack? My pulse was racing out of control.

Jack framed her face with both of his hands. He tilted his head and leaned in just slightly. He was going to kiss her. I had to do something.

Did he not know I would never wear that horrid shade of red lipstick?

Jonas! Go to the window overlooking the courtyard. Now!

I'm busy.

You're not too busy for this.

Fine. I'm at the win— Jonas stopped mid-word. *You called me to the window to watch Jack kiss you. That's low, even for you.*

I turned and looked up at the window. *That's not me, you idiot.*

Even my mindspeak came out through gritted teeth.

Jonas's eyes darted from Jack and the clone to where I stood behind a large bush, then back to the clone. *Who is that? Oh, my... Is that who I think it is?*

Bang on the windows. Get Jack to look up at you.

I stepped toward Jack and the clone—but it was too late. Jack leaned in and kissed her, and I hadn't done enough to stop it.

Their lips touched once, then two times. I could see him press harder, increasing the intensity of the kiss.

Jonas banged on the windows. Jack broke contact with the girl and looked up. The color of fresh blood was smeared across his lips.

I watched as realization dawned on him—probably with a few mindspoken words from Jonas. His smile faded, and his eyes darted around the courtyard.

I wanted to run, but I knew I couldn't. I had to face this clone and find out who she was, how she got the tracker. Would our troubles with rogue clones ever end?

At last I stepped out from behind the boxwoods and took a few steps toward the clone and Jack.

Jack saw me, then turned back to the clone. "Who are you?"

Instead of answering, she smiled. Not the sweet smile from earlier, but a knowing grin that screamed victory. She pushed past Jack and walked toward me, tugging on the lacy sleeves of her dress as she did so. The passionate kiss had dulled her lipstick a bit. When she reached me, she bowed her head, gathered a section of her dress, and curtsied. "Hello, Lexi. It's so nice to finally meet the princess of clones."

"You know who I am?" I already hated this girl.

"Of course I do. You're my long-lost sister clone. Sandra swears we'll get along famously, but I'm here to promise you... I have no intention of becoming your friend, let alone your sister."

"You have a tracker at the base of your skull. Who put that there?"

Her smile faltered. "How did you... Oh, right. You can see inside our brains."

"She has a tracker?" Jonas now stood behind me, and Briana hovered a short distance behind him. "Are you being controlled? Did someone lead you here?"

"Don't be so dramatic. No one forced me to come here. I volunteered. As far as who put the tracker inside my head...?" She turned to me. "You should ask your mother."

I gasped, and my spine tightened.

Jack reached out and grabbed the girl's arm. "Why are you here? And what the hell was that?"

She batted her eyes at him. "That... was 'Hello,'" she said in a low, sexy purr. Then with a wink, she patted his cheek. "Don't worry, sweetie. You'll be seeing a lot more of me. Now, if you'll excuse me." With another small curtsy, she turned and exited the courtyard.

A Lincoln Town Car I hadn't noticed before was at the turnabout waiting for her. We all watched wordlessly as a man opened the back door for her, she disappeared inside, and they drove off.

FOUR

We watched the Town Car drive toward the gated entrance of Wellington. By the time the brake lights faded and the car pulled away from the school, Jack, Jonas, Briana, and I were all facing my cloned twin's grand exit.

I stretched my fingers out straight before curling them into tight fists.

"Someone tell me what the hell just happened," Jack finally said.

I couldn't look at him. I squeezed my eyes shut. As I did, I was reminded of two things: Jack kissing another girl—my twin clone, a "gift" from Sandra—and the thumb drive that I'd received from Sandra earlier that day.

This had been Sandra letting me know that her note was no bluff.

"Apparently, there are two of each of us. Well... there *were* two of each of us." Jonas's voice was quiet. He stood right behind me.

My eyes snapped open, and I turned to face him. "Did you know about her? That clone of me?"

Jonas just stared at me, pinned by my glare.

"You *did* know." *This is what Sandra meant when she claimed you could give me the password. That clone was the second part of my gift.*

I knew a second clone of Sandra existed, Jonas mindspoke back, *but that doesn't mean I purposely hid her identity from you. You keep distancing yourself from everyone around you, Lexi. Keep picking fights. Eventually, you'll push us all away.*

Jonas turned to Bree as if his conversation with me was over. "Bree, how about we finish that dance?"

She nodded, and he reached out and grabbed her hand. But before they walked away, he looked at me again. The wide look in his eyes demanded my attention. "Just because we managed to run Sandra out of town doesn't mean she's gone from our lives," he said. "Obviously she's finding ways back in, and she's seeing to it that we're all at odds. This battle we're in isn't over, and we're all going to need each other."

Golden specks flickered like fire in the dark amber of his eyes. *If you need to break up with Jack, then do it. But stop pushing him and the rest of us away under the guise of mistrust. It's not us that you mistrust. We're just the ones within reach.* He and Bree walked off, hand in hand, back toward a party that was supposed to be a new beginning for all of us.

Jonas was right. I didn't want to push Jack away, but Sandra gave me no choice. She'd always get to us. And I knew she meant what she'd said.

Wait, Jonas. I need the password to the thumb drive.

I'll meet you later.

I practically growled when he brushed me off. Nothing was ever urgent with him. And he knew I wouldn't come after him right now, since Jack still didn't know the thumb drive existed, and I didn't want Jonas with me when I pulled up the files Sandra had sent. Sandra wouldn't have sent anything unless she had a plan to hurt one of us. And I wouldn't let Sandra hurt anyone else I loved.

"Why'd you do it?" Jack's voice was low, barely loud enough to be heard above the wind and the music from the party. "Why'd you let me kiss her?"

I swallowed hard. There was so much more going on here than that kiss, although Jack's lips on that clone of me would haunt me forever. "I don't know. I guess I wanted to see if you would know it wasn't me." I raised my fingers and wiped the cherry red from his lips.

He backed away from my reach and wiped his mouth on his sleeve. "You were *testing* me?" He asked it as if it was the most absurd thing he'd ever heard, because it probably was. What sane girl would let another girl kiss her boyfriend? "You wondered if my love for you was great enough to know the difference between your warm, tender lips and the lips of a cold, cloned replica?" To drive his point home, he ran a thumb lightly across my lower lip.

When he put it like that, additional guilt moved in where jealousy had settled minutes earlier.

His fingers brushed down my arm, then wrapped around my forearm and took hold. He tugged me closer, forcing my eyes to meet his. "I guess you'll never really know the answer now, will you?"

The slow burn of his gaze was much different from the short fuse I saw in Jonas's eyes. "I tried to stop it," I whispered.

"I don't think you did. I think this is just you picking a fight. What I haven't figured out is, why?"

"You're insane." I brought my other hand up and tried to push away from him, but he snaked his arm around my body until it pushed into the small of my back, holding me tightly against him.

"Let me go." I struggled against him. His closeness sucked the breath out of me.

He stared down into my eyes. I knew if he looked deeply enough he'd see the ugliness churning there: the hate and revenge that were manipulating my thoughts and actions. He'd see the many ways I dreamt of hurting Sandra Whitmeyer each night as I lay awake in bed.

"I loved you the minute I discovered you on this campus," Jack said. "You were larger than life. I didn't know at that time if you were like me in any way. I didn't know you were cloned from another, but I knew I had to find out. I was drawn to you. There was no escape."

"And tonight? Were you *drawn* to our newest cloned 'friend' the same way?" I regretted the words the moment they left my mouth.

He loosened his grip on me, allowing me to back away a step. I immediately felt the chill as his heat left me. "Let me ask you this," he said. "Are you attracted to Lin?"

I pictured Lin, Jack's identical twin clone. He was gentle, like Jack, but unsure of himself, a trait I didn't learn about until I got to know him a little. Even though he lacked Jack's confidence, the similarities between them were uncanny, yet I was in no way attracted to him.

Jack didn't wait for my answer. "And what about Jonas? Are you going to stand there and tell me you've never felt the least bit attracted to him?"

I looked away. I wanted to deny the pull I'd felt toward Jonas, a desire I didn't understand and one I tried to ignore time and time again. But I didn't love Jonas. "This isn't helping. None of this matters right now. What matters is that, according to the newest freak in our lives, my mom knows about her. And she has a tracker at the base of her skull." It didn't make sense.

What also mattered—what had always mattered—was that my best friend was dead. My father was dead. And the woman I held responsible was now sending me cryptic messages, including a clone twin with a tracker in her brain.

I hugged myself tighter, trying to hide the fact that I was shaking in my thin ball gown. I would not let Jack see the vile need to strike back at Sandra within me.

Jack crooked a finger under my chin and angled my face toward him. "This is just one more puzzle piece. We'll find a fit for it." He sounded so sure. So in control.

"I don't want to fight with you," I whispered.

"We're not fighting. We're just getting to know each other better."

"Is that what you call it?"

"It's better than what we've done the last two weeks." He leaned in and kissed my temple, and instead of pulling away, I let him. I relaxed in his arms. I wanted to tell him how much I'd missed him. I wished his warm touch could be enough to thaw the coldness that settled in with every contact Sandra had with me.

But instead I did exactly what Sandra wanted me to do. I picked a fight that would separate us. "Jack, you knew my mom had come to town, and you kept it from me." I leaned my forehead against his chest, then willed myself to back away and put needed distance between us.

"It's not that simple."

Nothing in our lives ever was. "It *is* that simple." My voice rose slightly before I reined it in. "I have to know you'll be honest with me at all times. And right now? Let's just say, this feels awfully familiar." I was throwing our past troubles—troubles I had long since forgiven him for—back in his face.

"That's so unfair. I didn't tell you about your mom because you were trapped inside The Farm. You were being held hostage, and you needed full concentration while you got away from Sandra." Jack backed away from me and tugged at his hair in clumps. "Come on, Lex. This is ridiculous."

"Is that supposed to be some sort of apology? Because all I'm hearing is how *you* decided—again—what was best for me."

He turned away, walked a few steps, then whipped back around. "No. It's not an apology. I'm not sorry for trying to protect you. I won't apologize for loving you."

The music suddenly got louder. I looked up at the window, where our classmates were dancing and having a good time.

"I know you would never intentionally hurt me," I said. What was I saying? I had to be strong. This was for his own good.

Jack shook his head. "I would trade my own health and happiness to make sure you didn't suffer. Hell..." He paced. "I would trade my own life to secure your safety."

I would trade *my* life to keep *him* safe, as well. And I would start by putting distance between us.

He lifted both hands and framed my face with his hands. "Please stop the silent treatment."

I nodded between his hands. "No more silence, but..."

"But?"

"I need time." Jack's brows inched closer together, and the pain in his eyes was like a scalpel to my heart as I said what I had to. "So much has happened, and I think we both could use the space."

His cheeks fell slightly. "Space." He nodded. "Do you realize how ridiculous this is? You don't want to push me away. I can see it in your eyes."

I looked down at my twitching hands in order to hide the real reason I was asking for time. "It's what we need."

"I don't know why you're talking about this horribly clichéd need for space, but fine. I'll give you space if that's what you need. Just don't tell me 'we' need it."

I met his intent gaze again. That had been too easy. "Great."

"Yeah, great," he said, though it sounded more like a frustrated "whatever." His eyes squinted like he wanted to say something else, but hadn't quite formed the words. But then he glanced up at the windows to the party. "Can I escort you back to the masquerade? As friends?" He held out his hand, and I wanted more than anything to take it, but that would just delay what I needed to do next.

"You go ahead. I need to find my shoes and mask. I'll find you in a few."

He started to walk away, but turned. His jaw was set. His shoulders rotated back like he was preparing to fight. "I'll respect your wishes for space for now, but Lexi? Don't think for a second that I think this has anything to do with your mom being back in town. You're hiding something." When I didn't argue with him, he continued. "Don't shut me out completely. Too much has happened. Sandra and my father are not gone." His words echoed what Jonas said earlier.

I didn't want them to be gone. Revenge is harder when you can't find the enemy. I smiled and gave Jack the nod I knew he needed.

We are not over, he mindspoke.

I turned away before he saw any moisture in my eyes. I hoped he was right.

~~~~~

I stared at myself in the mirror. Unshed tears cast a redness around my eyes, and color was absent from my cheeks.

I ditched the high-heels and the mask, then traded the party dress for a pair of sweats and one of Jack's T-shirts that I'd snagged while at his house once. Grabbing my computer, I headed to the common area down the hall from my dorm room. I sank down into the sofa, folding one leg under and sitting on my foot.

"Okay, Sandra," I said to myself, "what have you sent me?"

I had to believe Jack would eventually forgive me for pushing him away. After I got rid of Sandra once and for all.

I pushed the thumb drive into the side of my computer and braced for what I was about to see. When prompted for a password, I typed "Maya," the name Jonas had mentioned while lecturing me earlier.

The words *"The password you have entered is incorrect"* flashed across the screen.

I tried her name in all caps, in lowercase, in some caps and some lowercase. Nothing.

Ready to let me help? Jonas entered my head right on cue.
~~~~~

I sat up tall and listened for any sign of Jonas in the hallway. I didn't want his help, of course. *Where are you? You promised you would stay out of my head.*

When have I ever kept a promise? You should learn to shut me out better, Jonas challenged.

God knows I'd tried.

Do you know the password? I asked.

Yes. Come let me inside the dorm. I'm assuming you cast some sort of spell on the security guard here, because I've been unable to control his mind.

I smiled. At least some of my powers worked better than Jonas's. *Why would I do that?*

Because I'm not giving you the password unless I can watch the message with you. There had to be a very good reason why Sandra made sure only I could give you the password.

With a heavy sigh, I set my computer aside and went to the side door of the girls' dormitory. After convincing the security guard to take a walk around the perimeter of the building, I let Jonas in.

When I opened the door, laughter and voices carried from the direction of the art building. We climbed back up to the second-floor common area. "Is the party breaking up?" I asked as I scooped up my computer.

"A little. We probably should find a more private place to watch this."

I glanced toward my room—the room I lived in alone, now that Dani was gone. A room I avoided except to sleep. "Fine. We watch, and then you leave."

Jonas laughed. "You scared to be alone with me, Lexi?"

"I'm tired." I wasn't in the mood for Jonas's antics. And I wasn't interested in pretending that I wasn't heartbroken. I spun and walked to my room. Jonas followed.

Once inside, I set the computer on my desk and sat in the chair. Jonas stood behind me, looking over my shoulder. When the computer prompted me for a password, Jonas said, "Maya2.0Raleigh."

"Raleigh?"

"That's right. Where I was living when I met Maya. The password is something Sandra made me memorize for something else."

I typed in the password, and a video began to play. It was Sandra, wearing a white lab coat, her hair pulled back in a short ponytail. She'd obviously had her hair cut recently. Business as usual for her, I guessed.

"Hi, my lovelies," she said, with what most would call a genuine smile. "I see you're finally working together. And you got my birthday present, Sarah? Good." She spoke as if I were actually answering her. "Thought you might like her. I do hope you left Jack out of this little meeting. While the birthday presents are going to keep on coming for you, Sarah, I'm not sure Jack will appreciate this next one."

"Get on with it," I yelled at the computer.

Jonas remained silent behind me. When I leaned my head back to look at him, he was studying the screen in such a way that I was convinced he was seeing something more than just Sandra. I twisted in my seat to look at the screen again. Behind Sandra was a series of machines, different from anything I'd seen on UK's campus. "What is it?" I asked. "What do you see?"

Jonas shook his head. "I don't know." He squinted at the screen. "Nothing, I guess." His face relaxed.

Sandra continued. "Sarah, this took some work, but I convinced the International Intelligence Agency to release some surveillance tapes to me. I know you think I was responsible for your father's unfortunate death, but I'm not. Not only am I innocent of that heinous accusation, I have proof of who is guilty."

Sandra disappeared from the screen. The scene changed to show a set of doors.

"Is that an airport?" I said.

"That's the front of the Lexington Airport. And that," Jonas pointed at the corner of the screen, to a man exiting the far right door, "is Dr. DeWeese."

"What? We're supposed to believe that because there's video of Jack's father at the airport that he's responsible for planting a bomb in my dad's car?"

"Look at the date."

"So what? Anyone could have doctored this video."

We kept watching, and the video changed to show us a different camera angle. A man pushed through the large revolving door, and I gasped. "That's my dad," I whispered.

Jonas rested a hand on my shoulder, and I grabbed it and squeezed. I wanted to jump into the video and yell at my dad to not go to his car. When I saw Dr. DeWeese cross to him, shake his hand, and give him a one-armed hug, my heart began to thump loudly between my ears.

"He was there," I said. "He was his best friend."

The video went black, then Sandra appeared again. "Have you seen enough?" she asked.

I stood abruptly, and my chair, weighed down by bags and other junk hanging on the back, fell backward to the floor. "Just because Dr. DeWeese was there doesn't mean he killed my dad."

"No?" Sandra asked, her voice upbeat. "Well, keep watching." She replied to me as if we were having a conversation—as if she'd known exactly what I would say—which only added to the fire coursing through my veins.

The video switched back to a view of the airport. Dr. DeWeese and Dad were weaving in and around other travelers leaving the airport. They walked toward two SUVs, parked one in front of the other. Dr. DeWeese gestured, as if telling my dad to go ahead of him, and Dad did. He went to the vehicle in front and slid into the back seat. Another man closed the door, picked up a bag, and placed it in the back of the vehicle. When he closed the hatch, instead of walking toward the driver's door, he took a few quick steps and climbed into the other SUV.

The second SUV pulled out of the parking space and sped off.

The remaining SUV—the one my father was in—just sat there. "What's going on? Why doesn't he get out?" I yelled. I turned and pleaded with Jonas. He touched my face, but I jerked away and looked at the screen again. "Get out, Dad. Something's wrong. Please, get out." Tears streamed down my face.

The explosion filled the screen. My body flinched. I turned and buried my face into Jonas's chest as I sobbed.

Jonas rubbed my back.

Minutes passed before I pushed away and swiped the tears from my face. I began erecting walls all around my mind to keep Jonas out—and walls all around my heart to keep *everyone* out.

Jonas's arms dropped helplessly to his side as he stared at me. "I'm sorry."

"I need you to leave."

"Lexi?"

"Now, Jonas. I want you to leave, and I don't want you to breathe a word of this to Jack."

"We've got to tell him."

"This will kill him," I whispered. He might not like his father much anymore, but finding out he murdered my dad? "And did you not catch that threat from Sandra?" I shook my head. "I just can't risk her going after Jack." The memory of the explosion flashed before my eyes a second time, and I closed them. "I need time to think. And I need to be alone to do it."

"Okay." Jonas held up his hands and backed toward the door. "But I won't be far."

FIVE

The horse in front of me nickered as moisture from the cool autumn air pooled in my eyes. The nameplate on the halter read "Midnight Madness." The barn reeked of hay and manure.

It was the first day of November. The morning after I officially became eighteen. An adult. The day after I learned who killed my father.

And the day after I broke Jack's heart, as well as my own.

A sudden gust chilled a lone tear on my cheek and further stirred up the dirt and leaves that had drifted inside the barn. I lifted my opposite hand to brush Midnight Madness's forehead. He was a beautiful black quarter horse. "Who do you belong to?"

He lifted his head up and down in answer.

"Oh, it doesn't matter. You're not Cheriana." No, Cheriana, Jack's horse, was at my safe house. With my mother.

I backed up and sat on the bench across from Midnight. A neighboring horse pawed at the ground. That was when I felt Jack slide peacefully inside my head. He didn't say anything, nor did he invade my thoughts. He was just there.

At the sound of someone clearing their throat, I jumped up. Coach Williams, my long-time swim coach, walked toward me. His sports jacket barely hid the firearm I knew was tucked in a holster at his side. Coach was ex-FBI and, more recently, had been hired by my father to watch over and protect me.

"I thought you would be Jack," I said.

"Are you disappointed I'm not?"

I shook my head.

"He and Jonas are worried about you, you know. It seems you skipped breakfast. You skipped practice this morning, too."

"I know. I'm sorry."

"Pfft. You know I don't care about the swimming. That was just a front. And it kept you out of trouble for a while. You'll always have swimming for exercise when you need it though." Coach playfully punched my arm. "Jack sent me to talk to you once he discovered where you were hiding."

Jack had a knack for finding me with his mind ability, but fortunately, I had discovered how to shut him out of my thoughts for the past couple of weeks. He could probably still get in if he really wanted to—and obviously, Jonas still could—but I continued to get better at blocking them both.

Coach pulled something out of his pocket. After unwrapping what appeared to be a peppermint, he walked over and fed it to the horse. "Midnight is a retired lead pony from Keeneland racetrack. She's led many a racehorse to the gate."

"Coach, we never discussed something..." I stuffed my hands in the pockets of my jacket. "Will you stay at Wellington? You know... now that Dad is gone?"

"That depends." Coach had grown a goatee the past couple of weeks. He was good-looking, in a forty-something sort of way.

"On what?"

"On you, actually."

"Me? Why me?"

He unwrapped another peppermint and held his flattened palm out to Midnight, who quickly gobbled up the candy. "I now work for you, Lexi."

I cocked my head and looked at him like he'd sprouted a second nose. "How can you work for *me*? I don't have any money." I was just a kid. I felt like one, anyway. The only thing I had was this school, and that was only for a few more months. When Dad was murdered, I was told that he had made sure my schooling was paid for, and that Dr. John DeWeese was my new guardian. Of course, that last part had changed when we discovered that Dr. DeWeese had conspired with Sandra Whitmeyer, my clone donor, to trap me inside their genetic laboratory.

"You're eighteen now."

"Yeah? And suddenly I'm a trust-fund baby?" A sarcastic laugh escaped my lips.

"Actually..."

I narrowed my gaze.

"Lexi, I haven't always agreed with how your father did things, but now that you're eighteen and your father... has passed... the life you've known no longer exists. Your father's attorneys—*your* attorneys—are on their way to Wellington right now."

"To tell me what?" I wiped my sweating palms on my jeans and stood a little straighter.

"That's for the lawyers to say. I swore an oath to your father to keep his secrets and to stay near you, be his eyes at Wellington. And in the event that anything happened to him, it was my responsibility to continue to watch over you until your eighteenth birthday—at which time you would be responsible for making your own decisions. And one of those decisions is whether you'd like to continue to use my services."

Continue his services? I squeezed the bridge of my nose. "You said that Jack told you I was here in the barn. Does he know what the lawyers will tell me?" I knew the answer before I was even done asking it. I knew in my heart Jack no longer kept information from me.

"No, he doesn't." He jingled some coins in his pocket. "Listen, Lexi. When your father died, my oath to him carried over to you. I swear to you to keep your secrets and be your eyes when you aren't present. I will continue to protect you to the best of my ability."

"Did you tell Jack how to find my mother?"

"No. Your mother showed up out of the blue the day you were trapped inside The Farm. Jack just happened to be here. The safe house, as you are now aware, is hers. Well... it belongs to your family, technically. Jack refused to tell your mother anything, but he didn't stop her from going to the safe house and waiting for you. Didn't Jack already tell you all of this?"

"No." But I hadn't given him the chance. He'd kept so much from me since we met. And now, I had a secret of my own. One that could hurt. One that stripped me of all desire to eat, sleep, or tell the one I loved what a monster his father was. "So," I said, "all I have to do is say the word, and you'll keep my secrets and protect me the best you can?"

"That's right."

"What about payment?"

"You have the money, but that's all I can say for now."

"Do you swear to always tell me the truth, no matter how painful that truth might be, and no matter how bad the timing?" Coach had been a consistent presence in my life for years. There wasn't a bone in my body that doubted what he said.

"Yes."

"You're one of the few adults I trust." I reached out and scooped up his hand, prompting him to open his palm. I dropped the thumb drive into it. "That's a copy. It was delivered to my campus mailbox yesterday. Only Jonas and I have seen it."

"What's on it?"

"Missing surveillance from the Lexington Airport. John DeWeese trapping my father in the car that exploded."

Coach's eyes widened. "Are you sure?"

I shrugged, tilting my head side to side in answer. "I'm sure of what I saw in this video."

"You need to tell Jack."

"It would destroy him." I swallowed hard, but quickly shook off the sadness that threatened.

Coach's eyebrows knitted together. "He loves you." I nodded, and he said, "I'll pass this along to my contacts at the FBI."

"They'll only add it to their growing files. Call it circumstantial or something." I had no confidence in the FBI after they'd practically let Sandra and John confine me to The Farm. They simply had too much red tape to ever be able to determine that another arm of the government was supporting a Division of Human Cloning. They required too much evidence, and the IIA was better at covering it up than the FBI was at finding it. "I mean, Sandra could have doctored that video to make us see exactly what she needed me to see, for all I know."

"You don't believe that, though." Coach squinted at me. "That look in your eye makes me nervous. What are you planning to do?"

I zipped my jacket up further and attempted to hug away some of the November cold. "Honestly? I'm not sure yet."

~~~~~

The school chapel was only used for special ceremonies. It was small, held few people, and Wellington didn't have a full-time chaplain on staff. As a result, the chapel was almost always empty—the perfect place to have a private meeting.

I traced the letters on the shiny new plaque displayed outside the front entrance. "In memory of Danielle Gray. Daughter, Sister, Friend."

"Dani," I whispered. "You were my best friend—like a sister. I miss you so much. I want you to know that I will make them pay for what they did. I don't care how long it takes, or what I have to do, I will make sure your murderers are punished."

I heard Jonas's voice, and turned to find him and Jack approaching. "Good, you're both here," I said. "Let's go inside."

They traded glances. Jack held out a cup to me, barely making eye contact. Steam squeezed through a small opening in the cup's lid, a ribbon that carried the scent of cinnamon and cloves.

"Thank you." I took the chai latte, then turned and walked up the steps to the chapel.

Inside, the wooden pews were separated by a single aisle down the center. The air smelled a little musty from lack of
~~~~~

use. I sat in the second row, toward the altar. Jack and Jonas sat one pew in front of me and turned to face me.

"Want to tell us what this is about?" Jonas asked. His eyes held a million questions. *Are you going to tell him?*

I took a sip from my latte, the perfect blend of spice and cream. I knew Jonas was asking if I planned to reveal what was on the video Sandra sent me. *Not now.* "I'm meeting some lawyers at eleven."

"Lawyers? For what?" Jack stretched out a hand. It came close to touching mine before he retreated.

"They were my father's lawyers. I'm not completely sure what they're coming to tell me."

"Do you think they'll assign you a new guardian?" Jack asked.

Jonas picked a piece of lint off of his sleeve and flicked it to the floor. "You didn't tell him?"

"Tell me what?"

"That yesterday was Lexi's eighteenth birthday. She no longer needs a guardian... legally speaking."

I glared at Jonas in response to the dig.

The line in Jack's jaw tightened. "No, she didn't tell me." He faced forward, turning his back to me. "So, some lawyers are coming. What does this have to do with us?" His voice had chilled.

Jonas looked from Jack to me. With a shrug of his shoulders, he asked, "What do you need from me?"

"I need you both to come with me to meet with these lawyers." I reached a hand out and placed it on Jack's shoulder. His muscles stiffened, but at least he didn't shrug me off. "Jack, I want you to be there. I need you there."

I may have asked him for space, but I needed him there as a friend. I trusted him more than anyone else in my life. I had to believe I'd find a way to secure our safety so that we could be together.

He stood and faced us. "Why, Lexi? It's clear you don't need us both."

I stared down at my drink. "What are you talking about? Don't do this, please." It was so unlike Jack to act jealous. He knew nothing was going on between Jonas and me.

"Don't do what? Did Jonas ask you to include me?"

"What? That's stupid."

"Is it? He told you to break up with me last night. I just assumed..."

"How did you...? Addison." Addison was the only clone who could slip into our minds unnoticed. I was getting better at noticing her there, but I had to be looking for her.

"That's right, Addison heard Jonas and told me."

"Jack, asking for space had nothing to do with Jonas or anything he said to me, but everything to do with me and what I need."

"Oh, the old 'It's not you, it's me.'" Jack linked his hands behind his neck and looked up at the ceiling. "And are you going to tell me what Jonas was doing in your dorm room last night?"

My breath caught. "What?"

"Or how about... What time did Jonas leave this morning?"

My eyes shot from Jack to Jonas.

"I slept on the couch in the common area," Jonas explained. "We still don't know how Maya got in and out of Wellington unnoticed by security." He shrugged. "I was worried."

I stood, clenching my free hand into a fist, and I felt the cup in my other hand give a little under the pressure. "What, exactly, are you accusing me of, Jack?" This was not happening. Why would Addison tell Jack this when she had to know Jonas wasn't in my room? "I don't have time for this. These attorneys will be here any time now. I obviously misjudged who I could turn to this morning. I'm a little bit sorry I didn't tell you I turned eighteen yesterday, but that's the only concern worth addressing in your long list. A lot has happened lately, and given the fact that the boy I'm in love with and I haven't been talking the last couple of weeks, and the fact that my best friend is dead, I didn't feel like celebrating my stupid birthday." I turned to go, but then turned back. "I wanted you both there because I'm scared out of my mind wondering what they're going to tell me. And I thought I could trust the two of you, my best friends, to be there with me to hear what these lawyers say. I was wrong."

I was halfway to the door before Jack yelled out. "Lexi, wait! Don't—"

I let the heavy wooden door slam behind me before I stormed down the stairs and hurled my latte against a tree.

~~~~~

I sat on a bench outside Dean Fisher's office. Bent over at the waist, I buried my face in my palms, massaging my forehead with the tips of my fingers.

It was Saturday, so I refused to wear a uniform. Instead I'd dressed for success: black skirt, patterned tights, and boots. I'd completed my ensemble with a red-cropped jacket Dani had
~~~~~

given me after one of her many elaborate shopping sprees. I had no idea what Dad's attorneys were about to reveal, or who it would be revealed to, but I would be taken seriously.

"Lexi?"

My head snapped up. I had expected Dean Fisher's secretary, but it was the dean himself. I stood and smoothed out my skirt, wiping my sweaty palms. "Yes, sir."

"They're ready for you."

Instead of escorting me to his office, the dean led me through a set of double doors down the hallway and into a large boardroom.

As I entered, Cathy DeWeese—Jack's mom for all intents and purposes—was saying something to a man sitting at the head of a long table. "I have known everything from the beginning. Keeping me from hearing Peter's final wishes is unacceptable. I was listed as her guardian, for crying out loud!"

"Not once the young lady turned eighteen," the man said in a calm voice. "And, with all due respect, you don't know *everything.*"

Cathy flinched at his words. A woman I didn't recognize sat to the man's right, sorting through the papers in front of her, ignoring the exchange.

"Your job, Mrs. DeWeese," the man continued, "as her *co-*guardian, is over. And your husband's guardianship was over the second he made contact with Sandra Whitmeyer."

Beside me, Dean Fisher cleared his throat. Cathy straightened up, and her face softened when she saw me. "Lexi, darling."

I raised a single brow and simply stared. Who was she kidding with this multiple personality stuff?

"So nice to see you," she continued. "I hope you're rested. How was the Halloween party last night?" She spoke as if we'd had a children's costume party, complete with bobbing apples and zombie cupcakes.

"It was fine." I glanced sideways at Dean Fisher, who smiled in return.

The man who had just been receiving the earful from Cathy stood and made his way over to me. "Lexi, I'm David Finland."

The unknown woman followed. "And I'm Patricia Long. We were attorneys to your father."

I shook both of their hands, but remained silent. I was surrounded by four people: two lawyers I'd never met, Cathy DeWeese—who crossed both arms and pursed her lips until they disappeared—and Dean Fisher, who most likely knew more about my life than I did up until about six weeks ago.

"Lexi, these attorneys are here to read your father's final will," Cathy said. She reached a hand out and smoothed my hair as if I were a Golden Retriever. "I'd like to be here for you, sweetie. Can I get—"

"Sorry I'm late."

We all turned to find Coach Williams entering the boardroom. Jonas was at his back. "Me too." He winked at me.

"The two of you cannot be here," Cathy insisted. "This is a matter to be discussed with Lexi by her attorneys and her legal guardian. You were not invited."

I faced Cathy. "Um... actually, I invited them."

"But—"

"Mr. Finland, Ms. Long, I have no idea what you're about to reveal to me. Maybe you can tell me who should be present."

Mr. Finland looked from Cathy to me without so much as a twitch in his facial expression. "The only person that is required for this reading is you, Miss Matthews. But you may ask anyone you wish to be present—or *not* be present, as the case may be." He paused for a moment, throwing a quick side glance at Cathy before adding, "At least for part of it. Your father made it perfectly clear that you were fully capable of handling what happens next."

Cathy flashed an uneasy smile at me. "Darling, you need me here. I can help you make sense of the many secrets your father kept from you all these years."

My hands clenched into fists. I was sure my fingernails were leaving deep indentations in my palms. "Cathy, while I appreciate your tenacity..."—out of the corner of my eye, I saw Jonas mouthing the word "tenacity" and counting the syllables on his fingers—"...this is something I need to do on my own." Or with people I trust one hundred percent. "I'm sure you can understand. This has been a hard time—"

Before I could even finish my sentence, Cathy growled a heavy sigh and stormed past us all and out the door. Jonas chuckled. The attorneys remained expressionless, which was starting to freak me out a little.

The dean touched my arm lightly. "Lexi, I'll be in my office. I only know what your father wanted me to know. I am happy to share those things with you once you've heard everything these lovely people have to tell you."

"Thank you, Dean Fisher," I said.

"And Lexi..." The dean's face softened. "I'm sincerely sorry that you had to learn about your creation from anyone other than your father. It was always his desire to share everything with you himself. He just... waited too long. I do know this, though: your father was unbelievably proud of you, and the last time he and I spoke, I assured him that you were ready."

While the dean's words would normally have made me cry for my late father, today my eyes remained dry. I was ready to know everything.

After Dean Fisher exited, I stared at the empty doorway a moment longer, hoping Jack would appear. When he didn't, I swallowed hard and faced the two lawyers. "I would like Mr. Williams and Mr. Whitmeyer to stay."

Ms. Long's eyes widened. "Did you say 'Whitmeyer'?"

"That's right. Jonas stays."

Without another word, Ms. Long closed the door, then returned to the other end of the table, motioning for us all to have a seat. I took the chair next to Mr. Finland, and Jonas sat next to me.

"Lexi, this is a copy of your father's—Peter Roslin's—Last Will and Testament." I took the folder holding the thin document with a shaky hand. "And these"—he held up a second bound document, the thickness of two Harry Potter books—"are copies of trusts and other notarized documents that support and substantiate what's written in Mr. Roslin's will."

Jonas and I traded wide-eyed looks. My leg was shaking uncontrollably under the table, and I drilled my fingers into the spot over my wildly beating heart. "Mr. Finland..." My voice cracked. Jonas pressed a gentle hand to my knee to stop my bobbing leg. "Before we go any further, can you give me the short version of what you're about to tell me? I'm freaking out here." I slid my hand into Jonas's and squeezed, as if bracing for a major medical procedure.

Mr. Finland sat back. With his elbows on the arms of the chair, he steepled his fingers to his chin. "Miss Matthews, I'm here to tell you that you have inherited Wellington Boarding School... among other things."

Jonas and I gasped at the same time.

"Come again?" I sat up straighter.

"The fact that you have inherited Wellington Boarding School is only the beginning. Ms. Long is here to explain the rest."

SIX

I can't run a boarding school." And I didn't want to. "This is crazy." My voice cracked.

Jonas and I stood just outside the boardroom. After an hour, we had taken a break from the lawyerly meeting so that I could make sense of what I had learned so far and gather my wits before I heard more. Mr. Finland had read the will. In the midst of all the legalese was the basic message that I was now sole heir to everything my dad owned. That included Wellington Boarding School, several houses around the world, half of a house here in Kentucky, and, of course, money.

A cold sweat broke out across my neck as I stared up at Jonas's calm expression. I held up my two shaking hands.

"Look at me. Do I look like I'm capable of what they just told me? I'm a kid." I didn't want to be responsible for teaching cloned humans to use unnatural abilities—to mindread, mindspeak, control actions, or whatever else they could do. Not to mention the responsibility of honing the medical healing capabilities these clones might have. And what if these clones turned out to be more like Sandra? I couldn't even think about that right now.

After allowing me to rant for several minutes, Jonas rubbed my arms in an apparent attempt to get some circulation going. "I've seen you in action, remember? You are capable of anything you set that mind to." He tapped a finger to my temple.

"Did you listen to the rest of that will? I've been left some kind of trust fund that I'm in charge of. What was my dad thinking?"

"He was thinking he would be alive long enough to make sure you knew what to do, but in the event that he wasn't, he made sure there were people around to advise you."

"Like who? Who are we talking about? Those attorneys I just met? Cathy DeWeese? Dad left Dr. John DeWeese as my co-guardian, for crying out loud. My father may have loved me, but he obviously didn't know who he could trust any more than I do."

"That's not why he chose John as your guardian. In fact, he never expected John to advise you or take care of you." Coach Williams's voice startled me. I hadn't heard him return.

"What makes you say that?"

"Your father met with me the day after he spoke at the Association of International Physicians dinner. He thought someone was following him, and he wanted me to know that if anything happened to him, he had arranged for John DeWeese to be your legal guardian. But he warned me that if that were ever to happen, I would need to watch over you more closely than ever before."

"I don't understand."

"Your father believed in the old adage, 'Keep your friends close, but your enemies closer.' He thought that by bringing John DeWeese into the fold—by making him your co-guardian, a gesture of trust—that John would hang himself, so to speak. Your father knew John had been meeting with Sandra. I don't know how he knew, but he knew. Your dad just didn't count on dying before your eighteenth birthday. I'm sure he hoped to catch John in his secrets."

"So you're saying he gambled with my life?"

"Maybe a little, but I was watching. You were seventeen years old, after all—not a child. And Jack was looking out for you. He might not have known to keep an eye on his own father, but he was keeping an eye out for anyone who might harm you."

A knot formed in my stomach at the mention of Jack. "What are you saying?"

"Jack came to me shortly after your father died, and after you had discovered that you were a clone of Sandra Whitmeyer. He figured out that I was ex-FBI and questioned what I was doing there. I knew, then, that he would let nothing happen to you, no matter who the threat turned out to be."

I drilled two fingers into my temple. "What about Cathy DeWeese?"

"Your father believed that Cathy and her brother, Roger Wellington, had always had different agendas. And from what I've seen, they definitely have unique motives for being at Wellington. But I don't think they want to do experiments on you. Your father would have told me, or removed them himself, if he ever thought they meant you harm. I think they just want to be a part of using the school and the clones for the betterment of medicine."

I wasn't convinced. Dad's track record spoke for itself. But for now, I would keep Roger and Cathy "closer." "You say they have unique motives?"

Jonas rubbed the spot on the back of his neck where I had recently removed the tracker from the base of his skull. He was taking in Coach's and my words, but he remained quiet.

"I'm only speculating here, but instead of keeping your medical healing abilities a secret, I think Cathy and Roger want to exploit them—to use them for financial gain."

This didn't surprise me. Cathy DeWeese was a walking advertisement for Coco Chanel and Valentino Garavani. She screamed wealth, and that takes a lot of money.

Jonas tapped his lips before finally speaking. "Roger Wellington is the current president of the boarding school. The school bears his name. Does Lexi's inheritance change this?"

"That's up to Lexi. I think that once she hears about the rest of what she's inherited, she'll know that she has the power to do what she wishes with the school, and so much more."

Tight muscles were slowly taking up residence in my neck and between my shoulder blades. "I guess I need to hear the rest, then." Could I handle hearing more?

Jonas's hands drifted up to my shoulders and began to rub. *I'm here. I'll help you. We'll get through this together.*

I nodded. But as much as I appreciated Jonas being there—and I did—the person I really wanted was Jack.

Jonas and I took our seats while Coach informed the attorneys we were ready to proceed.

Mr. Finland returned to the head of the table and sat, but Ms. Long stood across from me and wrung her hands.

"Is something wrong, Ms. Long?" I asked.

The attorney pulled a one-sheet document from her stack and handed it to Mr. Finland. "This document is an affidavit, written and signed by your father, witnessed by me, and notarized by a member of my staff. It directs you to hear what I am about to tell you... alone." The way she said the word "alone" sent a chill down my spine. "After you hear the information, you can decide whom to share it with."

"Okay," I practically stuttered.

Coach and Mr. Finland immediately walked toward the door. Jonas leaned down and kissed the side of my head. *It's going to be okay.*

The intimacy in his touch felt wrong, but the smoothness of his mindspeak comforted me at the same time. Jonas was giving me what Jack had refused to this morning.

I shook off the feelings of guilt. I had enough to deal with without allowing those useless feelings in.

Ms. Long settled into her chair before pushing another piece of paper across the table.

I glanced down at a list of what appeared to be names of banks and other institutions. Some I had heard of, others I hadn't. Beside each one was a string of numbers—account numbers. "What's this?"

"This is a list of accounts where your father accumulated funds and investments before he died. Only a select few people know how to access these accounts. They require both passwords and DNA identification."

"'Select' people?"

"That's right. I don't know how to access the accounts. I only know who does."

My brain began to spin out of control. Who would Dad have possibly trusted with this knowledge? I stared across the table at Ms. Long. "Are you going to tell me? Or do I have to guess?" I was suddenly unable to keep the irritation from my voice as a strength from deep inside me surfaced.

"Only one person knows *how* to access the accounts, but she cannot access the accounts without you."

"Who?" I dug my fingernails into the wood of the table, bracing for what was coming.

"Alyson Roslin."

I closed my eyes, bowing my head, and a cold sweat washed over my body. After a deep breath, I looked back up at Ms. Long. "You're telling me the only way to access my inheritance is through my mother? And you said the accounts require a specific DNA? I'm guessing mine?"

"That is correct. She is also the owner of the other half of the property here in Kentucky."

My mother and I now co-owned the safe house where I found her two weeks ago. Perfect.

I stared down at a list of twenty or so bank accounts. "How much?"

Ms. Long stared back at me. I studied her. Just when I thought her expression had remained unreadable during this entire reveal, I noticed a slight twitch in her jaw and the tiniest hint of sweat droplets along her hairline. I cocked my head. "How much money is in these accounts?"

Without breaking eye contact, she said, "As of nine this morning, these accounts totaled 3.2 billion dollars."

The room began to spin. Dark spots clouded my vision. I tried to pull in air, but couldn't. Pressure closed in around my neck. I couldn't breathe. *Jonas,* I managed. *Help me.* I clawed at my throat.

Jonas pushed through the boardroom doors, but Ms. Long was already at my side. "Miss Matthews, are you okay?" She grabbed a pitcher of water and poured me a glass. "Here." She tipped the glass against my lips.

I gasped, shoving the glass and her hands away. The glass hit the floor with a thunk, spilling the contents.

Jonas grabbed my shoulders, spinning my seat so that I faced him. "What did you do to her?" he yelled at the lawyer.

"Nothing. I—"

"Apparently not nothing. Lexi..." He squatted before me. "Breathe. In... out..." He took in a deep breath and let it out slowly as if to show me how.

Finally, I sucked in. The air stung my throat.

"That's it. Nice and slow." Though his voice was calm, his brows knitted together. He sat in the chair beside me, keeping both hands on my knees as I continued to force breaths in and out. "Want to tell me what just happened?"

I inhaled and shook my head.

"You're very pale. Have you had enough for one day?"

I shook my head again. "I'm okay," I whispered. "Can you give me one more minute with Ms. Long? Then I think I'd like a break."

Jonas hesitated, but stood to leave. "I'll be right outside the door."

When the doors were closed again, I turned to Ms. Long and swallowed hard. "I just want to know why," I said in a hoarse voice. I also wanted to know *how*, but that seemed less important at the moment.

"Why?" Ms. Long repeated. Her forehead wrinkled in confusion.

"Why did my father accumulate so much?"

"Oh." The lawyer pursed her lips until they practically disappeared. "I'm simply the messenger. I would assume only your mother knows that."

"My mother?" I stood abruptly, causing my chair to roll backward.

"That's right. I'm told your mother and father divorced when you were young, but remained very close. Since she's the one who knows how to access the accounts..."

I didn't feel the need to hash out family drama in a boardroom, but apparently I was going to be forced to meet with the woman who had deserted me when I was young. I ran my tongue over my parched lips. More questions scrolled through my mind than I knew what to do with. "How many people know the size of my inheritance?"

"Two: me, and now you." She paused a moment. "Your mother knows that the inheritance is sizable, but for her protection, your father decided it was best to tell as few people as possible until the right time."

I glanced down at Ms. Long's hands as she wrung them at her waist. Her pupils were dilated. "You're scared. Why?"

I couldn't help but think of Marci. My dad had trusted the journalist with information. How much information? I had no idea, but she had been frightened the last time I saw her here at Wellington.

Just before she was murdered on the University of Kentucky's campus.

"Miss Matthews, my firm protects a lot of information for our clients, but the security measures surrounding this case are enough to make even the strongest a little skittish. There are instructions in place in the event something happens to me… or you." Her hands shook as she pretended to organize the documents in front of her. She looked back up at me. "I'm worried about you. You're young. And your reaction to the news…"

"It was a shock, that's all. It's a lot of money." I squeezed at the pressure point between my thumb and forefinger, a nervous habit I usually only did when I suffered a headache. "How about you give me a day to digest the information? Can we meet again in a day or two?"

"I am at your disposal. I work for you now, Ms. Matthews, as long as you desire me to."

"In that case, I'd prefer that you call me Lexi."

I looked down at the documents in front of me. Ms. Long must have followed my line of vision because she said, "An office has been set up for you. It's to the right of Dean Fisher's office. A copy of every document Mr. Finland and I brought here today will be placed in a safe in that office." She handed me a piece of paper. "Memorize this combination and then destroy it. I created the combination this morning and am the only other person who knows it."

"You've thought of everything." An office seemed like overkill.

"Your father paid us to." She began to gather documents, straightening loose papers and closing folders.

"Ms. Long, I have one last request."

"Anything."

"You said that you and I are the only two who know the value of my inheritance?"

"Yes."

"I want it to stay that way. No one can know the details of what you just told me."

"Of course. That's entirely up to you. Your father left you in charge starting the day you turned eighteen. Much of what he wanted you to know is in the journals he already gave you, and in this file." She held up a brown expandable folder. "I'll leave this in the safe for when you're ready."

When I was ready.

Would I *ever* be ready to know what Dad expected me to do with 3.2 billion dollars?

~~~~~

"What did that woman say to you in there?" Jonas asked.

I shook my head, refusing to look at him as I pocketed all my thoughts and hid them securely away. We wandered through the small cemetery adjacent to the chapel where we had started our day. Though neither my dad nor my best friend was buried there, I somehow felt closer to them. And right now I needed them.

"Fine. You don't have to tell me..." Jonas stuffed his hands in his pockets. "But Lexi, you scared me. You were so pale." He kicked at a rock that bounced off a headstone.

"You heard most of it. I now own Wellington Boarding School." Whatever that meant. How does someone own a school? "And I inherited money from my dad." Jonas didn't need to know I was now worth the gross domestic product of a small country. *No one* needed to know that information. Not yet, anyway. People close to me had been killed for less.
~~~~~

"That must have been some trust fund, to cause you to hyperventilate and practically pass out like that."

It was. But how had Dad accumulated that much money? And why? And what could I possibly need with it? And why would my father leave this school to me? The last time Dad and I spoke, I had been more than ready to graduate and move on with my life—go to medical school and become a caring and successful doctor.

But now?

My back to Jonas, I stared at a monument in the center of the cemetery: a life-sized sculpture of a girl with large angel wings. A book lay across her lap. Carved in stone below the sculpture were the words "In Memory of Father and Mother." Love poured out of the simple inscription.

Until recently, I had felt as if both my parents were dead, that all I was left with were distant memories of two parents who once loved me. But now that I knew the truth, I had to wonder: Had my mother *ever* loved me? Could a mother who loved her daughter leave her behind? And had I been given a chance to know that mother again?

The wind picked up, bringing me out of my daydream. Goose bumps spread down my arms. Being in the cemetery reminded me that death was real—and final. I would never forget the image of the neurons in Dani's brain turning dull like the brightest star fading from the sky. That image—of Sandra Whitmeyer killing my best friend—would be ingrained in my mind forever.

And now, that very woman was working hard to make sure I knew that her partner, Dr. John DeWeese—Jack's father—was the one responsible for the murder of my dad? I had yet to figure out why she would do that. What was her game?

Whatever she was up to, I needed to figure it out soon. Sandra Whitmeyer and John DeWeese had already taken away two of the most important people in my life. And now Sandra was hinting that Jack could be next.

Deep in thought, I didn't hear Jonas step up behind me. His hands rested on my shoulders, massaging the tension that knotted up between my shoulder blades. My muscles stiffened, but I settled into his touch, closing my eyes.

Yet behind the darkness of my eyelids, it was Jack I saw. He had shoved me from his life earlier that morning, at a time when I needed him. Of course, he'd had every reason to act the way he had, after last night.

Like always, Jonas was inside my head, but I knew by his frustrated sigh that I was successfully shutting him out. He bent his head close and spoke softly. "What did Ms. Long tell you today that scared you so much?"

"Does it matter?" I stepped away from his touch.

"What kind of question is that? You asked me to be there for a reason." He spun me around and stared into my eyes. "You were close to passing out when I got in there."

"Well, you heard the biggest part of it. I'm somehow the proud owner of a boarding school. I have no idea what that even means."

"You're not telling me everything."

"No, I'm not. And I don't have to." I backed up, putting distance between us. We should never have been that close to begin with, but he was right. I was scared. I had needed his touch. No, I needed someone else's touch: Jack's. And I needed to feel something other than fear.

The corners of Jonas's lips tipped upward in a sly grin. "Okay. Have it your way." He laughed in an aloof I-don't-care sort of way.

I crossed my arms. "Why are you smiling?" My voice escalated in volume. This was the Jonas that infuriated me—the same Jonas I had despised once upon a time.

"Oh, don't get that sexy black skirt in a bundle. I was just thinking that my initial instinct would be to force it out of you with my mind, just like you would force someone to tell you something."

"But we promised each other. No invading the other's thoughts."

"That's right. How could I forget? Is Jack exempt from that rule?"

"What do you mean?"

"I mean, he's not here. It's no secret you two haven't been speaking since just after the lab explosion, except to argue."

I frowned and looked away. Lingering autumn leaves fell from the trees. "Jack and I just need space."

"Is that why you're afraid to tell Jack what was on Sandra's video? Or about the note? You think he would let you push him away if he knew?"

I pushed loose strands of hair from my face and tucked them behind my ear. "You know I can't tell him. Sandra has followed through on every threat she's made." Turning, I walked along behind some gravestones, grazing shaking fingers along the cold, rough concrete as I passed.

Jonas followed. "You forget. I don't have to read your mind to *read your mind.* Your body language gives you away, and you're hiding something. More than Sandra's message. Answer me this... If Jack were here, would you tell him what Ms. Long revealed?"

I whipped around. "Well, it doesn't really matter, now does it? Look around, Jonas. Jack isn't here, is he?"

Jonas reached out and grabbed my hand, yanking me forward. He brushed his fingers along my hair and jawline. "No, he isn't." His calm tone deflated my anger a little.

I breathed heavily. "This isn't right, Jonas." I heard the weakness in my voice, but did nothing to stop him. Was he inside my head, preventing me from turning him away?

"No?"

"No."

"Why not? Because of Jack?" His breath feathered against my lips.

"Yes. And because of Briana. Because of lots of things." I tried pushing against him, to free myself from the straitjacket of his arms.

"What things? What the attorneys said?" Jonas tilted his head and leaned closer. "Tell me what they said. Let me help you."

I couldn't let this happen. Jonas's lips were millimeters from mine. His pupils were dilated, leaving only a thin rim of amber. I pushed against him. "Jonas, let go of me. This isn't you. What are you doing?"

Suddenly, an avalanche of cool air washed over me. My eyes sprang open as Jonas was jerked from me.

"What the hell are you doing?" Jack shoved Jonas, and Jonas nearly stumbled over a tombstone.

"Jack," I gasped.

Jonas grinned. His eyes were glued to Jack. "Well, well, well. So nice of you to join us."

"You set me up?" Jack walked in a circle, stalking Jonas like prey. "You called me here just so that I could watch you kiss my girlfriend?"

"What's he talking about?" I asked Jonas. *Why would you do this?*

"Girlfriend?" Jonas feigned a shocked hand over his mouth, ignoring me and belittling the girlfriend label. "I thought you two had broken up. 'Needed space.'" He placed air quotes around the last two words. "That's what you said this morning. Isn't that why you deserted Lexi when she practically begged you to be there for her?"

"Jonas, stop," I said. "It's okay." It was actually for the best, because now, I didn't have to feel guilty about all of the secrets I was keeping from Jack.

Jonas stopped smiling. "It's *not* okay. You needed him. We all need each other, and he left you alone."

"I told Jack I needed space. It's not his fault."

"But you're hiding things, and you just can't," Jonas said. "Sandra isn't gone. She'll be back. You think your twin clone showing up last night was a coincidence? It wasn't. It's a sign. This is not over."

"I know Sandra's not gone. You of all people know that I'm well aware that Sandra will be back... *is* back." I turned my back on both of them. I had to think, get my priorities straight. But first I wanted to know the truth. I faced Jonas. "What did Jack mean when he said you set him up?"

Jonas wasn't smiling. "I sent him a message with my mind. Told him he needed to come."

"To watch you try to kiss me," I said—a statement, not a question.

"No... well, yes, I did, but—"

I held up my hand to silence him. "Don't even bother."

"Lexi, you needed him here, and by staging that kiss and his reaction to it... I've proven that Jack still cares."

Jack's mouth fell open as he looked at me. "Is that what you think? That I've somehow stopped caring about you?"

"I didn't say that." I drilled two fingers into the center of my forehead. This was stupid. A laugh bubbled up through my throat and across my lips before I could stop it. "Are you hearing yourselves? We've resorted to staging kisses and arguing over who cares and who doesn't. I'm so done with this."

"All I was trying to say was that you needed Jack. And he needed to be aware of that, and of what you're going through. And now you've been left the responsibility of running Wellington, along with a group of crazy adults we don't even know we can trust."

I looked from Jonas to Jack and back. "You're right. I *did* need Jack. *And* you. That's why I met with both of you this morning. You're also right that I'm hiding things." I looked at Jack. "And after your reaction to my need this morning..." I turned to Jonas. "And after your typical games here just now... I'm right back to where I was when I first learned of my father's death. On my own."

"That's not fair." Jack's arms hung limp at his sides in defeat.

"Oh, yeah? Well, guess what? I don't care if it's fair. You both need to grow up. I'm being forced to, so why can't you?" I shoved past them, assuming they would know better than to follow me.

I had hoped to have them both with me this morning, learning with me more about this life we were being forced to lead—a life we would have to protect if we wanted to see our nineteenth birthdays. I had known that the meeting with the lawyers would be crazy hard. Asking Jack and Jonas to be there with me was my way of telling them that I believed we were a team—and at the same time, I had hoped it would keep them from invading my head uninvited.

But now that they knew I was hiding things, Jonas would constantly be looking for a way in, and I would have to work extra hard to shut him out. I couldn't have anyone knowing the amount of money my dad had left me. At least not until I knew why.

I made it through the wrought-iron gate of the cemetery before Jonas mindspoke. *I'm sorry.*

I threw my hand in the air, giving him a backward wave. *Whatever.*

SEVEN

Sunday morning, I jogged to Gram's nursing home—a place I once upon a time used as an escape from boarding school life.

Gram was sleeping when I entered her room. Her breakfast sat on a tray, untouched. I could see that she'd lost weight in the last month. Seth had told me that Gram's body was suffering the effects of cancer, but that Gram had expressly requested—before the Alzheimer's took over—that she not undergo invasive radiation or chemotherapy treatments, or major medical treatments of any kind. And Seth confirmed that surgery was not an option.

In short, I was losing Gram, the only mother I'd ever known.

I leaned over and gave my grandmother a soft kiss on the cheek. Her skin was silky smooth and smelled of moisturizer. After memorizing the peaceful look on her face, I turned and exited the room in search of the person that was supposed to meet me.

The nursing home was already humming despite the early hour. At the entrance to the common area, a sign read: *Church Service, 11:00 A.M.* The area was mostly empty, but I suspected that, come eleven, the home would be abuzz.

I continued further into the room. Around the corner, by a window overlooking the parking lot, was Seth Whitmeyer, sitting with one of the residents while she ate breakfast. I approached the table hesitantly, my running shoes squeaking on the tile floor. "Hello, Mrs. Whitmeyer."

Seth's and Sandra's mother paused mid-bite to look at me. Her cheeks lifted and her eyes brightened. "Sandra, dear."

"No, Mom." Seth grabbed his mother's hand. "This is Lexi. She looks a lot like our Sandra, but this is one of my students. The one I was telling you about."

Mrs. Whitmeyer's eyebrows tilted inward. "Oh." She stared at her warm cereal, and Seth gave her hand a squeeze and attempted to comfort her through the confusion.

I pulled a chair back and took a seat facing Seth. "Thank you for meeting me away from school."

He shrugged. "After recent events, I'd say you're finally starting to put a lot of pieces together."

My leg began its nervous bob. Seth had appeared in my life shortly after Jack, and had made no secret that we were *not* friends—not yet anyway. After first meeting him, I had even considered that perhaps he had murdered my father and was at Wellington to kill me. "Why did you come to Wellington?" I asked.

"I came in search of Jack and you, and the others."

"When did you know about us?"

"About ten years ago. Before Wellington even existed."

"Wellington is that new?" I didn't know why, but I had always assumed that Wellington had been around for a while. I never thought to question that.

"Wellington was opened for you. For all of you."

I thought of the list of clones Dad had been compiling. "Dad was searching for clones. He was searching for them even when I was only ten or eleven. Bringing them here."

"That's right."

"Do you know how many clones are at Wellington?"

He nodded. "Fifty-two. All younger than you and Jack and the rest of the original group."

"What about outside Wellington?"

"That's a little trickier. No one seems to know how many embryos survived after the lab burned down eighteen years ago." Seth glanced over at his mother, who seemed oblivious to our entire conversation. "Here's the thing, Lexi. Sandra is creating more cloned humans every day. She's been creating these clones since before the original lab burned. And she's getting better at it."

"How is she doing this? *Where* is she doing this? How many surrogates could she possibly have that are agreeing to this?"

"Those are huge questions. As far as the 'where,' I think a facility is already in place when she leaves one lab and goes to another. Hard to say the exact locations."

"You think *she* burned down that lab—the one where she, Dad, and Dr. DeWeese worked? The same way she destroyed the lab at the University of Kentucky?"

An orderly rolled a large cart down the hallway behind me. I stood and paced a moment, processing this new information. If Sandra had been cloning humans all these years, where were they?

I faced Seth. "So, did Dr. DeWeese know where Sandra was after the original lab fire?"

"Not at first. No one knew where she was. But John and Sandra had been in love—"

"Some form of it, anyway." I laughed under my breath, although nothing about this was humorous.

"I can't disagree that their connection is strange. But after the fire, my sister disappeared. John, your dad, Cathy, Roger, and even your mother—they were left behind to pick up the pieces. Everyone else pretty much scattered."

I squeezed the bridge of my nose, attempting to ignore the comment about my mother. "Why did Dr. DeWeese marry Cathy? Did he think Sandra was dead?"

Seth smiled. "Oldest trick in the book... so to speak. Cathy became pregnant with John's clone."

"So... what? You're saying John wanted Jack? And Cathy tricked him into marrying her?"

"Control is everything. Controlling the cloned humans that survived. Controlling future research. Controlling who knows what and when—"

"Controlling who gets to live or die." I watched Mrs. Whitmeyer slowly lift a spoon to her mouth and take a bite of her oatmeal, and I was struck by her gentleness. Her daughter was nothing like her. How had Sandra become so evil?

Then again, Dr. DeWeese, too, had seemed gentle and caring when I first met him. But after facing him and Sandra inside The Farm... and if he was responsible for killing Dad—his best friend...

"Mr. Whitmeyer." A nurse approached. "It's time for your mother's bath."

Seth leaned over and kissed his mother on the temple. "Good to see you, Mom."

She squeezed her son's hand with a palsied but firm grip. "I hope you'll both come see me again. Your voices are lovely."

"Of course we will." I smiled as I watched the nurse wheel her away.

When she was gone, Seth said, "I was sorry to hear about Danielle."

My heart constricted just hearing my best friend's name. "Were you?"

"Of course I was. I'm not my sister, Lexi. I'm hoping since you asked me to meet you here, you're figuring out that I'm here to help you."

Had I figured that out? "How do you know so much of this history if you weren't actually a part of the original lab?"

"Who said I wasn't?"

"So you were *there*? When Sandra decided to clone human beings? Did you know she planned to implant them?"

"I'm the twin brother no one notices, Lexi. Sandra was always the star, the one going places. But yes—I was there." Seth stood and faced the windows overlooking the grounds. "And I knew that she would never destroy those embryos once she figured out that she could not only clone a human, but actually alter their genetic makeup.

"We tried to stop her. A plan was in place—to destroy the embryos—but then the fire started. Everything was so chaotic. We had no warning. But Sandra knew. It was all part of her plan."

I stared at Seth's back as he remembered his sister's actions all those years ago. "Something obviously went wrong."

He faced me. "What do you mean?"

"Well, the embryos weren't destroyed, but she also lost control of them. In some cases, she didn't even know where they ended up."

"Not all of them," he corrected. "At least not at first."

"Jonas," I said, mostly to myself. Not to mention the non-altered clones: Dia, Lin, and Ty. "What about the other clones? The ones that don't seem to have the same abilities we have?"

"A control group to compare the altered clones against."

"How did Sandra keep control of those, but not the DNA-altered ones?"

"Good question. I don't know."

"And Addison? She seems different."

"That she is. An anomaly." Seth nodded. "She remains a mystery to me. She doesn't talk about her time in Sandra's facilities. However, she seems to escape every time. I don't even know who she was cloned from, or if she has any healing powers. So far, all I know is that she has incredible mind-altering abilities."

"I'm assuming her disappearances occurred once Dr. DeWeese was back in touch with Sandra. Why was Jack never taken to one of the facilities?"

Seth smiled. "Don't underestimate a mother bear protecting her cub. I'm fairly certain Cathy had no idea that Addison and her mother disappeared to one of the facilities from time to time, but Cathy knew her husband, and she was careful to never let Jack out of her sight. Not for long, anyway."

I stood and stared out the window. Two squirrels chased each other around the base of a tree. "Which is why she home-schooled Jack." I remembered how protective Cathy had been when Jack first met me and insisted on enrolling at Wellington. "But Dr. DeWeese seemed to be on board with Cathy's decision to keep Jack hidden. And they kept a lot of the truth from him. What changed?"

Seth joined me by the window. "It has always been important to both of them that Jack learn who he was over time. To become well-educated. And Cathy tried to maintain complete control over that. Educating Jack worked for both Cathy's plans and John's... in different ways, of course."

Cathy was definitely a control freak. "So, why The Program?" I asked.

Seth crossed his arms and rocked back on his heels. "Ah, yes. The Program was *my* invention. Once I discovered that some of the clones had survived, and were even thriving as human beings, I began watching everyone closely. I knew Sandra had gotten in touch with John in the last few years, so I suspected he knew that she hadn't stopped cloning. And Cathy and Roger had kept in touch. Of course, Roger was in touch with Peter since Peter was the money behind Wellington.

"Anyway, the lines were pretty clear, so I constructed The Program. It was my way of approaching Roger and Cathy separate from John and Sandra. And once I had The Program, I began building my database of what clones existed. I had the trust of all parties."

"What about my dad? Did you ever talk to him?"

"We were supposed to meet the day he died. But he knew about The Program, and had given Roger his blessing to start teaching you and the other clones."

I stared at Seth. "You were supposed to see him? That was the day you found me here."

"Yes. And for the first time, I was afraid for the future of the clones I knew existed. I already knew that Peter had been back in touch with John, and that they were best friends. The lines had blurred. I didn't know if Peter had been in collusion with John and Sandra, or if his loyalties lay with Wellington, the clones who lived there, and especially his daughter—you. Most importantly, I didn't know who would have wanted him killed."

I massaged the spot over my racing heart. *I* knew who killed him—the same man my father appeared to trust in his final days. I faced Seth. "Why would my dad trust you to teach me—to be anywhere near me—and the clones hidden at Wellington? I mean, being Sandra's twin brother and all."

Seth nodded, as if expecting the question. "I tried to warn him eighteen years ago that Sandra had her own agenda, that she had plans to destroy everything he, John, and Sandra had built. He didn't believe me back then. But now I had proof."

"Proof?"

"I had email correspondence between Sandra and the IIA. It linked John and Peter with Sandra and the project to clone humans and build the human clone robots the IIA wanted for some sort of foreign spy program."

Sandra had shown me a video of the spy robots. The International Intelligence Agency was helping Sandra with her cloning program in exchange for experimental weapons. The thought made me sick. But something else bothered me. "You sent me one of those emails. You were blackmailing me."

The corners of Seth's lips curved slightly. "Sorry." He shrugged. "You're a replica of a sister who stabbed her own twin brother in the back, figuratively speaking. And I needed those journals your father wrote in order to know everything I needed to know about their research—his, Sandra's, and John's. I still do. But when I realized you're nothing like my sister, despite almost identical DNA, I decided I would be patient."

A case of nature versus nurture, I supposed.

Everyone had their own agenda, it seemed, and it was a challenge to decide which agendas were beneficial to the existing clones' futures, which ones were harmful, and which ones needed to be crushed completely.

"Dad left me Wellington," I blurted out.

"The school?"

I nodded. "I don't know how to run a school." I didn't mention the fact that the school was almost insignificant compared to the amount of money Dad left me.

We were both silent for a moment, gazing out the window, until from somewhere down the hall outside our room, a man screamed, "Turn it on Kelly Ripa!" and reminded us where we were. After another beat, Seth touched my shoulder, bringing me back to focus on our conversation.

"I'll ask you the same thing I asked you about The Program," he said. "What do you want from me?" I must have paused a little too long, because he added, "Because last we talked, your strongest desire was to *not* need me or The Program."

I looked him in the eye. "My desires have changed. I still want to know everything about our history, but now I also need to know where Sandra Whitmeyer and John DeWeese are. I need help finding their new lab."

EIGHT

I stared at the still water of the campus swimming pool early the next morning, breathing in the moist air and the smell of chlorine. Practice wouldn't start for another hour, but I couldn't sleep.

I sat on the edge of the pool. My legs dangled in the cool water, and I watched the ripples move across the surface. Each one carried a piece of the puzzle that had become my life. As the water settled, the weight of my problems burrowed back into the muscles of my shoulders. I placed my goggles over my eyes, then lifted my body up and propelled myself into the pool, allowing the water to engulf me.

I hoped the hollow sounds of swimming would drown out all the other thoughts screaming in my head. The desire to discover the location of Sandra's new lab was at the top of that list. I would take her down one way or another. I had no idea how—yet—but I figured that being a billionaire was bound to work to my advantage.

I moved my arms and legs as I crawled from one end of the pool to the other. Flipping at the other end, I vowed not to stop until I physically couldn't go any further.

One. Two. Ten. Fifty. A hundred laps. Whatever it took.

At about my thirty-fifth lap, I heard the distant thud of a door closing. Sure that it was just another swimmer showing up for practice, I didn't stop swimming. My muscles were looser than they'd been in weeks. I was feeling no signs of tiring.

Ten strokes from one end of the pool, I cocked my head to the side to take a breath, and a loud screeching noise broke through the barrier of the water, reaching my ears. I stopped and looked up. Through the smoky color of my goggles, I could just make out a figure standing at the head of my lane.

Lexi, do not remove your goggles, and do not come any closer. The voice entered my head, and there was no mistaking who it was. Maya.

What do you wan— I attempted to mindspeak back to her. The screeching noise cut me off. My hands flew to my ears.

You will listen. Sandra insists that you join her. You and your friends. She will not stop until you do.

You know where she is? My twin allowed me to speak. I couldn't believe we were back to this: Sandra being so arrogant as to think that I would willingly join her.

There is a video in your inbox. Once you've watched it, I'll find you again. I'll give you a few days to come to your senses and realize that surrendering to Sandra is your only choice.

My look-alike raised a hand over her head, her fingers spread wide, then lowered it. As she did so, I felt pressure on the top of my head, and I was shoved under the water. I thrashed about, reaching my arms up, grabbing at nothing but air. Why was she trying to drown me when she was supposed to be a messenger from Sandra? I stared up, seeing nothing but fuzzy shades of aqua.

I couldn't get a breath. *Jack! Jonas! Bree!*

Two more things... Maya spoke through the deafening thunder of water raging against my ears. *Sandra wants you to know that none of your friends will be able to save you if you don't surrender.*

And though I could terminate you right now, I'm not the one you should be worried about. Someone else wants you dead.

Suddenly Maya left my mind, and Jack entered.

Lexi? Where are you?

Jack! Help! Unable to stop myself, I took in a breath. Instead of air, water hit the back of my throat, and like fire, it traveled through my body to my lungs.

I heard the mumblings of voices in my consciousness before darkness washed over me.

~~~~~

"One. Two... Thirteen... Twenty-nine. Thirty. Breathe."

"One. Two..."

Suddenly I was coughing and throwing up water.

"That's it."

I felt a strong hand on my back, rubbing my skin in circles. In less than two months, I had nearly drowned twice. I could now say with certainty that if it came down to it, drowning would *not* be my top choice of a way to go. I'd heard people say that it would be a peaceful way to die. It wasn't.

I threw up again. When I was done, I looked up and discovered Jack, Jonas, and Briana hovering over me.

If you wanted me to touch your chest, all you had to do was ask. A smirk spread across Jonas's face, and I blushed, realizing he had just performed CPR on me.

You're an idiot. I sucked in a painful breath, letting it out slowly.

"What the hell were you doing swimming alone?" Jack stood and paced. "I'm trying to give you distance, Lexi, but if
~~~~~

you keep insisting on making these idiotic decisions, I'll stick a twenty-four-hour bodyguard on you myself."

"Jack," Briana said. "Give her a break. Give her a chance to tell us what happened before you threaten to lock her up."

"No. He's right." Jonas squared his shoulders, looking down on me. "She's not being smart. And a bodyguard is not a bad idea... in light of recent news."

"What recent news?" Briana asked. Her red curls hung down the front of her swim team warm-ups.

Jonas looked from me to Jack to Briana.

She shrugged, raising an eyebrow. "Well? What news?"

I pushed to stand. No one moved to help me. "Dad left me Wellington Boarding School. As in, the entire school—everything about it—mine."

"And some amount of money that sent her into the mother of all panic attacks."

If I'd had the energy, I'd have punched Jonas. I hadn't seen him since the morning I was given the news of my inheritance, and actually I was a little shocked that he'd given me space after witnessing my hyperventilation.

"Are you kidding?" Briana asked. "That's awesome."

I rolled my eyes at her.

Jack rotated his shoulders. His brows furrowed, casting a darkness over his eyes that made me stand taller. I stuck my hands out to the side, a little dizzy.

"Hey." Jack wrapped his hand around my forearm, offering me some support when he realized that I was off balance. His expression softened. "Take it easy. Let's get you over to the infirmary. Seth or a nurse can check you out."

"I'm fine. I couldn't have been out long."

"You were floating head down in the pool when I ran in," Jonas said. "But you're right. I wasn't far when I heard your screams in my head."

"And why is that? How did I get that lucky?" I narrowed my eyes. Jonas's eyes darted toward Briana, whose face turned fire engine red.

"Jonas walked me to practice. I was in the locker room when I heard you." She thumbed toward the doors over her shoulder.

"So what happened?" Jack finally asked. The edge of his voice had returned, scalpel-sharp.

"Maya was here. She had a message from Sandra. After delivering the message, she tried to drown me. It seems that Sandra likes to have her minions submerge me in water for some reason." Probably her way of telling me that she can get to me, even in places where I'm most comfortable.

"Come on." Jack placed an arm around me, giving me support, and began leading me toward the locker room. "Let's get you a warm shower and some clothes."

"What was the message?"

Jack and I stopped at Jonas's question.

I turned. "That she's not done with us. That she insists we join her."

Oh, and that someone besides Sandra wanted me dead.

~~~~~

For breakfast, the lovely food specialists in the cafeteria had concocted a green smoothie complete with spinach, banana, and frozen mango, along with some kind of vitamin supple-
~~~~~

ments. It was quite the departure from my high-sugar cereal favorites, but handy since Jack insisted we get our breakfast to go.

And I needed to get to my computer. The thought of another video message from Sandra was enough to send my pulse racing.

November had brought with it cooler temperatures and grayer skies. I hugged my winter jacket tighter as I thought about how to ditch Jack. "Where are we going?"

"Coach is waiting on us." He was a step ahead of me. "He wants to talk to us before class." He hadn't looked me in the eye since we were by the pool.

I took a sip of the smoothie, letting the cold liquid soothe my scratchy throat, damaged from coughing up all that water. "You're mad."

From behind, I could see his shoulders rise and fall from a deep breath. Without turning, he thought, *I've seen you nearly killed so many times now that I've lost count. You can't imagine what it felt like to walk in and see your lifeless body by the side of the pool.*

"I'm sorry." It was all I could think to say. And I was positive he knew I was apologizing for more than almost dying.

He stopped abruptly and faced me. I jerked backward a little, and his lips tugged downward. "When I walked in and saw Jonas performing CPR on you..." His voice was barely above a whisper. "All I could think was, 'This is it. She's going to die, and I did nothing to make sure she knew how much I loved her.'" Tears formed in his eyes.

The pain in my throat from holding back sobs was almost too much to bear. Would he still love me when he discovered that I was already actively searching for his father? That I planned to make John DeWeese and Sandra Whitmeyer pay for the lives they took from me? That I planned to destroy their labs, one way or another?

A part of me didn't think he would object to part of my plan, but I hated for him to see this darkness in me. A darkness I didn't even know existed until recently.

"What is it?" Jack asked.

I shook my head. I continued to fight back tears. I would not cry.

"I know you still love me," he said.

"Of course I do," I said without thinking. My eyes shot up to his. "But..."

"But what?" He slid a hand behind my neck, forcing me to look at him.

In my mind I brought up the image of the dulled neurons of Dani's brain, just after Sandra had shut off the lights that represented her life. Just remembering that image was enough to let coldness into my heart—to remind me that I had already set a plan into action. Seth and Coach were actively searching for wherever it was that Sandra may have moved her labs. And I now had the means to do whatever I wanted to do with those labs. I could destroy them, and everyone in them, including Sandra and John.

My neck stiffened under Jack's touch. "Love won't be enough. Too much has happened. *Is* happening." Our love wouldn't stop Sandra from hurting Jack, if that's what she set out to do.

He shook his head. "You're wrong. We'll fight together. Like we always have." I knew he meant what he said, but I could also see the doubt slowly creep into the trenches forming on his forehead, his face scrunching up in worry. "We'll find this new clone. We can remove her tracker. It's gotta be the tracker that's making her come after you."

I pulled away from him, stepping back. "Don't you get it, Jack? This will *never* be over. We'll never be free of this life. You once thought we could run, but you know we can't. We're still at Wellington because there is no escape."

"It doesn't have to be like this—"

"Oh yeah? How's it going to be, Jack? Tell me. Because from where I'm standing, every time I turn around, someone new is getting inside my head. I'm exhausted. I can't keep fighting every new path Sandra finds into my head. And I won't let them kill someone else I love." I would find a way to protect what was left of my loved ones—and this school that my dad had fought so hard to preserve.

"What are you saying?"

I let my eyes close while I took a deep breath. I had said too much. "Nothing. I'm saying nothing." I pinched the bridge of my nose. When I opened my eyes, Jack was staring at me, waiting. I sighed. "I'm tired," I said. "And I need to do something before I meet with Coach."

"I'll go with you."

"No," I said, a little too quickly. "I'll meet you there. I just need a few moments alone."

He closed the distance between us, standing so close his body appeared taller and larger. "Fine. But listen to me, Lex. I don't know what's going on inside your head or what you're planning, but I won't let you shut everyone out."

"You don't have a choice." My voice had taken on a permanent edge.

"Oh yeah? You're forgetting something."

I placed a hand on my hip, refusing to step away, refusing to be intimidated. "And what might that be?"

"I don't need a tracker to get inside your head. Sure, you can shut me out, keep your secrets. For a while. But you won't do it for long."

"You wouldn't break the trust we've worked so hard to build."

"I would rather break our trust and risk losing you than see you self-destruct or put yourself in danger."

And with that, he turned and stormed off.

"You can't get inside my head anymore," I yelled after him, but even I knew my words didn't carry much weight.

NINE

I didn't want to think about the possibility of Jack sneaking inside my head and discovering the truth about his dad, or about the fact that I'd sent information to the FBI. As I raced through the administration building, I vowed to tell Jack everything. Today. We'd have to be ready to protect ourselves from Sandra.

However, classes started in an hour, so first I would find out what else Sandra had emailed me.

I passed a secretary on my way to my new office, and she gave me a quick nod. Voices carried from the conference room where I had met with the attorneys.

"She doesn't know how to run a school! Let alone all the programs we have going on here. Peter didn't know what he was doing when he left her the school. Or anything else." It wasn't hard to place Cathy's voice. It was like poison on top of an already poor day.

"I can only guess, but I suspect he knew *exactly* what he was doing." As always, Seth's voice was calm, in control.

"We have no choice but to help her," Dr. Wellington added. "We can still get what we want out of this."

I placed a flat hand on the ornate wooden door and slowly pushed it open. Roger Wellington and Seth looked up. Cathy sat taller in her seat. Her face completely transformed, the thick lines in her forehead disappearing, a weightless smile suddenly forming on her lips.

"Oh, Lexi, darling," she practically opera-sang in a multiple-personality kind of way. "How *are* you this morning?"

I took a few steps into the room, studying each of the three people seated at the table. Leaning against the edge of the table, I set my green smoothie on the wood. Sweat from the cup immediately began pooling around the base. I focused on Cathy.

"Are you insane? Bipolar?" She straightened and pursed her lips. I looked at Dr. Wellington. "You were explaining how you could still get what you wanted out of *this*. And what is it that you want out of *this*? Exactly."

He stood, clasping his hands in front of him. "What we've always wanted. To create amazing doctors... no, not doctors, healers... from the most intelligent humans ever created."

I stared at him. He spoke like this was just another day at boarding school—like I hadn't almost been captured for Sandra's own personal experimentation a couple of weeks ago.

"I think I'm starting to understand," I said. "This is all playing out exactly how you intended, isn't it? You cloned human embryos, modified their genetic makeup to suit your purpose, and now you're attempting to control those *humans* like they're your property." I emphasized the word "humans" in the hope that I would point out the obvious: that we are not machines built based on planned specifications. "You're no different than Sandra Whitmeyer."

"Now, wait just a minute." Dr. Wellington's face reddened. "We thought the cloned embryos were destroyed eighteen years ago. Even your dad thought they were destroyed. From the moment we learned of your existence, we have done nothing but try to protect you and the other clones. This has not been easy."

"*What* hasn't been easy, exactly?" I asked.

"Keeping you, Jack, Kyle, and Bree a secret. Especially after we discovered that Sandra hadn't stopped cloning humans."

"So, when you discovered the truth, you—what? Thought you'd gather us together and see what you could gain from the situation?"

Seth's lips tipped up as he calmly lifted his coffee mug and took a drink.

Dr. Wellington's hands curled into fists against the table. "It's not—"

Seth lifted a hand. "Just stop, Roger. Lexi knows it's not like that. She wouldn't have stayed at Wellington if she actually thought you meant her harm. Am I right, Lexi?" He winked at me.

I stared at the three of them. Seth had a point. Though I found Cathy annoying, Roger questionable, and Seth a little too mysterious and a little too related to Sandra, I didn't fear for my life when I was around them. Maybe because I knew they couldn't do much to me here at school with Coach nearby, or without someone else witnessing something.

Seth continued. "What Lexi needs... what we *all* need... is for Wellington to continue to operate. Business as usual. The students here need consistency and normalcy. Many of the younger clones we've found still don't know what they are. And we're still figuring out if Sandra altered them in any way. If we discover more clones, or if more escape Sandra, they'll need a place to seek asylum."

I crossed my arms, processing. Seth was right. I needed Wellington—the only home I'd known for the last eight years—to keep going while I searched for Sandra. My dad had set this school up to shelter unsuspecting kids from what they were while they learned to be who they were supposed to be. That's what he'd done for me, and that's what I was going to do for others like me.

"Dr. Wellington, I have a question." He raised a brow when I spoke. "Is Wellington self-sufficient? Can it support itself financially based solely on the tuition it charges?"

He smiled, and after casting a smug glance at Cathy, he answered. "Yes, my dear. Your father and I, along with many parents of the other... uh... *students*..."—his pause told me that by "students" he actually meant other clones—"...set up Wellington to operate without the need for external support. Not from the state or... anyone. That's why the tuition is rather... well, steep. And thanks to your father's continued work overseas, he set up a trust to cover anyone who comes our way without the means to pay that tuition. A board is in place to ensure Wellington functions as an elite school for the super-wealthy, complete with security and privacy for those who need it."

I was sure the information regarding this trust was located in the documents left by my new lawyer, Ms. Long.

"Speaking of which..." Cathy fiddled with the coffee mug in front of her, turning it round and round. "Your mother has been in touch. She insists that you need around-the-clock security."

"My mother." Like I would take the advice of a mother who left me when I was barely a toddler, then left her own mother—my gram—to be cared for by Dad and me.

"That's right. Apparently Ms. Long, one of your attorneys..."—Cathy's face seemed to morph through several emotions before she lifted sad eyes to me—"...well, honey, she was found in her office last night. She'd overdosed on some sort of medication she was on. They're ruling it an accident, but..."

My heartbeat picked up speed. "But what?" I asked when Cathy didn't continue.

She waved a hand through the air. "Your mom... well... I think she's overreacting, but she thinks it may have been murder, and wants more protection for you. Anyway, she says not to wait much longer to get in touch with her."

I fought hard not to ball my hands into fists. A woman, an innocent woman, had been murdered... because of me.

I picked up my smoothie and took a sip, letting the cool liquid slide down the back of my throat again. I hoped that the more I pretended to be calm and in control, the more I would actually believe it.

"Anything else? Because I need to speak to Seth alone before I go to class."

And I wasn't about to discuss my mother with Cathy DeWeese.

~~~~~

Alone in my new office, I powered on my computer. My hands shook, and my stomach reeled thinking of Ms. Long. According to her, she and I had been the only two who'd known the exact terms of my inheritance. She'd also had hinted at measures put in place in case anything happened to her
~~~~~

or me. But what measures? And what information did she have that might have resulted in her murder?

Seth entered and closed the door behind him. "Nicely done in there. Equal parts snarky and mind-your-own-business attitude."

"A woman was murdered, Seth."

"I know." His lips thinned into a straight line. "I'm sorry."

I brought up my email; I had to focus forward. Sure enough, just as Maya promised, there was an email waiting for me from an unknown address with an attached video. "Any leads on where Sandra and John DeWeese may have gone?" I asked without looking up. Even I was starting to notice a change in my demeanor as I addressed Seth, a doctor twice my age and arguably twice my level of maturity. "Have they set up a new lab?"

"There's no question they've set up a new lab. They would have had to have. Or, more likely, they had a lab in place well before coming here."

I lifted my eyes. "So UK was just a stopover on their way to another place. They never had any intention of staying there?"

"Definitely. Remember, Sandra's main reason for coming to Kentucky was to try to bring you, and others from the original seven, on to her team. And from what Jack and Jonas have told me, the lab at the university showed no real evidence of having bred any new clones, only developing the ones she already had into weapons for the IIA."

Sandra had verified that she needed me for her research. And the IIA was obviously willing to help Sandra in exchange for the work she did for the military. But why did the IIA care so much about me? Or was I just the means to keep Sandra working on the projects she did for the government? That made much more sense. "So you have no idea where she would have moved to?"

"No, not yet. But Coach Williams has discovered where they may have been before they came to Kentucky."

I clicked on the email and brought up the video, pausing it so that I could get my headphones out and untangled. "Where?"

"Auburn, Alabama."

"Auburn University, maybe?" He nodded. "Why there? And why another university?" I tried to recall anything I knew about Auburn from the materials I received while accumulating college brochures over the last year and a half. "Because it has the top veterinarian school, possibly? Would she have been cloning animals again and needed their facilities?"

"That's an idea, but a hunch tells me it's more than that. A lot of stem cell research and therapeutic cloning studies are done inside animal science labs. However, I'm working to draw some correlations between the two places."

I squinted at him. "How did Coach discover this?"

Seth narrowed his eyes. "Your mother told him."

That was just perfect.

Redirecting my attention to the computer in front of me, I held up a finger. I had decided I wanted to view the video first before allowing Sandra's brother to see her latest message. "Give me just a minute." After placing the earbuds in my ears, I pushed play.

Sandra appeared on screen. Her hair blew in a breeze, and a palm tree stood in the background, reminding me that she had told me I would like the "beach location" of the next lab. "Hi,

Lexi. I hope this video finds you well. That was a nice stunt you pulled back at the labs. I was impressed, and I don't impress easily."

My heart rate began a slow climb. I didn't chance a look at Seth, who had to be wondering what I was watching.

"I trust you received my messages," Sandra continued as the muscles in my spine tightened. I assumed she meant the other video she sent and the message delivered by Maya. "I know you're wondering why I would expose John as your dad's murderer."

The thought *had* crossed my mind, but I'd dismissed it since I couldn't possibly figure out the mind of a crazy person—even if I had seen every firing neuron inside it.

"I want to make you a promise, Lexi. And I have something to show you." The corners of her lips twitched a little—a subtle grin that sent a cold chill over my entire body. "First, the promise," she continued. "I will let you confront John for what he did to your daddy. Then I will allow you to turn him over to the authorities—in exchange for your help with my project."

Sandra somehow knew I would want revenge on the person who murdered my dad in cold blood, but did she think I could just forget what she'd done to Dani and Ty? Plus, she didn't just want me to join her. She still wanted the information hidden in my DNA. The information she told me herself she'd been unable to replicate.

"I know that you have the intelligence to process the good that I'm doing. Good that you can be a part of. I've discovered how to save the world from all illness..." Sandra's voice rose, and she was talking with her hands now. "To cure people who have been injured. Just by tweaking your DNA slightly, you have been gifted with an unbelievable talent for healing—even greater than what you've unlocked so far. I saw Addison's injuries after her accident. I even made them a little worse just before I went into that unfortunate coma of my own."

An audible gasp escaped my mouth. Seth, who was scrolling on his phone while waiting patiently, looked up and started toward me. I yanked the headphones out of the jack so he could hear the rest.

"I know. I know. That was evil of me," Sandra continued, her voice now filling my office. "But I knew you were going to heal her. You and Jack were growing closer. Seth was in place to teach you what you could do. It was all going according to plan. Everyone was working toward giving me everything I'd ever wanted, and they didn't even know it. I'm just sad I wasn't there to see how you actually healed Addison." She smiled and appeared lost in her own thoughts for a moment—like a mother relishing in a child's triumph.

Bile rose to the back of my throat. The room began a slow spin. I had done exactly what she'd wanted of me. I was nothing more than a marionette, and Sandra was pulling all of the strings.

"Anywho," she sang. "Now I'm just rambling."

Sandra was not rambling. She was purposefully stating what she wanted me to know.

"I have one more thing to show you." She began walking.

The camera followed her as she turned to her right and approached a grey metal door. She punched in a code and opened it. The camera must have been stopped briefly, because suddenly Sandra was in a different place—a lab—and she was dressed in a puffy white suit and had a protective mask of some sort over her head. Behind her were men dressed the same way, standing over large machines that looked like horizontal freezers. Rows and rows of rectangular-shaped boxes, white with dark glass on top.

Sandra leaned in close to the camera. "This is so exciting. I know how much you love human life, Lexi. I saw it in your eyes while you were with me at the UK lab. And it was evidenced by you stealing Dia and Lin."

"I didn't *steal* them," I yelled at the computer. "They left because you're a demented, certifiable lunatic!"

"What are those?" Seth was leaning closer to the screen.

"What?" I had been so focused on Sandra that I had forgotten the rectangular machines behind her.

As if hearing us, Sandra asked, "So, do you want to see what's inside?"

I stared at the machines. I so badly wanted to hover above them and look inside. Yet I was terrified at the same time.

"Oh my God." Seth placed his hands on the desk beside me as if to steady himself. "Those are incubators."

"Incubators?"

"Open it." Sandra was no longer talking into the camera but to a lab tech.

A cold sweat broke out across my neck. Seth's fingernails dug into the wood of the desk beside me. I stared wide-eyed at the scene unfolding in front of me.

The lab worker punched something on a keypad, a task that appeared difficult with those clunky protective gloves covering his hands. The lights along the edge of the machine changed from red to gold to green, and then a clicking sound was followed by the whoosh of air as a door over half of the machine opened like the lid of a coffin.

Sandra peered into the machine, then turned and seemed to look straight at me before grabbing the camera from whoever had been doing the filming. She held it out at arm's length so I could still see her face. "Lexi, I'd like to introduce you to a clone of your best friend."

For the second time that week, I couldn't breathe. Sandra guided the camera to give me a look inside the incubator. Beneath a layer of glass was a clear liquid, but in that liquid was what appeared to be a human baby.

"What has she done?" Seth gasped beside me. "She's growing humans outside of a human body! True test tube babies."

I stood sharply, knocking my rolling chair backward against the wall, and pulled in a deep, labored breath. "Look at how many there are." My voice came out hoarse and breathy. Had Sandra truly cloned Dani? "Oh, God." I dug the heel of my hand into my chest.

Sandra's face filled the screen again. "Well, that's it for today. Bye!" Just before the screen turned to snow, she actually raised her hand in a friendly wave.

"She can't get away with this," I whispered. A large lump burned the back of my throat.

"She *is* getting away with this." Seth moved around the desk. He linked his hands behind his neck and tilted his face toward the ceiling. "The International Intelligence Agency is *allowing* her to get away with this."

"What do you mean?"

"How else could she fund such a facility? To run a laboratory big enough, sophisticated enough to clone humans in large quantities... that would take an enormous amount of money. Government money."

And it would take a large amount of money to take that kind of operation down.

Money I now had.

TEN

I rushed across campus to get to class on time, but slowed when I saw two vehicles—an older-model SUV and Jonas's car—parked in the drop-off lane. Jack leaned against the SUV, aviators covering his eyes. His visage was unreadable.

On the sidewalk behind the vehicles, Jonas and Briana stood with Georgia, Fred, and Kyle. I hadn't seen Kyle in two weeks. I had meant to stop by his dorm room to make sure he was okay. I knew he was still mourning Dani. We all were. How would I tell him what Sandra had done? How would I tell any of them?

They all had strange facial expressions, like they were scared to tell me something. "What's going on?" I asked Jack when I got closer. Jonas acted like he was listening to the others' conversation, but he was staring at me.

"A field trip." Jack pushed off the truck and took three steps toward me.

"We have classes," I said, stating the obvious.

"We're cutting. Not like we need any of those classes to graduate."

He was right. The advanced classes we all took were formalities. Those of us who had been enrolled at Wellington had completed all of our AP classes by junior year. We were now taking college courses, or classes such as art, for fun.

He reached for the strap of my backpack, I assumed to take the weight off my back, but I shrugged away and out of his reach. For some reason this "field trip" felt like some sort of intervention.

"Why are we cutting?" I couldn't hide the defensive tone in my voice.

My mind and stomach churned from the vision of incubators growing live human babies into whatever scientific beings Sandra wanted them to be. I wanted so badly to tell Jack, to let him comfort me. But Sandra had such a hold on me. She was going to hurt someone I loved; I knew it.

He let his hand drop back to his side. "Because we are. The seven of us, plus Dia and Lin, need to get out of here."

His face remained expressionless. His lips didn't move up or down. I couldn't see his eyes behind his dark aviators. But I knew he was holding something back.

Jonas clapped his hands together when Dia and Lin pushed through the doors of the guys' dorm, hand in hand. "The gang's all here. Let's hit the road."

I'm not going. I have things to do. Heat crept up the back of my neck and spread down my arms. I couldn't do this and keep what Sandra was doing a secret. Jack and Jonas would see right through me. And Jack's coldness was scaring me.

Yes, you are. Jack was not to be argued with. *Get in the car.*

I folded my arms across my chest and stared Jack down. He opened the back door of one of the SUVs and gestured for me to get in.

Then, after readjusting the weight of my bag, I did what any self-respecting girl would do: I turned and stormed off. I was *not* going to be ordered around. *I* held the power at this school now, and no one—not even Jack—was going to give me orders.

Jack let me get about twenty yards before he caught up to me, slid his fingers around my upper arm, and spun me around. With his free hand, he removed his sunglasses. His pupils were dilated, making his irises the color of midnight, with thin layers of sapphire on the outer edge. Instead of anger, I saw pain beneath his furrowed brows. "I'm sorry, Lexi, but you're giving us no choice." *Jonas, Kyle, make her get in.*

I quickly tried to rearrange all of my thoughts to keep Jonas out, to keep him from seeing what I had watched on the video from Sandra. Then I attempted to block him out altogether, to keep him from controlling my actions. But I was too late. I hadn't expected what happened next.

Jonas grabbed my arms from behind, holding me in place, while Jack stuck a needle into my bicep.

I won't forgive you for this, I managed before my legs buckled. Jonas was all that kept me from sliding to the ground.

Lexi, I'm sorry, too. We really hoped it wouldn't come to this. Kyle's voice wove in and around the tiny space of my consciousness.

Then why are you doing this?

Kyle slid my backpack off my shoulder. I was conscious enough to see him stick it in the back seat of the vehicle. Then Jack slid an arm around my back and another one under my legs, and lifted and cradled me to his chest.

Jack, I can make her get in the car, Kyle said.

It's fine. We don't need you going blind on us. Anyway, it still might come to that at some point.

Unable to fight what I was truly feeling while under the influence of whatever drug Jack injected me with, I laid my head against his chest. He smelled of ocean breezes, and I mentally berated myself for enjoying the scent.

Kyle climbed into the driver's seat, and after placing me in the back seat, Jack climbed in beside me. I assumed everyone else filled the two vehicles, but I was too groggy to look.

Jack stroked my arm as I snuggled against him.

I meant it when I said I'd never forgive you for this.

No, you didn't. Besides, it's a risk I'm willing to take. He leaned his face into my hair and kissed the side of my head.

I usually feel more loopy on this drug. I was surprised to find that my thoughts still felt very clear, and I was less controlled than I had been the last time Jack and Kyle had drugged me—when they'd gotten me away from Jonas's and Ty's mindsiege. The fact that this was becoming a "usual" thing told me that I was obviously hanging out with the wrong friends.

It was a very low dose. I wanted to be able to talk to you and get honest answers.

It wasn't a truth serum. When Jack didn't respond, I added, *Was it?*

I felt his body vibrate as he chuckled. *You should rest. We'll have plenty of time to talk when we get where we're going. And I suspect you're going to be pretty pissed when this mild depressant wears off. We'll both need energy for the fight we're going to have.* He leaned closer and placed a gentle kiss on my cheek, then pulled my body a little closer.

He was right about one thing. He would deal with an avalanche of anger from me when this drug wore off, but until then, I would enjoy the soothing sound of the highway and the comfort and strength of his arms.

~~~~~
~~~~~

I woke in a haze in the back seat of the SUV. I was alone. The sun, high in the sky, warmed the vehicle. Voices carried through the small cracks left in the windows.

I sat up and took in my surroundings. Trees on three sides. We were parked in some sort of gravel lot. Georgia, Fred, and Jonas appeared to be studying a piece of paper.

Where the hell are we? I mindspoke to anyone who would listen.

They all turned and looked at the vehicle. Georgia rolled her eyes. A smirk spread across Jonas's face. He folded the paper and stuffed it in his back pocket.

The door beside me opened, and Jack held out a hand to help me out. I ignored his hand and pushed past him.

"All right, everyone know where we're going?" Jack walked around to the rear of the SUV and reached inside. "No one should get too far ahead or fall too far behind."

When Jack turned to face me, he thrust my own hiking boots at me. *You're going to want to put these on.* The sweetness from before was gone. His entire demeanor was that of someone on a mission, preparing for battle.

I took the boots. I had no idea how or when he managed to get them. "Will someone please tell me what we're doing here in the middle of the forest? Where are we exactly?"

"Red River Gorge," Briana said as she walked toward me. She put an arm around my shoulders. "Come on. Let's get your hikers on. Jack and Jonas thought it would be a good idea for us all to get away from school for a while." She cast an evil look over her shoulder at Jonas, and maybe Jack. "I don't know why they're being such jerks about it. Hiking will be good for us."

I said nothing and didn't make eye contact with Jack or Jonas the entire time I changed shoes, though Jonas managed a couple of smirks my way. He was not himself. This was a perfect opportunity for him to make sarcastic comments, yet he remained quiet.

And Jack... Minus the few tender moments before I fell asleep, Jack was a different person, too. He had practically manhandled me into the back seat, and he had yet to tell me why he was slamming things around and speaking with an edge that would cut even the least sensitive.

"You okay?" Briana asked as I pulled my laces tight.

"Fine."

"I'm just as confused as you are about why Jack forced you to come without discussing it with you first, but Lexi?" Her voice lowered to a whisper.

I looked up at her. A curl of red hair hung down in front of one eye.

She glanced toward the others, making sure they were out of earshot. "Jack loves you. If he's not acting like himself, it's only because you've cut him out of your life lately. He and Jonas have both acted weird the last two days. I've seen them huddled in corners, or leaving the dining hall together before they've even had time to finish their meals."

I nodded, then continued to tie the laces of the second boot.

Once my boots were all laced up, I walked toward the vehicle where Jack was tightening his own shoes. When he saw me approach, he went to pull his pant leg down over his boot, but not before I saw the leather sheath holding a knife at his ankle.

I took a step back, my pulse quickening. *Why are you carrying a knife?*

Jack turned and met my fearful eyes. *We're in the middle of the wilderness,* he stated matter-of-factly. *It's just a precaution.*

I proceeded to set my shoes in the rear of the SUV. That's when I noticed two large backpacks, complete with what looked like camping gear. I turned toward the other vehicle. Kyle was placing a backpack on Lin's back, and another one sat at his feet.

What's going on, Jack? Enough's enough.

Are you ready to listen without freaking out? The minute you freak out, we start hiking and stop talking. And if I have to sedate you and let Kyle lead you on this hike, that's what we'll do.

Stop talking to me like I'm ten. Why was it so important to get me away from school?

"Wellington is being evacuated this afternoon."

"What? Why?" My voice came out a little louder than I'd planned.

"Oh, here we go," Fred said from somewhere behind me.

"My money's on Jack sedating her before this is done." Georgia crossed her arms and leaned against a tree to watch the conversation.

"Coach Williams received intel from his contacts at the FBI. They've been monitoring phone lines, and apparently there's been some chatter about someone taking the entire school out."

"Taking it out? Who? What does that even mean? Like bombing the school?"

"Or a major shooting. We don't know. But Coach felt it was reliable enough, and Dr. Wellington suggested that the nine of us get away from the school before the evacuation even began."

"Why did he suggest we leave before the others? I should be there. That's my school now."

"Dean Fisher is running things just fine. You've owned Wellington for like two minutes." Jack's words reeked of condescension.

"You're not telling me something. Why did we sneak away before the evacuation was even announced?"

Jonas moved to stand directly beside Jack. "Your name was mentioned repeatedly in the wiretap. The FBI believes there's a bounty on your head."

"A bounty?" I nearly laughed. Not because this was funny, but because a bounty seemed so... absurd. "You mean there's a reward for my capture? That's ridiculous."

Jonas and Jack traded glances.

"What?" I placed a fist over my heart.

Jack stepped closer and cupped my cheek. "Someone wants you dead, Lexi."

I searched Jack's eyes. This wasn't news. It wasn't that long ago that someone ran us off the road. But hearing Jack say the words made the threat seem more real. "Sandra?" Which didn't make sense. Why would she go to such trouble to share information with me, entice me to join her, if she wanted to kill me?

"I don't think so. I don't think she or the IIA ever intended to kill you, only to lure you into her web. According to Coach, this is different. It's a threat from an unidentified source."

I rubbed my chest above my racing heart and concentrated on keeping my breathing slow. "Sandra knows who wants me dead. Maya mentioned something before she nearly drowned me."

Jack placed his hands on either side of my head. "We are not going to let anything happen to you."

I nodded. "Why not tell me this from the beginning?"

Because I think you know why someone wants to kill you. I was pissed when Coach and I couldn't find you earlier. You were with Seth, learning more information that you're planning to keep from me.

I'm not—

Jack held a hand up. *Don't bother. If you were about to say 'I'm not going to keep anything from you,' then you'd be right. Before we leave this forest, you* will *tell me everything. Whether that's tomorrow or next week will depend on you.*

Fine. Let's hike. I hadn't wanted to keep everything from him. I was scared. And now, all I could think about was Ms. Long. If someone had murdered her because of the information she had regarding my inheritance, was I in danger for the same reason? Was my mother?

Wait. Take this. Jack grabbed my hand and slid a ring onto my finger. I looked—it was the same ring I'd used to paralyze Sandra inside The Farm. *I believe it will work on bears as well.* He winked.

I turned and stalked off, while rubbing the underside of the ring with my thumb. I should have been scared, but Jack looked worried enough for both of us. And anger trumped fear.

Georgia shrugged at Fred like she was impressed that Jack and I hadn't come to blows. "What?" I said to her, practically provoking her into a verbal argument.

"I'm just surprised how easily you gave in, that's all."

"She hasn't given in," Jack said. "But she will."

~~~~~

Kyle led the way, followed by Dia and Lin, then Briana and me. Georgia and Fred laughed from time to time behind us. Jack and Jonas brought up the rear.

We had been hiking for well over an hour when it was decided we would stop for a late afternoon lunch. I leaned against a tree, setting my pack on the ground at my feet. Jack handed me a bottle of water.

"Thanks."

"We're going to camp tonight."

I had already guessed that was the plan, given that all four guys had heavy packs on their backs, complete with tents and other supplies. The girls also carried camping supplies. Well... except for me. I hadn't been given enough notice to prepare for anything. *Whatever,* I thought.

"Take a walk with me." Jack grabbed my hand and tugged gently.

I studied him for a minute. He wore a black and white flannel shirt over a tight black Under Armour shirt. It was the perfect combination of sporty and rugged. His eyes pleaded with me.

I pushed off the tree. Jack turned and, without dropping my hand, led me farther along the path and away from the others.

After ducking through a tunnel of low-hanging tree branches, the path opened up to reveal a clearing beside a creek that ran through the center of the gorge.

Jack dropped my hand and walked backward while appearing to size me up. "How about a light workout?"
~~~~~

A light workout, huh? I quirked an eyebrow. What he meant was, he wanted to do a round of taekwondo while he played mind games with me. I gave my head a little shake.

"Scared?"

Very, but I wouldn't tell him that. A breeze picked up and blew wisps of hair away from my face. The air was crisp and carried the scents of damp leaves and moss growing on the bark of trees preparing to go dormant for winter.

"I'm sorry I wasn't there for you when you listened to the reading of your dad's will. I'm sorry I haven't been with you for a lot lately." Jack unbuttoned the cuffs of his flannel shirt and rolled the sleeves up to his elbows. "Jonas thinks that whatever you inherited is the reason someone wants you dead. And I suspect it has very little to do with your new ownership of Wellington."

"I suspect you're right."

"Talk to me, Lex."

I walked toward the stream that ran rapidly over large rocks. Like a little kid, I grabbed a small, fallen tree limb and poked at the mud beneath the bubbling rapids. Jack didn't deserve the hypocrite I had become. He also didn't deserve to know that the reason I was keeping so much from him was because I believed his father was the one who killed my dad.

He grew so quiet behind me, I wasn't sure he was still there.

"Tell him, Lexi."

I jumped, almost falling in the water. Jonas had snuck up on us. I faced them both. Jack looked from Jonas to me. "Tell me what?"

Jonas nodded encouragement.

Tears flooded my eyes. *I can't,* I mindspoke to them both. A lump the size of a mountain formed in my chest and threatened to cut off my air supply. I swallowed hard against it and looked up through the shedding trees to the blue sky overhead. A tear spilled over and slid down my cheek. Sandra always followed through on her threats.

Jack took two giant steps forward to stand right in front of me. "Whatever it is, we'll be fine. We've survived so much already. I can't help you if I don't know what it is."

I stood straighter, swiped at the tears that revealed sadness instead of the anger that burned deep in my gut. "You say that like there's nothing so big that it can't take us down, but you're wrong."

"I'm not wrong. There's nothing you can tell me that will change that. I haven't made the best choices where you're concerned the past few days, but my feelings haven't changed."

"It's not your feelings for me that I'm worried about." I turned away again. I was about to destroy any hope of a happily-ever-after with Jack once and for all.

Jack placed hands on my arms and rubbed up and down. When I remained silent, he flipped me around. Jonas had disappeared. "This is ridiculous. Just tell me. Nothing will change between us. I promise."

"Don't you get it?" I lifted my arms in a move that broke the contact between us. "Everything has *already* changed. We won't recover from this. And that was exactly what Sandra wanted."

And that's when it dawned on me. Sandra fed me this video about Jack's father, and sent Maya into our lives, at a time when we were already vulnerable. Not that she could have known just how vulnerable we were, but she had certainly intended for my twin clone to cause problems, and surely she knew that discovering that John DeWeese killed Dad would drive a thick wedge between Jack and me. "This is what she wants," I said. "She wants to drive me away from you." I turned and started to walk away, but Jack stopped me.

"Then don't let her. Don't let her win, Lexi. Tell me right now. Just say it." His fingers wrapped around my wrists, holding me in place as I stared up into his eyes. "Spit it out, Lex."

"Your father killed my dad," I whispered.

"What?" His jaw tightened. "How do you know this?"

I stiffened under his touch, then said in a low voice, "Sandra sent me a video so that I could watch him do it. It was my birthday gift."

Jack's eyes searched mine. What was he looking for? Truth? Deceit? For any sign that I might be mistaken? His grasp on my wrists loosened, and this time it was Jack who turned away.

And after a few beats, he stormed off into the forest.

ELEVEN

I don't know where he went!" I screamed at Jonas. "He just walked away after I told him."

I turned on him, and he backed up a step. "This is *your* fault. I *told* you this would destroy him." I hadn't even gotten the chance to tell Jack that I'd made sure the FBI knew John DeWeese had killed Dad.

I looked around the campfire Kyle had built. Kyle had kept himself busy constructing a campsite from the moment we decided where to camp for the night. Staying busy was his way of coping with the heartache he suffered the day Dani was stripped from us.

Dia and Lin, who huddled together on a log, seemed to only have each other. Jonas, Georgia, and Fred supported and protected each other. Briana hardly ever spoke of her family. We all suffered in our own way.

And now Jack faced the realization that his parents were not what he once believed—that his father was responsible for taking the one family member I'd had left who was capable of loving me.

We all had lost. Each in different ways, but we suffered nonetheless.

"I'm sorry," Jonas finally said, but he didn't sound sorry. "He needed to know. That, and so much more. This camping trip is about more than us escaping some unrealized threat on the school. It's about you finding a way to trust again—for us *all* to trust each other. Sandra wants you to feel alone, but you're not alone in this."

"Don't you think I know that?"

"Do you? Then start acting like it."

"That's enough," Briana said. "You both have to stop this."

Jonas raised a flippant hand and stormed off toward the fire, joining the others.

"What's going on between you and Jonas?" Briana asked.

I glanced sideways at her. "I'm not sure what you mean."

"You know exactly what I mean. I can't decide if you two fight like a brother and sister protecting each other, or a couple in love."

Jonas looked up from where he was stoking the fire. Was he hearing our conversation? I thought I had successfully kept him out of my head lately, but I had no way of knowing. I only knew that he had stopped controlling my movements. And that he didn't seem to know certain things I had learned recently. His eyes drifted back and forth between Briana and me, eventually landing solely on Bree. His cheeks relaxed, and his lips lifted into a smile.

"Is that answer enough for you?" I smiled at her.

"For now." She left me and joined him on a log beside the fire.

~~~~~

I tossed and turned for hours. Just after four a.m. I gave up. Trying not to disturb Briana, who snored softly beside me, I unzipped the tent and slipped out into the sounds of the forest
~~~~~

waking up around me. Birds chirped, trees creaked, and something wrestled in the leaves behind the tents.

A light fog hovered along the ground at the base of the trees. Someone shifted in the tent beside ours—someone else who couldn't sleep, maybe. Had to be Jonas or Jack, because theirs was the only tent that hadn't been up when I'd gone to bed the night before.

I'd heard Jack's voice when he'd returned. It had been well after dark. I could have punched him for scaring me like that, which is why I turned over and pretended to sleep when he looked in on me. He mindspoke my name, and, fighting against tears I refused to let fall, I ignored him.

Now the fire, smelling of charred beech and the lingering scent of roasted marshmallows, smoldered in the middle of our semicircle of tents. I zipped my parka all the way to my chin and, relishing in the peacefulness of the early morning, went in search of a spot to think. I found it on top of a large boulder overlooking the creek.

Not long after I settled into a morning meditation, Jack entered my mind. *I'm sorry I worried you last night.*

Not knowing how to respond, I remained silent.

I understand if you don't want to talk to me right now, but please don't wander far. It's dangerous in the dark.

I mentally scoffed at that. *Is that why you were gone several hours past sundown?*

I wasn't far. I just needed time to think and... space. You of all people should be able to understand that.

I guess I deserved that. Since I had asked him for space not long ago. *So, did you think?*

Yes. We should talk.

I nodded, though he couldn't possibly see me. *I'd give anything for a chai latte right now.*

There's tea in my pack, but we'll have trouble with the latte part. I'll make you some as soon as we get the fire going again.

You want to join me? I asked. I was so tired from keeping Jack at a distance. My heart ached knowing I had been the one to hurt him the day before. Or ever.

A scuffle of feet in the foliage alerted me to someone approaching.

Please tell me that's you behind me and not some stalker in the woods come to slice my throat.

"Don't even joke." He climbed up on the large rock and sat behind me, placing his legs on either side of mine. He slid his arms around my waist and pulled me back to lean against his chest. "I so badly wanted to sneak into your tent last night," he whispered into the crook of my neck. He kissed me there, his breath warm against my skin.

"We would only have fought. I was so mad at you for staying away after dark. I was scared for you."

"I know. I said I was sorry." He squeezed his arms around me a little tighter, and I welcomed the touch. "I'm sorry for my father's part in your dad's murder."

"Don't be. You're not your father. You're not responsible for his actions."

"Yeah, but I had suspected he had something to do with it."

I shifted my body and tried to look back at him. "And you didn't say anything?"

He held me tighter, like I might flee at the first sign of conflict between us. "I only just began piecing elements together the last few days. I didn't want to believe it. And you haven't been talking to me."

He had a point there.

"The morning you asked me to join you for the reading of your dad's will, I had just confirmed with my mother that she had no idea of Father's whereabouts the day of Peter's death."

"That's why you were so out of sorts."

"How could I help you—hold your hand through that—if my own father was responsible in the first place? I was the one who told you of his death. I watched my own father console you and take care of you for weeks after."

I climbed down off the rock and turned to Jack. He scooted closer so that I stood between his legs. I placed a palm on his cheek. "You're not responsible for your parents' actions."

"Neither are you."

I cocked my head. "What do you mean?"

"You hid this from me because you were scared of hurting me. We can't keep these things from each other." Jack grabbed both of my hands and brought them up to his lips, then rubbed them between his own hands, warming them. "I know you're hiding more right now."

I pulled away from him and walked a few steps toward the bubbling stream. The forest was starting to lighten just slightly around us. Jack followed me.

"What are you so scared of?" His voice was so close I flinched.

What makes you think I'm scared? I was sure my voice would betray me. A chill moved through me and I visibly shivered.

"Because you and I don't keep secrets anymore. We're beyond that." He ran his hands down my arms. "And before you bring up how I kept your mom's reappearance from you, save your breath. We both know I took you to see her the minute you were safely away from Sandra and the IIA. I admit I could have handled the situation better, but I know that's not why you're hiding things from me now."

I turned in Jack's arms and searched his face for reassurances—for proof that he would still love me when I revealed the true me.

"You're shaking." He continued to rub my arms up and down. "Does this have something to do with Jonas?"

"Jonas?" I didn't understand.

"Why have you trusted him and not me?"

Was that what he thought?

Jack backed away from me, breaking contact. His face hardened. He swallowed hard, as if just realizing something for the first time. "You're in love with him, aren't you? That's why he urged you to be truthful yesterday. He saw the video Sandra sent you. The two of you have grown closer. I knew it was happening."

I shook my head. "No." He looked away from me, toward the sky, but I reached up and forced him to look down at me again. "No, Jack. I am not in love with Jonas. The only reason he saw the video of your dad was because Sandra made sure he knew I had it, and he was the only one who could tell me the password for it." It was just another example of Sandra trying to drive a wedge between Jack and me.

"You're not in love with Jonas?"

I smiled. "No, I'm not. What I am is stubborn and confused and—"

"Scared."

"Terrified." My vision turned fuzzy from uninvited moisture. "Of so many things."

"Of what? You can tell me."

"Sandra told me that if I shared my birthday gift with you—that if I told you about the video she sent me—that the next gift she sent would be sent directly to you."

"She's manipulating us."

I searched his eyes. "I know. But she hurts or kills everyone I love. I already hate her so much." I said the last part through gritted teeth. I covered my heart. "It would kill me if she did anything to hurt you."

He framed my face, rubbing my cheeks with his thumbs. "She's only doing these things to drive us apart. We're stronger together. She knows that. Of course she would try to separate us."

I nodded, then looked down at my feet and back up. "There's more." I braced for the hurt I would put in his eyes, then took a deep breath. "I gave the video that Sandra sent me to Coach. He passed it along to his FBI contacts. Your father is now wanted for questioning in the murder of my dad, and for an act of terrorism outside an airport."

TWELVE

I watched Jack's face for any changes—for any sign that this would be the end of us, because I had broken his trust in such an unforgivable way.

Jack's silence seemed to stretch between us for hours, though surely it had been only seconds. The sounds of the rapids inches from our feet thundered in my head. Every sound of the forest—birds chirping, squirrels scrambling up the trunks of trees, leaves rustling—was magnified as I waited for Jack to yell at me for my betrayal.

Instead he wrapped his arms around me and crushed me into his chest. "I know," he whispered. His chin rested on my head while he simply held me.

"You know?" I could barely hear my own voice. I pulled away to see his eyes. "But... how?"

"Coach called me last night. I told him you had a video that I wanted sent to the right authorities for analysis. I told him that if my father had anything to do with Peter Roslin's death, then he needed to answer for it."

"You told him all that?"

Jack nodded. "And it's the strangest thing." He crooked a finger under my chin and angled my face toward his. "Coach told me that it had already been turned over."

"I'm sorry." I tried to pull back, but he wouldn't let me.

"Like we already agreed, you and I are not responsible for what others have done." He smoothed out my hair, which was blowing in the morning breeze. "You and I can only control how we react, and what we choose to do with our own lives. And..." He pushed hair behind my ears. "We are responsible for each other. So please: Stop. Pushing me. Away."

I slid my arms around his back and leaned my head into his chest. "Did you ask Coach if anything had happened back at school?"

"Yeah. Nothing. Students have been under lockdown in the tunnels under the school, and no new communications have been intercepted. He said it had been eerily quiet."

"You find that odd?"

"Very. Coach will call us later, but he thinks maybe it was a false alarm."

"I hope so."

He wrapped his hand around mine and pulled me toward the large rock. Reaching down, he placed both hands around my waist and lifted me up onto the rock, then climbed up beside me. "Now lay down," he whispered.

I did. He leaned in, and his breath warmed the skin just below my ear. I lifted my head, giving him access to my neck.

His lips grazed the sensitive skin below my hairline, and his body became a warm blanket over mine. "God, I've missed you."

I allowed my hands to slip under his thick flannel shirt, where he was covered by a layer of thermal. The need for skin was too great, so I pulled at the hem tucked into his pants until my hands found skin.

He flinched at first. Raising his head, he revealed the smile there. "Your hands are cold."

I giggled. "I'm sorry."

"Don't be," he whispered with a smile against my mouth. He tilted his head one way, then the other, before he finally pressed his lips against mine.

My hands roamed his back, slowly warming to the temperature of his skin as he deepened the kiss with slow, mounting pressure. He pulled back and studied my eyes, then brushed his fingers along my hairline and let them float down to the zipper of my jacket next to my neck. Slowly, he unzipped the fleece and let his hand wander down the side of my body, stopping at my waist, never once taking his eyes off of mine.

"Jack," I said softly.

His thumb roamed over my ribcage, and I about lost all concentration for what I wanted to say. "Mmm?" He kissed the corner of my lips.

"I'm really sorry." I played with the straw-colored hair that lay across his forehead. "I never meant to give you the impression that I didn't trust you. I know that you and I are way past that."

"I believe you." He kissed me again.

I placed my full hand on his cheek. "Jack, I'm serious."

"I know you are." He leaned into my touch, then lowered his head to smile against my neck.

"I'm just so worried that—"

Lifting his head again, he placed a finger on my lips. "I know. Sandra is a threat. A real threat. But right now, we're the only two who matter. No one else. You and me. And I have you all to myself for a very short period of time."

I also had more to tell him. But he was right. None of our worries were going anywhere while we were in the middle of the forest. And we did have a rare moment alone.

Finally, I smiled and let him resume his exploration of my lips and my body. He shifted us so that he was on his back and I was on top of him. My right leg fit perfectly between his as I lay across his chest. I leaned down and covered his lips with mine. When I sucked his lower lip in gently, his hand fisted in my hair, sending shockwaves through my chest and stomach.

I didn't know how long we stayed like that before we finally settled in, and I fell asleep with my head tucked in the crook of his shoulder.

~~~~~

"What the hell, Lexi?"

The sound of Jonas's voice made me jump. I lifted my head to see him rushing at us.

Jack looked down at me. He was disoriented, as was I. Just waking up, and it being just barely past dawn, made Jonas's yelling seem all that more harsh.

I shifted so that I could climb down off of the rock. Jack followed. I smiled when I saw how tousled Jack's clothes were. *You should tuck your shirt in.*

After glancing down, Jack returned the grin.

As Jonas got closer, I could sense anger coming off of him in waves. Jack stuck out a hand to slow him. "Hey. Take it easy."

"Take it easy?" Jonas's chest rose and fell in fast movement. "I just got off the phone with Seth."

I crossed my arms across my chest. "Yes, and he told you that your lovely mother sent me another video."

Jack turned on me.
~~~~~

"What? I was getting to it. I can only confess one thing at a time." I glared at Jonas. *Nice job, idiot.*

"Just because the two of you seem to have made up doesn't mean you get a get-out-of-jail-free card. You should have told us about this the minute you saw us yesterday."

"When? Before or after you drugged and kidnapped me? If I'm in jail, it's because you guys"—I pointed at the two of them—"put me there."

At that, Jonas's lips lifted in a grin.

Asshole, I directed at Jonas. Then to Jack, *Or would you have liked for me to have stopped our "make-up" session?*

Jack tilted his head side to side, weighing the choices. "What was on this video? Would it give us a hint as to why someone might be going after Lexi?"

"The opposite, really." I placed a hand on Jack's arm. "First, are we okay?"

He wrapped an arm around my neck and leaned in to kiss my hair. *We're more than okay.* "How much are you still hiding, though?"

Jonas rubbed his hands across his face. A low growl escaped.

"I'm not hiding anything else on purpose. The video Jonas is referring to just happened. Ten minutes before you stuck me with a needle."

"So, spill it," Jack ordered.

My jaw hardened slightly. "It would be better if I showed you. It's on my computer. I think everyone needs to see it."

Jonas led the way, and Jack held my hand as we hiked the short distance back to camp.

When we got back to the campsite, I dug through my backpack, pulled out the laptop, and handed it to Jonas. "It's a good thing I had this with me when you decided to kidnap me."

The weight of a hundred elephants sat on my chest as the group crowded around my laptop, watching the video Sandra sent me. I stood in the back, gnawing on my cuticles.

Jack pulled my hand away from my mouth and slipped his fingers into mine, tugging me closer to him. *I'm sorry. This is what you were dealing with when I drugged you and packed you up for a day of hiking?*

It's okay. I squeezed his hand. I tried not to think about the fact that my boyfriend felt the need to drug me in order to get me out of town to talk to him. In a way, he probably saved me from myself in the process. Besides, we probably needed to fight it out to get back on track. Stubbornness never got us anywhere.

It's not okay. We're supposed to help each other.

And we will. Starting again, now, I mindspoke.

Jack's facial expression turned grim when we got to the part where Sandra explained that she had produced a clone of Dani.

He turned to me. *Does she realize what she's done?*

I had no idea how to answer Jack's question. The hate in my heart was growing with each interaction I had with Sandra, or Maya, or with anyone who had contributed to the operation that the IIA was seemingly funding.

"Why is she doing this?" Briana asked, staring straight ahead, when the video ended.

Kyle stood and kicked one of the backpacks. His face reddened. "She can't get away with this."

Dia and Lin, who shared a log directly in front of the laptop, remained extremely quiet.

Jonas was in deep thought across from me. "I saw the incubators in the first video she sent. I couldn't remember where I had seen those before, but now I remember."

"Yeah? Where?" Jack prompted.

"The previous lab, in Alabama. These machines were delivered just before we moved to Kentucky. Sandra and a lab tech unpacked one of them. They obsessed over it for several days. Then, the day we were to leave for Kentucky, I overheard her tell some guys to send them all somewhere..." Jonas's voice died off.

"You don't remember where?" A fire erupted in the pit of my stomach. I had to know where Sandra and John had run to. Where they were growing clones and manipulating the DNA and minds of humans. I had to stop them.

Jonas's eyes darted from side to side. His head angled toward the ground. "It was a person's name. But she made it sound like a place." He combed his hands through his hair, making it stick up in places.

"Maya, or something," Dia said. Everyone jerked their heads in her direction.

"Oh, look everyone, she speaks," Georgia said from her place against a tree.

Fred elbowed her. "Be nice."

"You're saying Sandra sent these machines to Lexi's clone twin?" Jack asked.

That didn't make sense.

Dia, who was nothing like her clone twin Briana, didn't look anyone in the eye. She wrung her hands. "I remember them talking about Maya around the same time that these machines arrived. I even heard a lab tech refer to them as Project Maya—or something that sounded close."

"She's right." Jonas circled the group. "It was close. Mia... Maria... Maya... *Myra*. That's it. She said, 'Send them to Myra.'"

"Who is Myra?" Kyle asked from his spot by the campfire. He had been trying to get the fire going again so that we could eat breakfast. The way he stoked it, though, it was like he was stabbing a wild animal about to attack.

"I don't know. I don't remember anything else," Jonas said. "Sandra acted like she kept me in the loop about a lot of things, but she really didn't."

"Well, we should eat if we're going to do some training exercises before we head back to school." Kyle's voice was hoarse, like he was fighting back rage. He dug through his pack, pulling out some granola bars and packs of instant coffee. He shoved some things back in before turning away from the group.

"I'm going to get you that tea I promised." Jack kissed the side of my head and went in search of the supplies he'd brought.

I approached Kyle from behind and put my arms around him. "I know it hurts."

He grabbed hold of one of my arms and clung to it while his body shook slightly. "I should have been able to save Dani."

I squeezed tighter. "You couldn't. You would have if you could've, but you couldn't."

He stepped forward and out of my embrace. Wiping his face with his sleeves, he went back to busying himself with the fire. We were both drowning, each in our own grief and anger.

And on top of that, I couldn't shake the horrible feeling that this camping trip had torn me away from something important I should have been doing back at school. All I had learned was that there seemed to be another person—another clone maybe—whose name was awfully close to Maya, my evil clone twin.

Something didn't add up.

Before I could think more about it, Georgia and Briana approached me. Georgia spoke first. "What do you know about Dia and Lin?"

"I know they were victims of Sandra, the way we all have been."

Briana spied Dia and Lin as they helped make coffee for Fred and Jonas. Lin laughed at something Jonas said. "They just seem a little too reserved for my liking. It's like they're hiding something."

I laughed. Weren't we all guilty of being reserved? Of keeping our thoughts to ourselves? "Guys, I'm the most non-trusting person in this group"—I glanced sideways at Georgia—"well, except for possibly Georgia."

"Ha ha." She smiled at me.

I continued, "But I trust Dia and Lin. They've been locked up inside a lab their entire lives. I'm sure they don't know what to make of all this. And they totally helped me when I was inside The Farm." Well, Lin had. Dia hadn't trusted me then, but I thought we'd moved past that after I'd helped Georgia remove their trackers.

That seemed to appease Georgia and Briana. They continued to discuss, but I tuned them out as I took in the others. That was when I noticed that Jonas and Jack had disappeared.

I scanned the campsite, and when I didn't see them, I headed off in the direction of the stream where Jack and I had talked earlier.

The sun was up now, hanging low in the sky and filtering through the trees overhead. We had camped out at the bottom of the gorge. To leave, we would be hiking mostly uphill today.

As I rounded a large tree toward the clearing by the brook, I heard their voices. I ducked back behind the tree, and cleared my head in the hope that they wouldn't hear my thoughts.

"You've lost your mind if you think I'm going to allow you to send her in there as bait again. Lexi and I will disappear before we'll take on your crazy mother again."

"What if Sandra is growing super-powered healers, Jack? What if we could cure the diseases that are killing so many these days? Lexi doesn't want to hear this, but even if Sandra is the devil herself, what she's creating could be a good thing. Can you imagine the possibilities?"

"But you're suggesting that Lexi is the missing link to Sandra's entire mission to create the perfect healer."

"*I'm* not suggesting that. *Sandra* is the one who claimed Lexi is the key. And now she'll do anything to get Lexi to come willingly to her. That's why she's sending Maya in with empty threats. That's why she's antagonizing her with video evidence of who killed her father, with images of a clone of Dani. Sandra could have killed Lexi when she had her inside The Farm, but she didn't."

"No, she didn't. Instead, she killed Lexi's best friend, and your clone twin, right in front of her." I didn't have to see Jack to know his face was growing red and that he was grabbing the back of his neck in frustration.

"What I was going to say is that, instead of killing her, it seems like she's *provoking* her. Trying to get her to seek revenge. Don't you see it? Sandra can clone anyone she wants. All she needs is a DNA sample, which she can get from a simple strand of hair. No, Sandra specifically chose to clone Dani because she's someone Lexi has loved and lost."

I peeked around the tree. Jack opened and closed his hands into fists. He was taking in Jonas's words. Jack knew Jonas was right, and I knew Jonas was right—Sandra *was* provoking me. She was adding gasoline to an already stoked fire. What none of them realized was that I didn't need provoking. From the moment I saw Dani's lit-up neurons go dark, revenge had settled into my heart.

Until recently, I just didn't know how I would get it.

~~~~~

We were halfway back up the gorge before the group began making chitchat again. Prior to that, the forest had been eerily quiet. I'd heard every twig crack beneath the foot of each hiker, oftentimes causing me to flinch for no apparent reason. We single-filed up the path. Jack and I brought up the rear.

I racked my brain for possible locations for top-secret laboratories. I didn't think Sandra could continue to hide what she was doing at large research universities the way she had at the University of Kentucky and Auburn University. Sure, she could argue to the universities that she was simply researching diseases and DNA patterns. And that might have sufficed at UK, where, from what I had witnessed, she wasn't actually growing human lab rats. But now that she was doing the un-
~~~~~

speakable to human life, I had no doubt she had moved to a remote location under high security.

But where?

I think you're right.

I jumped at the sound of Jonas's mindspeak. I had left my mind open.

I'm thinking she's left the country, Jonas joined in.

Did you ever live outside the country with her before? I stared at the back of Jonas's head. He was helping Briana climb up a small embankment.

Not that I remember.

Jack and I came to the same embankment. Placing a hand on my waist, he guided me up.

"Thanks." I glanced at our group, a line of hikers. Kyle, Lin, and Dia were getting a bit ahead of us. I wanted to tell them to slow down and stick together.

I realized that it had been smart for us to get away from school. Jack and I had been able to clear the air. We had all bonded as a group. Even if we didn't all fully trust one another, we had definitely grown closer. It was a start. And after re-watching Sandra's video this morning, there was no doubt in my mind that we were all struggling in our own ways with the truth of what we were—and with our feelings toward those who had created us.

Jack was just starting to climb the embankment behind me when bark shattered above my head, followed quickly by a popping sound echoing through the forest.

I ducked, and my breath caught.

Jack barked, "Get down."

In front of me, Jonas pulled a gun from his waistband—a gun I hadn't realized he had. He pointed Briana toward some trees. "Go that way. Hide."

"No. Not without you." Briana spoke in a loud whisper. Her eyes widened in crazed panic.

Jonas's face hardened, then he ran gentle fingers down her cheek. "God, you're infuriating." He ducked his head and looked back at Jack and me.

I also turned my head to look at Jack. He gripped a knife with his left hand, poised to attack.

"Go back," Jonas quietly hissed. "There was a small cave opening a hundred feet back. Maybe we can fit in there while we figure out what to do." Jonas reached out, grabbed Briana's hand and guided her to pass him and follow us.

Shots rang out again, echoing through the trees, this time multiple shots in quick succession. They came from somewhere above us, and sounded like some sort of semi-automatic rifle.

My stomach lurched. The adrenaline running through me promoted a thought very new to me: as many times as I had turned down guns in the past, I wanted one now. I wanted to fire back at these shooters.

Jack held my hand as I climbed back down the embankment, but I looked up just in time to see Kyle duck behind a large tree, Lin clutching his chest. Dia screamed, then scrambled up the path to where Lin landed awkwardly against some tree roots.

A gasp escaped my throat, and I moved to climb back up.

"No," Jonas said through gritted teeth. "You can't help them."

Jack reached around my waist and pulled me backward, then urged me ahead of him on the path. We ran the short distance until we found the small cave, and the four of us climbed in. It was roomier inside than it had looked from the outside.

Jack, we have to help them. My heart pounded wildly inside my head. I drilled my fist into my chest while trying to find my breath. *What about Georgia and Fred?*

We're okay for now, Georgia mindspoke. *We went down through some thick trees off the path. We're hidden. Who do you think that is?*

Jonas looked from Jack to me.

They're here for me, *aren't they?* I squared my shoulders, still breathing hard. *I can't let you guys take bullets for me.*

Jack spun me around and placed a hand on each of my cheeks. "This is not your fault," he whispered. "You hear me? We don't even know what they want."

Two quick shots were fired, and Jack's eyes widened. His entire body shuddered, and then he crushed me close to his chest, holding me there.

The sound of fast-moving footsteps made us all stop breathing. I didn't dare move from Jack's embrace.

They're coming your way, Georgia said.

We hear them, Jonas answered her. *Did you get a good look at them?*

Yeah. There're two of them. I've never seen them before. They're young, early twenties maybe.

By the sounds of heavy hiking boots against the dry path, they were just outside the cave where we hid. I wished Briana could make us all disappear. It was theoretically possible for all we knew: Jonas thought she would eventually learn additional mind tricks, much like Addison.

We're with Kyle now, Georgia reported. Then, with a quieter voice, she mindspoke: *Dia and Lin are dead.*

I gripped the fabric of Jack's coat in my fists. My body shook as the effects of grief took immediate hold. Jack held me tighter, and I buried my face into his chest to suppress my sobs.

Why did everyone around me keep dying? I thought of the attorney who presumably lost her life because of information given to her by my father. Why would someone kill her? And what information did she hold that would make her killers come after me?

And then I knew.

Georgia—you, Fred, and Kyle try to keep going, Jonas instructed. *Stay behind trees while they're down here. We'll let you know if they head back that way. Stay out of sight until you hear from us.*

Briana sniffed quietly. I turned to find her in Jonas's arms.

A voice spoke from outside the cave, and not far off by the sound of it. "Two of them are dead." It was one of the shooters, and he sounded like he was on the phone. "I don't know. The redhead, and Jack DeWeese I'm afraid... Couldn't be helped. He got in the line of fire, and we couldn't get a clean shot on Matthews... No, she disappeared with the Whitmeyer boy. I understand... Yes, sir, we'll find her."

"Well, what did he say?" asked the second shooter.

"We have to find the Matthews girl. We are not to return until she's dead, or we don't get paid."

I looked to Jack with frantic eyes. *They think you're dead. They were obviously aiming at me.*

Jonas squatted and searched silently through his pack. He pulled a piece of metal out and screwed it onto the end of his gun. A silencer. Next he lifted a second handgun and handed it to Briana, who examined the chamber. He stood and looked her in the eye, and after a silent exchange, she nodded.

What did you just tell her? I asked.

I told her not to be a hero. This is for self-defense only. Her goal is to get out of these woods. As is yours. He reached down and pulled out a third gun, then held it out to me. I stared at it for a moment. *Lexi, it's you or them.*

Jack squeezed my hand. *You also have your ring. The gun is for when you don't want to get that close. These people are here for one thing only: to kill you. I don't know why they want you dead, but we're not going to let that happen. This gun is for 'just in case.'*

I eyed the gun once more. I was so sick and tired of being fired at, threatened, and controlled. I knew how to shoot. And I had become a pretty good shot, too, thanks to Coach and Jonas. I grabbed the gun and expertly tucked it into my waistband.

"Let's split up," one of the shooters said. Their voices grew quieter and the footsteps faded. When they were gone, the four of us began planning our escape.

"The two of you are going to hike up the path," Jonas whispered, pointing at Briana and me. "Jack and I are going to find out who these guys are."

"What? How are you going to do that?" I asked.

Jonas cocked his head. "Don't worry about how. We have to know who's trying to kill you and why."

I turned to Jack, frantic. *I won't let you put yourselves in danger for me. I wouldn't be able to live with myself if something happened to you or Jonas.* I whipped around and faced Jonas. "Bree and I can help. With her trick of making them see something that they're not. And I can convince them to lower their weapons."

"She's got a point," Jonas said.

"No. I will not—" Jack began.

I placed a finger over his lips. "This isn't your decision."

"Lexi's right." Briana cocked her gun. "We'll help. You can thank us later." She managed a wink.

Bree got on my nerves often, but I liked her spirit. I smiled despite the danger that lurked.

Jonas shook his head, stifling a laugh.

"Fine." Jack framed my face with his hands. *If something happens to you, I'll kill you.*

If something happens to me, you'll fix me right up with your magical healing powers.

He leaned his forehead to mine, then brushed a kiss across my lips.

"All right," Jonas started. "We venture out. If we can disarm one of them—"

"But don't kill," I interrupted.

"Right." He pursed his lips, then continued. "If we can disarm one of them, maybe we can get him to talk—to tell us who wants Lexi dead."

Although I was pretty sure I already knew.

THIRTEEN

We stayed off the main paths. Without being able to see or hear the shooters, I couldn't use my power to control their minds. And it took too much energy for Briana to change all of our appearances for long. So Jonas and Jack tracked the shooters the old-fashioned way, by noting fresh footprints and snapped twigs.

My heart shattered as I thought about Dia and Lin. The shooters thought they had killed Jack and Briana. I was racked with guilt as I realized I was thankful that both were still with me.

The heavy metal of the firearm Jonas gave me burned through my shirt at the small of my back. The thought of using a gun on another person had at one time frightened me, but the more people who died close to me, the more I imagined my own hands wrapping around the weight of the gun, aiming it at the person who haunted me, and pressing a single finger to the trigger.

At the sound of a sharp crack of a stick behind me, I flinched, and Jack held up a hand to halt our forward motion. After placing a finger to his lips, he motioned us to walk left. He led us to a large uprooted tree trunk, large enough that it completely shielded us. We all crouched down and listened for the men to approach.

Jonas peered around the tree. *They're about twenty yards away.* He pointed the barrel of his gun toward the sky. His back was straight against the tree roots, and he was poised on his haunches and ready to attack.

Footsteps grew nearer. I took a deep breath in, attempting to calm my racing pulse.

Jonas stuck out a foot and sent a man flying over his leg. It was a large man, dressed in camouflage, and he failed to get his arms or hands out in time to break his fall, landing hard on his shoulder and not very gracefully. Yet he regained his feet with lightning speed and immediately had his rifle pointed straight at Jonas.

Jonas's hands flew up, his gun dangling loosely. *Lexi, see if you can control his head.*

Jack ducked around the other side of the tree root and surprised the other shooter by punching him in the face. The man stumbled backward, but then charged Jack.

While they wrestled, I slipped inside the mind of Mr. Grace. *Point your gun at your buddy's head.* Mr. Grace hunched his shoulders as he redirected his aim. Just as his friend raised a gun and pointed it at Jack's chest, Mr. Grace cocked his rifle and touched the barrel to his friend's temple.

"Bernie, what are you doing?" The second man's chest rose and fell in deep breaths beneath his army green jacket. Instead of lowering his gun, he raised it, pointing it straight at Jack's nose. Jack didn't dare look away from the firearm aimed at his face.

"We killed you," the man said, confusion spreading across his face. His eyes darted toward Briana and widened.

Tell him you'll shoot him if he doesn't do what we tell him to do, I ordered Bernie.

"I will shoot you if you don't do what these kids tell you to do."

Bernie's partner glanced at me out of the corner of his eye. "You're controlling his mind, aren't you?" His lips twitched. "We were warned about you. It won't work. I've been trained to resist all forms of mind control, even with the worst kinds of torture and manipulation. You could even kill us, but eventually, the man who wants you dead will kill you."

Tell him to drop the gun.

"Drop the gun, Don," Bernie deadpanned.

Don ignored the order. "Who are you exactly?" he asked me. "What did they do to you to give you this power?"

Ignoring his questions, I asked, "Who told you about my powers?"

He grinned. "The man who was willing to pay an enormous amount of money to see to it that you ended up dead."

Jonas pulled his own gun and aimed it at Don's leg. "Drop the weapon, or I shoot your foot."

The man smiled.

Jonas pulled the trigger.

The bullet formed a crater inches from Don's foot, and Don danced like he was on fire. "Dammit, man!"

"I missed on purpose that time." Jonas adjusted his aim. "This time, it'll be your knee."

Briana, can you walk away and come back as Cathy DeWeese?

Why her?

Just do it, Bree.

They know about the powers, Lexi. What makes you think that will work?

I don't know if it will, but I've got to know for sure who's trying to kill me.

And you think Jack's mom might be behind this. Behind killing her own son?

I glared at her. *Just do it.*

"Who contacted you?" Jack yelled, still staring down the barrel of a gun, breathing evenly somehow. "Who ordered Lexi killed?"

Jack, please don't antagonize him while he has a gun pointed at your head.

Jonas started to raise his gun. I motioned him to wait. If Don panicked or twitched in the wrong direction, Jack was dead.

I couldn't control more than one person at a time. But at least my nose remained dry—so far. I was getting better at this. I walked around Bernie. "Bernie, who wants you to kill me?"

"Don't tell them," Don warned. "We'll both be dead."

"What makes you think *we* won't kill you?" I asked.

A grin spread across Don's face. "You don't have it in you. Besides, I'm the one with a gun pointed at your friend."

I cocked my head. Don's arrogance sent a fire through my blood. I twirled my paralyzing ring around my finger.

I'm going to switch minds. Jonas, you prepare to take Bernie down. But don't hurt him. I think he'll be the one to crack and give us information.

I let go of my hold on Bernie.

Now, Jonas. I then slithered into Don's brain. The inside of his brain was a darker place, its blackness matching his head-to-toe outfit. *Don, lower your gun.*

He seemed to fight my command. His hand shook. Trenches of worry formed across his forehead as he furrowed his brow and scrunched up his face.

Jonas took two steps and kicked Bernie behind the knee. The man's legs buckled. Before he could fall all the way to the ground, Jonas had him in a headlock. Beads of sweat formed along Bernie's hairline.

I spread myself further into Don's brain, touching every part of his mind with mine, taking control of his actions. *Lower your gun,* I mindspoke again. His hand twitched. Jack's eyes darted back and forth between me and the barrel of the gun. *Remove your finger from the trigger.*

Finally, Don's finger slipped away from the trigger, and his arm lowered slightly. Jack took the opportunity to sweep Don's legs from under him.

I rushed toward them both. *I got this.*

I bent down over Don and, cupping my hand around his neck, stuck him with the small needle from the ring, injecting about half of the paralyzing liquid into his blood.

Once Don was incapacitated, we turned back to Jonas and Bernie.

"Way to go, boys," said Briana, disguised as Cathy DeWeese, as she rounded the corner. She was dressed in pencil-thin jeans and a designer barn jacket.

Jonas raised his head, lifting Bernie's in the process. A smirk touched the corners of his lips. "What the..."

I raised a brow. "Well, well, well. If it isn't Cathy DeWeese." I watched for any change in expressions from the two hit men.

"Let them go," Cathy ordered.

Jonas tightened his hold on Bernie. "I don't think so."

"You did this, didn't you?" I asked. "You paid these men to kill me."

"I don't know this woman," Bernie grunted through Jonas's chokehold.

So, maybe Cathy wasn't involved, but I was almost certain this threat to my life and the murder of my attorney was directly related to my inheritance. *Bree, make Jack look like Roger Wellington,* I mindspoke to Bree and Jack.

Change him right in front of these guys?

Yes. We had no choice. Besides, they knew we had supernatural mental capabilities.

Right before my eyes, Jack's facial features, clothes, height, and hair morphed into that of Roger Wellington. As he transformed, Don's eyes, the only part of his body capable of movement, widened.

Bernie's body convulsed. "What the hell?" His eyes darted from Roger, to me, to Bree, and then back to Roger.

Roger knelt before Bernie. He fisted a handful of Bernie's hair. "I ordered you to terminate this girl." He lifted his head in my direction. "What happened?"

Confusion washed over Bernie's pale cheeks. His head began to shake back and forth. "That's not possible."

"What's not possible?" Jack stood and took two quick steps toward me. *I'm really sorry,* he mindspoke, then grabbed me by the arm and yanked me to stand in front of him. "Killing this little girl is not possible?"

I was sure that wasn't what Bernie meant. I grunted and pretended to be scared of Jack. *Tell Roger the truth, Bernie. He wants to know why you failed so thoroughly at getting the job done.*

"I... we... tried." Bernie stuttered. "Their mind powers are just too strong."

"How much did this asshole agree to pay you?" I asked.

Jonas shook his hold on Bernie. "Answer her, or I promise, you'll feel a bullet in your leg."

"Five hundred thousand."

I gasped.

"That's it?" Jonas asked. He looked up at me. "Personally, I think you're worth so much more than that."

"Ah. Thanks."

"Now, you got anything left in that ring of yours?"

I stepped forward and emptied my ring into Bernie's neck.

You thought my mother had something to do with wanting you dead? Jack asked. He had returned to looking like himself.

I'm sorry. I knew it had to be someone close to my dad, someone who wanted Wellington school for themselves. Your mom and Dr. Wellington were the first two people to come to mind.

"Now what?" Bree asked. We all turned to her.

"Now... we go see my mother, Alyson Roslin."

~~~~~

Two hours later, we arrived at a gate decorated with the initials "R & R."

"Roslin and Roslin," I whispered. I hadn't noticed the gate the first time I'd visited—the first time I'd seen my mom in many years. I glanced at Jack, who sat beside me in the back seat. *My parents lived here together once upon a time. I remember that gate.* This was the safe house Dad had mentioned in his letter to me, after he died. He'd brought me here several years ago.
~~~~~

Jack linked his fingers with mine.

Fred pulled up close to the gate and began studying the keypad outside his window.

She's made some changes, I noted. Fresh black paint coated the fencing. The landscaping had been cleaned up.

Jack ducked his head and peered through the windshield. He pointed to a video camera hidden in a tree to the left of the gate, and another to the right. *She's ramped up the security for sure.*

As if on cue, as soon as I spotted the camera, the gates began to slowly open inward.

"Lexi, this is your place?" Fred asked. His red hair curled around his ears. We all had a little extra shine to our hair and skin. We could use showers.

"Sort of," I answered. "I own it with the person who was my mother." I stared out the side window at the pear trees that lined the drive. The remaining yellow leaves blew in the wind.

Cheriana sprinted up to the fence like she knew Jack was in the vehicle, then stopped and dangled her head over the rail. *Why did you bring Cheriana here?* I asked.

She needed space to run. They wouldn't turn her out in the fields at school for very long.

And you clearly had a long enough conversation with Alyson that she invited you to board Cheriana here?

Jack's brows knitted together. *Your mother made it clear to me that this house was as much yours as it was hers. I didn't want to take Cheriana to my father's farm. Alyson and I didn't think you'd mind.*

First-name basis, even.

Stop it. I'll support your decision if you never want to see your mother again after today. But I think you owe it to yourself to give her a chance.

I dropped the subject and glanced back out the window at Cheriana. *She's beautiful.*

Fred stopped the SUV in front of the house. He quickly looked toward Georgia in the passenger seat. She had been very quiet on the road trip. We'd all been quiet. Not surprising since two of our friends had been shot and killed.

Kyle, Jonas, and Briana pulled up behind us in the second vehicle.

It suddenly dawned on me. According to the notes in Dad's journals, we were the original seven.

Slowly, I pulled my hand from Jack's grasp and reached for the door handle. He touched my arm. When I turned back, he said nothing, but his expression was the reassurance I needed to face the woman I had put so much energy into hating.

I gave him a small smile. "Let's do this."

I approached the front door. Jack stayed behind me, and everyone else stayed in the vehicles. I reached my hand up, pausing before letting my fist make contact with the wood.

As I waited, it occurred to me: I was knocking on my own door. I owned half this house, and yet it felt as foreign to me as a stranger's home. Which is exactly what it was: a stranger's home. And that stranger was my own mother.

My house. My mother. And I didn't know the first thing about either one of them.

The door swung open, and my mother greeted us with a smile. Her warm expression confused me. She wore casual yet stylish knit pants and a sweater that draped elegantly around her neck and shoulders.

I glanced at Jack and then back to her. "Hi."

"Hi, Lexi." She started to lift her hand, but then thought better of it, I guessed, and crossed her arms across her chest instead. "I'm so glad you're here."

"We need your help," I said.

She stood back, opened the door wider, and allowed us to pass. "Of course."

Jack motioned for everyone else to follow, and they piled out of the vehicles.

Alyson said nothing as we filed into the living room. All of the blinds were closed, and very little light got through. A fire burned in the gas fireplace.

"Roger Wellington tried to have me killed." I turned and stared at her. "Any idea why?"

My mother looked around the room at my friends. "Can you give Lexi and me a moment alone?" They all traded glances. "There are towels and anything you might need to shower and freshen up in the guest bathrooms upstairs."

"I could definitely use a shower," Georgia said.

Jack slid his hand into mine. *I'm staying.*

I nodded.

They headed back out to the trucks to grab a change of clothes, then proceeded up the grand staircase toward hot showers. With one foot on the first step, Jonas glanced at me. *You okay with this?*

I think so.

Yell like a maniac if you need me. He grinned.

Jack looked from Jonas to me. Squeezing my hand tighter and rotating his shoulders back, he moved closer to me, if that was possible. When I looked to my mother again, I caught her examining Jack and me. She was looking at our clasped hands, and at the way my other hand crossed my body and rested on his elbow. Her eyes drifted upward until they found my eyes. "I'm glad you found each other."

"Really? Why's that?" My defensive tone came out involuntarily.

"Because the odds of your survival, or of either of you having a normal life, have always been grim. You're stronger together."

I cocked my head. Jack moved to stand just slightly in front of me, part of his body shielding mine. "She would have been stronger had a parent warned her about this life. What kind of mother deserts her newborn baby?"

My mother's jaw hardened, but then her cheeks relaxed again, and her voice came out as softly as before. "I'm the kind of mother who gave up her daughter in order to protect her," she said.

I narrowed my eyes. "To protect me? Right," I scoffed. "And just how did disappearing from my life *protect* me?"

She turned a bracelet round and round on her wrist. "I've been working with Sandra for the past twelve years. In doing so, I made sure she didn't find you."

An audible gasp escaped my lips. Surely I had heard her wrong. "You've been working with *Sandra*? Doing what?"

"I've been pretending to be pissed that your father ran off with you and hid you from me. I agreed to work with Sandra to find you and your father for her. I made her believe that my anger ran so deep that I would do anything. I also convinced her that what she was doing to further science was important and necessary work. Because I'm an electrophysiologist and a neurolinguist, I was helpful to her. I study the way—"

I held up a hand. "I know what the words mean."

She opened her mouth, then shut it with a smile. "Of course you do. I'm sorry. You have grown into a beautiful and intelligent woman, Lexi." Her hands fidgeted with the draped material of her sweater.

"That doesn't explain how you protected me."

"I continuously threw Sandra off her search for you, Lexi. In addition to giving my medical and electrophysiology knowledge to Sandra's cause, I worked tirelessly to create evidence that you were in places that you weren't. That you were in Europe and Asia with your dad, or with nannies and bodyguards he'd hired. And every time we seemed to get close to either of you, you would be gone—or at least that's what I led Sandra to believe. Your father would sometimes even make sure he was spotted by IIA in these places to make the whole thing believable."

I swallowed hard. If what my mother was saying was true, she'd given up her life for me.

"Where does Maya fit into all of this?" Jack asked, still standing in such a way that made it clear he would never allow this woman to touch me. "She claimed to be Lexi's sister."

"Ah, yes. Maya." She looked at me. "Maya and the other beta clones were created at the same time you were."

"We're the alpha clones?" Jack asked.

Alyson nodded. "I didn't know about her for a long time, of course. We didn't know a lot of what Sandra had done until well after you were born. She set everything into motion, implanting the two of you and the other original clones into surrogates. I had no idea that you weren't my biological daughter from my own eggs until Sandra found us again." Her lips tugged downward and lines formed across her forehead, her sadness apparent.

"That doesn't explain why Maya claimed to be my sister."

"I don't know why she said that. Maya was just another way for Sandra to play with life, to clone her own DNA."

"That's what Sandra does," I said. "She uses people and things to manipulate everyone around her."

"You know Sandra well." My mother smiled. She really was beautiful. Her hair hung in loose, blond waves that ended at her shoulders and framed her face. She wore minimal makeup, just enough to highlight her high cheekbones and her cat-like eyes. "I want to tell you everything, but I'm sure you and your friends are hungry. I have a lasagna I can put into the oven." She turned slightly and gestured toward what I assumed must be the kitchen.

I nodded. "We'll graciously accept." My mother turned and walked toward the kitchen.

Jack raised a brow. *We will?*

"We'll be right there," I said to my mother. When she was gone and presumably out of earshot, I said to Jack, "You don't think we should stay and hear what she has to say?"

"I do. I was just surprised to hear *you* say we should. You're the one who stormed off the first time you saw her."

"My mother may well know more about Sandra's operation than anyone else. Maybe she can tell us where this new laboratory is."

"So we can do what?" he countered. "Let's say we find out where this lab is. Then what?"

"We destroy it."

"And how do you propose we do that?"

"I'm working on it."

"You're working on it." Jack squinted at me. "I'm not going to like your plan, am I?"

I stood up on my tiptoes and kissed his cheek. "Of course you will."

I started to head toward the kitchen, but Jack grabbed my elbow and stopped me. Bringing me back, he leaned in and brushed his lips across mine. I closed my eyes and savored the warmth of his touch. When I opened my eyes, his face was close. He smiled. "You seem... I don't know... less affected by all this than I expected you would."

"Maybe I'm getting good at life on the run. And investigating the mysteries of our creation."

"I'm still ready to live permanently on the run. Just say the word."

FOURTEEN

The delicious smells of garlic and basil had brought everyone to the kitchen, and we'd all squeezed in around a large farm table. I played with the salad on my plate, and hardly touched my lasagna. Jonas mopped up every last bit of tomato sauce and cheese with his garlic bread.

Briana's nose scrunched up in disgust as she watched him. "You're disgusting, you know that?"

"I am not. I was starving. We hardly ate on our little camping trip."

I snickered. For the past forty-eight hours I'd watched how Jonas and Bree had grown closer, more so than they ever had in the past few weeks. He still made eye contact with me from time to time, but the look in his eye when he did was changing. It was less... intense. Our relationship had always been confusing. It had been difficult to decide how much of what he felt for me stemmed from the tracker Sandra had placed at the base of his brain, and how much was real.

Jonas wiped his mouth on a cloth napkin, then folded it neatly beside his plate. He looked up at me. *My feelings are only changing because you're in love with my best friend.*

I straightened. *Dammit, Jonas, stay out of my head.*

I can't help it. It's a lovely place to be. He smiled, then reached for his water glass. *You're the one who left it open to me that time.*

Alyson stood and began clearing things from the table. She hadn't spoken much while everyone ate. I had a gazillion questions for her, but I wanted everyone to eat first. She stopped by my chair. "Did you not like the lasagna?"

"I'm sure it was fine." I pushed away from the table and gathered up my dishes. "Just not hungry." I didn't have to look at Jack to know he was following me with his eyes as I walked to the sink.

"I'd be happy to eat your portion," Jonas announced.

I glared at Jonas. Nothing seemed to bother him for long. Or perhaps he was just better able to hide it than I was.

After the dishes were cleared, at Alyson's instructions, we all moved toward the living room. I stopped just inside the room and leaned against the doorjamb. Georgia and Fred squeezed into a large chair-and-a-half, and Kyle spread out on a pillow on the floor, the soft glow from the fireplace lighting their faces. Jonas motioned for Briana to join him on the sofa, and Jack stood with his back to the fire, his hands stuffed into his front pockets. Alyson picked up a remote control and began pushing buttons. From the ceiling on the wall adjacent to the fireplace, some sort of long, skinny compartment opened, and a white screen lowered.

"Are we watching a movie?" Fred asked.

Kyle threw a small pillow at Fred's head.

When the screen was in place, Alyson opened up a laptop on a desk on the opposite side of the room from the fireplace. A ray of light shone on the big screen. I followed the line to a small projector coming out of the ceiling on the other side of the room. White in color, it was nicely camouflaged into the decor.

"Jack, will you get the light, please?" Alyson asked, pointing to a switch on the wall.

I looked from the blank screen, to my mother, and back to the screen, not knowing what to expect. She pushed a pair of glasses up on her nose, then typed away on the computer.

After Jack dimmed the light, he returned to the fireplace. The silence in the room was deafening. What was my mother about to show us? Could I actually trust her to help us take down Sandra?

I almost laughed hysterically just considering the magnitude of that thought—the idea that I had any idea how to take down a division of the IIA, a powerful government organization that had protected Sandra and her secret medical experiments all these years.

Alyson continued to type as a large map popped up on the screen. "Seth called to tell me you were coming." That explained why she didn't seem surprised to see us, and how she knew to have enough dinner ready to feed a small army of clones. "He said you'd been asking where Sandra could possibly have located the lab in the video she sent you."

"Did you watch the video?" I asked. "Did you know she was growing human clones outside of a human body?"

She typed for a few more seconds, then stood, grabbed a small item off the desk, and walked toward me. Several inches taller than me, she faced me, demanding that I look at her.

"I knew as far back as my early twenties that Sandra Whitmeyer was capable of doing anything she wanted. She used and hurt everyone around her to further the medical research that she finds more important than human life. I knew she was capable of cloning a human outside of a surrogate, but I had no idea she had begun cloning en masse like this."

"Is it about money?"

Alyson leaned against a wall beside me and stared at the blank screen. "For some, medical research is about money..."

I thought of Cathy and Roger. They wouldn't hesitate to hang a sign saying "The Doctor Is In" if we agreed to cure the many things we were cloned to do. And they would pocket every bit of the profit in doing so, without giving a second thought to how sick the supernatural powers made us. The consequences of Georgia's power might even kill her.

"For others, like your father, it's about advancing medicine and saving human life." She closed her eyes briefly. Was she taking a moment to remember Dad? "Cloning human DNA all those years ago was about studying how certain cells worked together, and how manipulating certain genes—or let's say removing a mutated gene—might affect the viability of an embryo to survive."

"And Sandra?" I asked, though Sandra's motivations were evident.

"For Sandra, it's about prestige and influence. Power. It's about winning the race to gain knowledge no one else in the world has. To do something no one else in the world is even capable of. It's ironic, really." She laughed a little under her breath. "Sandra set out to prove she could help further medicine by studying the genetics of intelligent people. By cloning already proven geniuses, and enhancing their DNA, she thought she would be the most powerful person on the planet."

"So she made a bunch of brilliant freaks?"

She tilted her head. "You really believe that?"

I looked away, squeezing my eyes tightly.

My mother placed a gentle hand on my arm. I reopened my eyes. "Lexi, you are beautiful, and intelligent, and strong-minded. It doesn't matter how your life was created, or how messed up your childhood seemed as you were living it..." She paused a moment, and I searched her eyes. I craved whatever it was she would say next. "I'm sorry for how my leaving affected you. I swear I only did what I thought would keep you safe. And I made sure you were surrounded by love. You felt loved, didn't you?"

I immediately thought of Gram. "Yes. Gram loved me like I was her own daughter."

"That she did."

I suddenly realized that everyone was staring at us. "What do we do? I want to destroy Sandra's operation. She can't continue to hurt people." And I wanted to make her pay for the people she'd killed.

"If that's what you want to do, then we will." She drew her hand away, then approached the screen, which was now showing a map of North America.

Just like that? This mother that had deserted me as a small child was going to help me take out Sandra Whitmeyer and her government operation? How could she be so calm about it?

Alyson held what appeared to be one of those remote controls I'd seen my teachers use for PowerPoint presentations. She clicked a button and began pointing with a red laser. "Right here," she said as she pointed to a spot over the northwestern part of the United States, "is where Sandra first started studying DNA, along with Peter, John, Seth, myself, and several others, including some of your parents." She pointed to the others in the room. They looked on in surprise. "This is also the location of the lab where all of your embryos were created."

I spoke up. "This was the location of the large lab explosion. And then you all scattered and Sandra disappeared."

"That's right."

Briana leaned forward. "Washington? Why there?"

"The University of Washington in Seattle, to be exact. I'm not sure why Washington in particular." Alyson turned back to the map and pointed to another part of the United States: Texas. "When I found Sandra again several years later, she had an entire research facility here in Austin, on the University of Texas's campus."

I moved closer, tilting my head and studying the locations she was pointing to.

"We stayed there for seven years. And then one day the alarms sounded, and we packed up and moved."

"Where did you go this time?" I asked, searching for common links.

"Raleigh, North Carolina. Home to North Carolina State University." The red laser dot darted west. "Then Auburn University in Alabama."

"So, are we trying to decide what these universities have in common?" Kyle asked.

Any ideas? I mindspoke to Jack and Jonas.

They both shook their heads without taking their eyes off of the map. Jonas had a hand on Briana's shoulder, his fingers massaging a tension spot. Jack clasped his hands behind his neck. Both were staring intently at the map.

"They're all major research universities," Jack finally said.

"As is the University of Kentucky," I added. "Which could mean she's moved to another university town."

"It could mean that." Alyson tapped the laser pointer to her chin. "But I don't think so."

I studied her for a few seconds. "What did you do for Sandra? Besides throw her off her search for me."

"Why do you ask?" Alyson turned so that I couldn't see her face.

"You said she found the fact that you were a neurolinguist and an electrophysiologist useful. In what way?"

Alyson's hands twisted and turned the remote control for a few beats as if she was considering how to answer, then she returned to her computer. She typed a few keystrokes before the map was replaced with a new picture: a blown-up diagram of a tracker.

Jonas sat up straighter, dropping his hand from where it had massaged Briana's shoulder.

"That's one of the trackers." I moved closer. "It's one of the newer ones, isn't it?"

"What do you mean?" Jack asked.

"It's not like the trackers we removed from Addison or Jonas. It's more like the one Sandra almost put in me."

"That's right." My mother twirled her glasses in her hand. "This is what I designed for Sandra. And it's the type of tracker Maya has. It doesn't just communicate via the cell towers, the way the old ones did, but can also use satellite signals."

"This one doesn't have the same prongs that the old ones had." Georgia cocked her head, studying the picture.

"Oh, they're there." Alyson kept typing. The diagram spun around to a different angle, one that revealed a close-up of wires very much like the ones on the older model of trackers, except that these wires were as thin as a strand of hair. "These thinner wires ground the tracker at the base of the skull, wrapping around bone or muscle or whatever they can grasp hold of. You cannot remove these trackers once they're implanted. At least, not without killing the subject."

"You *designed* these?" I swallowed hard. I was giving her a chance to prove she was someone that should be in my life, yet here she was telling us how she'd helped Sandra with her evil plan to use and abuse every human clone within her reach.

Alyson lowered her gaze. "I didn't have a choice. My only objective at the time I created this tracker was to keep Sandra from discovering Wellington Boarding School... and you."

Dad had never made me feel like I was in hiding, although he'd always instructed me that I should keep a certain level of privacy. That changed when he returned to Lexington to give that speech. He knew, then, that someone was close to discovering Wellington.

"So this was meant to distract Sandra?" I asked.

"It's difficult to distract someone as intelligent as Sandra, but yes, I was attempting to appease her in hopes that she would realize she didn't need the clones that weren't already under her control."

I went back to studying the ultra-thin wires of the tracker. "So even if we wanted to, we couldn't remove Maya's tracker?" I had wondered if during one of Maya's escapades to torture me, we might catch her, remove her tracker, and study it. I had hoped we could extract information from the tracker about the whereabouts of the new lab.

"No, but we could still tap into Maya's tracker for information."

I faced my mother. "You think she would know where this lab is?"

"I'm positive she knows, but you'll never get her to admit it. These trackers will shut her down if she even appears to be giving you information that Sandra doesn't want you to know."

"You mean Sandra would kill her," I said, and Alyson nodded. How could I be responsible for another death at the hands of Sandra Whitmeyer? "You created one of these for me." It was now in the side pocket of my backpack.

"Yes, but it's special. It has a mechanism that would allow me to take it over, if it came to that." She paused a few beats. "I never considered that you would voluntarily march into Sandra's lab."

The doorbell rang, making me jump and interrupting my thoughts. "Who's that?"

Alyson stood slowly. As she passed, she gently touched my arm. "It's Seth and Mr. Williams." I didn't know if I should be offended by her motherly tone—since I hardly knew her as a mother—or relieved that the people I trusted far outnumbered her.

She left the room then returned with Coach Williams and Seth. Seth had a five o'clock shadow. His eyes appeared slightly bloodshot.

"Did you find them?" I had tried to block out the thought of the men who had tried to kill me. The men who had succeeded in murdering Dia and Lin.

Coach rubbed the back of his neck. His tie had been loosened. "Yes, we found them. They were just able to walk again by the time we arrived on the scene. They're in custody. They were screaming some nonsense about some kids injecting them with a paralyzing drug." Coach eyed me sardonically. "Most of the agents thought they were just crazy."

I smiled, but I didn't mean it. "And Dia and Lin?"

Coach and Seth shifted at the same time, trading uneasy looks. Jack came over and stood beside me.

"The bodies that were pulled from the gorge today have been identified as Jack DeWeese and Briana Howard."

"What? Why?"

I turned to Jack, noting that he didn't appear the least bit surprised. "Jack—you knew this?"

"Only because Seth texted me an hour ago. I had Jonas break it to Briana before dinner."

Briana's eyes were directed to the ground in front of her.

"But we're going to set the authorities straight, right? Why would you let that happen?"

Coach pushed the lapel of his sports jacket aside to put a hand in his pants pocket. "There is no record of Dia's or Lin's existence. And when the authorities mistakenly identified the kids as Briana and Jack, we wondered if there was an opportunity here."

"An opportunity for what?" I asked.

Jack grabbed my shoulders. "To verify that my mother had nothing to do with the shooting."

"To make sure she wasn't part of wanting me dead," I whispered, and he nodded. "Are you sure? If she did have nothing to do with this, then believing that you're dead... it'll break her heart."

"She'll understand why we had to do it."

True. It wasn't like she hadn't manipulated those around her. If we proved Roger Wellington was reckless with Jack's life, she wouldn't care that we'd lied to her.

"This doesn't answer the question of why Dr. Wellington wants me dead." I turned to Alyson. "You started to tell me earlier."

Alyson glanced around the room, clearly uncomfortable. She spoke in a low voice, though I was sure everyone could hear. "I don't know the extent of your inheritance. Given my residence at the time your father had his will drawn up, we thought it best to keep me out of the mix. However..."

"You're shaking." I grabbed my mother's hand.

"I visited with Ms. Long shortly before her... death. I was the secondary beneficiary to your father's will."

"Meaning, if something happened to me, then the school and everything went to you?"

"As long as I was not still inside one of Sandra's compounds."

"And if you were?"

"If I was still working for Sandra, and if something happened to you, then everything would go to Roger. Your father trusted him until just before his death. But apparently he never got the chance to change the will."

Coach stepped closer to us. "Shortly before he was killed, your father had suspicions that Roger's intentions were no longer pure where the clones were concerned. That was why I watched Roger closely, but until today, I truly hadn't thought he was a danger to you."

"Dad was getting ready to move me," I said, more to myself than to Coach. "That was what Marci had said. I always thought it was the IIA that was trying to kill me, but—it was Roger Wellington all along?"

I thought of the size of my inheritance. Roger had to have known it was enormous, even if he didn't know the exact amount. I turned my frantic eyes back to Alyson. "That's why you added the security around this place."

She nodded.

Jack placed a hand on the small of my back. "Now we just have to prove my mother's not involved in Roger's plan."

~~~~~

You ready to put on the performance of your life? Jonas asked as we entered the main administrative building on Wellington's campus.

Seth had put numbing drops in my eyes to make them appear red and watery, and I had let mascara run down my cheeks.

If it means we get rid of Roger Wellington and finally prove that we can trust Cathy DeWeese—whether we like her as a person or not—then yes. I'm just sorry that if she is *innocent, that we're making her suffer the greatest loss a parent can suffer. Even if it's only temporary.* Though my voice sounded calm, my heart felt heavy and too big for my chest.

Let's do this, then. Jonas turned the handle and pushed open the door to Dr. Wellington's office. Trepidation weighed on me as I stepped into the room. Seth and Coach were already there with Roger and Cathy.

"Finally, you're here," Cathy said, rolling her eyes at me. "So, will someone please tell me what this is—" She suddenly
~~~~~

stopped, zeroing in on my face. "What's happened? Why are you crying?"

Coach stood behind Roger. One hand rested on his gun, tucked inside a holster on his hip, a gesture I'm sure no one noticed but me.

Seth walked toward Cathy. "Cathy, the kids were shot at today while they hiked through the Red River Gorge."

Cathy's eyes grew big. "What do you mean? Who shot at them? Where's Jack?"

I turned and buried my face into Jonas's chest. His hand rubbed my back. *I can't do this.* Trying to pretend that Jack was dead was cutting right to my heart. My pulse sped up.

You're doing fine. She'll just assume you're too upset to talk. Jonas gripped me tighter when my knees buckled slightly.

"Cathy, why don't you sit down." Seth gestured to nearby chair

"I don't want to sit down. Tell me where Jack is. Tell me he's okay, Seth."

"The FBI pulled two bodies out of the forest and identified them as Jack and Briana Howard."

Okay, that was true. I rotated my body to watch their reactions. Jonas kept a loose hold on me.

Roger paled. I was pretty sure he hadn't meant for Jack to die. But the tears coming down my face became real when I saw Cathy's stunned face. She stared at the floor for a few seconds before she looked up. Tears welled in her eyes. Her hands balled into fists at her side. Then, just like the transition from day to night, a dark cloud of anger fell over her face. "This is *your* fault, isn't it?" she hissed at me through clenched teeth. "Everyone you touch *dies!*"

My spine stiffened. She was right. Everyone was dying around me. I tried to back up even more, but Jonas only squeezed harder. *Be tough. She's just angry. And heartbroken. She's lashing out.*

Cathy walked a few steps closer to me. "They were shooting at *you*. You know that, right?"

I started to shrug, but then nodded. *She hates me. Look at her eyes.*

"Cathy, the FBI is here." Coach had stepped up beside me, his hand still on his holster. "They have no choice but to assume that this is related to Peter's death. They'll have questions, but I have one first. Do you know who would want Lexi or any of these kids dead?"

"Why would I know any more than you already know?" Her voice came out hoarse. "I knew I should never have let Jack come here. Sandra is toxic, which means any *thing* that shares her DNA is toxic, too. I'm sorry he ever met you." Tears streamed down her face, and my heart constricted in my chest as the coldness of her eyes penetrated mine.

As much as I hated to hurt anyone like this, Cathy was showing me just how much she despised me. Did she hate me simply because I was the clone of Sandra Whitmeyer, or had I earned that hatred in my own right?

Roger, who had yet to react to the news of his nephew, walked over to his sister and put an arm around her. "What is being done to search for whoever did this?"

Coach placed himself between Roger and the door. "The FBI took both shooters into custody. The agents who were first to respond believe the men were mercenaries acting on behalf of another."

"What makes them think this?"

Coach only shrugged. "That's privileged information."

"Well, you can let the authorities know that I and this school will do whatever is necessary to cooperate with their investigation." Roger squeezed Cathy close. "But for now, I'd like to get Cathy home where she can mourn and make arrangements."

Cathy started to walk toward the door, but stopped beside me. Her eyes were already red and swollen. "*You're* the reason my son is dead. This is your fault."

At some point while those two sentences were spoken, I stopped breathing. I stared into Sandra's eyes, then looked to Dr. Wellington. He stood over his sister's right shoulder, his hand resting at the small of her back.

"Look at the two of you," I finally breathed. "My father trusted you." I looked to Dr. Wellington. "He trusted you to manage this school and watch over the clones he'd found over the years." I met Cathy's glare again. "And he trusted you and your pathetic excuse for a husband to take care of his only daughter. Yet you both wanted only to get your hands on my father's money and to use the clones for your own selfish motives. You have no one to blame for what happened today but your own selfish selves."

Dr. Wellington dropped his hand from Cathy and stepped around her to tower over me.

I hope you know what you're doing, Jonas mindspoke.

"What are you talking about?" Cathy asked between sniffs, then turned to Dr. Wellington. "What is she talking about?"

Coach whispered something to Seth, who immediately left the room.

"She's upset," Dr. Wellington answered. "We're all very upset. We need—"

"I need you to shut up!" I screamed at Dr. Wellington. "You're a liar and a murderer!"

Dr. Wellington tilted his head from side to side, cracking his neck. He took in a large breath. "Lexi, we know how much Jack meant to you. You're tired, and you're not making sense."

This wasn't the plan at all. But why stop now? Jonas asked. *I think you're making perfect sense.*

Several suits filed into the office, each one appearing to make very calculated steps.

"It's over for the two of you," I said. "I have evidence that you put out a hit to kill me." I only knew for sure that Dr. Wellington was involved, but I directed my statement to Cathy, too.

"A *hit* on you? What are you talking about?" Cathy faced Dr. Wellington. "What is this nonsense?"

"She's crazy, Cathy. You know that. She's just like Sandra. You said so yourself."

"Roger Wellington, Cathy DeWeese." One of the FBI agents approached. "You're wanted for questioning in the deaths of Jack DeWeese and Briana Howard."

I swallowed hard.

Suddenly Cathy turned and lunged at Dr. Wellington. Her fists beat at his chest. "What did you do? Did you kill my son?" She was crying and screaming. She clawed at his face.

Dr. Wellington said nothing, did nothing to defend himself while Cathy assaulted him. After she got in a few good licks, the agents pulled her off of him. "Mrs. DeWeese, we need you to come with us."

Dr. Wellington and Cathy were led from the room. They weren't cuffed. Coach followed them out. As soon as they were gone, I collapsed into Jonas's arms.

"Shhh." He rubbed my hair and cradled me in his arms. "It's going to be fine."

"Watching her react made it feel real, Jonas. I imagined what it would be like to know I would never see Jack again. And I don't ever want to feel that. Ever."

"I know. And you won't."

I raised my head and looked at him. "You don't know that. She was right. Everyone I touch dies."

He placed his hands on either side of my face. "No, they don't. I'm still here. You have lots of friends around you. And Jack..." Jonas swiped a thumb across my cheek, wiping away what I was sure was black mascara and tears. "Jack is still here. And he's not going anywhere."

I swallowed and let Jonas hold me. I so badly wanted to see Jack, but I knew I couldn't until we were sure about Cathy. "I'd like to go back to my room. I need to be alone. And I could really use a shower."

"I wondered what that smell was."

A weak laugh passed my lips.

"That's better. Laugh a little. We won't have to pretend that Jack and Briana are gone for long. Promise."

FIFTEEN

A hot shower washed away the ickiness of camping and hiking, but it did nothing to cleanse the ache of my heart. Not only was I mourning so many lives lost, now I had to pretend that the love of my life was dead. And I knew that Cathy was right, even if she had the names of the victims wrong: it *was* my fault that Lin and Dia were dead.

Dani was murdered because I didn't answer Sandra quickly enough and do exactly as she had ordered.

Dia and Lin were dead because someone had been shooting at me. Because of money? I never asked for this money.

I pulled on sweats that said "Wellington" down one pant leg and a simple cashmere sweater my dad had brought me from Europe. It was late, but I knew I would struggle to fall asleep, so I grabbed my computer and headed up to my favorite spot on the roof to clear my head. If that was even possible.

The air was cool and crisp against my face. I pushed back thoughts of Jack and tried to focus on possible locations of Sandra's new lab. What I couldn't figure out was, if Sandra wanted me to come to her so badly, why didn't she just tell me the location?

I leaned against the side of the roof and looked out over campus. I saw a security guard in the distance doing a routine check, shining a flashlight along the outside of the classroom building. Otherwise, the campus was still.

You up? Jonas entered my mind.

I immediately pocketed my thoughts like Jonas had taught me to do. There was no reason to keep him up with the many things going through my head. *Yes.*

Georgia and Fred decided not to return to campus. They went back to our house near UK.

I don't blame them. And I didn't. Who would willingly get mixed up with this stuff? If I were them, I'd probably have left a long time ago and not looked back.

They're not leaving, Lexi. They want to help. They're just not sure what it is we're asking them to do.

I'm not sure what I'm asking, either.

Get some sleep. There are guards outside the dorm. Roger Wellington is not getting near you tonight. Let's meet in the morning and discuss how to go forward.

Something told me that when Jonas slipped out of my head that time, he was actually gone. Maybe he'd slipped into Briana's head. I didn't know. Jonas's mental reach was greater than mine and Jack's. I was just thankful to be alone with my thoughts on what to do about Sandra.

She wanted me with her for some reason. She had made that much clear. And she wanted me alive. Yet I didn't think her "protection," if you could call it that, had been extended to anyone else. Would she and John even be upset to hear that Jack might be dead?

I turned and sat with my back against the wall. After digging my laptop out of my backpack, I logged on to the internet. I typed Washington, Texas, Alabama, North Carolina, and Kentucky into the search engine. The first sites that popped up were related to state laws: seat belt and smoking bans. Most of the other sites had to do with sports teams. I continued to scroll.

Then, fairly far down on the list, I came across an article titled: "The World's Biggest Military Bases." I clicked on it. It turned out that five of the world's largest military bases are located in the United States: Ft. Bragg in North Carolina, Ft. Campbell on the Kentucky-Tennessee border, Ft. Hood in Texas, Ft. Lewis in Washington, and Ft. Benning on the border of Georgia and Alabama.

I pulled up maps for each of the military bases, and compared them to the locations of each of the schools. Was it just a coincidence that military forces were stationed so close to every one of the labs where Sandra had operated a cloning operation? I remembered the video Sandra showed me at The Farm—how she cloned young boys, turned them into droids and trained them to spy on military officers. She had mentioned how the U.S. government paid her a lot of money to supply them with intelligent weapons.

"Oh my God." I sat up and closed the laptop. The reason the military and the government hadn't shut down her unethical and evil operation was because they needed what she was supplying. "They're helping her," I whispered.

But how deep did this federal involvement go? Would the FBI be privy to this? Maybe the FBI was throwing us off, the same way Alyson had worked to throw Sandra off from finding me? No, that was too farfetched. But I did believe that the IIA was capable of covering up this operation, moving it anywhere in the world they desired.

I placed my hands over my face and drilled my fingers into my forehead. Conspiracy theories threatened to make my neurons misfire. But I knew: we were all in one giant chess match. And the biggest problem was that there were too many kings and queens.

~~~~~

When I woke, I smelled a familiar scent. I couldn't hide the smile that immediately stretched across my face. *When did you break into my room?*

Around two a.m. You were restless most of the night.

A lot on my mind. How did you get in?

Addison. She made me invisible and helped me get in.

I opened my eyes. The only light came from campus lighting outside my windows. Jack sat at the end of my bed with his back against the wall and his feet draped over mine. His hair was slightly tousled, as if he had run his hands through it a hundred times. I sat up to face him. "Glad you're not dead." My voice came out a little raspy.

"Not as glad as I am."

"Your mom took it hard."

"I heard. I'm sorry she treated you so badly."

"Hardly your fault." I moved to slide from under the covers, but then realized I was wearing only a T-shirt and panties. When I paused and looked at Jack, he raised a single brow. "Close your eyes," I said.

The corners of his lips lifted in a sly grin. "What if I said 'No'?" He shifted and climbed up to lie beside me. With his arm, he guided me back down to my pillow, then rolled so that the weight of half his body lay across me. He traced my hair-
~~~~~

line until it met my neck, then his fingers lingered across my jaw on their way to my lips. "Why didn't we run months ago?"

I only stared into his eyes. His irises were bright blue in the dim lighting.

"Is it possible to already know what you want more than anything else in life by the time you're eighteen?"

"It has to be." I raised my head and brushed my lips across his.

He slid his hand under my neck and supported my head as he kissed me deeper. When he released me, he rested his forehead against mine. "I know that I'm sometimes overprotective of you, but it's only because I don't think I would survive if something happened to you."

I rested my head back on my pillow and studied the worried trenches of his forehead. "I'm not completely incapable of taking care of myself. And you can't guard me against all harm."

"I'm trying."

"That you are."

A smirk reached all the way to his eyes. "Why, Miss Matthews, did you just make a funny?"

I giggled. "Now close your eyes *and* turn your head."

"What are you wearing under here?" He picked up my comforter between his forefinger and his thumb and proceeded to pretend to peek under the blanket. I slapped his hand away.

He huffed out a breath. "Fine." He lay back on the pillow and placed an arm over his eyes.

I laughed as I slipped from under the covers, grabbed my sweatpants, and scurried off to the bathroom.

When I returned, Jack was on my computer.

"What are you looking at?"

"Your latest searches. I think you might be on to something with the military bases."

I should have been angry that he was snooping around my computer, but I wasn't. I was ready to let him in on everything. As long as Sandra was still around, manipulating our lives, we wouldn't have the full ability to make our own life choices. We would need to work together if we had any chance of putting her out of business.

"What do you make of it?" he asked.

"I can't decide if the military is requiring Sandra to work close to a base, or if she's calling the shots with the help of the military. If she is, in fact, selling experimental cloned spies to the military to fund her operation, like she showed me that day inside The Farm, then—"

"The government knows and is covering it up."

"Exactly. But probably not *all* of the government. I'd say the IIA is fully capable of covering this up all on their own." Jack's phone rang in his back pocket. I reached down and pulled it out. "It's Seth."

"Answer it."

Before I even got the word "hello" completely out, an angry Seth asked, *"Where's Jack?"*

"He's right here. What's wrong?"

"Cathy is demanding to see the body. We told her it was not a pretty sight, but she's insisting. Does Jack have any markings she'll be looking for?"

I handed the phone to Jack. "Seth needs to know what markings you have on your body that will be different from your clone. Your mom's insisting on viewing the body." I shrugged when he furrowed his brow. We still didn't know if Cathy was aware of Dr. Wellington's plans to kill me in order to take over Wellington and inherit Dad's money—but could we really let Cathy go on thinking her only son was dead? What if she was innocent?

"Hey, man. Did the FBI question her?" Jack stared at me as he listened to Seth. "I'll be right there. It's time I confront dear ol' mom."

After he hung up, I touched his cheek. "Do what you have to do."

And while Jack went off to slay his demon, I had my own to draw out and smite.

~~~~~

I opened my mind and directed thoughts to Maya as I weaved in and around headstones in the school's old cemetery.

During the two weeks after I left The Farm, Jonas had taught me how to open my mind to one person but close it off to others. I had practiced the technique with him and Addison, since I wasn't speaking to Jack at the time.

I also sucked at it, but I was getting better.

The air felt damp and had the smell of impending rain. I hugged my heavy sweater closer, having refused to dig out my winter coat so early in the season.

Birds chirped, and I jumped when a squirrel dropped an acorn from a tree and it cracked against a tombstone. Maya had told me she would find me again. I suspected Sandra would grow tired of waiting and would soon send someone for me.
~~~~~

Two more clones were dead. How many more people had to die before we regained control of our own lives?

The desire to hurt Sandra burned like a raging inferno inside my heart.

"Well, well, well... look who's off wandering alone."

My back stiffened at the sound of Maya's voice behind me. My plan had worked. Now I just needed to get inside her head without her sensing it.

"Is that smart? I'm surprised Jack and Jonas let you out of their sight."

I turned slowly, facing my twin. She was dressed in a denim jacket, black skirt, and boots. A stylish scarf was wrapped around her neck, and her red-streaked hair was piled high on her head in a jumbled mess.

"How do you know they're not close by watching us? I mean, look how predictable you are." She stood just a little straighter at the word "predictable." "I call out, and you come running. I hope Sandra treats you well for being her little errand girl." Did Maya even realize that she was just a pawn in Sandra's little game? That we *all* were?

Her eyes narrowed. She looked like she wanted to say something, but couldn't. She opened her mouth and took a breath, then closed it and looked away. Did the tracker in the back of her neck have so much control that she couldn't even speak her own original thoughts?

I tried a different angle. "How are you getting in and out of Wellington?"

Her eyes met mine again. A smirk lifted at the corners of her lips. "Wouldn't you like to know?"

Hoping she was irritated and distracted enough, I slipped inside her head while trying to keep the conversation going. "Yes, actually, I would." Her neurons were crazy bright red, like the paint in her hair, and similar to Jonas's. I wondered if that had anything to do with the tracker. "Obviously, some security person needs to be fired, and since this is my school now, I plan to keep the people in it safe."

"Is that what you told Dia and Lin?"

A slow fire erupted in my veins and began to spread. "You really are a perfect clone of Sandra, aren't you?" Pure evil.

Her neurons were firing chemical signals, or messages, across thousands of synapses. Yet all of these "messages" seemed to both originate from and return to a central location—the tracker at the base of her skull. It was as if the tracker had some sort of magnetic force on one side, but repelled fiery neurons from the other. Or maybe it was that the information traveling inside her head circulated through the tracker. If that was the case, Sandra would know everything a tracker clone did and thought.

"I'm not like Sandra."

For the first time, Maya said something that made me see her a little differently. I had always thought that any clone under the control of Sandra was a victim, but when one tried to drown me in a swimming pool just for fun, I had no choice but to put up a wall until I could decide whether the person was worth saving.

Keeping distance between us, Maya began walking through the cemetery like a shark circling her prey. "I told you someone wanted you dead. Why didn't you listen?"

"Do you know *why* Roger Wellington wants to kill me?" Did Sandra know the kind of money I stood to inherit?

"No. Only that he does. And it must be for a very good reason, because he was willing to pay a shitload of money to see that it happens. Of course, he hired two idiots who couldn't even tell the difference between Jack and Lin."

I cocked my head. "Jack and Lin are identical. So tell me, Miss Smarty Pants, how should they have been able to tell?" I could tell the difference because I knew the exact cut of Jack's hair, recognized every sun-created freckle on his nose, and sensed each firing neuron of his mind when he was near.

"Because he's always one step away from you." She looked around. "Except now, I suppose. You've told his mother that it was Jack in the forest, not Lin." She made a clucking noise with her tongue. "That wasn't very nice, now was it? And it leaves you vulnerable out here."

I was growing tired of this conversation. "Where is Sandra hiding?" I asked. "If she wants me to come to her so badly, why is it she hasn't revealed where she is?

"All you have to do is say the word, Lexi, and I'll have you to Sandra by tomorrow morning."

"Why not today?"

Maya broke eye contact with me for a couple of beats. "Because today doesn't work for me."

Uh-huh. Could it be that the new lab was more than a day's travel? "I'm surprised Sandra hasn't set a deadline for me to join her, like she did last time."

"Oh, she will. To be honest, Sandra hasn't been ready for you quite yet. But once she decides she's ready, you won't have a choice but to comply."

Which was why I needed to find her first.

"She's worried you'll get yourself killed before you realize that joining her is your destiny."

I slid inside Maya's head again and focused harder on the tracker that controlled her thoughts and words. It was very much like the tracker Sandra almost placed inside my head. Looking closer, I saw the micro-sized wires snaking in and around the network of veins. I had proven that I could extract the tracker from Addison by using telekinetic powers similar to Georgia's, so I now used that ability to shift Maya's tracker over a bit. As the tracker began to move, the wires, which had been flowing freely from the base, stopped as if on alert. When nothing further happened, I moved the tracker a little more. That was when the wires suddenly clamped down tightly around the veins and muscles within reach.

Maya's hand flew to the back of her neck, and she cried out. "What the—"

I stopped. "What's wrong?" I backed up slightly.

Her face reddened and the muscles around her eyes tightened. "What are you doing?"

"What are you talking about? Nothing." I held both hands out in front of me as I took another step back.

She straightened her posture and took a few steps toward me. The vein in her neck pulsated. "I've been nice to you, and *this* is how you repay me? By messing with my tracker?" She took another step. The neurons in her head fired in an unbalanced firestorm.

Nice to me? She really was delusional. "I'm sorry. I didn't mean—"

"You didn't mean to what?" Maya was on me quick, clamping a hand around my throat and cutting off my air supply. "Hurt me? Manipulate me? You don't get it, do you? Sandra will kill me if she thinks you can remove my tracker and get the upper hand."

My hands flew to my neck, clawing at her hand. I couldn't get a breath in. Maya was abnormally strong, and I couldn't pry her fingers away.

How was this clone of me so strong? Her face was inches from mine. I could see my reflection in her eyes, and I was sure my face was turning blue.

"Let her go, Maya," Jonas said as he entered the cemetery.

"Stay out of this, Jonas." Maya loosened her grip for a second, allowing me to get a breath in, then squeezed tightly again. Gagging sounds escaped my throat. I was losing my grip on consciousness, and my vision was starting to go fuzzy.

I heard the clicking sound of a gun being cocked. "Maya, I will kill you."

"How did she get under your skin so fast? You were Sandra's pride and joy. What happened?"

As Maya spoke, I felt her grasp slip ever so slightly, but it was enough of an opening for me to raise my arms through hers and break her hold on me. I had just enough strength left to slam a knee into her stomach, knocking the air from her lungs. When her head went forward, I grabbed the messy bun on her head and pulled her back up, holding her in place by her hair.

Breathing hard, she met my glare. "I've given you two chances to kill me. Now you're going to wish you had."

Without letting her go, I pulled my phone from my back pocket and called Coach. "I've got Maya... In the cemetery... Yes, Jonas is here. We'll wait for you." I hung up and returned the phone to my back pocket.

Jonas raised an eyebrow. "What was that about?"

"Alyson thinks we can extract information from Maya's tracker. But we needed Maya to do it. Coach and Seth have a room ready for her inside The Program."

"You came out here alone on *purpose*? To trap Maya?" I wasn't sure if that was disappointment or admiration in his voice.

"Yes. And mission accomplished. Now we can lock her up until Alyson figures out how to get what we need from her."

Jonas made no move to help me with a struggling Maya.

"You won't get away with this!" Maya screamed. "Sandra will kill me if you even *try* to mess with my tracker."

"I'm willing to take my chances."

SIXTEEN

Kidnapping an eighteen-year-old girl and holding her hostage was probably wrong. Although, in my defense, she *had* tried to kill me. Twice.

I studied Maya through the one-way observation window. Coach and Seth had locked her in the same exam room where I'd healed Sandra. She stood like a statue on the other side of the window, staring back at me. I knew in my head she couldn't see me, but that didn't stop her cold glare from chilling the blood that ran through my veins.

Have you lost your mind? Jack mindspoke.

I cringed, and my eyes slammed shut. *You heard already?*

How do you think Sandra will react when she hears?

Sandra isn't calling all the shots here. This is my school. And this girl trespassed, impersonated me, and tried to kill me.

Seriously? She stands accused of impersonating you? What? Of kissing your boyfriend?

Well, when he put it like that, it seemed petty. *And she tried to kill me.*

Okay, well hang her up by her feet and flog her.

I chuckled. We both knew we had no intention of hurting Maya. She was only following orders being fed to her through her tracker. If anything, I wanted to save her—to remove that tracker from her skull. She was just another victim of Sandra.

She knows where Sandra's lab is, I mindspoke. *I need to know.*

What exactly do you plan to do if you find out where this lab is?

Good question. *Why do you ask?*

Don't be coy, Lexi.

Sorry. We can talk about it later. I turned away from the window. *What happened with your mother? Did you see her?*

Yeah, he mindspoke slowly.

I guess she was pretty emotional?

Understatement of a lifetime.

It seemed Jack wasn't going to offer much of an explanation where his mother was concerned. *Well, did she know about her brother's plan to kill me?*

She knew you had to have inherited a lot of money. She couldn't tell me how much. But she seemed genuinely shocked that her own brother would put her son at risk by shooting at the group of us.

I nodded in understanding, knowing Jack couldn't see me. I was surprised he didn't ask me about the inheritance. *So, what do we do? If you tell me to trust that your mother doesn't want me dead, I will. Because I love you.*

Jack went silent.

Jack?

I asked her to leave campus.

Okay.

She was so angry at you for lying to her about my death. She wouldn't see reason or believe that it had been a group decision.

I'm sorry. I closed my eyes and imagined his tousled blond hair.

I know. I am, too.

Meet me later on the roof?

I'll be there.

I was so busy concentrating on Jack that I had forgotten about Maya. When I turned around, I found her her standing with her face just inches from the glass. She cocked her head and appeared to see directly into my eyes. She intimidated the hell out of me.

"What information do you have locked inside that tracker?" I asked. She couldn't hear me, of course. I fiddled with the tracker inside my jacket pocket. I carried it around as a reminder of how close Sandra had gotten to controlling me.

Maya's chest rose and fell in large breaths. Her face was red. She began banging on the window and, though I couldn't hear her, I could see her mouth move. She was screaming like a mad woman and shaking her head. She was losing it. She turned, grabbed a chair, and flung it at the glass. The glass didn't break.

The door to my left opened, and in walked Coach. He stood beside me and observed our guest. "She's a little upset."

"Ya think?"

"What do we do about her?" he asked, as if it were my decision, and I guessed, in a way, it was.

"I need Alyson to come here. I have a plan."

~~~~~

Jack wasn't going to like my plan.

I had the cooks prepare Jack's favorite meal of pizza and hot wings. Briana helped me move a table and chairs to the roof. We found a white tablecloth and some candles in the cafeteria—supplies from the many parties they'd put on for us over the years. We strung twinkle lights along the railing around this corner of the roof, providing the perfect lighting and transforming the rooftop into a tranquil oasis.
~~~~~

I brought a blanket and some throw pillows. I spread them out for us to lie under the stars after dinner.

"If I didn't know you better, I'd think you were about to get super personal with Jack." Bree waggled her eyebrows at me.

I picked up a pillow and threw it at her head. She caught it. "You don't know me *that* well."

"Our friendship may have had some rocky spots, but I think we know each other pretty well." She glanced around at the transformed roof. "I also know a bribery meal when I see one. What are you telling him tonight?"

"You'll know soon enough."

Her brows lifted. "I can't wait."

I continued to fluff the pillows and spread out the blanket. I wanted everything perfect. This could be the last time Jack and I would be together like this for a while. Maybe the last time ever. And I didn't want to take him for granted. I planned to treat every moment we spent together from here on out like it might be our last.

I gave my head a shake, attempting to shut out any doubt, any notion that my plan wouldn't work. Briana had gone silent. "Hey, you okay? Where did you go just then?"

She smiled, but it barely reached her cheeks. "I want what you have." Her voice came out flat.

I sat back on my heels. "What do you mean? You want your only family to be a mother who left you as a young child, and a dying grandmother who doesn't know your name? Or do you want a bounty on your head so that you spend your life looking over your shoulder or wondering when the next person is going to try to kill you?" It was meant as a joke, but neither of us laughed.

"I want someone to love me unconditionally," Bree said simply. "I want someone to love me for *me*, and I want that person to love me so much he'd be willing to do anything for me, and I for him. I'd die for any one of you, you know." I knew Briana was talking about the six of us—the original clones. She was near tears. I'd never seen her look so melancholy.

"Hey." I jumped up and pulled her into a hug, a gesture very new to our friendship. And extremely awkward given that she was many inches taller. "You have us. We protect each other. That's what this dinner is about. I'm going to make sure nothing happens to any of us, or any of the rest of Sandra's clones." I knew that Briana had mostly been referring to what Jack and I shared. I wasn't so sure that Briana and Jonas weren't on their way to having that same kind of special bond, but maybe it was still too early to speak it.

Good or bad, these were our lives. And without Sandra around to make everything difficult, we would find a way to live these lives much more easily.

I held Briana at arm's length. "Now, help me get this set up. I've got some smooth talkin' to do."

~~~~~

I placed the mask on my face. It was the same mask I had used the night of the Halloween party, but Briana had fixed it so that I could attach it instead of having to hold it.

I lifted my dress and stepped through the door, onto the transformed oasis.

Jack turned. The blue of his eyes popped through his simple black mask, and a gasp escaped my lips. Seeing him like
~~~~~

this—his bright, reassuring smile, the way his dark suit fit snug to his body, the way his presence dwarfed the beautiful atmosphere Briana and I had created on the rooftop—made me forget the challenges that continued to haunt us daily.

"You're beautiful." His voice came out in a whisper, as if he was trying to hide some emotion.

I glanced down at my dress, the lace blending into the silk underlay. I was suddenly bashful. I wasn't sure how I could go through with this. He was going to freak.

Jack closed the distance between us. He crooked a finger beneath my chin and lifted. "You. Are. Beautiful," he said, his voice much stronger this time.

"So are you."

He smiled. "So... you got me up here. And I'm thrilled that you did, but what's this all about?"

"Awfully pushy, aren't you? Let's eat first?"

He turned and gestured with his hand, then pulled out one of the chairs, allowing me to sit. As I scooted in, he leaned down and kissed the top of my head.

After taking his seat, he reached for the lid to the plate in front of him. "What are we having?" He removed the lid, revealing several pieces of homemade pepperoni, sausage, and mushroom pizza and a pile of extra-hot buffalo wings. The spice from the wings made my eyes water even from across the table. He raised his eyes. "Not what I was expecting."

"Oh yeah? What were you expecting?"

He looked around the rooftop. "I was expecting something a little more... sophisticated."

"Are you disappointed?"

He laughed. "Are you kidding? These are my favorites." His smile slowly disappeared. "Which makes me wonder even more what I'm being set up for."

I removed my lid. My plate consisted of a couple of slices of the same pizza, except with added banana peppers, and no messy buffalo wings. "Can't I do something nice for you? You're always doing nice things for me. I figured you were due."

"Mmm-hmm."

We ate our dinner slowly, limiting conversation to casual chitchat. However, we both knew the lightness of the atmosphere around us wouldn't last.

When we had finished dinner, Jack took my hand and led me to a spot away from the table. He pulled my body flush with his. We'd had a break in the cool temperatures, giving us a bit of warmth for our date on the roof, but I was still thankful to have my cashmere shrug over my shoulders.

Jack slid his hand under the shrug and placed it on my back between my shoulder blades. The feel of his strong hands next to my skin made me shiver in his arms.

He pushed me away for a moment. "You cold?"

I gave my head a little shake and bit my lip. I surprised myself with the shyness I was feeling with Jack tonight. We were both changing. Each day, Jack and I were growing up a little bit more. Our relationship had gone from high school sweethearts to something much more, and I wasn't sure I would ever be able to let go of him, even if we were separated.

He leaned his head down into the crook of my neck. His lips rested near my ear. "What are you thinking about?"

"You can't hear my thoughts?"

"No. You asked me not to... and you've gotten better at blocking me out." I felt him smile against my cheek. "I don't try to invade very often. Only when it's necessary to keep you safe." The muscles in my back tightened. "Relax. I only enter because I'm in love with you. And if you don't tell me what this romantic date is all about soon..." He began a line of kisses that began along my shoulder and ran all the way up to my earlobes. I leaned my head to the side to give him access. "...I will be forced to distract you while I begin extracting your thoughts."

Jack's hand wandered from its place on my back to the base of my neck. His fingers spread into my hair as he guided my head back. He leaned in and pressed his lips against mine.

His lips were soft, and the kiss was gentle at first. As he pressed harder, kissing me more deeply, I knew my guard was collapsing. I pocketed my thoughts and all the crazy things going on in my mind. My fingers dug into the fabric of the suit jacket covering his biceps as I concentrated hard on keeping my thoughts to myself. The last thing I needed was for him to grab hold of the wrong thought. I needed time to tell him my plan in a certain order, in a certain way.

As hard as I worked at pocketing thoughts, I never felt Jack enter my mind.

He broke the kiss. We were both breathing heavily. His hand grazed my arm, brushed against my ribcage, my waist, and took my hand. With a gentle pull, he led me to the blanket I had spread out earlier.

He knelt, grabbing the pillows and fluffing them for us to lie on. When I joined him, he directed me so that I was on my back looking directly into his eyes. His pupils were dilated, like two giant orbs of onyx surrounded by bands of blue sapphire.

He began kissing me again, and I knew my defenses were weakening. I tried to tell myself that I hadn't brought him up here to make out, but I also knew that it might be the last time we did. Guilt was settling in as I spread my fingers through his hair. Unable to control the emotions that erupted in my chest, tears sprang to my eyes. I swallowed hard, breaking contact.

"What's wrong?" His eyes narrowed. His voice was soft, gentle. "Hey, why are you crying?" He cupped my face, rubbing the tears away with his thumb. His eyes never moved from mine.

"I just need a minute to breathe."

He rolled over on his back, squeezing my hand in his and holding it over his heart. We both stared up at the sky.

I tried to find the very few constellations I knew: Orion, Ursa Major, and the Big Dipper—which I knew wasn't a constellation at all, but an asterism that made up part of Ursa Major.

If only the stars would align for us in life.

Jack rubbed his thumb back and forth over the surface of my skin. It was soothing.

"Why didn't you force me to run from Wellington?" I asked.

He took in a deep breath. "I guess I knew there was no way of escaping who we are. Even if we ran, it would catch back up to us eventually."

I nodded slightly. "I think you knew, as I'm finally realizing, that in order for the younger clones at this school to survive—or for any of us to live normal lives—we'd have to stop Sandra and your father."

Jack shifted. He placed his opposite arm up behind his head. Several beats passed before he spoke again. "I tried to believe it wasn't our job to stop them, but Sandra continues to taunt you and send weapons in after you. First Jonas, then Ty, and now Maya."

"Three of the secondary clones are dead," I said. "And my father. Dani. The reporter Marci. And now Ms. Long, the attorney who knew the details of my inheritance. Sandra is directly or indirectly involved in the deaths of more than half a dozen people. And those are just the ones we know about. She disposes of anyone who gets in her way, and others have gone absolutely crazy trying to control what Sandra began all those years ago."

"Like Roger?"

"Roger wanted control of us, along with your mom. He also wanted my money, and he was willing to settle for whatever clones remained after getting it."

Jack sat up and turned to me. "So, the money your dad left you... Was it enough to keep the school running?"

"And then some." I pushed myself up to my feet and paced. Jack was up and next to me in the blink of an eye. He wrapped his fingers around my elbow, stopping my motion and forcing me to look at him.

"What are you afraid of?" He searched my eyes. "You think your inheritance will change things between us?"

I nodded. Moisture collected in my eye, but I blinked it away. "Money always changes things. This will change everything."

"How much?" When I tried to look away, he said, "Look me in the eye." I did, and he continued. "I promise you. Nothing you say will change the way I feel about you. Nothing will make me stop looking out for you. For us. Stop trying to put a barrier between us just because you're scared."

I breathed harder. I couldn't find the right words. I blinked up at him, swallowed hard again. And when I opened my mouth to speak, his cell phone rang.

"Ignore it," he said. "Now tell me."

His phone stopped ringing, but immediately started up again. It wasn't Jonas. He would have mindspoke. "Answer it. It could be important."

"*You're* important." His eyes searched mine, and then, growling, he took his phone out of his pocket. "It's Coach." He slid the bar across his phone and answered. "This better be good." Jack's eyes widened. "When? Okay. We're on our way."

"What is it?" I asked after he replaced his phone in his pocket.

"Jonas is missing. He was supposed to meet Coach and Seth at dinner. He told them that he and Bree have figured out where Sandra's new lab is located."

"Where's Bree?"

"She's lying in the infirmary. They found her unconscious outside your office."

SEVENTEEN

Jack and Coach leaned over an oversized map spread out on the conference table in my office. Seth typed on a laptop at my desk.

Alyson stopped me with a light touch to my arm when I entered. "How's your friend?"

I looked down at her hand, then back up at her face. "Alive." I closed my eyes, immediately regretting my shortness with her. "I'm sorry. She's got a nasty headache. And she's scared. She doesn't remember much right now." She didn't even remember what she and Jonas had been doing before someone cracked her on the head.

Jack raised his eyes from the map he was poring over. The hardness in his jaw said everything. It was bad. All indications pointed to Jonas being abducted.

I walked closer. They were examining some islands off the west coast of the United States. "What are you looking at?" It wasn't Hawaii. It was too far south.

"This was on the ground next to some blood spatters over there." Jack handed me a crumpled-up piece of paper as he pointed to some spots on the carpet.

"And the sea will tell." I looked from Jack to Coach. "What does it mean?"

"It's a book," Jack said.

"Jonas wrote down the name of a book just before he was taken?" I didn't understand.

"*And the Sea Will Tell* is a true-crime novel about the Sea Wind Murders, a double murder from the 1970s," Coach explained. "They happened on an atoll south of Hawaii called Palmyra Atoll."

"Palmyra," I said to myself. "Myra." I looked at Jack, who was clearly already a step ahead of me. Jonas had told us while in the gorge that Sandra had ordered the incubators delivered to Myra, which could be short for Palmyra. "You think this is where Sandra located the new lab."

"It makes sense." Jack shrugged.

"What kind of island is this? Is it part of Hawaii? Meaning, is it part of the United States? Is it protected by our government?"

Seth looked up from the computer. "It's not governed by Hawaii. It's an unorganized incorporated territory of the United States. So technically it is governed under our Constitution."

"How about non-technically?" I asked.

Seth bowed his head toward the computer again. "A portion of the atoll is owned by the Nature Conservancy. The rest by the federal government. According to the information I've found, no one is allowed to travel to Palmyra Atoll without prior approval from the U.S. Fish and Wildlife Department and from the Nature Conservancy."

"So if Sandra has built a lab there and is running a controversial scientific operation, she's gotten approval from the federal government?"

"More likely, she doesn't care what laws she's breaking," Seth answered. "However, yes, she does appear to have the protection of the IIA."

~~~~~

Even though it was three in the morning when we got to my room, Jack insisted I take a hot shower. Thought it might relax me. Little did he know, I did my best thinking in the shower. The heat soothed my tense muscles, but the steam went straight to my head as I thought about what someone would have to do to get the upper hand on Jonas.

Was he hurt? Would they kill him?

Those questions turned into thinking about the desperate look on Briana's face when I'd visited her at the infirmary. She had received a severe blow to the back of the head, giving her a nice knot and a mild concussion. But her only concern had been finding Jonas. "You have to find him, Lexi," she told me. "This can't keep happening."

While the shower cascaded over me, a sob escaped my throat, and I slammed my hand over my mouth, trying to suppress the sound. I was tired. And angry. And most of all, I knew what I had to do.

I finished my shower and dried off quickly. After pulling on a T-shirt and sweats, I went into my room. Jack was sitting in my desk chair, his chin on his chest. He had fallen asleep sitting up.

I couldn't help but smile. He had refused to go back to his room. Said there was no way he was leaving me alone, yet the poor guy couldn't keep his eyes open. What I needed to tell him would have to wait until morning.

I touched his cheek gently. He started at my touch, and I jumped backward, giggling. "Sorry," I whispered. "Let's get you
~~~~~

to bed." I grabbed his hand and led him to Dani's bed. He crawled in, and I covered him up. Leaning down, I brushed my lips across his.

After making sure my door was locked, I set a proper booby trap: my desk chair with an unsteady stack of puzzle boxes balancing in the seat. If anyone opened that door, the boxes would tumble to the ground, making a terrible racket.

I crawled into my own bed, and listening to the soothing sounds of Jack's breathing, I drifted to sleep.

~~~~~

The sound of a familiar voice woke me from a deep sleep. I sat up in bed. "Jonas!"

I looked to my right. Jack jumped out of bed and stumbled backward a little. "Lex, what's wrong?"

We stared at each other for a moment. We were both extremely groggy. Neither of us looked sure of what had woken us.

"I… I guess I was dreaming." I looked down at my covers; they had fallen to the floor. I was wearing nothing but a T-shirt and short pajama shorts. I quickly gathered up my covers and pulled them back on the bed and over top of me.

Jack came over and crawled behind me on top of the covers. He pulled me against him, my back to his chest. "Sleep." He kissed the back of my head and held me tight.

I stared out into the room. My chair was still by the door, the boxes still piled high. I had just closed my eyes when I heard him again.

Lexi. Can you hear me?
~~~~~

Jonas? Where are you? I smelled the familiar scent of smoke—a scent I remember only from the times when Jonas had a tracker. My eyes sprang open, but I remained very still. Sitting on Dani's bed was a figure leaning forward, his elbows on his knees, holding a cigarette. Memories of Jonas controlling my mind and actions flooded back. My pulse quickened.

Lexi, listen to me. The figure took a drag, then looked over at me as he blew the smoke out. *Sandra has me. She plans to come back for you.* His voice sounded strained, like he was in pain. *You have to fight her.* He grimaced.

What is she doing to you? I can't let her hurt you because of me.

Don't worry about me. I'll figure something out. She won't do permanent damage.

Are you still close? I found the note you left. We know where the lab is. I know what I need to do.

No! Lexi, don't go near Palmyra. Promise me. I shouldn't have left that note. If I had known.

But Jonas, I can—

No. Promise me. If she catches you there, she'll never let you leave. I finished reading your dad's journals. He hid the formula inside you. Your DNA has the key to producing the perfect healer. We had only just begun to figure it all out. Your dad, Lexi... He made sure you were the key. Sandra knows this. If you die, she destroys any chance she has of perfecting the healing mechanism that can be placed inside the trackers.

That's why she hasn't killed me yet, despite all the chances she's had, I thought mostly to myself. *She's only tried to scare me into needing her.*

Or into running. If you were to run, you'd be vulnerable. You're somewhat protected at Wellington.

I tensed, and Jack's arm held me tighter. *Until Roger tried to kill me.*

He got greedy. But he's locked away now.

Which was only a tiny relief: smart, rich people tended not to stay locked up. *Tell me where you are.*

I don't know. With a shaky hand, he lifted the cigarette to his lips. The end of the cigarette flared as he inhaled. *I'm okay for now.*

How did Sandra get into Wellington? Furthermore, how had Maya been getting in?

There must be someone on the inside. Be prepared, Lex. Sandra'll be coming back for Maya, too.

What makes you say that?

Because she hasn't killed her yet. She would have terminated a tracker clone if she wasn't right where Sandra wanted her. Haven't you wondered why Maya hasn't forced someone to let her out yet? You can't lock up a tracker clone without disabling the tracker.

I sat up. *Oh my gosh, you're right.* Maya would have simply used mind tricks to force someone to let her out. She must *want* to be here. Or Sandra wants her here.

"Lex?" Jack placed a hand on the small of my back. "Can't sleep?"

Jonas disappeared, and the smell and haze of smoke went with him. "I have to see Maya." I threw the covers back, grabbed a pair of jeans off the floor, and shimmied into them.

"Right now? You need more sleep. We're no good to Jonas or anyone else if we're zombies."

"I can't sleep. Jonas says he's okay for now."

"Wait. You talked to Jonas?" Jack sat up. "Did he say where he was?"

"He didn't know." I grabbed my weapon-ring from my desk and faced him. "We have to stop Sandra, Jack. She won't stop until she's won. We can't let her."

"I'll go with you."

EIGHTEEN

"Are you sure you can do this?"

I nodded once. "I'm sure." Jack had his hands on my shoulders, and his gaze was directed at me, looking for any sign I wasn't up for a one-on-one mental battle with Maya.

Seth unlocked the door, ushered me in, then closed and locked the door behind me. Maya sat on a sheet on the floor in the lotus position. She appeared to be meditating. *Good morning, Lexi. You're here awfully early.*

"Don't you sleep?"

I slept.

"What are you meditating about?"

She opened one eye and directed it at me. Heat spread across my neck. I broke eye contact and began circling the room, stopping briefly by the one-way window. I knew Jack was on the other side of it.

He can't protect you if you go to Palmyra, you know.

I spun around. "Palmyra?" It was the first time Maya had mentioned the island. "Have you been there?"

She cocked her head. A sly grin reached all the way to the evil sparkle in her eyes. In one fluid motion, she lifted her body from lotus to a standing position. I flinched, and hoped she hadn't noticed. Someone had given her some blue scrubs that she'd rolled at the ankles.

Yes, I've been to Palmyra. You're going to like it.

"What makes you think I'll go there?"

Because that's the only way to save Jonas. She smiled again. *Does he know?* She nodded to the large window where Jack stood watching us.

I turned my head and looked over my shoulder at the window. When I turned back, she was standing slightly closer. "Does he know what?"

That you have a connection with Jonas.

"You don't know what you're talking about." Sweat covered my palms. I wiped them on my jeans.

Don't I?

"How long has the lab been at Palmyra?"

A while.

Stop being so vague, I mindspoke as I entered Maya's head. Her brain was an organized web of red neurons. *Tell me now. How long has the lab on Palmyra existed?*

Instead of mindspeaking, Maya spoke aloud in a monotone. I had her. "I was taken to Palmyra as a baby. The lab has existed since before you and I were born."

When we first met, you called me your sister. What did you mean?

"We were created at the same time. We were supposed to be implanted in the same surrogate, but after the explosion, something happened. We were separated."

Maya's neurons began firing a little more, and changing in color. Darker.

How can I get inside Palmyra without being seen?

"You can't. Not without help." Her neurons darkened further, but only momentarily before they sparked again. She gave her head a shake before slipping back into a trance. She was fighting my control. "Why would you want to sneak in? I can take you there. They're not going to hurt you. They're expecting you. You're going to love it there."

Sandra had said the same thing—that I would love the beach where the new lab was. Only it wasn't new, just new to the clones she had here at the University of Kentucky.

How have you been slipping in and out of Wellington unseen?

Maya closed her eyes. Her head twitched to one side, then the other. Another presence invaded her mind and pushed against me. This presence was like a water balloon. When I pushed against it, it moved, but barely. Who was it?

Tell me who's inside your head, I commanded.

"No. I can't." She shifted. Her eyes remained closed. She brought both hands to the sides of her head, and screamed. "Gaaah!"

Jack, someone else is inside Maya's head. Can you see who it is?

No. The presence is too elusive. I can't get a good read. Wait a minute...

What? Who is it? I slipped back inside Maya's brain. I recognized Jack's presence immediately—straight-edged, easier to move and shove out—yet this other presence was familiar, but constantly changing. Who was that powerful? One of the seven? No.

Who is it, Maya?

And then I realized. I spun around and stared at the window. I didn't have to see through the glass to know Jack had already fled in search of the one person capable of stopping my mind invasion and getting Maya in and out of the school. How could we have been so stupid?

I heard the noise behind me, but by the time I reacted it was too late. Just as I lifted my elbow, preparing to nail Maya in the face, her arms were around me, and a needle was in my arm. I only just managed to turn the switch on my ring and drive it into her neck before I sank to the ground. My only consolation was that she went down with me.

~~~~~

"Hey, Lex. It's Kyle. Can you hear me?"

My eyes fluttered open. "Kyle?"

His figure knelt beside me. "Jack sent me. Let's get you out of here. I need you to stand." He placed a hand on my back and helped me to my feet. I swayed, and my vision was off.

Maya was beside me. Her glassed-over eyes stared blankly up at me, barely blinking. I had no idea how long I'd been out, but she was still paralyzed. I bent down and whispered in her ear. "I would have helped you." She remained motionless. I must have gotten enough of the paralyzing agent in her before I crashed to the floor. I rubbed the spot on my arm where the needle stuck me. "So, am I unconscious?" I asked Kyle. "Are you controlling me in my sleep?"

Like before, he spoke out loud to me, and because of his mind control, I was able to move and speak despite the drug Maya injected me with.

"Yes, and I'm not sure how long you'll be unconscious. I don't know what she gave you, or how she got it." He put an arm around me. "Now walk. We're getting out of here. Coach is on his way to deal with Maya."

"I know who it is, Kyle." The volume of my voice climbed. "I know who's been helping Maya and Sandra."

"Shhh. Calm down."
~~~~~

"It's Addison. That's how Maya and Sandra have gotten in and out of Wellington unnoticed. Addison made them invisible."

"I know. Jack's looking for her."

Kyle guided me through the door and down the hallway. We had just reached the stairs that would lead us to the main floor of the infirmary, when Addison appeared from out of nowhere.

I stopped, and curled my fingers into my palm until my nails broke the skin.

Lexi, if she does anything to me, I won't be able to stay inside your head. You'll go back to being unconscious, and I'll be blind.

"Hi, Lexi. Long time, no see." Addison always sounded older than her eight-year-old body looked.

"Jack's out looking for you."

"Oh yeah? Why's that?"

I cocked my head, studied her. She didn't yet know we'd figured out she was the one getting Sandra and Maya in and out. "Well, he said he hadn't talked to you in a while. Wanted to make sure you were okay."

"I'm sure you've all been busy. It's all right."

"No, it's not. We need to stick together."

Keep her talking. Invite her to breakfast. I'll tell Jack.

"Kyle and I are on our way to breakfast. You interested?" My words slurred slightly. I always sounded a bit drunk when drugged and under Kyle's control.

"Sure." She wrung her hands, glancing periodically around me to look down the hallway behind me. "What were you guys doing down here? I heard we had Sandra's clone locked up here on campus."

Wave your hand like it's no big deal, Kyle instructed. *Tell her Maya's sleeping.*

"Pfft. Oh yeah. I just checked on her. She's sleeping. I'd like to get that tracker out of her. I think she'd be relieved to be away from Sandra and out of her control."

A wrinkle formed across Addison's forehead.

Now lead Addison out of here. I'll do my best to keep you on your feet. She's not getting inside your head because you're unconscious. It's frustrating her. Don't let on, but I'm having trouble finding Jack.

I reached out and grabbed Addison's hand. "Come on. Let's go eat." Even while I was unconscious, my heart caught in my chest at Kyle's words. What had happened to Jack?

Kyle kept me walking toward the dining hall, and I led Addison and tried to keep our conversation going. It was early in the morning. Most students weren't even up yet, and the campus was quiet. We were halfway across campus when she slowed.

I don't know how much longer I can keep this up, Lexi. I'll go blind the minute I lose my grip on your mind. And once I'm gone, if you're even the least bit conscious, she'll know what you're thinking.

So what do we do?

Speed her up.

"I'm freezing." I crossed my arms and rubbed the goosebumps that formed there. "Let's hurry."

She looked toward the turnaround in front of the dorms, then back at me. "Wait. Jack's coming."

I looked up. "From where? How do you know?"

"He just told me, silly."

She's playing you. She's trying to stall. Jack hasn't answered me.

Just keep me conscious, okay?

Kyle sighed. *I'll try.*

Just as we reached the sidewalk, a dark car sped to a stop in front of us. *Kyle?* Panic sent my heart into overdrive.

I can't hold on much longer. You have to relax.

It's Sandra. I swallowed hard, and glanced at Addison. Her hands shook. She stuffed them in her coat pockets. I decided it was time to stop pretending. "At least you have the decency to look scared. You can stop the games."

Addison's crazed eyes found mine. "You knew? Why can't I read your mind?"

"Because Maya drugged me. I'm unconscious."

"Kyle's directing you." She glanced behind me to Kyle. "But he's about to lose you, isn't he? That's why his face is scrunched up in pain."

Which was definitely unfortunate. "I brought you out of that coma. I broke into The Farm to save you. And this is how you repay me? Repay Jack? After everything we did for you, you're working with Sandra?"

"I had no choice." Her voice was meek, quiet.

"We always have a choice."

"She has my mom," she whispered.

Anita had been at The Farm when we were there. "What? Why didn't you say something? We would have helped her."

The back door of the car opened, and out stepped Sandra. "Hello, Sarah."

"You can't win," Addison said. "Sandra always wins."

"That's right, Sarah. Surely you're starting to realize this. Addison, where's Maya?"

Addison glanced over her shoulder. "She's back at the infirmary."

Sandra narrowed her gaze at me. "You did something to her, didn't you?"

"Nothing she didn't deserve."

Sandra pulled a stun gun from somewhere behind her, walked up to Kyle and stung him in the arm. As he fell to the ground convulsing, my legs gave out. I had regained a little bit of control over my body, but not enough to keep from hitting my head on the sidewalk as I slumped to the ground.

My fingers and hands were numb, and I couldn't move my legs; and in my state of impaired consciousness, I couldn't even mindspeak. Kyle rolled back and forth on the ground in pain, and I knew that when his pain subsided, the blindness would prevent him from helping me. I was caught, helpless.

"Addison, go get Maya, now."

Addison's gaze ping-ponged between me and Sandra before she turned and sprinted toward the infirmary. For someone so little and young, she was fast.

Sandra stood over me. "This would have been much easier had you simply accepted your fate. Maya understands this already. What happened to you?"

My eyes opened a little. I brushed my fingers across my lips. "I guess you messed up my genes when you altered them."

Sandra laughed. "That's funny." A frightening chill moved through my body. Sandra knelt beside me and traced my cheekbone, my chin, and ran her fingers down my neck. "You're my masterpiece, Sarah. There's nothing imperfect about you. You're the key to the future of stopping the world's most deadly diseases. We're going to make a great team. You can either participate willingly, or I can force you. You thought it was rough having Jonas in your head before? Wait 'til you see what changes I've made to his tracker. It's going to be brilliant."

My heart constricted. *Oh, Jonas, I'm sorry.* I hadn't heard from him since earlier that morning. How could I help him, help the other clones, if I was under Sandra's control?

Sandra opened the door of the car and said something to the driver. He exited the car and circled the hood. He was a tall, bulky man, not someone I had any desire to mess with. He bent down and started to scoop me up off the concrete.

"I wouldn't do that if I were you." Mr. Bulky paused.

Sandra snapped her head in Jack's direction, followed by the slow rotation of Mr. Bulky, who had one hand up, one hand reaching under his sports jacket.

Jack. He's got a gun. Finally, I was able to use my mind to reach out to Jack. I tried to reach Mr. Bulky. *Do not touch that gun,* I ordered. *Raise both hands and turn around.*

He did as he was told.

"Nice trick, Sarah." Sandra looked about as worried as a cat taking a nap. What game was she playing?

Jack held out a hand to me. "Can you stand?"

"I think so." The drug seemed to be wearing off. I reached out and grabbed hold of his hand and let him pull me to my feet. I swayed slightly then touched my hand to the back of my head. My fingers came away bright red. "Shit. I hit my head pretty hard."

Motion to the left caught my eye. It was Addison and Maya, running toward us. I pulled on Jack's arm, supporting myself while he continued to watch Sandra and the driver for any movement.

As Addison and Maya got closer, they slowed, both seeming to take in the situation. Addison refused to look at Jack or me, but Maya's eyes shot daggers.

"Okay, Sarah." Sandra had been calmly gnawing on her cuticle, but now she dropped her hand. "This is your chance to choose to come with me."

"What crazy planet do you live on that you would think I would come with you?" Although I'd go to her island eventually. I'd rescue Jonas, take control of the clones she was growing, and make her pay for the pain she'd caused. But I wouldn't go there with her. When I went, it would be on my terms.

She stepped closer to me, ignoring the gun Jack had pointed at her head. "You will join me eventually. I can be patient for now. But if you come now, I won't send my next gift." She smiled.

Don't listen to her. You know this is a trick.

I stepped even closer, rotating my shoulders back. "Your gifts don't scare me."

Laughter erupted from deep inside her. "Oh, Sarah. This one should." She reached up and patted my cheek. "You call me after you receive it, okay? We'll talk then."

One blink later, Sandra, Addison, and Maya vanished.

NINETEEN

Days later, we still hadn't received any messages or "gifts" from Sandra. And I was pissed at myself for constantly glancing over my shoulder and jumping at every sound. Meanwhile, I was moving forward with what I called "Operation Sandra Smackdown."

The only problem: I still needed to tell Jack the plan.

He held my hand tightly as we walked across campus. He had reverted to touching me a lot since Sandra came for Maya.

"I know what you're doing," I told him. I sipped my tea. The sky was overcast, and the warmth of the tea and the soothing effects of the honey comforted me.

"You do?" He placed his free hand over his heart, feigning shock.

"You think you can protect me from Sandra just by shielding me." We had discovered that Jack had the ability to keep people like Jonas, Ty, and Maya out of my head as long as he was touching me. The issue, though, was that it wasn't feasible for him to be touching me at all times. Although that didn't stop him from trying.

"Mmm."

As we approached Wellington's admin building, we passed a few government vehicles—some black Crown Victorias and a smaller SUV, all with official government license plates. My guests had arrived.

Squeezing my hand, Jack halted my forward motion. "What's going on here?" he asked.

"It's okay. I invited them."

Jack maneuvered his body to stand in front of me, keeping me from proceeding. "What do you mean, you invited them? Who are they? What's going on?"

"Just some government peeps I thought could help." I was purposely vague. "It's time we take Sandra, your father, and their operation down."

Jack twisted his neck, popping it twice. "What are you talking about? How are *you* going to do that?"

"I have some ideas."

I sidestepped Jack, but held on to his hand and pulled him behind me. "I've been resisting everything we've been dealing with since the beginning. But now it's time to face it head-on. We'll never be free to move forward with our lives with Sandra constantly trying to brainwash me, trying to steal me away from my life here at Wellington."

"So what's the plan, then? Are you going to let me in on it, or do I have to stand in the background and make the have-you-lost-your-mind face?"

"I haven't lost my mind."

"Okay then, let me ask you this: how did an eighteen-year-old girl talk a team of 'government peeps' into showing up for this meeting?"

"I got Coach to help."

"You asked Coach Williams."

"And I may have threatened them a little."

"Right. You threatened them. With your paralyzing ring?" He chuckled.

"You think this is funny?"

His smile only faltered a little. "No. I don't think it's the least bit funny. More like terrifying."

I dropped his hand and sped up. Before I reached the door to the building, he grabbed my arm. "I'm just wondering how you might have 'threatened' a group of government officials. Officials who have done *nothing* to help us with anything that's happened so far, and who we'd rather not know that much about our gifts. So what do you have that made them listen?"

"Information. And money."

"Money? Your inheritance."

"I've tried telling you. We keep getting interrupted. My father left me a small fortune when he died."

"I gathered that. What kind of small fortune are we talking?"

I turned my head into the breeze, and the cool air blew some rogue strands away from my face. I took a deep breath in, preparing to blow Jack's mind.

Jack touched my cheek and directed my gaze back toward him. "How much?"

"Three point two."

"Three point two what? Million?"

"Billion."

Jack dropped his hand and took a step back. He cupped his chin, rubbing his hand back and forth across his five o'clock shadow. The vein in his neck began pulsing rapidly.

"Say something." I couldn't hide the shakiness from my voice.

He opened and shut his mouth three times, then turned away from me, looking out across campus.

"Jack?"

He whipped back around. “Let me get this straight. You’ve known since the day those attorneys came to meet with you that you were the heir to a few *billion* dollars? Do you have any idea what kind of money that is?”

I didn’t even bother answering those questions. The last one didn’t even deserve an answer. How could anyone—especially a teenager sheltered inside a boarding school wearing uniforms half her life—comprehend what that kind of money meant? All I knew was that it meant *power*. I just wasn’t sure how much power.

“Are you mad I didn’t tell you? I tried. I wanted to. It was just, you were angry at me. And I was mad at you. And then people were shooting at us. Someone *did* shoot two of us. Jonas was taken. Maya tried to kill me. Twice. Then Sandra almost kidnapped me.”

Jack closed the distance between us. He slipped an arm around me and raised a finger to my lips. “Shhh. I’m not mad that you didn’t tell me.”

“You’re not?” I searched his eyes. “This changes everything, doesn’t it?”

“Money doesn’t change things between you and me. I just wish you would have trusted me with this sooner.”

“It wasn’t that I didn’t trust you. I wanted to tell you the other night. I started to, but then Jonas was taken. I tried again when we got back to my room. But you fell asleep while I was in the shower. And—”

“I would have protected you better had I known. This is why Roger wants you dead, isn’t it? He stood to take over more than just the school if he got rid of you.”

"It appears so. My father's biggest mistake was trusting the wrong people."

"I'm sorry I wasn't there for you when you found out about your inheritance."

"It's okay. I forgave you for that a long time ago. We've both made our share of mistakes."

"I don't want to make any more." He tucked an errant strand of hair behind my ear. "Can't we just use this money to run away?"

I cocked my head. He and I both knew we couldn't just run. "I'd love nothing more than that, but Jonas needs us."

Jack nodded. "That he does."

"And Sandra has the backing of the government on her side."

Jack took in a deep breath and let it out slowly. "So, we meet with and threaten that same government? That's your plan?"

"More or less."

"Well, then..." He gestured with his hand out. "Lead the way."

~~~~~

At five feet two inches, there were times when I had to be bigger than myself.

Several men and one woman gathered in Wellington's conference room, and almost all of them carried guns. They were dressed in dark suits and held small Styrofoam cups. The smell of coffee filled the air. I'd never understood the lure of hot coffee in the afternoon.
~~~~~

Not one of them looked our way when we entered.

"Oh, good, you're both here." Alyson walked in behind us, along with Coach. "Are you sure about this?" She placed a gentle hand on my arm.

I nodded. It was surreal to have my mother ask that question and touch me with a gentleness that I was coming to know in her. Had I forgiven her? Or had I simply put my anger on hold while I conquered the real monster?

Coach cast me an uneasy smile. "This isn't going to be easy. I called in all my favors. You've got a tough crowd before you."

I scanned the room, studying each person. My eyes finally fell on a woman dressed in a lovely dark red suit. Evelyn Meyers, the president's deputy chief of staff. She was flanked by two men in navy suits—Secret Service, I presumed. "I'm ready," I told Coach.

"Okay, then. Let's do this." He faced the room. "Ladies and gentlemen, if you could, please take your seats."

"Actually," I stepped forward, placing a hand on Coach's arm, "there's no need for all of you to sit." I met each of their stares before landing on the one female in the room. "Ms. Meyers, I believe? I would love it if you and I could have a private conversation."

The other suits in the room traded raised-brow looks. One of the men chuckled under his breath, then with a toothy grin, said, "And who might you be, pretty lady?"

"I'm Lexi Matthews. Who are you?" I answered with a smile to match his, though mine had a touch of smart-ass to it.

He glanced to Coach Williams, then back to me. "Agent Mackelroy, FBI."

"Agent Mackelroy is the agent who is working your father's case," Coach explained. "He also was nice enough to call the office of the president's chief of staff, which resulted in Ms. Meyers and a couple of Secret Service agents attending this meeting." Then he added, "As you requested." There was a touch of warning in his voice not to piss these people off.

"I see. Well, Mr. Mackelroy, I appreciate you being here. I'm thankful that you're still trying to solve my dad's murder." Though I still hadn't heard if they had done anything about the video I'd sent them. "I'm even more grateful for the call you made to the president's chief of staff. For now, I need to speak with Ms. Meyers. Alone. You and your friends are invited to take a walk over to our campus coffee shop and have a latte on me."

One of the men standing directly next to Ms. Meyers spoke up next. "We're not leaving Ms. Meyers."

"Why? Do I look like I'm a threat to her?" That got an amused grin out of Ms. Meyers.

I made eye contact with each of the men, one by one. *I need each of you to exit the room. You will walk across campus and find the coffee shop there. Have a latte. Otis, the barista, is expecting you.*

They each made their way to the doors behind me. Ms. Meyers looked on as the men filed out of the room, leaving Jack, Coach, Seth, Alyson, Ms. Meyers, and me.

Ms. Meyers's eyebrows slanted inward, almost touching. "What just happened?" She was a middle-aged woman, African-American, and by her size and build, I suspected she was an avid runner.

"I asked them to leave." I pulled out the chair next to her and sat.

A knock sounded behind me, and the door opened slowly. "Sorry I'm late." Briana entered, looked around the room, and headed over to stand beside Jack.

How's your head? I asked.

Better, thanks to you. Any word from Jonas?

I shook my head.

Ms. Meyers clasped her hands together. "I think it's time someone told me why this meeting was called." Irritation was evident in her tone.

I drew in a sharp breath. "Ms. Meyers, have you ever heard of Palmyra Atoll?"

"I know it. A small island in the Northern Pacific Ocean."

"That's right." I could feel Jack's eyes on me. We had talked about how much or how little to divulge to anyone in the government, which is why I'd asked everyone but Evelyn Meyers to leave. I had researched her online and found her to be trusted by her colleagues and respected by the news media. She was married with three children. A career woman who still made time for family. "Correct me if I'm wrong, but this island is partially owned by the Nature Conservancy. The other part is owned by the United States and run by the U.S. Fish and Wildlife Department."

"I believe that's correct. It's an unorganized, uninhabited territory."

"Unorganized, maybe. But there *are* residents of this atoll."

"All right. Why don't you tell me why we're discussing this island?" Her smile told me she was struggling to take me seriously.

"The secretary of the interior is responsible for whatever happens on Palmyra Atoll. And the secretary, who sits on the president's cabinet, answers to the president. This indirectly makes the president responsible for what happens on this atoll. Isn't it partly your job, as deputy chief of staff, to protect the president?"

"What exactly do you want, Miss Matthews?"

"I want to purchase Palmyra Atoll."

Ms. Meyers's face turned stoic. "Let's pretend for a minute that you could possibly have enough money to purchase a private island. Palmyra Atoll is not for sale. Even if it were, why would the United States of America sell it to you?" She enunciated each syllable. "Besides, what would a young girl like yourself want with an uninhabited island in the middle of the Northern Pacific?"

I chose to ignore the "young girl" comment for now. "I assure you, money is not a problem." I nodded to Seth. He flipped on the projector, and Alyson dimmed the lights. I gestured for Ms. Meyers to direct her attention toward the screen now lit up with a photograph. "This is a satellite photo of the atoll, taken yesterday." I picked up a laser pointer and walked to the wall. "As you can see here and here..."—I pointed to a few fuzzy spots in the picture—"...people are, in fact, currently on the island."

"Okay, so what?" She turned her hands out, then let them fall back to the table. "I obviously am not completely in touch with the goings-on of this island. The Nature Conservancy might have a project in progress."

"I mean no disrespect when I say this, but I'm willing to bet that no one working under the president is aware of what's happening on Palmyra Atoll right now."

She shifted in her seat. "What are you suggesting?"

"I'm not suggesting. I'm *telling* you that there is something happening on this island that I plan to put a stop to, and the International Intelligence Agency is covering it up right under the president's nose. And because the president is ultimately responsible for this island—and for what the IIA does on U.S. soil—a political and PR nightmare will erupt if, or should I say *when*, the American public finds out."

"And just what is happening on Palmyra that you think is so serious?"

"The IIA is allowing a group of doctors and scientists to clone human beings and experiment on them." I decided not to add the fact that this was being done in exchange for robotic and cloned human weapons to be sold to military around the world. Not yet, anyway.

A hysterical laugh passed Ms. Meyers's lips. "Human cloning. That's not possible. Where would you get such an absurd idea?"

"It *is* possible. I'm proof."

One, two, three beats passed while she tapped a manicured fingernail against the table. "What do you mean, you're proof?"

I nodded to Seth. He changed the slide on the screen to show three side-by-side pictures. With my laser, I pointed. "This is a photograph of me. The next one is Dr. Sandra Whitmeyer when she was my age. And the third is Sandra Whitmeyer today." A chill produced goose bumps across the back of my neck and down my arms. It was the first time I had seen myself directly next to the donator of my DNA.

"That doesn't prove anything. You could have created an age-enhanced photo."

"I could have, but I didn't. I can prove that my DNA is nearly identical to that woman's. Just as I can prove that Jack's DNA"—Jack nodded behind me—"is identical to Dr. John DeWeese's DNA. Dr. DeWeese is the man who raised Jack, and he's this woman's partner in every insane thing being done on Palmyra Atoll. The FBI agents who were here today also know this information to be true. They've simply not been able to prove it fully."

Coach, who had been leaning against the wall the entire time, stepped up to the table again. "What Lexi is failing to mention is that Sandra Whitmeyer and John DeWeese have repeatedly asked Lexi to join them. When she has declined their request, they have threatened her life. They need Lexi as a subject, in order to enable the types of DNA modifications they want to make to the cloned humans they're creating."

"And they're killing hundreds of embryos for every one that survives." My heart ached just saying that out loud. As if voicing the horrific truth made it even more of a reality.

"If what you're saying is true, I'll take this information to the president. We'll launch an investigation. The U.S. government will not allow this to continue. If necessary, the military will get involved."

My stomach tightened. "No. That won't work." The military was liable to take the entire island out if they discovered the kind of craziness that was happening there. "Doing that brings attention to the island. Too many people will discover the horrific experiments these doctors are doing. Neither the president nor I have any interest in the public knowing anything about what is going on there. That's why I decided to bring it to his attention—to *your* attention—before the public discovers this unfortunate information and forms their own opinion."

I was taking a risk by bringing this to her—if the military were to get involved, I would fail.

Ms. Meyers stood. She was at least five foot eight, a good six inches taller than me. "Are you threatening the president, Miss Matthews?"

My pulse was sprinting at full speed. "On the contrary. I'm trying to protect him. And myself. I'm saving your boss from a public relations disaster if news of the experiments being done to Americans on this island were to leak to the press—experiments that have nothing to do with the mission of the Nature Conservancy or U.S. Fish and Wildlife."

"And what makes you think anyone in the press would believe anything you were to say to them?"

"Because I have proof of every experiment ever done by the IIA's Division of Human Cloning. And I have proof that at least one segment of the U.S. government has allowed immoral and unlawful experiments to take place in exchange for the creation of unorthodox weapons." Not to mention that those weapons were being sold to other countries' military.

Though I wanted to retreat backward into the dark corner behind me, I took two steps closer to the deputy chief of staff. "I also have proof of murders, and attempted murders, committed by representatives of the IIA or by people currently protected by the IIA. These murders have been covered up by agencies of the U.S. government, as have the repeated threats on my life."

Panic erupted in Ms. Meyers's eyes and across her face. "Do you realize you are blackmailing the president of the United States?"

"I'm not blackmailing anyone. I'm offering our government the chance to do something right before the public discovers the truth. The truth about the American lives that have been lost due to the horrific experiments being performed by the doctors on Palmyra Atoll."

Ms. Meyers frowned. "I can see that you've put a lot of thought into this. But this is not a job for a little girl. This is a job for the U.S. military." She stood and placed her hands on the table to brace herself. "I appreciate you bringing this information to the president's attention, but this meeting is over."

I glanced behind me to Alyson, Jack, and Briana. Jack nodded encouragement. "Before you decide to turn your back on us, we need to show you one more thing."

She stared at me a few seconds, then sank back down into the leather chair.

Jack and Briana stepped up to the table. "The reason I know so much about the experiments being done on the island is because Jack, Briana, and I are just a few examples of what these doctors are capable of creating. We have... supernatural abilities that these doctors want to reproduce—even if it means killing one hundred times the number of humans in the process, including small children."

"*Supernatural* abilities?" she repeated. "Like flying? Running faster than a speeding bullet?" She laughed, but I could tell she didn't really mean it.

"Our abilities are more of the mind control and medical healing kind."

It was time to bring out the big guns.

Ms. Meyers, please tell me something highly sensitive the president is planning right now that the public doesn't know about.

Ms. Meyers cocked her head. "The president has invited Palestinian-Israeli leaders to a summit to take place at Camp David next week."

"Interesting." *And the press hasn't gotten wind of this?*

"No. It's very important that no one knows these leaders are coming to the United States, for fear of the conflicts that could arise."

I released her mind. Her eyes grew to the size of silver dollars. She covered her mouth as if she could take back what just spewed from it. "Why did I just say that? I could lose my job."

"For the same reason the FBI and Secret Service agents exited earlier. Because I asked."

She stared at me, dumbfounded.

I turned to Briana. "Bree, can you please demonstrate your ability to Ms. Meyers?"

Briana stepped up beside me, then morphed into a replica of me.

Ms. Meyers's chest rose and fell in quick succession. I could hear her shallow breaths.

"Briana can make anyone think they're seeing something that they're not. We both have the ability to manipulate the minds of others. We try not to use these powers to do harm, but, as I'm sure you can imagine, not everyone would use these abilities for good."

I had one more demonstration. "Jack."

I only had to say his name, and he was by my side. He handed me a knife, and Briana laid a white towel on the table, beneath where I held my hand. I took the knife and, without hesitation, drove the sharp point of the blade into my hand, slicing directly across the palm. I suppressed a wince from the biting pain.

I lifted my hand so Ms. Meyers could see the wound; blood dripped down my arm and onto the towel. Ms. Meyers could only stare open-mouthed.

Jack lifted two fingers and followed the line of the cut, healing the wound as he went.

"Oh my God," Ms. Meyers whispered. "You just healed her cut."

"Our abilities go way beyond what we've just demonstrated. And in many ways, we're still just learning. These abilities—or at least the healing ability—may appear at first to be a force for good. But the cost to human life is just too great. We can't let these doctors create more like us. We can't let them treat innocent human beings as unwilling test subjects. And we can't let someone with such obvious ethical deficiencies be in control of such powers. Can you imagine if our abilities reached the wrong people at high levels within our government? Or our enemies' governments?"

Jack spoke for the first time. "And the public can't know about these abilities. It's a Pandora's box. Other scientists of dubious ethics—financed by those with a thirst for power—would be drawn to try to repeat these experiments. Once the secret is out, there's no way to ever contain this kind of research again. Genetic manipulation will become the world's next WMD."

"Further, a large part of the population would demand that we heal everybody of everything," I added. "And we wouldn't be able to. There would be too many." My voice cracked with emotion. A part of me wished there was a way to end pain and suffering, but that's just not the way of this world.

Ms. Meyers leaned back in her chair and let out a large breath. "I just don't know." Her smiles from earlier had faded. Her cheeks appeared heavy.

I sat beside her again, on the very edge of my seat. My leg bobbed rapidly. I placed a hand on hers. She took it away and tucked it in her lap.

Jack touched my shoulder. He knew what I was thinking—that this was the first time an outside person had been repulsed or frightened by something I'd demonstrated.

"And all you want is to purchase this little island?" Ms. Meyers said at last.

"That, and I want the chance to stop these doctors and scientists from murdering more embryos and cloning humans." And from ever murdering or controlling the mind of another.

A grin touched her lips, but not her eyes.

"And you think you can use your powers to stop them?"

"Yes." I have to. "And do you see why I asked everyone else to leave? This isn't something we can risk leaking."

"Why not just find a quiet corner of the world to hide in? We can help you disappear. The military can stop this operation." She was attempting to understand us. "We have a wonderful witness protection program. If you have money to purchase this island, you have the money to disappear. Why risk your life?"

"That's a lovely offer, Ms. Meyers, but no thank you. The woman behind this is responsible for taking away almost everything I've cared about in my life, including my father and my best friend. And she's doing unspeakable things to human beings. I *will* stop her."

Ms. Meyers seemed to consider this. "What do you need from me?"

"Besides ownership of the island? I'm not one-hundred-percent sure what we need quite yet, except that we'll need someone ready to take in the guilty once we've discovered them."

"And how do I know you won't just be taking over the performance of the same experiments?"

"I will personally invite you to visit the laboratory once we've taken over and secured the facility."

"Why should I trust *you* to take over this facility? No offense, but you're just a kid."

That was a great question. I had absolutely no idea what I was going to do once I had in my possession this tropical island in the middle of the Pacific Ocean, let alone the responsibility of a lab I knew very little about—other than that I didn't want its experiments to continue.

"She won't be alone," Seth said. The fatherly tone in his voice struck me. "We've already assembled a team to take over the lab."

We have?

Jack linked his pinky finger with mine. *Just go with it.*

"Take over? But I thought you said the lab was doing illegal and immoral experiments on humans."

"They are," I said, "but someone has to find a humane way of dealing with the aftermath. My only goals are to make sure the innocent are protected." I swallowed hard. "Once we remove the doctors responsible, someone will still have to see to it that the humans created within this lab survive the best they can—that they'll be given the best shot possible at a normal life."

"And you're capable of that job?"

I closed my eyes for a brief moment before meeting her gaze again. "Yes. I have to be."

TWENTY

I woke to loud banging on my door. When the door opened a little and the stack of puzzle boxes tumbled to the ground, my heart raced at triple speed. Every muscle along my spine tightened.

"Lexi, wake up," Seth yelled through the crack in the door.

My shoulders slumped forward. The relief was quickly replaced with anxiety as to why Seth was breaking into my room in the middle of the night. I stumbled out of bed and over to the door, then moved the fallen boxes out of the way with my feet and pulled the chair back. "What's wrong? Is it Jack?"

"Yes. And Georgia. Get dressed."

The clock glowed 3:00 a.m. I swallowed against the swell of emotions forming in my throat as I searched for clothes. "Tell me what's happened."

Seth turned his back to me while I quickly slipped into a pair of jeans and changed into my favorite green sweater. "Fred called. Said Georgia had a massive attack. Jack went to help, and is now throwing up. He can't stop."

I shoved my phone into my back pocket and rushed past Seth and out the door, pulling my hair back into a loose ponytail. As we jogged down the hallway, I looked at my phone. No missed calls. Why hadn't Jack called me? I had fallen asleep right after dinner last night around eight o'clock. Jack had agreed to return to his own room and get a good night's sleep if I promised to lock up and booby trap my door again. "Where are they?"

"They're inside The Program."

"Here?"

"No, on campus." As if I needed further explanation, he added, "At the UK Hospital."

~~~~~

Jack was sitting on the floor, one foot bent at the knee, the other stretched out in front of him, and leaning against the wall. His arm was draped across a toilet seat, and his head was pointed toward the ceiling, eyes closed.

Fred paced. "I don't know what happened. They told me not to call you, but..."

"Jack told you not to call me?" I knelt beside Jack and placed my palm against his forehead. He was clammy. His hair was wet, I presumed from sweat. "Did he say why?"

"I don't know. I don't know what Jack wants me to tell you."

A queasy feeling erupted in my stomach at the thought that Jack was keeping things from me again.

I'm not keeping things from you, Jack mindspoke. *I wanted you to get sleep. I thought I could take care of whatever this was.*

I studied his face. He didn't move. *Are you okay? Tell me how you're feeling.* I could be mad at him later.

I feel like a thousand monkeys are dancing in my head, throwing my equilibrium off.

What happened?

Is Georgia okay? he asked, ignoring my question.

I glanced to the other side of the room. Seth was inserting an IV into Georgia's arm. He made eye contact with me and
~~~~~

shrugged. Fred looked on while wringing his hands at his sides.

Seth's working on it. Tell me what happened.

Georgia thought she saw you. She mindspoke to me. Said you told her that Sandra had trapped you and inserted a tracker into the back of your neck. You were scared, but you wanted the tracker removed. Georgia panicked and brought you down here to try and remove it. She said that when you screamed bloody murder at the first movement of the tracker, she tried to stop, but you forced her to keep going and to cut a small incision into the back of your neck. I realized that it wasn't you but Maya, but by the time Georgia reached out to me, the damage had been done.

Where is Maya now?

She was here when I got here. She was bleeding from the neck and crying, and Georgia was having the worst epileptic attack I've ever seen. I tried to heal Maya's wound, but then I started throwing up and couldn't stop.

Why did you try to heal her? She deserved what she got.

It was strange. She asked me to, and I couldn't say no. She looked so pitiful, and all I could see when I looked at her was you.

I rose and crossed the room in search of supplies. After finding some paper towels and wetting them, I returned to Jack and began patting his forehead down with the cool moisture. *You're going to be okay.*

The room won't stop spinning. My head is throbbing. I don't understand it. Lately I've been suffering less when I've healed. But this is the worst I've ever felt.

And you say you've never seen Georgia have such a strong attack?

Never.

This reeked of Sandra's mind games. She was somehow using Maya to make the consequences of our powers worse. But how?

"Is he going to be okay?" Fred asked, and I nodded. "That girl who looks like you—Maya—we thought she was you at first. She said Jonas was taken. Was she lying to us, or was that true?"

"It's true." I stood. "But we're going to get him back. I promise. We *will* find him."

Worry swam in his eyes and in the trenches along his forehead. "Maya also said that Sandra took him to a lab far away."

"We don't know if that's true, but we'll find him," I repeated. I hadn't heard from Jonas in a while. I prayed Sandra didn't hurt another person I loved because of me.

Georgia coughed, bringing me out of my thoughts. Her eyes remained closed.

"She's not slipping into a coma, so there's that," Seth said.

"Can I do something that will make her feel better faster?"

"No. Can't chance another of you getting too sick to function."

Seth opened a cabinet over the sink and began sorting through some pill bottles there. He removed the cap on one of them and shook a pill out into his hand. "Here." He handed me small pink pill. "See if you can get Jack to swallow this."

I found a small Dixie cup and filled it with water. Back by Jack's side, I placed a hand on his back. "I've got a pill for you to take. Seth says it will help."

Jack leaned forward, took the pill in his mouth, and took a slow drink of water. He swallowed like it was the hardest thing he'd ever done.

"Can I help you get into a bed?"

No. Maybe in a minute. Can't move yet.

"Okay." I went to the bed and grabbed the blanket and pillow. I fluffed the pillow and gently placed it behind his head, then covered him with the blanket. I leaned into his ear and whispered, "I'll be back soon."

Before I could stand, he snaked his hand around my wrist and squeezed. *Where are you going?*

"I'm going to find Maya. She's going to help us get into the Palmyra lab whether she likes it or not."

He didn't even try to argue with me. He just whispered, "Lexi, before Maya left she told me..." He swallowed hard.

"What? What did she tell you?"

"She said, 'Sandra hopes you enjoy your gift.'"

TWENTY-ONE

I didn't know what Maya meant by "gift," but so far, Sandra's presents had gotten exponentially worse.

The emergency room at the UK Hospital was bustling with people waiting to be seen. Perspiration bubbled along my forehead, and heat flared on the back of my neck after running the three blocks from The Program at a full sprint. I stood just inside the door, unsure where to look for Maya, or if she was even there. Since neither Maya nor Addison was capable of healing wounds (that I knew of) I figured she'd have to go to a medical facility to stitch up the cut from the botched tracker removal attempt.

Someone bumped me from behind. I turned as a man led a young boy past me while holding what appeared to be a hand towel to the back of the boy's head. Blood colored the tan cloth a mixture of dark and light red. The sterile smells of iodine and alcohol from the hospital mixed with the coppery smell of blood.

The man approached the triage desk. The woman behind it lifted her head. She had to have seen the blood coming from the little boy's wound, but her bored facial expression remained constant. She handed him a clipboard. "Fill this out. A doctor will see you shortly."

His hands full and his look desperate, the man just stood there, dumbfounded.

I rushed over and took the clipboard. “Let me help.” I didn’t have time for this, but I couldn’t consciously stand there and watch this little boy lose so much blood.

“Thank you,” the man said. “My son... he fell... thank you.” The man didn’t look much older than Jack. A few years, maybe.

He led me to a set of chairs. As he did, I quickly tried to diagnose the boy, unbeknownst to the worried father. I first looked inside his skull for any damage or internal bleeding. When I found none, I examined the wound from the inside out. It was a simple gash on the back of his head, but because of the location of the injury, it was bleeding heavily.

“Daddy, I’m dizzy,” the boy said.

“I know, champ. We’re gonna getcha fixed up as soon as we can.”

“What’s your name?” I asked the small boy. He looked to be no more than four or five years old.

“Henry,” he said softly.

This was more the level of injury for Jack to heal, but I was certain I could close the gash without feeling ill thanks to all the training Jonas and I had done. “The doctors here will get you fixed up, Henry.”

He looked up at me with big blue eyes, once again reminding me of Jack and how I needed to find Maya and Addison.

As we sat, I lifted my fingers to touch the cloth. “May I? I need to describe the wound for the doctors.” It wasn’t a complete lie.

The man was slow to answer, but then nodded.

I carefully pulled the cloth away and studied the cut from the outside this time. It was deep. Thankfully, the boy’s dad was on the opposite side from me and didn’t have the angle I did. I concentrated hard. Slowly, the separated pieces of skin moved closer until the wound closed and the bleeding stopped. I pushed the cloth back against the boy's healed wound.

I was relieved to find that my head ached only slightly from the process. The side effects from using my abilities had definitely lessened recently. "Just keep pressure on it," I instructed the father. "Let's get the paperwork filled out quickly."

"Are you a nurse? You're so young."

"No, but both of my parents are doctors, and I've seen lots of injuries in my lifetime." That seemed to appease him.

I began asking him a series of questions—name of patient, name of parent or guardian, address, social security number. As he answered each question, I made mental note of the doors where patients were being admitted. After he'd answered the basic questions, I described the wound for the triage nurse. I knew the kid no longer needed to be seen, but I didn't need to draw any more attention to myself. Hopefully, I'd be long gone before anyone discovered the "miracle."

"That should do it," I said. "I'll just give this to the triage nurse."

The man looked completely worn out. "Thank you," he said.

After handing the clipboard over, I stood and made my way over to a door that appeared to lead back to the emergency exam rooms. Hospitals always had a way of making me feel like I was trespassing. That any minute someone would stop me and tell me, "Wait! You can't go back there." But when a doctor in navy scrubs and a nurse dressed in hot pink exited the exam room area, I slipped by them, doing my best to act as if I belonged.

Beyond the waiting room, doctors walked about and nurses typed away on computers at their stations. No one looked up or seemed to care that I was there. I peeked around curtains and through doors, looking for any sign of Maya.

As I neared the end of the hallway I heard a man yell, "There she is!"

I whipped around. The father of the young boy was standing by the door with a security guard. He was pointing, but not at me. I followed the line of his outstretched arm down the hallway—to Maya. She stood close to a wall at the far end, one hand gripping a metal railing.

Maya, can you hear me?

Her eyes popped wider, looking from the screaming man to me.

"I don't know what she did. All I know is my son came in with a gash on his head, and now he doesn't after that girl touched him." The man had to realize how crazy he sounded.

Maya was still staring at me. She slowly backed away from the crazed man and the security guard who was trying to reason with him.

"What's going on here?" the nurse dressed in hot pink scrubs asked. "Mister, you need to calm down. We can't have you yelling back here."

The little boy, whom I hadn't noticed until now, was walking toward me. His head was cocked, studying me. He turned and looked past his father to Maya. Then back at me. "Daddy," he said softly.

"Just a minute, champ." Rationality seeped back into the father's voice.

"Daddy," he said louder. "There's another one. That's the girl who—"

I bolted around the corner and out of sight. I hoped I hadn't scarred the little boy, but I wasn't sticking around to be questioned about who Maya and I were.

The emergency room was laid out in a big square. I followed the walls around until I came to the corner where Maya had stood. As I inched closer and peered around, I felt a tap on my shoulder.

I turned and no one was there. However, I felt the familiar presence. *Show yourself, Addison,* I ordered.

Don't be mad at me.

Mad at you? You've been helping Sandra. And you got Maya in and out of the school. She almost drowned me. Mad doesn't begin to—

She wouldn't have killed you.

Is that supposed to make me feel better? You betrayed Jack, the one person who would have died for you—who fought for you when you were in a coma. What about Jonas? Because of you, he's back in Sandra's evil web.

Sandra has my mother. She sounded so small inside my head, her voice full of regret.

Anita. We hadn't been able to find her when the lab began to blow up. Addison thought Anita would get out in time, but she hadn't. *Have you heard from your mother?*

She's at Palmyra. Dr. Whitmeyer and Dr. DeWeese told me that if I led either you or Jack to them, they would let my mom come home.

Addison made herself visible. Because she was so intelligent, it was easy to forget how young she was when she was only a voice inside my head. But as she stood before me now, I could see the slumped shoulders of a small child, her face tilted toward the ground. When she looked up, her eyes filled with moisture. “I’m sorry. I didn’t want to hurt you or Jack. Or anyone. But I had to save my mom.”

“I’ll give you a chance to make it up to us. Right now, we need to prevent Maya from being questioned by this man and hospital security.”

Addison leaned around me.

The father and the security guard were trying to talk to Maya. “I’ve never seen this man in my life,” she said. “I was back here getting my neck stitched up.” She leaned forward to show them the large white bandage on the back of her neck.

I aimed my mindspeak at the father. *Tell the security guard that you’re sorry and that you’ve made a mistake.*

“You know what? I’m sorry. I was so distraught when I brought my son in, I must have made a mistake.”

“Okay,” the security guard said with a southern drawl, his face a mask of confusion, but most likely relieved to have the crazy man walk away. “Do you need help back out to the waiting room?”

Tell him no. You’ll be fine.

“No, we’ll be fine.” The man turned and put his arm around his son’s shoulders. They exited toward the waiting room.

I had healed the boy, and kept him from a painful procedure of staples or stitches. And it had felt good. With everything that had happened since I’d discovered what I was, I had never really stopped to consider just what it would mean to use my power for good, even if only in small ways. Jonas and Jack had tried to get me to see a different point of view, but I didn’t want to listen. It had always felt too overwhelming, knowing I couldn't heal everybody or every illness in the world.

Maya was walking slowly toward me. *Nice work, sis.*

Don't call me sis. You and I are not family. I reached around and grabbed the back of her neck where the bandage covered her stitched-up wound. She flinched. *If you move or call attention to us, I will shift your tracker such that Sandra will know that I have control of you, and she'll be sure to terminate you.*

Maya's eyes widened as she nodded, grimacing in pain.

What did you do to Jack?

Her head shook vehemently. *Nothing. I don't know. Sandra was in complete control of me.*

I squeezed harder. *You're lying. What did you do?*

Addison grabbed my arm, but I kept my grip on Maya.

"Lex, she's telling the truth. She doesn't know what she did, only that she was being controlled by an outside force. She begged Jack and Georgia to remove the tracker. When they got so sick, and the presence controlling her left, she bolted."

Maya's breathing was shallow. She pleaded with her eyes for me to let her go.

With a frustrated sigh, I released her.

She backed away and leaned against the wall, placing a gentle hand on the back of her neck. "I hate you, you know," Maya said. "But I think it's because I've been taught to hate you."

"The trackers are so powerful." Addison touched my hand. "You and I have some power against them, and some power to resist others invading our minds, but to someone whose DNA wasn't altered like ours..." She glanced toward Maya, who was an exact clone of Sandra, but whose DNA remained pure. "To them, a tracker is like a prison sentence. With that tracker at the base of her skull, Maya has no hope of ever being who she wants to be. Only who Sandra commands her to be."

I thought of Jonas. Not that long ago, Ty had gotten inside his head, and at Sandra's direction—through his tracker—he had convinced Jonas that he was in love with me one minute and wanted to kill me the next. The lines between what was true and what was a lie had blurred for Jonas. "So you think Sandra forced Maya to do something to Jack and Georgia?"

Addison shook her head. "Maybe. But she always programs someone else to do the dirty work. Wasn't Ty manipulated to come after you through Jonas?"

Attracted to me or not, Jonas had nearly killed me at Ty's direction. Jonas eventually fought Ty off, which led to Sandra discovering that Jonas's natural mental powers were stronger than Ty's tracker. So she killed Ty.

I let that sink in as a pregnant nurse approached us from the right. "Are you girls okay?" she asked.

"Yes, ma'am," I answered. "We were just leaving." I wrapped my fingers around Maya's forearm and pulled her with me toward the exit. Maya may have been a victim, but that didn't make me suddenly trust her.

You're hurting me. She sucked in a harsh breath through clenched teeth.

But I didn't let her go until we exited the hospital. As soon as I did, she whipped around and came at me like she might challenge me to a catfight. I stood taller. *I dare you to hit me right now.*

"What makes you so important?" she said. "What does Sandra want from you?"

I didn't know how to answer that. And Maya didn't deserve an answer even if I had one. When I stepped toward her again, she recoiled. Good. I needed her to fear me, even if only a little. "Right now I'm important because I have power. Your evil DNA donor wants me. She wants me so badly that she's threatening the people I love. And that pisses me off. I also have power because no matter how badly you want to hurt me, you can't, or Sandra will kill you."

After a few deep breaths, she backed away and eyed Addison. "What now?"

Addison twirled her long black hair around her forefinger. "That depends on Lexi."

Maya's eye twitched with an evil glint. "Why would *any* part of my future depend on Lexi? She doesn't control me."

I studied Addison. There was worry behind her cold gaze, a vulnerability that came with being too young to make decisions on her own, yet being forced to do so nonetheless.

"Sandra's gone." She let go of the lock of hair she'd been fingering and wiped her palms on her leggings. "She took Jonas, and they left today."

"What do you mean, they left?" Panic settled into my heart. Addison was still capable of mentally tracking people's physical locations—clones and non-clones. And she'd just confirmed that Sandra had officially taken Jonas into her faraway lair.

"I tracked them to a private plane at Bluegrass Airport. They're gone."

"They went to Palmyra," Maya whispered. Her eyes seemed to focus on the sidewalk in front of her. "They left me here."

It was weird watching Maya. Sometimes it was like looking in a mirror. In that moment, I wanted to feel sorry for her. But

I didn't. She'd tried to kill me. And now she'd done something to Jack.

She raised her head, and her cold eyes found mine. "Could you remove the tracker in my skull?"

I gawked at her. Removing her tracker could kill her. "Why would I do that? You've brought nothing but harm to us since you arrived."

She nodded. "You're right. You don't owe me anything—"

"But she knows Palmyra inside and out," Addison interrupted. "And she would no longer be a threat to you without the tracker."

This was exactly what I wanted from Maya and Addison—my ticket into Palmyra undetected. "That might be true, but for all I know Maya would be leading me straight into a trap."

"I'll help you." Maya's voice sounded panicked. "You need me to figure out what's wrong with Jack. I can do that."

"Why would I ever trust you? What's changed?"

"It's not about trust. It's about *need*. You need me. And I need you."

I thought about that for a minute. "That may be. I'll consider it. But first, the two of you will need to find a place to stay while I make plans. You're not welcome at Wellington." I couldn't possibly trust them where I sleep. "And if you sneak in using your mind tricks, the deal is off."

"What about my tracker?" Maya asked.

"I won't make promises. But I'll see if I can figure out how to safely remove it."

TWENTY-TWO

"You think they'll sell the atoll to me?" I asked Coach as I kicked into the punching mitts strapped to Jack's hands. A roundhouse left him stumbling backward a little, and I eyed him funny. I hadn't kicked that hard.

"Frankly, I don't know why they would."

I straightened. "Why *wouldn't* they? My money not good enough?"

Coach cocked his head. "Money isn't the issue. The president's staff and the Secret Service are currently analyzing every angle and possible threat that could arise from selling that island. And they're balancing that against every possible threat that could arise from *not* selling that island."

"What about Ms. Meyers? Surely she impressed upon them what's at stake."

"Oh yes, I'm sure she did. I doubt she'll soon forget your little demonstration. I'm going to take a wild guess that Evelyn Meyers didn't sleep much last night after that performance."

I chuckled.

Jack removed a mitt and tucked it in his armpit. He wiped his forehead against the sleeve of his T-shirt. I was the one working out, and he was sweating?

I reached out and touched his arm. "Hey. You okay?"

Instead of answering, he said, "You think Sandra did something to cause my and Georgia's severe attacks?"

Noticing the beads of sweat across his nose, I crinkled my brow. Clearly, Sandra did *something*. But I had no idea what.

Jack's hand shook as he tipped a water bottle back and squirted a power drink in his mouth. He'd been trying to replenish his electrolytes for two days. "I need to take a break."

Coach held his phone up as he backed away from the conversation. "I'm going to make some phone calls. And Lexi, your mom is making dinner tonight. We're supposed to be at the house by seven. I have a surprise for you."

I hated surprises.

When coach disappeared through the door, I zeroed in on Jack. "What's going on with you? Something's not right."

"I'm fine."

"Bull." I brushed my fingers along his forearm and started to grab his hand, but he yanked it away.

"I said, I'm fine." His tone cut straight through to my heart.

"Okay." I reached for my own water.

He closed his eyes briefly. When he reopened them and found mine, his expression softened. "I'm sorry. I'm just tired from getting so sick. I feel like I just got over the flu."

"It's all right. I've had enough for today anyway." I took a drink of water. "Why don't you take a nap before we meet with everybody." We'd be discussing our plan to save Jonas and destroy Sandra's operation. I was ready to confront her, and the sooner the better, if we wanted the element of surprise on our side.

"That's a good idea. I think I will take a nap." He leaned in and brushed his lips across mine. "I'll call you later."

I took another drink of water as I watched him exit the room. I had examined the different areas inside his head after the run-in with Addison and Maya. Everything seemed to be intact and functioning normally, but I had a horrible feeling.

Jonas, I wish you could hear me. Something's not right with Jack. I need your help.

Silence. What had Sandra done to Jonas? Or to Jack? I walked to the corner of the workout mat and pulled my cell phone from my backpack. Maybe Georgia had thought of something.

"What do you want?" Apparently Georgia's mood was no better than Jack's.

"How are you feeling?"

"Like I've been hit on the head a few dozen times with a baseball bat." A confusing pattern of noises followed. "What? No. Fine, you talk to her."

"Lexi?" It was Fred. "She's not herself. I don't know what Maya did, but Georgia has never taken this long to recover from an episode. Never. She's mostly slept since we brought her back to the house. She's been confused a lot, extremely thirsty, and I just watched her take four ibuprofen. I don't know what to do to help her."

"Don't leave her alone, okay?" All of those symptoms were side effects of the epileptic attack, but they should have already subsided by now. "I'll call you back."

I grabbed my bag and took off in the direction of my dorm room. On the way I called Kyle. "Any luck finding the Skype or cell phone number for Sandra? I need to talk to her. Now."

"As a matter of fact..."

"Give it to me."

He rattled it off without a second of hesitation.

"How did you find it so quickly?" I asked.

"I asked Seth."

"Seth? Are we sure it's current? Why would she keep the same number?"

"Why not? Seth figures she's arrogant enough to think everyone will eventually bow to her awesomeness."

I thought about that for a few beats. It was true. She'd expected me to join her. "Thanks for the number." I hung up.

A few minutes later I entered my dorm room and headed straight to my computer. I pulled up the Skype interface and typed in the number.

It rang and rang, but there was no answer. I tapped my fingers on my desk in a nervous pattern. We were leaving for Hawaii soon, and I was going to need Jack's and Georgia's help.

I decided to use the free time to pack for our trip. It somehow seemed stupid to pack for a trip to take down an evil empire of scientists and IIA operatives, but I did need some necessities, after all. I pulled my suitcase out of my closet and began throwing in clothes and a few toiletries. When I was almost done packing, a ring sounded from my computer.

The muscles in my neck clenched. I turned to find Sandra's number flashing across the screen. I quickly sat and angled the screen so that my suitcase and packing mess was hidden. Then I answered the call.

"Hello, Sarah. I'm so thrilled that you called. What's new at Wellington?" Sandra was as cheery as a mother calling to catch up with her teenage daughter.

"Cut the crap, you evil witch. What did you do to Jack and Georgia?"

"Why? Are Jack and Georgia feeling a little... off?" She fake-frowned. If I could have reached my hands through the computer screen, I would have wrapped my fingers around her neck and wrung it until she blew out her last breath, her body fell limp, and her eyes went glassy.

"You know, you think you're going to win this, but you won't," I said. My voice came out calm and even, but the war inside my chest was anything but. "You might even think you've won if I were to come to Palmyra, but if Jack becomes one of your casualties, you will lose. I would rather sacrifice myself and die than let you get whatever it is you think I have."

Sandra made that annoying clucking sound with her tongue. "You sound like you're giving up, Sarah. That's the last thing I want." She leaned in closer to the camera so that her face filled the entire screen. "I have a deal for you, Lexi. Jonas is already here. But if you and the other original clones come to Palmyra, I will make sure we get Jack and Georgia all fixed up and back to normal. And not only that: if you work with us, then I promise we'll allow all the other clones around the world to live normal lives."

I scoffed. "Why would I believe you? The last time I entered your web, you murdered your own son in front of me." And my best friend.

"He was malfunctioning; it needed to be done. However, you can rest assured that I will not kill any of the original clones. But beyond that... you have no idea what I'm capable of, Sarah." Her words were coated in infinite threats. And I believed each and every one.

"No deal. I will come. Just me. I'm the one you want. Leave the others alone. But first, you have to tell me how to make Jack and Georgia better. *Then*, and only then, I'll do whatever it is you need at Palmyra." The horrible taste of bile rose to the back of my throat. I was selling my soul to the devil. But I couldn't live with myself if something happened to Jack. What had she done to him? And why couldn't I see whatever it was?

I wanted to find Maya and Addison and punish them for their part in this, but I knew in my heart that this was all Sandra's doing. She had found ways to control both Maya and Addison. I honestly didn't think either one of them had a clue what Maya had done to Jack. That's not to say I could completely trust either of them. That they were under Sandra's thumb was reason enough to be wary. But I needed Maya and Addison to help me get inside Palmyra. I had to trust them at least that much.

"Deal," Sandra said. She sat back, crossing her arms in arrogant triumph. "Except... you come first, and *then* I'll give you the cure. And you'd better come soon, dear... or Jack and Georgia will die."

TWENTY-THREE

"Can you do it?"

"Yes, but Lexi, this is a terrible idea," my mother said. "We might not be able to remove the tracker after it's been implanted."

I'd worry about that if and when I ever got away from Palmyra. "It's the only idea I have that protects everyone else."

"I'll be right back," my mother whispered. "I'm going to check on dinner. The others will be here soon. And you still need to figure out a way to tell them the plan." By "them," I knew she meant Jack.

Alyson turned quickly to go, but before she got to the kitchen door, I heard her pull in a labored breath. She swiped at her face. My heart squeezed at the sight of her crying.

I leaned back into the oversized chair, my feet propped up on the ottoman in front of me. It was difficult to admit this to Alyson, but it was nice to be in a comfortable home instead of the cold, stark infirmary basement.

I lifted my flattened palm in front of my face. The tracker sat on its edge in the middle of my hand. From this angle, I had a view of its tentacles. If Alyson could program this tracker to mirror Maya's, but trim the tentacles to give them less gripping power, she could then place it at the base of my skull and make it indistinguishable from Maya's implant. Then all I had to do was make sure my appearance and personal knowledge were identical to Maya's. We'd have an eleven-hour flight to go over the details. Of course, I still needed to entice Maya to cooperate.

The theory was that if I could pretend to be Maya, then I could get inside Palmyra. And if I could do that, then somehow I would find Jonas, and the cure for Jack and Georgia, and then get out. Easy, right?

I sighed. It was impossible. But I had to at least try.

And unfortunately, I would have to do it alone. Georgia and Jack were still ill, seeming even sicker than before, and I'd never get Fred to go to Palmyra without Georgia. And I needed Kyle to hack into the system and be my voice from the outside. I might be able to use Briana, but she was so very new to using her abilities, and I wasn't sure I could risk something going wrong.

The doorbell rang. Alyson passed from the kitchen to the foyer behind me. When she returned, Kyle, Jack, and Briana followed. They all glared at me as if I'd told them Wellington would no longer serve dessert in the dining hall.

"What?" I asked.

Jack traded glances with the other two, then stepped forward. His face was pale, and a grey hue darkened the skin under his eyes. "You'll go inside that place by yourself over my dead body."

I crawled out of the chair. "Jack, I—"

"Save it. Alyson called. She told us what you're planning."

I glared at my mother. *Snitch.*

She wrung her hands. "I didn't come back into your life to help you walk into a death trap. I knew you'd listen to your friends before you'd listen to me."

"Tell me what this is about." Jack linked his pinky with mine. "What's changed?"

I stared down the laces of my running shoes a moment before I found the strength to meet his gaze again. "Sandra... she did something permanent to you and Georgia. Well, Maya did it, but it was Sandra who forced her to do whatever it was."

"What do you think she did?"

"I'm not sure. I examined your head, but I couldn't find anything."

"Then how do you know she did something?"

"Because she told me. That was the 'gift' she mentioned." This was my fault. If I had just listened to her after she'd sent the very first "gifts" on the night of my birthday party. She had warned me to leave Jack out of it.

"What exactly did she tell you?" His jaw hardened.

"That if I'll join her inside Palmyra, she'll reverse whatever it was she did to you and Georgia." I left out the part about what would happen if the effect wasn't reversed—that he and Georgia would die. I'd make sure that didn't happen.

"Lexi." Kyle sat his laptop on a nearby writing desk. "Briana and I have studied the layout of the full lab. It's not very big. It's not as intricate as the lab she had at UK."

Briana nodded. "I've memorized the faces of the doctors and lab techs that appear to be current residents of the island." Her voice was low, which was strange for her. "There aren't many."

"And security seems to be light," Kyle added.

"Maybe because it's on an island that's supposed to receive very few visitors, and never ones who aren't announced by the government." Jack spoke as if he'd researched the island himself.

There was a knock on the door, and Alyson answered it.

"We brought dessert," Seth announced as he lifted two large grocery bags. Coach walked in behind him with a couple of oversized black briefcases.

"What're those?" I asked.

"New toys."

An irrational excitement bubbled up in my chest; I loved the unique weapons that Coach came up with. And this time, I was going to need something inconspicuous. I would never enter Sandra's lair packing a gun—I might as well just announce that I was the enemy.

"You guys start without us," Jack said. "I need to talk to Lexi a minute."

Jack pulled me toward the door. On the front porch, he dropped my hand and turned to me. "Did you search my entire body?"

"No. I didn't have time. I knew you were off a bit, so I did a quick search of your head before you left to take a nap. When I didn't find anything, I Skyped Sandra. She was expecting my call." I averted my gaze from Jack's. I couldn't stop the moisture from pooling in my eyes again. "I can't lose you," I whispered. "I'll do whatever I have to."

Heat radiated from his feverish body as he pressed himself against me. His arm snaked around to my back, bringing me even closer. He leaned his forehead against mine. "You are not going to lose me. We'll figure this out."

I let his lips find mine. After kissing him, I snuggled my face into his chest and breathed in the scent of the ocean. "I want you to help me figure this out, and I want you close, but I need to enter Palmyra alone. Jonas is already there. He knows how to control his actions and fight anything Sandra is doing to him." I hoped so, anyway. "He can help me find the cure for you and Georgia."

Jack pulled away and ran a hand through his hair. "Why didn't we kill them when we had the chance?"

I knew he spoke of Sandra and his father. "Because that's not who we are."

"I'm not sure I'd make the same choice if given the chance to do it over. We're in constant danger. Why won't they just leave us alone?" he asked, exasperated.

"Because they want something from me. But Sandra made a mistake."

He cocked his head. "What mistake?"

"When I first returned from The Farm, I wanted nothing but revenge. Dani was dead. Sandra sent me evidence that your father killed mine. I would have been happy to go in, guns blazing, to take out everyone on that island and in the lab. And then disappear forever." I paused, thinking about how angry I'd been—how angry I still was.

"What changed your mind?"

"Sandra's mistake was showing me just how low she would go. She showed me how she had cloned my best friend just to get back at me—for no other reason than to punish me for not giving her what she wanted. And she's not going to stop experimenting with human life. She's producing more clones." I gritted my teeth. "And a division of our government is letting it happen."

"The IIA."

I nodded. "I'm pretty sure the IIA killed Dad and made sure it looked like your father was involved. I think Sandra orchestrated it that way, the same way she's playing me at every turn."

"You don't think my father killed Peter?"

I squeezed the bridge of my nose. "I just don't know. I don't think your father is innocent..." I met Jack's gaze. "I'm sorry. But the way the agents seemed to surround him in that surveillance video... your dad's face was the *only* face visible in that video. Everyone else looked like anonymous agents who never looked at the camera. Like they knew where *not* to look."

"Still, he's been a large part of Sandra's team."

"True, but a murderer? He was shocked when Sandra killed Ty. I saw his face when he found out."

"It doesn't even matter if he murdered Peter. He's still heavily involved in Sandra's plan to produce these healing machines. And they're killing innocent lives every day in that process."

"And they must be stopped. But instead of making them face a firing squad—because that would be letting them off easy—I want to take them down bit by bit. And I want Sandra, John, and everyone else involved to watch me do it."

~~~~~

The University of Kentucky campus was dark, and the dropping temperatures sent everyone inside. I had told Maya and Addison to wait for me inside The Program. I'd be surprised if they had, but one could hope.
~~~~~

I rounded a corner and made my way along a sidewalk between two buildings. The wind picked up along this dimly lit walkway between two rows of thick evergreen trees. Leaves from neighboring maples blew in a swirling pattern. A plastic bag was caught against the leg of a nearby bench.

A presence entered my mind. *Where've you been? We've been waiting for you.* It was Maya, her words reeking of entitlement and abruptness. *Can you get this tracker out of me?*

We'll discuss it. I would not be removing Maya's tracker until Jack was better and Sandra and John were safely in prison. I continued along the sidewalk.

An unexplained shiver moved down my spine, and I shuddered. I looked right, left, and behind me. I didn't see anything, but I couldn't shake the feeling that I was being watched. I sped up.

Addison, are you and Maya inside the building?

Yes, why?

I'm almost there.

I reached the side door to the building, the entrance closest to the steps of the basement where The Program had been temporarily located before the move to Wellington. In hindsight, I probably shouldn't have come alone, but I'd needed everyone working on their part in tomorrow's trip, and I wanted Jack to rest.

I took the steps up to the building two at a time. As I reached out my hand to pull on the metal handle, I heard a noise behind me. I didn't even have time to turn around before a large hand clamped down over my mouth.

Instinctively, I screamed through the fingers, but it came out in a muffled cry. An arm wrapped around my body and dragged me back down the steps. I tried to dig my heels into the sidewalk as I felt for my ring. It wasn't there. I had forgotten to wear it, and I'd left my new weapons back at school because I hadn't thought I'd be needing them until I got to Palmyra.

A man's hushed voice whispered in my ear, "I'll remove my hand, but don't scream. No one's out this late to hear you anyway. And if you scream, I'll be forced to shut you up sooner rather than later."

His hand dropped slowly from my face and joined the other in its hold on my body. He continued to drag me backward. "What do you want?" I couldn't hide the shakiness in my voice.

The only other sounds were of his feet shuffling against concrete. I squirmed and fought against his strong arms. I was being carried backward in the direction from which I had just come. I had to relax. Think.

I tried mindspeaking. *Who are you? What do you want?*

The person stopped and stood me on my feet, but didn't loosen his grip on me. I felt his head lean in closer. "I want *you*. Dead, if necessary." He shoved me away from him.

Once I regained my footing, I spun around. "Dr. Wellington?" The muscles in my back and neck clenched.

"Apparently if you want a job done right, you have to do it yourself. But first, we need to talk." He held up a tranquilizer gun and pointed it at my face. "Your father made a big mistake when he changed the terms of his will. He should have left me Wellington Boarding School and the money to run it, like he promised."

I sucked in a deep breath and let it out slowly. "You want me dead because you want the school?"

A deep laugh reverberated from his throat. "Not just the school. The money to own the clones inside of it, too. And I want his journals."

"The clones are people. You can't *own* them." And why did everything always come back to those journals? Had I missed something?

"You always were naïve. You think the parents of those freaks care about them? No, they're all for sale. All I had to do was locate them and convince the parents to let me take them off their hands. And with you dead, I can finally have the school. This school that *I* built, with my own hands."

And with my dad's money. I curled my fingers into fists. I wanted to punch him in the throat and cut off his air supply. "Why do you need the journals?"

"Your father and I gathered extensive data on many of the clones created in the last ten years. As recent as Addison's group. But your dad kept the records."

So it was my fault that Dr. Wellington wasn't smart enough to keep his own set of records? "And you think I would just *give* you my dad's journals? Why? Because you asked nicely?"

He lowered the gun. "It doesn't have to be this way. You have so much to gain from partnering with me and Cathy. You and Jack, along with Cathy and me... We could create a medical empire with clones trained to use their healing abilities."

"Why do you think Cathy would want any part of your scheme? You almost killed her son."

A grin lifted the corners of his lips, sending a chill down my spine. "You don't really believe Cathy didn't know about the hit put out on you, do you? She knew the risks. She's just Oscar-worthy at playing the victim."

"Are you saying she *knew* that you sent snipers into the gorge where we were hiking?"

He laughed. "Of course she knew. She never believed the snipers would shoot at anyone but you, though." He raised the gun again, pointing it at my leg. "So what's it going to be, Miss Matthews? You can agree, and come with me willingly... or we can do it the hard way." His finger shifted, then curled firmly around the trigger.

Just as I'd had enough of Roger Wellington and was about to tell him to drop his gun, I saw a shadow of movement behind him. Roger must have noticed my quick look, because he turned, waving the tranquilizer gun around.

"Who's there?" he asked. He turned back to me and, grabbing my arm, pulled me into a headlock while redirecting the gun to my arm.

Giving me no time to use my own mindspeak ability, Jack emerged from the trees with a *real* gun pointed at us. "Let her go."

Roger pressed his weapon harder against my arm. "I'll give you to the count of three to drop your gun. One... two..."

I squeezed my eyes tight and held my breath.

"Three." A girl's voice came from my right. The tranquilizer gun flew from Roger's hand. He turned in a circle, but no one was there.

Addison.

"Over here, jerkface." Definitely Addison's voice, but she remained invisible.

Roger spun toward the sound, then fell forward in pain and grabbed at his knee. I assumed Addison kicked him.

I smiled. "Roger, I'm afraid you've been had by a kid."

Coach appeared from behind me and pointed his own gun at Roger's temple. "And now you're going back to jail. Police are already on their way." Coach had handcuffs on Roger in a matter of seconds. He eyed me like an irate father. "Jack stays with you."

I nodded.

Jack took a few steps forward. "You'll tell the feds what Roger claims about my mother?"

Coach sighed, but agreed.

"If she's guilty of what Roger says, I want her locked up." Jack swayed slightly, apparently still off-balance from Sandra's handiwork.

A couple of police officers came running up the sidewalk. Coach shoved Roger in their direction, forcing him to walk toward his fate.

I grabbed Jack's hand to steady him, then put my arm around his back for support. *How did you find me?*

Coach got a call that Roger had been released due to some fancy work done by his attorney. He was on his way to tell you when he saw you exit the dorm and get in a cab. He followed you and called me.

"Addison?" I called out.

Addison appeared. "I thought you needed help."

"*Now* you help?"

She shrugged. "I was watching you all those times Maya was on campus. You didn't need help then."

That was one opinion. "You'll have to forgive me if I don't believe you." I was arguing with a kid.

"I need Sandra to think I'm doing everything she's asked. She hasn't had contact with Maya or me in a couple of days. Not since—"

"Since Maya delivered her 'gift.'" I couldn't stop the anger that flared.

"Sandra made her—"

I towered over Addison. "I don't care that she *made* her do it. Look at Jack, Addison. Whatever Maya did to him... Sandra's killing him." My voice cracked.

Jack grabbed my hand. "Addison didn't do this to me."

I stared up into Jack's bloodshot eyes. There in the dark, his irises looked almost onyx. I brushed my hand along his cheek, then pressed a little harder, making sure I had his full attention. "I don't care. She played her part. She also helped give Jonas over to Sandra." Addison was the only way Sandra could have gotten on campus to take Jonas.

Addison sniffed, and tears fell from her eyes. "I'm sorry. I didn't mean to..." Her voice trailed off. She took a deep breath. "I will do whatever I have to do to make it right between us."

"I'm glad to hear you say that, Addison. Because you're going with me to Palmyra."

TWENTY-FOUR

The flight to Honolulu was long and tiring. Jack slept through most of it, thankfully. A hot, humid island breeze greeted us the minute we stepped off the airplane.

Jack crossed his arms while he watched the ground crew unload the plane. Drivers pulled up and began loading our luggage into a couple of SUVs. Jack's eyes glazed over, and he wobbled on his feet a bit.

Wake up. I nudged him playfully, yet gently, for fear I would add to his instability. *We're in Hawaii.* I tried to sound excited, even though this was far from the ideal way to see a tropical paradise for the first time.

His eyes lifted and found mine. *I'm trying.* He removed the jacket he had needed while still in Kentucky and tied it around his waist. His pants hung at his hips loosely. He was losing weight.

I know. I'm sorry. You feeling okay? A stupid question.

He lifted his hand and rocked it side to side. *So-so.* He smiled.

I was thankful Seth had thought to bring plenty of antinausea medicine and other medical supplies we might need on the trip.

I looked down at my watch. The captain of the boat—an ex-marine Coach had found to take us to Palmyra—expected us at the marina by six p.m. We were early.

Our entire group—Seth, Coach, Alyson, Kyle, Briana, Addison, Maya, Jack, and I—looked like we needed a good night's sleep. We were missing Georgia and Fred, but I'd left instructions in case they changed their mind and could join us. I refused to force anyone to participate in this mission who didn't want to. Well, except for Addison and Maya.

I continuously searched the area for anyone who looked like they might be interested in our group. I counted on members of International Intelligence Agency to be present wherever we went, but I wasn't too worried. Briana had altered our appearances so we looked like a college group going on a holiday excursion.

Once the luggage had been loaded into the vehicles, Coach, Kyle, Addison, Jack, and I climbed in the front vehicle. Alyson, Seth, Briana, and Maya piled in the second. I put Briana in charge of Maya.

We left the airport and rode through the streets of Honolulu. As we traveled, I caught Coach glancing over my shoulder to the vehicle behind us several times, verifying that it was still with us.

Jack's eyes were closed again, his breathing slow and even. I brought up an image of the inside of his head and began examining every nook and cranny. His neurons and synapses were firing normally for a person sleeping. His skull was intact. His brain appeared normal. I saw nothing that would cause his constant vertigo and lethargy.

Beads of sweat formed along his hairline while he slept. My mind immediately began thinking of all the things I might do to Sandra if anything happened to Jack—the many different ways I could make her suffer slowly.

"We'll be at the marina in five," Coach announced from the front seat.

"Is everything in place?" I asked.

"Ready and waiting for us."

I nodded, and brushed my fingers down Jack's cheek. He started, drawing in a deep breath.

"I'm sorry. I hated to wake you. We're almost there."

He nodded, then grabbed my hand, rubbing his thumb over mine. *You must think I'm the weakest boyfriend ever.*

I cocked my head. *Weak? Because you tried to help someone who didn't deserve it?* I looked out the window briefly. I couldn't swallow the anger that heated the blood coursing through my veins.

When I turned back, Jack was staring at me. I unbuckled my seatbelt and scooted closer. *Sandra is going to pay for everyone she's hurt in our lives. She'll pay for doing this to you. She thinks she's weakened me by making you sick, but she'll soon know I'm stronger than I've ever been. So, weak? No.* You *are my strength.*

Would you have come if I had asked you not to? Jack asked.

I chewed my lower lip while I considered how to answer that. I opened my mouth, but immediately closed it.

Jack smiled. *I know you would have.*

Yes. This is something I have to do. My father made it possible for me to be the voice for the innocent souls that Sandra murdered, and for the many others she continues to harm.

How much of coming here is to save Jonas? Jack asked.

Before I could answer, Coach spoke up. "We have a problem." The alarm in his voice had me scooting off of Jack's lap and looking out the front windshield. Lights flashed in front of us. "It's a roadblock of some sort." Policemen and men and women in dark suits were leaning down into vehicles in front of us.

"You think it's for us? Could those suits be IIA?" I didn't even give him time to answer. "I'll take care of it." *Bree, you seeing this?*

Yes.

Can you alter our appearances from where you are?

I'm on it. But my energy level is running low. Don't know how long I can keep it up.

Do your best, I encouraged.

Our driver rolled down his window. "Is there a problem, officer?"

"No, just looking for a group of kids in the area causing mischief tonight."

They're blocking the entrance to the marina. Do they know I chartered a boat? How could they know? I mindspoke to Jack, panicking.

He placed a hand on my knee.

The officer looked carefully from our driver, to his ID, and back to the driver again. "Where're you people headed tonight?"

"Oh, just taking my group here down to a dinner cruise."

The officer handed back the ID. "Okay. Have a good night."

Our driver put up his window and moved forward. My shoulders slumped forward as I let out an anxious breath. Jack eased his death grip on my leg.

I resisted the urge to turn around and watch the second vehicle. A vein pulsed on the side of Coach's neck. His head was angled in such a way that I knew he was watching through the side mirror, and I saw the driver's eyes keep darting to the rearview mirror.

"What's happening?" I asked.

"They're talking—shit! They're making Seth exit the vehicle." Coach directed our driver to back into a nearby parking spot. From here we had a direct, although distant, view of the interrogation.

Bree? What's happening?

Not now, Lexi. Her voice was strained, angry.

Bree, give us something. Jack leaned forward to watch out the front window.

They're just talking to him. Her voice was softer now. I rolled my eyes. *I'm trying to make them think they're seeing someone they're not. It's almost as if they're trying to intimidate him or get a rise out of him—asking questions about where he's going, what he's doing in Hawaii and at the marina...*

"I should have just asked our government contacts to drop a bomb on the island and be done with this," I said out of frustration. I couldn't mindspeak to the officers because, as I'd found out while inside The Farm, many IIA agents had been trained to recognize when I had gotten inside their heads. These officers may or may not be IIA, but I couldn't take the risk.

"But then innocent lives would have been lost, including Jonas's." Jack didn't look at me, but I knew he was letting me know that, although our discussion had been cut short before, it wasn't over.

He was right, though. I had no intention of allowing harm to come to Sandra's victims. The cloned humans of the world hadn't asked for the lives they were given. If I could give hope to any of them at the end of this, I would have fulfilled my purpose. And if I could get revenge on my evil DNA donor in the process...

Is that what this is to you? Jack asked as he overheard my thoughts. *Revenge?* He ran a hand through his hair. *You're putting your life in danger for revenge?*

I refused to look at him, just stared straight ahead at Seth and the officer while I worked hard to close off my thoughts. I couldn't be angry with Jack for invading my thoughts. For anything, really. I wouldn't waste my energy on anger when I only wanted him to feel loved. I knew that Sandra could take anyone from our lives without notice.

My eyes welled up. *Is it so wrong to want revenge on the person responsible for so much pain and suffering?* And I wasn't just talking about Dani, Ty, and my father, if she had any direct responsibility for that. I was talking about the hundreds or thousands of souls she extinguished every day inside test tubes.

"He's getting back in," Coach said. No one in our vehicle moved while the officers walked around the SUV. "That's it. Let them go," he said, mostly to himself.

Only when the vehicle pulled forward and passed us in the parking lot did we all relax. The officers didn't seem too concerned with the passing vehicle and went back to checking others.

Coach turned in his seat to address Jack and me. "We probably shouldn't all be seen loading the boat and climbing aboard together. Alyson and Seth will get members of the crew to help. I've instructed them to act like a married couple. If anyone asks questions, the crew won't look guilty since all they know is someone chartered their boat for an extended vacation off the coast."

"Lexi and I will take a stroll around the docks." Jack opened his door and, after grabbing my hand, pulled me out after him. "We have things to discuss before we set sail."

~~~~~

"The sunset is beautiful." I leaned against Jack, my back to his chest. He circled his arms around me to rest his palms against my ribs. We had found a deck outside the restaurants and retail stores surrounding the harbor. We looked out past the sailboats and other vessels to the sun sinking into ocean.

"When this is over, I want to take you somewhere like this where we can just be."

"I want that, too," I whispered, scared that the fear of something happing to him would show in my voice.

He rested his chin on my head. "Nothing is going to happen to me. We'll figure out what Sandra has inflicted me with, and you'll heal me."

I wished I had his faith. But all I could think was, what if this was my punishment for not embracing my ability to heal sooner? If I had been spending more time honing my abilities, I'd have figured out how to identify the problem and cure him already.

I closed my eyes and savored the feeling of being held by the strongest man I knew. He had to survive this.

After several beats of silence, I turned in his arms and looked up at him. "I began planning this trip the minute I discovered I had the means to take Sandra down. When the attor-
~~~~~

ney told me the amount of money my father left me, and when Sandra continuously showed me the monstrosities she's capable of, I started brainstorming a thousand different fantasies of shutting her operation down and freeing everyone she's trapped inside her world."

"What about Jonas?"

"I'm beyond mad that he's not with us right now helping us plot against that evil woman. I hope I can free him from his mother forever. Yes, a small part of me kicked this plan into a higher gear when he was taken, but not because I'm in love with him."

"I didn't say—"

I placed a finger over his lips. "You have nothing to be jealous of when it comes to Jonas and me. Sandra did something to his tracker, forcing our closeness, and yes, I have had feelings for Jonas. I have no idea how he gets under my skin, but he does. But I love *you*. Not him. And he knows that." I turned my head to look beyond the dock, out into the great ocean. "Jack, I know in my heart that Jonas would put his own life in danger to save either one of us."

"He would." Jack brushed a loose strand of hair off of my face. "And we'll do the same for him."

I rose on my toes and brushed my lips across his. "You and I are going to survive this, and after that we'll spend the rest of our lives making sure our love is an epic romance that no one can touch." I smiled.

"I think I can handle that challenge." He matched my smile with one of his own, but it didn't mask the worry in his eyes. "Now, where is this boat you chartered?"

I pointed toward the dock. "See that dinghy?"

"You got us a dinghy?"

I gently elbowed him, laughing. "No. Look past that, do you see the boat just beyond the three sailboats?"

"That's nice. That could get us there."

"Yes, but that's not the boat I chartered. I got the one beside it."

"That triple-decker?" Jack attempted, but failed, to mask the excitement in his voice.

"Mm-hmm." I had chartered a two-hundred-foot yacht capable of sleeping fourteen guests comfortably and twenty crewmembers if necessary. "Her name is *La Luna y el Sol*."

"The Moon and the Sun," Jack whispered into my hair. "I like your little boat."

I smiled. She most certainly could not be described as "little." But he could call her whatever he wanted, as long as she got us where we needed to go.

~~~~~

"This is not a boat," Briana said after asking for permission to come aboard. "This is a freakin' mansion on water."

"I thought we needed the space." I shrugged and leaned against a pillar supporting one of the higher decks. It would take several days to reach Palmyra by boat, but it would be a quieter approach than arriving by seaplane or landing a private jet on the small landing strip on the atoll.

"Wow," Kyle said as he walked across the plank from land to boat. "I must be keeping good company these days."
~~~~~

Alyson and Seth traded pleased glances. I narrowed my gaze toward them. Alyson caught my look and moved to stand beside me.

"What's with the smiley face?" I wasn't sure I'd seen her with a happy look since she'd arrived in Midland.

"It's just nice to hear happy sounds coming from you and your friends. I hope to hear more of them in the future."

"Mmm." Even though the group did sound more joyful than usual, there was still an underlying sense of urgency and sadness. We knew what we were up against.

"I'm going to start setting up the control room for our mission," Alyson said. "We need to be ready. If I know Sandra, she already knows we left Wellington and is looking for us, which is why those men were at the marina."

"You think those men knew it was us?"

Alyson played with her short ponytail. "I don't know. We have to assume she knows all."

A crewmember appeared. "We can depart immediately, Miss. Dinner will be served in an hour."

Jack raised a brow at me. *Not too shabby.*

Yeah, well, I spared no expense. It might be the last nice thing I get to experience.

Don't say that.

"Got room for us?" a familiar voice asked.

I spun around. Fred and Georgia stood on the dock.

"Always room for two more," Seth said.

Better late than never, I mindspoke to Georgia, giving her a smile. She looked similar to Jack: sunken eyes, dark circles, ashen cheeks. *How are you feeling?*

Meh. I've been better. She walked onto the boat and directly over to me. *We go get Jonas, and then we destroy that bitch.*

I laughed. *Okay, then. Let's do it.*

TWENTY-FIVE

We pushed off from the dock before I was out of the shower. The yacht had the staff of a boutique hotel, so I had someone bring soup to my cabin. My stomach was in knots. I wasn't sure I could even eat.

Dressed in a T-shirt and shorts, I exited the bathroom while towel-drying my hair. The smell of mango from my shampoo wafted through the room.

"I don't think you should go to Palmyra."

I spun around, my wet hair whipping behind me, my hand covering my heart. Addison sat criss-cross in the middle of the bed. "Sheesh, Addison. Ever heard of knocking?"

"That would defeat the purpose of sneaking around, now wouldn't it?"

"What do you want?" I draped the damp towel over a nearby desk chair and began brushing my hair.

She climbed off the bed and began walking around the room. "I don't want you, Jack, or anyone to go to Palmyra."

I set the brush on the desk and grabbed a bottle of body lotion, then slowly climbed up on the bed. I sat on one foot while the other leg dangled. "We'll be okay. We can handle it."

"Let me go instead. I'll figure out what the cure is for Jack and Georgia, and I'll get back out. I can move around much more easily than you can, being invisible and all."

"Why would I let you do that? You're a kid. You wouldn't even know how to get there. You think you can just row a boat up to shore?" I squirted some lotion into my palm—the label promised the smell of the ocean breeze—and began spreading it on my arms and legs.

Addison fidgeted with her hands. She wore a hot pink tank top and black leggings. Her pixie size no longer deterred me from seeing the real Addison: a self-confident, intelligent adult in a child's body. I would not underestimate this little girl no matter how nervous she looked.

After much deliberation, she finally said, "I owe you and Jack. I hurt you both, and I want to prove to you that you can trust me. You never would have traded me to save someone else, and I'm truly sorry that I did that to you. But it was my mom."

There was a knock at the door.

I don't know if she did it by instinct or habit, but by the time I'd crossed the room to the door, Addison had disappeared. I opened the door to find Jack standing on the other side. His hair was damp, and he had changed into a fresh T-shirt and khaki shorts.

As he walked in, I scanned the room for any sign that Addison was still there. *Coward.* She was too afraid to face Jack. I didn't even get a chance to tell her that, yes, she would be going to Palmyra to find a cure.

But she'd be going *with* me, not *instead* of me.

~~~~~

The makeshift control room had been set up by the time Jack and I arrived. Alyson had skipped dinner, refusing to take a break. She'd assembled the computers, configured the satel-
~~~~~

lite WiFi connection, hung large screens on stands in the corner, and placed a projector on a table.

I set a covered plate on the table and knelt down beside her. She was fighting to untangle a bundle of cords, gripping a bright yellow one and jerking it hard to free it from beneath a table leg. Her face reddened.

I placed a hand over hers. "Alyson," I whispered. Her hand shook beneath mine. "Why don't you eat something."

She looked up at me and, with a puff, blew long strands of hair from her eyes. She fell back on her butt. "I just wanted to get everything set up. If we're not completely prepared for anything and everything, Sandra will try—"

"It'll be okay."

Alyson shook her head. "No, it won't. She'll terminate anyone who gets in the way of her plan—including you, once she has what she wants from you. You have to be ready."

I squeezed her hand harder and pulled her to her feet. "You need to eat. You're no good to any of us if you're too weak to monitor the computers and process the information coming in."

After a little more protest, she sat at the table and began eating the salad and grilled tuna the chef had prepared.

Jack pulled up a chair beside her. "I need you to level with me," he said to her. "What are the chances that Lexi can pull off pretending she's Maya while inside Palmyra?"

Alyson stopped chewing and swallowed hard. "I don't know."

"If it were your choice, would you allow her to do this?"

She stared at Jack with determined eyes. "It's *not* my choice. Sandra has something Lexi won't live without." The cure for

Jack and Georgia. "And Lexi has something Sandra wants. Sandra won't kill her yet. Not until she gets what she needs. But if she discovers her, she won't let her go this time. She'd prefer for Lexi to choose to work with her willingly, but even if Lexi refuses..." She didn't need to finish the thought. We all knew that Sandra wouldn't hesitate to use force if it came to it. "So we have to make sure she's not caught."

"Sandra's my Darth Vader," I chuckled. "Come to the dark side, Luke," I said in my best deep voice.

Jack stood abruptly and took two steps toward me, towering over me. "You're laughing about this?"

I flinched at his harsh voice and my smile faded. "No, Jack, I—"

"Good. Because this isn't funny. If you're expecting me to support your decision to fight Sandra, my father, and the entire IIA, at least take this seriously."

I touched his cheek. "I'm sorry." He jerked away from my touch and tried to take a step back, but I was faster. I put myself in front of him. "We *laugh* at this crazy shit, remember? We can't control what they do, but we can choose how we react. Sandra Whitmeyer and John DeWeese will never kill my spirit. And I am *done* letting them hurt those I love. They have to be stopped. *I* will stop them. One way or another."

After a few beats, he broke eye contact and returned to Alyson. "Will you be able to control her tracker when it's implanted? Sandra won't be able to obtain complete power over her, right?"

"That's the idea." Alyson wiped her mouth and took a drink of water. "It took me five years to perfect the tracker system. I know it inside and out. No one else will be able to override a tracker once I have control of it."

"What about Maya? What's the status of her tracker?" I asked.

My mother's face seemed to light up with an energy I had been looking for since we first came aboard this vessel. "I was finally able to tap into information stored on her device, and redirect the signal from Sandra's system. Now anytime Sandra sends a signal to Maya, I'll know about it first. *We* can decide what Maya receives, and what she doesn't."

"That's good news," I said, giving myself a minute to digest what she was saying. "Does that mean you could also redirect the signal to another tracker?"

She smiled. "That's exactly what it means. And I could send *information* to a tracker without sending it as a *command* to manipulate the host. In other words, once your tracker is in place and I'm running it, I'll be able to send you the information that Sandra's sending Maya. You can alter your interaction with her accordingly. But there's one problem."

"What's that?" Jack asked, his voice severe. When Alyson began fidgeting with her hands again, Jack continued. "You said 'Once you have control of it.' You don't currently have control of Lexi's tracker, do you?"

"No, I don't."

A growl erupted from somewhere deep within Jack. He scrubbed his hands over his face.

"The trackers are all synced with Sandra's system on the island," Alyson explained. "And the newest trackers were designed for quick getaways and multiple methods of communicating. When Sandra blows up a lab, she needs to be able to move fast, and she can't afford to give up control of her trackers—not even for a second. Most of the trackers—the ones scattered around the world—communicate with Sandra's control system via satellite links. But when a clone is in close proximity to the system—basically, if they're on Palmyra Atoll itself—the system is set up to communicate with them via a local cell tower instead. The satellite system then serves as a backup."

"Okay, so Lexi's tracker will sync up via the cell tower. That means we just tap into the cell network, right?" Jack asked. "That shouldn't be any harder than accessing a satellite."

I studied my mom, and saw the set of lines running vertically on her forehead between her eyes.

"I tried. The cell tower on Palmyra is off the grid."

"Meaning?"

"It's not part of the public network. As of right now, we can't intercept the signal, and we can't pull information from it."

I looked at my mom. "Tell me what I have to do."

Alyson took my hands in hers. "You'll have to find the server on Palmyra and switch the tracker communications from cell tower to satellite before Sandra discovers that you're not Maya."

I didn't dare look at Jack after hearing this. "How am I supposed to do that?"

"I'm hoping Kyle will be able to tell you how to get to the server room. He's been trying to hack into the computers, looking for a layout of the building. There should be some sort of switch—like a circuit breaker—somewhere in the room that houses the servers. Once the connection with the cell tower is disabled, the system will automatically default back to satellite communications."

"As easy as that? Just flip a switch? 'On' for satellite, 'off' for cell tower?" A hysterical laugh threatened to break through the surface of my sanity.

From the look on Alyson's face, it wasn't going to be as easy as turning a light on or off. "Physically flipping the circuit breaker may sound easy. But finding it, getting to it, and remaining undetected until you do so, will definitely not be. Make no mistake, Lexi. This is very dangerous."

I nodded. "I'll just have to find this room, while pretending to be Maya, and pray that Sandra doesn't discover my true identity."

The door to the control room opened, and in stumbled Maya, followed by Coach, who had a hand wrapped around her upper arm.

"Speak of the devil's spawn," Jack mumbled under his breath.

I straightened at the sight of Maya. Her hair was pulled back in a sleek ponytail, chocolate brown mixed with ruby red hanging around her neck and down the front of her chest. Jack's fingers curled into a fist.

I covered his hand with mine. *Down, boy. I know it's hard, but remember, she's just a victim. And Alyson has control of her now.* Of course, Maya didn't know that part.

Fred and Georgia entered next. Georgia crossed the room and sat in a chair facing everyone. Fred stood behind her and massaged her shoulders, his brow scrunched up with worry.

"What do I have to do to convince you I'm not going to jump off this ship and swim away?" Maya asked, jerking her arm away from Coach and putting space between them.

"As soon as we've figured out how to remove your tracker, you'll be free to go wherever you wish," I assured her. "But for now, we can't risk the chance that Sandra will find another way inside your head."

"I haven't received any orders from her in days."

"And that works in your favor." I looked at Alyson, who nodded, confirming that no information had been transmitted from Sandra to Maya in some time. So either Sandra knew that Maya had been compromised, or she was simply too busy destroying other lives.

The biggest problem with my plan to crush Sandra and her project was the number of variables I had no control over. What if I didn't find what I needed to cure Georgia and Jack of whatever was affecting them? What if I couldn't find Jonas? What if Sandra found a way inside my mind again, or figured out that it was me instead of Maya on Palmyra? What if I couldn't get the trackers on Palmyra switched from their cell tower to the satellite system Alyson could control?

I massaged the spot on my chest over my heart.

"Lexi," Georgia said with a scratchy voice. "I'm afraid I'm not much use to you right now, but I'll gladly keep Maya busy and out of the way."

Maya crossed her arms across her chest and tapped her foot. "I hardly need a babysitter."

"That would be perfect, Georgia. You and Fred are in charge of Maya. I'll keep you in the loop about everything going on and what the plan is as we near Palmyra."

"Maya," I added, "if you give us any trouble, we'll make sure that the FBI records reflect your involvement in helping Sandra kill thousands of human clones."

Maya gasped, but surely she saw in my face how serious I was.

Just as I was about to ask Coach to go over my new weapons, Kyle and Briana burst through the door, both panting. Briana fisted a hand over her heart as if she was encouraging it to slow down.

"What is it? What's wrong?" Jack asked.

"I was wrong," Kyle breathed. "There's more."

I cocked my head, studying him.

"More what?" Alyson threw her napkin on her plate and pushed away from the table.

"Buildings," Briana said loudly. "The lab and facilities are much larger than we thought."

Kyle's frantic eyes narrowed in on mine. "This place is huge. She's built a giant complex in the middle of the island. But it's not just that. I tapped into a lot of government documents, Lexi. Your dad knew about the facility. He knew, and he told the FBI. They've been sitting on the information."

~~~~~

"I didn't see anything about Palmyra in my dad's journals, did you?"

Jack walked two steps behind me along the upper deck of the yacht. "No, nothing."
~~~~~

"If the FBI knows about the facility at Palmyra, does that mean the NSA knows? Does the president?" I turned when Jack didn't answer.

He grabbed the railing of the boat and bowed his head as if catching his breath.

"Jack?" I went to him.

He lifted his head slowly, and his eyes pinned me where I stood. A tropical breeze blew blond hair off of his forehead. His face was flushed. Beads of sweat dotted his nose and cheeks. "I don't want you to go to Palmyra, Lexi. I want you to drop this crusade for revenge against Sandra and my father. They're not worth it. But *you are*. I want you to have the life you deserve, and it will never be possible if you keep this up. Sandra will steal your soul, or she'll kill you. Either one is not the life I want for you." Moisture pooled in his eyes. He stumbled forward, keeping one hand on the railing.

I put my arm around him and steadied us. "Why are you saying this? Why now? We're almost there. I can do this. You need this cure."

A tear fell down his cheek. "I know Sandra told you the truth. I'm dying. Georgia and I are going to die. Whatever she did to us is eating away at our insides."

I swallowed hard. "No, you're not. I won't let you." A sob rumbled through my throat. "You know Sandra has the cure. She did this to draw us here. We'll get it. You're going to be fine."

Jack about lost his balance again. "Don't you get it? She doesn't care about me. Or Georgia. She only cares about you. *Using* you. And you're walking into a trap. If I'm going to die, I want to rest knowing that you're going to live a long, happy life—away from her." He closed his eyes briefly, then reopened them.

"Let's get you back to your stateroom," I said.

I slipped an arm around Jack's back and let him put some of his weight on me. There was no way I could hold him, though.

"Lex?"

I looked up. Kyle stood in front of us. I didn't know how much he had heard. "Can you help us?"

Together we got Jack into bed. He fell asleep almost instantly.

"What are you going to do?" Kyle sat in a winged back chair by the balcony door. It was a lovely room, one of the master suites. I wanted Jack to have it, to be comfortable. I had taken a small neighboring guest room.

"You heard him?"

"Yeah."

I watched Jack's breathing even out, become almost peaceful. I faced Kyle. "I love him more than I ever thought possible."

"I know."

"If he dies..."

Kyle rested his elbows on his knees, bowed his head. He had to be thinking of Dani.

I walked over and added a blanket on top of Jack and tucked it in around him. I brushed my fingers along his forehead and trailed it down along his cheekbone. "I'm going to destroy that woman," I whispered. I turned to Kyle. "You in or out? And don't say in unless you're *all* in."

"I'm in," he said without hesitation.

I nodded.

Jack moaned in his sleep. I sat down on the bed beside him and picked up his hand. “I’m sorry, Jack. But you’re wrong. I wouldn’t be able to live with myself if I let Sandra get away with killing the last person I’ll ever love.”

TWENTY-SIX

Beautiful azure skies welcomed us on our second day in tropical paradise. As I looked out over the vast open water, my hand kept feeling for the starfish that usually hung around my neck—my last gift from my father.

It had been there last night. But when I awoke that morning, it was missing. I'd searched my bunk for it, ripped off all the sheets, but it wasn't there. I wondered if losing it was some kind of sign.

If it was, it wasn't good.

I blinked back the coating of moisture in my eyes. I had bigger things to worry about now. Hopefully the necklace would turn up. And I couldn't wear it where I was going anyway.

To my left, Briana was sunning in an oversized lounge chair on the deck as if we were just a group of tourists out for a private cruise. Coach, Seth, and Alyson sat at a nearby table, and by the way they hugged their coffee mugs, it looked like it had been a late night for them. Their occasional glances in my direction told me they were discussing my life without me. Typical.

"Bree," I whispered.

She raised a hand and shielded her eyes from the harsh early morning sun. "Well, well, well. If it isn't Little Miss Trust Fund Baby herself."

"Cut the crap." I glanced over my shoulder to make sure no one was listening. "I need your help."

"With what?"

"I need you to put red streaks in my hair. I need to look exactly like Maya."

~~~~~

The captain and I stood on the bridge, located on the upper level of the expansive and exotic yacht. A host of crystal clear windows offered a panoramic view of the Pacific Ocean. Below the windows were a multitude of gauges and navigational instruments that would have given a passenger jet cockpit a run for its money. I had requested a personal tour of my high-priced transportation, and the captain had been thrilled to personally play the role of guide.

"Can you show me on a map exactly where we are?" I asked, hoping to disguise my simple question as common curiosity.

"We're here." He pointed to a spot in the middle of the blue, far from any landmass. "That, of course, is Hawaii, where we started. My instructions were to sail toward American Samoa, which is about twenty-six hundred nautical miles from our origin. We should be at about the halfway point by first light tomorrow."

Palmyra Atoll lay at the halfway point between Hawaii and American Samoa.

We were almost there.

~~~~~

The crew hustled about, setting a table for nine on the deck. We would have dinner under the stars. And afterward, I would allow my mother to insert one of Sandra's trackers into my neck.

We'd be near Palmyra by morning, and I needed to be ready.

Dressed in jeans and a loose white button-down, sleeves rolled to the elbows, Jack stuffed his hands in his front pockets and stared out toward the ocean. His coloring looked better in the dim light of the lanterns. I circled the deck, admiring the set of his jaw, the lines of his shoulders and how, though sick, he still stood with an air of confidence.

I stayed hidden in the ship's shadows as I memorized everything about him in that moment. My hands shook at my sides. I couldn't tell him that tomorrow I would leave him to face Sandra.

I felt the soft touch of a hand on my arm. "Lexi." Seth pulled me backward into the shadow of a balcony overhead. He looked straight out into the dark depths of the ocean, not making eye contact with me for even a second.

"What is it?"

"I ran blood tests on Jack."

"Yeah? Did you find anything?"

He rubbed his hand back and forth across his unshaven jaw. Finally, he met my stare. Hope spilled from his eyes, leaving them dull and empty. "Yes. His white blood count is through the roof."

"What does that mean? Infection of some sort? Can we give him stronger antibiotics?"

"It can mean a huge number of things, but based on how fast his white blood cells are crowding out his red blood cells, his body seems to be acting like a person in the late stages of leukemia."

"Leukemia? As in cancer? How could Sandra have given Jack cancer?"

"I don't think he has cancer. I think his body's been instructed to *act* like it has cancer. Or as if it's been overtaken by a severe infection. And if we don't stop the multiplication of these diseased white blood cells, or force his healthy cells to crowd them out, he'll die."

My heart constricted, leaving me nearly breathless. "Do you have any ideas?"

"A few, but we aren't at a hospital, and I'm afraid that even if we were, we would still need a miracle."

"A miracle," I repeated. I grabbed onto a railing and looked out across the ocean. There wasn't a single light anywhere other than from our own boat. Waves and crests of water lapped against the hull, rocking us in a soothing motion. "Or perhaps a clone who has the ability to heal cancer or diseases of the blood."

"Jonas."

I whipped around. "What did you say?"

"Jonas is supposed to have that ability."

"Supposed to? Why didn't I know this? He never mentioned it."

"I had been working with him. It's a tricky power—healing cancer. He hasn't been successful at it yet."

"If he can heal such medical catastrophes, does that mean he could also cause them to happen?"

Seth remained silent as I stared at him with eyes that could drill through steel.

"Could he have instructed Maya to do this to Jack?" The same way Ty instructed Jonas to almost drown me?

I took Seth's continued silence as confirmation. But why would Jonas do this? Sandra had to have forced him, which meant he had been unable to fight her invasion through his tracker. I lightly grazed Seth's arm before turning to find Jack. Now, more than ever, I had to get to Palmyra.

I padded softly up to Jack and slid my arms around him, resting my chest against his back and my cheek between his shoulder blades. He had lost so much weight so quickly. His hand lifted and caressed my forearm.

You've been busy today. I haven't seen you much.

I swallowed hard, working hard to keep all of my thoughts private. *I've been sunning and enjoying all that this floating country club has to offer. Besides, you needed rest.*

Jack turned in my arms. *Don't lie to me, Lexi. I know you're going to Palmyra despite my begging you not to.* He lifted strands of my hair, revealing the red streaks Briana had helped me with.

Let's not talk about that right now. I linked my fingers with his. *Follow me. I've got something a little more private planned for us.* I flashed my best attempt at an easy smile.

I led Jack past the others and up the stairs to a higher deck on the bow of the boat. There, a table was set for two. Several lanterns cast a soft, candlelit glow around the table. Soothing music came through several hidden speakers.

"Dance with me," Jack said.

"Of course." I walked into his arms.

He drew my hand in and linked it with his over his heart. We swayed to the sounds of the music and the lapping of water below.

"What a strange world we're sailing through," he said. "On one hand, we're experiencing an adventure aboard the kind of boat most people never even see from a dock. On the other hand, we're here because we've faced terrible loss, the kind I wouldn't wish on many of our worst enemies."

I chuckled at his wording. "Yeah, we might wish the pain of loss on *some* of our enemies, but we'd be picky about it."

Jack crooked a finger under my chin and angled my face toward his. "I'm sorry," he said.

"What are you sorry for?"

"I'm sorry that I'm sick. I'm sorry that I didn't take you away from Wellington the moment I figured out that we were both part of some giant government cloning project." He looked up toward the stars then back down at me. Moisture pooled in his eyes until a single tear slid down his cheek. "Most of all, I'm sorry that our time together is going to get cut short."

"Don't say that," I whispered. Tears threatened to fall—tears I had been fighting since the moment Sandra told me Jack would die without her help. I swallowed against an unforgiving lump in my throat. "I'll fight for you. I'll fight for us."

"I know." He pulled back just enough to reach into his back pocket. He pulled out a small, slender, silver box with a thin ribbon tied into a bow. "A present."

I tried to smile, but my lips tugged downward. I opened the box to discover three hairpins, each decorated with beautiful red stones. "Rubies?"

"To match your new hair." He fingered the streaks of bright red hair that extended behind my normal brunette. "But there's more." He took a barrette from the box. "Each pin has a rubber coating at the stick end of it. Pull that coating off like this." He demonstrated by sliding the rubber covering away from the pin and holding it up in front of me.

"And it becomes a needle," I said softly. "Does it have the paralyzing agent inside?"

"Yes. Enough to take down twenty or so people with each pin. It doesn't take much."

Conveniently, I had a ponytail holder on my wrist. I quickly wove my hair into a long side-braid, then, one by one, stuck the pins into the braid. Each had a protective clasp to secure it into my hair.

As I was clipping the third pin into the braid, a horn sounded below. I faced Jack, his eyes wide.

"What was that?" I grabbed Jack's arm and held tight.

"Sounds like another boat." He grabbed the silver box.

From below, we heard yelling, followed by a man's voice through what sounded like a megaphone.

I ran to the side of the boat and leaned over the railing. Sure enough, another boat, one smaller than ours, had pulled up alongside our stern.

"It's the Coast Guard. We have to go." I started toward the stairs to the lower deck, but Jack stopped me.

"Wait." He pulled something else out of the box. Something red.

"A ribbon? Jack, we don't have time."

"It's not just a ribbon." Any other time it would have been funny that Jack was giving me a silly red ribbon for my hair. "See the wire running through it? It's a GPS tracker. Turn around."

I did as he ordered. He inserted the wire through my hair and seemed to sew it into place throughout the braid.

"It'll hold, and it's waterproof. This will tell us where you are at all times—in case you decide to leave the boat."

I cocked my head. "You knew I planned to leave in the morning, didn't you?"

"I didn't know when, but I knew nothing was going to stop you. Not even me, which is why—"

A loud, shrill scream cut through the air.

Jack and I stared at each other, our eyes panicked. We both went quickly to the stairs and practically fell as we scurried down them. At the bottom, we slowed, trying to assess the situation before we showed ourselves.

Out on the main deck, a body lay on its side, and Addison was draped over top of it. *Jack! It's Anita. Why would the Coast Guard bring Anita to our boat, unless—*

That's not the Coast Guard. And Sandra knows we're here.

Is she alive?

Addison cried over her mother's body. Her mom seemed to move her hand, but only barely.

"We have a message for Sarah Roslin from Dr. Sandra Whitmeyer," the man with the megaphone announced. "We know you're listening. Sarah, if you have not arrived at Palmyra in two days, Jonas Whitmeyer will be terminated, along with your clone twin and the twin of your best friend. Every hour after that time, if you have still not arrived, we will terminate an additional clone."

I have to go, I mindspoke to everyone capable of hearing.

I know, Jack answered.

I'm ready. Addison sat up from comforting her mom and turned her tear-streaked face toward where Jack and I stood.

Her power of knowing where we were at all times always caught me off guard.

I have to go, now, I said only to Jack. I turned and kissed him hard on the lips. He pressed his palm to the back of my braid. We kissed like it was our last. When he released me, I searched his eyes. *Promise me you'll hang on. I'm going to get that cure. That's my promise to you. Promise me you'll keep fighting. I won't say goodbye to you. Never goodbye.*

He leaned his forehead against mine. *I'll see you soon.*

Soon.

~~~~~

Addison, make me invisible to the men on that boat.

Done.

The captain of the other boat—the boat that I didn't believe for one second was actually the Coast Guard—returned to the bridge. They were leaving. I had to get on that boat.

Without giving myself time to think, I slipped behind Alyson. "Don't turn around," I whispered. "Addison has made me invisible to those men. I'm getting on that boat."

Her back tightened. She started to turn her head toward me, but stopped herself. Her jaw hardened. "You can't. You don't have the tracker inserted yet. Besides, they'll kill you."

"They won't know we're there. Give me the tracker and I'll take care of the rest."

Alyson hesitated, but then reached inside her jeans pocket and pulled out the tracker. "But... How are you going to insert it?"
~~~~~

"I'll manage. Sandra told me at The Farm that the trackers were self-directing once they slipped beneath the skin."

"That's true. You only need a small incision."

I nodded. I'd just have to figure out a way to make that initial cut.

"And Lexi, don't forget. You *have* to get this tracker on the satellite communication system and off the island's cell tower as *soon* as you can. You cannot allow Sandra to gain control of your mind."

I scooped up the small device from her hand, and she took hold of mine. "Lexi, I know I haven't been a good mom, but... I want you to know how proud I am of you. And that I never stopped loving you. And your father... he'd be so proud of you, too."

Lexi, they're leaving, Addison mindspoke.

I swallowed hard. "I have to go. Take care of Anita for Addison." Leaning in, I gave my mom a quick hug.

I hurried over to the side of the boat and climbed up to sit on the edge of the railing. The men on the Coast Guard boat were laughing and yelling. Before I could change my mind, I pushed off from the yacht and hurled myself toward the smaller boat below. I nearly missed and plummeted into the water, but thankfully I just made the distance. And thankfully, they were making too much noise to hear me land with a heavy thud. I turned and urged Addison over.

She climbed up onto the railing and did a graceful, ballerina-like leap onto the back of the boat.

A guy yelled, "Let's get out of here."

The boat pulled away slowly. I turned and looked up at Jack. *I love you.*

And I you.

I'll see you soon, okay? Promise me.

See you soon.

"Never goodbye," I whispered to myself. I blew him a kiss. As I lifted my hand away from my lips, gunfire rang out, and sparks flew from the top of *La Luna y el Sol.* I covered my mouth to stifle a scream.

What was that? Addison asked.

Everyone on *La Luna y el Sol* stared above them, except for Jack, whose face continued to point in my direction. I stared from him to the spot where sparks still flew in small bursts of light.

Lexi, Jack yelled inside my head. *They just took out our satellite. We've lost all communication.*

TWENTY-SEVEN

The sun was rising on the port side of the boat. I crawled to a cushioned bench.

I'm going to puke, I mindspoke to Addison. I slapped a hand over my mouth, as if that would stop it, willing my body to suppress the overwhelming waves of nausea.

I can make those guys think they're not seeing you spew into the ocean, but I can't stop the sound or the smell.

Two men sat on tall chairs just a few feet away from us. One of them sliced a green apple with a pocketknife. The other finished off a granola bar and tossed his trash toward a metal tub, but missed.

Sitting up straight and looking to the front of the boat, I concentrated on the horizon in front of us, trying to settle my equilibrium.

My world tilted slightly. A waft of rotten fish smell made me gag, and my mouth continued to water. Without notice, the boat hit a large swell, sending us up and back down again. My stomach did the same thing. I grabbed hold of the rail and leaned over the side of the boat. I couldn't hold it back. A ridiculous amount of liquid flew up my throat and out of my mouth, splashing into the water below. The wind sent some of the liquid splattering down the side of the boat.

"What the hell was that?" The man with the apple put his pocketknife away and peered down at the water.

I moved quickly to the other side of the boat, hoping I wouldn't throw up again.

Addison, help, I said when I thought I was done for a moment. I couldn't easily mindspeak when I was spending all of my energy concentrating on not being sick.

Exactly what am I supposed to do? Hold your hair? She stayed out of the way, curled into a tiny ball on the edge of a bench in the back of the boat. *Find the horizon. Concentrate on that. That's what everybody says when you're carsick, anyway. I don't get motion sick, so I wouldn't know.*

Of course you don't.

When at last I thought I was done vomiting, I lifted my head slowly and watched the horizon again. The boat went over another large swell. This time I handled it okay. The two men continued to look over the other side of the boat, confused.

After another wave, I thought I saw something up ahead. I stood up. It was land. And not all that far away.

"Hey, Dave, I think this is puke," Mr. Granola Bar yelled.

"What are you talking about?"

"Didn't Dr. Whitmeyer say one of the clones could make themselves invisible?"

The two men began looking around the boat. Mr. Granola Bar called out to the guys on the open bridge above.

I stared at Addison. She shrugged. *What are we supposed to do?*

I looked around and found a couple of life jackets. They were bright orange—not exactly inconspicuous. But they would help us float.

A couple more men climbed down from the bridge. "What is it?"

"I think one of those clones is on board," Mr. Granola Bar whispered, as if being invisible made us hard of hearing, too.

It was starting to get crowded on the deck. One wrong move, and someone would bump right into us. I glanced at the life jackets again, then noticed an emergency life raft beside them. It was packed into a sunshine yellow rectangle.

"Have you two been into the shine? There's no one down here." One of the men waved Granola Bar off.

Another man pointed to Mr. Granola Bar's wrapper. "And clean up your trash. We'll be on land in ten."

I whipped my head around to face Addison. We both leaned over the side of the boat and peered ahead. Sure enough, we were drawing nearer and nearer to land.

What do you think? Palmyra? Addison asked.

Has to be. But I hadn't implanted the tracker yet. What with the hiding and the nausea...

What do we do? Jump in the water? Wait 'til they've parked this stupid boat?

I closed my eyes as another wave of nausea hit me. *Let me think.* I drilled fingers into my temples.

The boat turned and seemed to be heading toward the western side of the island. Before we did anything else, I had to get that tracker implanted. If we arrived at the island without the tracker at the base of my skull, Sandra would know immediately that it was me and not Maya. *Addison, you have to help me implant this tracker into my neck.*

What? Are you crazy?

Probably. *If I have any hope of moving around Sandra's facility, I have to make her think I'm Maya.* I just hoped Alyson had gotten the satellite back up and running. I wouldn't be able to fool

Sandra for long. And I had no way of knowing if Jonas was being controlled by Sandra.

Several hundred yards from shore, the boat's engine was cut. My back stiffened. The men moved about the boat, covering and securing loose items.

I swallowed against another wave of nausea. *Hurry, find something sharp to make an incision.* The tracker itself was designed to do most of the work.

Lexi, I'm not going to cut your neck open with anything from this boat. No telling what types of bacteria you'd be putting into your blood. Oh—wait. Addison stood and started walking toward the front of the boat. *There,* she pointed. *A first-aid kit. There's got to be something in it.*

Mr. Granola Bar turned and stumbled in Addison's direction. She sidestepped him just in time, but her arm grazed his ever so slightly. He lifted a hand and scratched where the contact was made.

"Hey, Dirk," a man yelled from someplace outside the boat.

I darted to the railing. A bald man in a tank top rowed a dinghy up to the Coast Guard boat. *Hurry, Addi.*

I've got it. She opened the kit, searching through it. *There's nothing sharp in here.*

Bring the entire kit. We moved to a quiet corner in the back of the boat, where hopefully we would be safe from running into anyone.

The first aid kit had alcohol and antiseptic wipes, as I expected. After dousing both my hands and Addison's with alcohol, I pulled a hairpin from my hair. *We can use this.* I grabbed her hand and urged her to look me directly in my eyes. *Don't touch the ruby, okay?* If the paralyzing agent were to leak out into my skin... disaster.

She raised both eyebrows. *Got it.*

I removed the plastic that covered the tip of the hairpin, then scrubbed the entire needle with antiseptic. After handing the needle over to Addison, I brushed my long braid to the side and used a separate wipe to clean a spot on the back of my neck. Next, I cleaned the tracker that Alyson and I had carried around for so long. I'd never imagined the day would come when I would actually allow it to work its way through my neck and latch onto the base of my skull. Would it even work?

Okay, cut.

I reached for a couple of packages of gauze as Addison made the incision.

Here goes nothing, she said.

I reached out and covered her shaky hand with mine. *You can do this. I trust you.* Addison grabbed the gauze from my hand to mop up the blood from the wound. I closed my eyes tight as she touched my neck with her small fingers. When the needle first sliced my skin, I flinched.

I'm ready for the tracker.

I handed it to her. *This better not kill me,* I said, attempting to keep things light. Then the cold metal touched my skin, and I knew this was it. No turning back. I also knew that once it was inserted, I might be stuck with this foreign object inside my head forever.

The pressure of the tracker's insertion was almost too great. If my equilibrium wasn't already off, the burrowing invader had me gripping the railings along the side of the boat until my knuckles were white.

You okay? When I felt Addison press more gauze to my neck, I knew it was done.

I shook my head. The pain of the tracker moving little by little through my neck brought on another wave of nausea. I fought back tears from the biting pain.

Talk to me. I'm scared. Addison's voice came out in a whimper.

While the tracker did its thing, I fought through the pain and homed in on the wound in my neck. I could actually see the separation of skin. With my mind, I closed the gap, stopping any additional bleeding. I did it. I healed my own wound.

Finally the pain subsided. I reached for the last package of clean gauze and soaked it with alcohol. Addison took it from me and cleaned my neck. *You're good,* she said. We traded a glance—it was a combination of unspoken relief, and a prayer that I hadn't just inflicted my own fatal wound.

The men continued to move about the boat, occasionally tossing something in the dinghy. I hadn't even considered the fact that they wouldn't drive the boat directly up to some kind of dock.

Beyond the beach, a thick forest of palm trees lined the shore. From this distance, I couldn't see a lot of detail, but it looked wild, untamed. I suddenly imagined the sandy beach being littered with seashells and other debris washed up from the ocean.

I looked down at the dress and flip-flops I had chosen for last night's romantic dinner, and I wished I had on something more suited for traipsing through razor-sharp seashells and making my way through a jungle of tropical wildlife and foliage.

Addison stepped back from me, sticking her arms out to her side to balance while standing in the back of the rocking boat. *Are we going to have to swim to shore?*

Another wave of nausea hit me. I had to get off the boat, and fast, before I threw up again. *Can you swim?*

As in, do I know how? Yes, but—

Then let's go. I have to get off this boat. I climbed up to sit on the edge of the craft and swung my legs around. Then, as silently as possible, I dropped into the water, minimizing my splash as my entire body slipped under the surface.

Almost immediately, my body's balance leveled out, and I floated on my back, using my arms to distance myself from the boat.

You can do it, Addi. Come on.

Two men—Granola Bar and another man—stepped toward Addison, their legs wide to keep their balance. I returned to an upright position in the water. They must have heard my splash off the side of the boat. *Watch out.*

Addison dodged to her left and was almost out of their way when one of the men's arms brushed against her.

The man fell backward against Mr. Granola Bar. "Holy shit, what was that?"

"Get off me, dude." Mr. Granola Bar pushed his friend away, this time sending him right into Addison.

"It's one of them. They *are* here." The man waved his hands through the air in front of him. Addison ducked.

Jump! Don't let him catch you!

Addison turned and grabbed onto the side, then she very awkwardly rolled over the side of the boat and belly-flopped into the water, making a loud and lovely splash. *Graceful,* I said when she surfaced.

The men were yelling obscenities and pointing.

Are we still invisible to them?

Yes.

Addison struggled to keep water out of her mouth as small waves tossed her small body about. I reached out a hand to steady her long enough for her to get a breath. *Let's get to land.*

As we swam—being careful not to splash—I looked back at the boat, where four of the men were now climbing into the rowboat. They seemed to be in no hurry, so I assumed that Mr. Granola Bar and his friend had kept the information about our presence to themselves. *Men and their egos,* I laughed. Hopefully, their pride would keep us safe a bit longer.

We swam another hundred yards and then the waves began to help us along the rest of the way. Once on the beach, we both collapsed in the sand. The sun had now risen higher in the sky, and its harsh rays beat down on us. The area on the back of my neck throbbed, and I couldn't even think about the flesh-eating bacteria that might have crawled into the wound.

Sure that Addison had to be getting tired from keeping us invisible, I was about to suggest that we find a shady spot among the palm trees when, suddenly, the sunlight dimmed behind my closed lids. I opened my eyes to find two feet directly in front of my face.

Addison was gone, and I was no longer invisible.

I slowly lifted my head. A dark figure towered over me, the sun glowing behind his head.

Jonas.

~~~~~

Jonas lifted my braid, examined it, then tossed it aside. He circled his fingers around my upper arms and, with a tight grip, lifted me to my feet. "What are you doing here?" His voice was stern, scary. "How did you get here?"

This was it. I had to convince Jonas I was Maya. He'd already seen the red streaks running through my hair. "I..." I glanced over my shoulder toward the boat anchored just off shore. "I obviously came on that boat."

I smiled, attempting to take on the personality of a smart-ass, when everything in me wanted to scream and yell and force him to tell me if he had anything to do with how sick Jack was. But I couldn't break my cover. Not yet.

He shoved me forward, pushing me toward a path leading away from the beach.

I grunted as I my foot landed on a pointy palm leaf. "Ow! Watch it." I had lost my shoes in the swim to shore, not that those flimsy flip-flops would have done much good anyway. I kept my eyes to the ground, watching for crabs and biting insects.

Addison had deserted me the moment Jonas showed up. I wasn't sure Jonas even knew Addison was there.

I also didn't know how much of what he was doing was the work of Sandra. I used every technique he had taught me to keep him closed off from my mind. I needed him to truly believe I was Maya if this was going to work.

We followed the path, Jonas right behind me, until at last a building came into view. It was even bigger than I had imag-
~~~~~

ined—two stories but wide, nestled in and around the trees and tropical foliage.

Jonas led me to a metal door that appeared to be a side entrance. He placed his hand flat on a scanner—similar security to The Farm—and after a clicking sound, he opened the door. He placed a hand on my back, and when I hesitated, he pushed me harder through the entrance.

"Hey!" I stumbled.

He said nothing as he grabbed my elbow again and led me down a hallway, almost running me into the wall three times. It was like he was purposely keeping me to one side. That was when I scanned the ceiling and discovered the cameras. I glanced toward Jonas. He, too, was watching the video cameras. We slowed, then sped up, then slowed again. He was deliberately keeping me off of the video. But why? Did he know that I was Lexi? Was he trying to protect me?

We turned a corner, and he pulled me down another hallway to another grey metal door. After opening it and pulling me through, he shoved me against the wall and jammed a forearm into my neck, pinning me where I stood. "Where is Lexi? What did you do to her?"

My eyes must have widened to the size of sand dollars. I shook my head. "What are you talking about? I didn't do anything to her."

He pressed harder against my neck, cutting off my air supply. My hand clawed at his arm, struggling to wriggle out of his chokehold. I couldn't breathe or talk.

"If you don't tell me what happened to Lexi, I will make sure Sandra sees you as a traitor and a spy." He loosened his arm enough that I sucked in a labored breath.

"I swear I didn't do anything to her." I coughed right in his face. He closed his eyes in disgust. "I snuck on the boat with the agents who delivered Addison's mom. They didn't see me, but I managed to slip down below on their boat and stayed hidden until we got here. I slipped into the water before any-one caught me and swam to shore."

"How did they not see you?"

I tried to think about how Maya would act. It had to be different than how I would react to Jonas. I smiled, and instead of clawing at his arm, I began massaging it. "Because, Jonas, I'm that good."

He loosened his hold even more. "And Lexi wasn't on the boat with you?"

I shook my head, not letting my grin falter in any way. "I might have drowned her again if she had been."

He let go and took a step back. I sucked in a huge breath and let it out slowly while I massaged my neck. I flattened my hand against my chest, the place where my necklace used to be, losing my concentration briefly as I mourned the last gift my dad ever gave me. Lost in thought, and just when I thought Jonas had believed me, his hand came at me so fast that I didn't even feel the slap across my face until a second had passed.

I gasped, and my hand covered the smart. "You hit me!"

"That was for Lexi—for drowning her the first time. And for basically being a thorn in our sides since we discovered your existence. If I find out you did anything to harm Lexi or any of the others, I will make sure Sandra terminates you."

I rubbed at the sting. I couldn't believe he had hit me—or hit Maya, I guessed. He'd better not be just pretending that he hadn't recognized me. "And here I thought we could be friends," I purred.

I stepped around him. Only then did I notice we were in some sort of bedroom. The bed was dressed with white sheets and a dark grey blanket. All of the furniture was silver or grey metal or painted black. I knew I had to pretend I knew exactly where I was—that I knew my way around Palmyra—or my cover would be blown. "So, you seem to be settled in quite nicely. I bet Lexi would love to know you're fighting her battles while working so close to your mother again."

"You don't know anything about my relationship with my mother, but you'll find out soon." He gave me a cold smile, then turned and walked out the door.

When the door slammed behind him, panic rose in my chest. I ran to the door. Locked. I banged on it a few times.

Jonas stared at me through the small window. "Sandra will be here to see you shortly."

TWENTY-EIGHT

For the first twenty minutes of my captivity, I searched the room for anything useful. I lifted the mattress off the bed, pulled out every dresser drawer, and checked the attached bathroom for supplies. There were very few.

Other than a fresh toothbrush and toothpaste, the room had nothing I could use. Though it *was* nice to brush my teeth.

Addison, can you hear me? I hadn't heard from her since we'd crawled up on the beach. *Jack? Briana?* They were too far away.

I had to assume that my tracker, the tracker I stole when I fled The Farm—the same one that was now embedded at the base of my skull—was still connected to Sandra's system. And according to my mother, that would mean Sandra could control my tracker—and me—through the cell tower here on the island. *If* she discovered it had been activated. I just had to hope that Sandra didn't look closely at the computer software that controlled the trackers. Somehow I had to get my tracker connected to the satellite so that Alyson could assume command and send me all the information being fed to Maya.

But first, I had to get out of this room.

I was staring up at the ceiling when the doorknob jiggled. I jumped up and stared at the door.

Sandra blew in, followed by two women twice her size, and therefore twice my size. "When Jonas told me my cloned beta prodigy had come home, I just had to see it with my own eyes," she said.

I stared at her, wide-eyed and nervous, shifting on my feet to hide the fact that my legs were shaking.

Sandra was wearing a white lab coat. Circles darkened the area under her eyes. I forced my own face to soften and my lips to stretch into a smile. "That's right. And boy, am I glad to be home."

She stepped up to me, studying me, and a sweat broke out across the back of my neck. This was it. She was going to figure me out. How did I ever think I could get away with this?

"Where is Sarah? Your job was to ensure she came to Palmyra. Where is she?"

I repeated, *What would Maya say?* over and over in my head. Whatever I said next had to be convincing. "I did my job," I snapped. "Lexi will go through hell and high water to get the cure for Jack. She'll be here."

"Why are you here, then, without her?"

"I couldn't stay with them any longer. They locked me up. They threatened me. Lexi almost killed me when she tried to remove my tracker. She's scared. She won't risk something happening to Jack. She'll be here."

Sandra paced back and forth a few times. "Well, welcome home." She rested her hand on the gun at her waistband, I hoped out of habit and not out of doubt for who I said I was.

Jonas entered the room. "You rang," he said, practically bowing before Sandra. Surely he was joking. As he lifted his head, he shot a quick look my way. Not a very friendly look, either.

"Yes, Jonas, I want you to get to know Maya better. Let her tell you everything she learned from Sarah and the others. I need to know when to expect our Alpha healer. It's time she stopped fighting her destiny."

"What makes you think she's coming at all?" Jonas asked.

"Because she needs to know how to cure her precious Jack, who by now ought to be in seriously poor condition."

If I hadn't been watching Jonas so closely, I would have missed the lift of his eyebrow followed by the slight look of panic. Had he known Jack was ill? Based on what Seth had told me about Jack's medical abilities, I still wondered if Jonas had had something to do with Jack's and Georgia's predicament.

Resisting the urge to massage the space over my aching heart at the mention of Jack's sickness, I cocked my head and studied Sandra. "Do you plan to cure Jack?" I kept my voice even—disinterested but curious. "He's quite ill, you know."

Sandra seemed to bounce the question around in her mind. "Meh. Yeah. Probably. I'd hate to have to tell his father that his son is dead."

I squeezed my hands into fists. "Well, I'm glad to be back at Palmyra." I smiled, but there was no joy behind it. When I glanced toward Jonas, he was staring at me with one eyebrow raised.

"Well. I'm sure you're tired from your boat ride, so I'll leave you to rest." Sandra looked from Jonas back to me. "I'm just glad to have you both under the same roof. I think you'll get along famously once you get to know each other."

Jonas continued to stare daggers at me as Sandra moved toward the door to leave. Just before she stepped over the threshold, she turned. "Oh, and Maya, when you see Addison, please tell her that she can't hide forever. She should have stayed with her mother on that boat. Because once I find her, she won't be leaving again." And with that, Sandra let the door slam behind her.

A shudder moved through me as I took in and released a large breath. Sandra hadn't even questioned my identity. I glanced sideways at Jonas. "She's amazing, isn't she?" I tried to sound sincere, even though I practically choked on the words.

"Uh-huh. And obviously distracted." He crossed his arms. His eyes pinned me where I stood. "You're hiding something."

"What? I am not," I scoffed. I shifted under his gaze. "And stop staring at me. Didn't Sandra ever teach you any manners?"

"Actually, no. She taught me anatomy and medicine. And how to obey the commands of my tracker." He walked around the room. "Speaking of which, you've had your tracker a long time, right?"

"Yes." Where was he going with this?

"Are you ever able to disobey the orders fed to you through your tracker?"

"Why would I want to?" Maya didn't strike me as someone who would fight Sandra, and did the twin clones even have the mind abilities to disobey?

"What if Sandra ordered you to do something hurtful to someone you liked?"

I figured that was an easy one for Maya. "I've never been around people I like, so I wouldn't know. What about you?"

Jonas stepped close. So close that I could smell the tropical scent in his hair, see the amber specks in his chocolate eyes. "That's an interesting question. One I'll answer for you soon. But I'll tell you this. You better hope Sandra doesn't ask me to hurt you in any way."

A chill galloped down my spine. I raised my head so that my eyes met his. His breath warmed my cheek. "I'm a little tired," I whispered.

"Sandra would like for me to get to know you. I'll be back in an hour." He looked down at my dress. *And try to wear something equally hot.*

His mindspeak caught me off guard. I curled my toes, trying to concentrate on some other part of my body and not react to his words inside my head. I had no idea if Maya was capable of hearing Jonas's mindspeak.

"I'll be ready."

~~~~~

I had an hour before Jonas would be back for me. *Addison, where are you?*

"Right here." She popped into existence, sitting cross-legged on the bed.

"Let's go."

Addison made us invisible, and together we headed in the opposite direction from where I'd entered the building. It took only turn and we were in the middle of activity.

We must be in the center of the building, I mindspoke to her. *I need to find the room with the servers controlling the trackers.*

There. She pointed to a door where a man in a white lab coat was scanning a badge to enter. We jogged to catch up, and slipped through the door behind him.

I stopped dead in my tracks so suddenly that Addison ran into my back and practically knocked me over.

What are *those things?* she asked.
~~~~~

Those are incubators.

Addison and I were facing rows and rows of the rectangular machines: actual human clones being grown in a human-sized test tubes. Several people in lab coats milled about, carrying clipboards. They appeared to be checking gauges and settings on the machines and then earnestly jotting down notes. Tubes and pipes in white and sky blue ran from the machines to the ceiling. I chose a thick blue tube and followed it with my eyes across the ceiling to where it connected to a large white machine in the corner. *Oxygen.* I padded closer to the incubators, my fingers rubbing the spot on my chest where my heart beat erratically. I had to remind myself to keep breathing.

The machines were much larger in person than they appeared on Sandra's video. I had to rise to my tiptoes to peer into the window on top. When I did, a gasp escaped my lips. A human child lay on his side in the fetal position. Not a baby, but a child: a one-year-old, maybe. His hands were folded near his face, his thumb in his mouth.

I continued down row after row of incubators. Every machine housed a human body. Sandra was *growing humans.* Not just fertilizing eggs and developing embryos, but growing humans from embryo to baby to child.

A door on the opposite side of the lab opened, and John DeWeese entered. Instinctively, I ducked down.

Addison touched my arm. *Relax. He can't see you.*

A moment later, Jonas entered by the same door, following closely behind Dr. DeWeese as he walked down the rows.

We have to get closer. I want to hear what they're saying.

As I neared them, I heard Jonas ask, "What if you can't figure out the problem? What if the children keep dying?"

"Don't call them that," Dr. DeWeese answered. "Don't humanize them."

I stood straighter, walked faster until I was right behind them. I wanted to take one of my paralyzing pins out of my hair and empty a full dose into Dr. DeWeese's neck.

"What would you like for me to call them?" Jonas curled his hands into fists, but his voice remained calm.

"They're just delta clones."

Delta? As in fourth generation? I wondered.

Jonas paused his forward motion. His head turned to the side a bit before he continued walking.

Sandra entered the lab and sped toward them. Her face was red, her lips spread into a thin line. "Representatives of the Nature Conservancy are paying us a visit. It seems someone told them there was activity on the island that didn't fit in with their 'preservation of nature.'"

"What are you going to do?" Dr. DeWeese asked.

"I'm going to play the perfect hostess. This room needs to be sealed off. It can't even look like it exists. No one gets in or out while the Conservancy reps are here. And if anyone other than the Conservancy arrives, they'll be in for a big surprise. IIA has implemented a twenty-four-hour watch in the tower and at the beach."

"When do they arrive?" Jonas asked.

"By boat, midday tomorrow."

It was happening. I smiled.

"Which is about the same time we should expect Sarah," Sandra added.

~~~~~
~~~~~

I only had fifteen minutes before my meeting with Jonas, and I had yet to locate the server controlling the trackers. Which meant I still hadn't heard from Alyson. I was totally shut off from Jack, Alyson, and everyone else on *La Luna y el Sol*.

Since I didn't need to be invisible, Addison and I split up. If I met anyone, I would just have to carry on as if I were Maya.

After finding nothing but medical labs behind each of the doors in the hallway I was in, I stopped and leaned against the wall. I closed my eyes and massaged the bridge of my nose. It was useless. I needed Kyle and Briana. They had studied the layout of the buildings. I should have waited until I could bring them with me, or at least until I had studied the maps more myself.

"You look a little lost."

My eyes snapped open. Jonas stood in front of me, grinning. "Uh... no."

"Thought you were going to rest and wait for me in your room."

I rotated my shoulders back and reminded myself that I was not Lexi Matthews. "Since when do I answer to you? You said you were coming back to pick me up. I never agreed to stay in my quarters until then."

"Fair enough. So tell me... why is a girl who's supposedly spent so much time on Palmyra lost in the middle of the main hallway?"

Sweat broke out across my neck. "What makes you think I'm lost?"

"Because I just watched you open every one of those doors and peer inside, only to let the doors close again." He walked closer until there were only a couple of inches between us. "You're looking for something, darlin', and you can't seem to find it."

I glanced in both directions, looking for anyone who might see us.

Jonas followed my gaze, then returned to staring at me. "There's no one there. No one to help you."

My head was pushed hard against the wall, and my chest rose and fell in labored breaths. This was the Jonas I knew—playful yet intimidating. Only instead of the old Jonas, the one I knew I could handle, this one had a tracker in him controlled by Sandra. And I still didn't know if he was able to override his orders. "Why would I need help, Jonas?"

"You just look scared, that's all. What are you scared of, darlin'?"

I had to change my approach if I was going to keep up the ruse that I was Maya. *I'm not scared of anything,* I mindspoke to him. Maya had mindspoken to me several times, so her tracker must have given her that ability. *You make me nervous, that's all.* I batted my eyelashes and almost puked when a grin spread across his lips. Though I pretended to be Maya, I couldn't help but feel I was betraying Jack by flirting.

Jonas brushed hair back from my face and tucked it behind my ear. His demeanor toward me was the complete opposite of how he'd acted earlier that day. He leaned in and whispered, his breath hot on my neck, "You have nothing to be afraid of. I'm here to help you."

"I just got turned around, that's all. Where are the computer labs?"

He leaned back, cocked his head. "Why do you need to know that?"

I brought my hand to rest on his chest, pushing back a bit. "Look, Jonas, I don't answer to you. The quicker you realize that, the better you and I will get along."

One corner of his lips lifted. "Okay. We'll play it your way." He grabbed my hand and pulled. "I'll show you."

If only I was playing. It had been a while since I had seen Jonas act this way.

Jonas led me to a stairwell that led to a second story. No wonder I hadn't been able to find the computers. The second level was laid out similarly to the first. He took me down a few hallways to a set of double doors. The doors were windowless and looked to be made of steel. I was fairly certain we were directly above the incubator lab.

Jonas turned and stared down at me. "Want to see where the trackers are kept and controlled?"

I shrugged. "I've seen the computer rooms before."

"Not this one. It's new. The entire second floor just went online." He raised an eyebrow as if he was surprised I didn't know that. "According to Sandra, you haven't been on Palmyra in months."

Again he pressed his hand on a scanner. The doors opened, and Jonas pulled me after him.

The air was cool and smelled of overheated machines. Like the space below it, this room was large. But instead of rows of incubators, this room had three rows of floor-to-ceiling black machines. Blue lights glowed from each one.

"So all of the trackers placed inside Sandra's clones are controlled from this room, right?"

"Well, this is where the information stored on each tracker lives, but the trackers are controlled from those computers"—Jonas pointed to a long desk with multiple keyboards and rows of flat screen monitors—"and from a remote app on Sandra's phone."

Alyson had said nothing about an app. I wondered what else was new to the system.

I walked slowly toward the screens. They were all lit, each one showing a different view, like we were watching sophisticated security footage. One TV caught my eye: it showed me in profile, standing in this room. My heart sped up. I slowly turned my head; the face on the screen turned, too.

"They can see everything someone with a tracker sees?"

"That's right." Jonas turned and walked down to the end of the row of TVs, then made his way back toward me. His eyes remained fixed on the monitors the entire time. "There's something missing from these monitors, don't you think?"

Yeah, *my* line of vision. Shit.

The sound of footsteps stopped just outside the lab doors, and Jonas and I traded panicked looks. When the beeping of security approval started, Jonas grabbed me by the elbow and led me away from the door and away from the computer monitors. We ducked behind the tracker servers. I breathed heavily. Jonas lifted a finger to his lips, then closed his eyes.

I squinted at him. His actions confused me. He was obviously allowed in the room—his handprint was recognized. So why were we hiding?

He remained flat against the server we hid behind. His lips tugged downward. He slipped a hand around my waist and pressed it against the small of my back, bringing me closer so that my chest was against his body and I was hidden from whoever just entered. When he leaned in, his mouth next to my ear, I thought he was going to whisper. Instead he mind-spoke. *We're hiding, my dear Lexi, because when Sandra figures out that you aren't who you say you are, she will do unimaginable things to you to extract the DNA information she needs to complete the next generation of trackers.*

How did you know?

That doesn't matter at the moment. What matters is why you were searching for this room.

I need to switch the communications system, so the trackers route through the satellite instead of the cell tower.

Jonas's eyes remained closed. And suddenly, the reason we were hiding dawned on me. He didn't want whoever was standing in front of those monitors to know that he was with me.

Why? Jonas asked. *Sandra can control the trackers just as easily through the satellite as she can through the cell tower.*

Yeah, but the system is more vulnerable to an outside hack when the trackers are on the satellite.

And by outside hack, you mean...?

My mother.

Jonas nervously drew circles on the small of my back. *I don't know, Lex. I can't believe Sandra would leave this new system open to that. Your mom hasn't seen the improvements that have been made since Sandra and her minions returned from UK.*

But she designed *the system. I just know I have to try.*

Okay. There's a panel to the left of the computer stations. It's on the wall beside the monitors. Inside that panel are three switches, one for each row of tracker servers we're standing in now. You simply have to move the switches from one side to the other.

That's it? It seemed too easy. Now I just needed to hope that Alyson had regained her satellite connection.

I leaned over Jonas and peeked around the edge of the server. My body stiffened under Jonas's hands. I took in a breath as my heart constricted and a sweat broke out across my neck.

What is it? Jonas asked. *Who's over there?*

I jerked back behind the servers. I had to get out of here. *Is there any other way out of here? This is bad, Jonas.*

Tell me who's over there.

Can you see inside Addison's head and see what she's seeing, like you've done with me in the past?

Yeah. As long as she's not invisible at the time.

Then see for yourself.

Jonas went silent for several seconds, though it seemed like hours. I knew what he was seeing. He was looking through Addison's eyes at the tracker monitors—along with two other people.

Sandra and Maya.

TWENTY-NINE

Oh my God, Lexi. Close your eyes. If they tap into your tracker, they'll see exactly what you're seeing.

Jonas's eyes remained shut, and I did as he ordered. *How the hell did Maya get here? And Addison's still helping them?* I had had my doubts about Maya, especially under the influence of Sandra's tracker, but Addison? *Sandra's going to find me here.* I knew the time would come when I'd turn myself over to Sandra, but I wasn't ready yet.

We have to get out of this room, Jonas mindspoke. *Come on. Keep your eyes closed.* He dropped his hand to mine and pulled me down the row of servers. I let one hand graze the servers to my left so I knew where I was. I stumbled slightly, but managed to keep my footing.

As we drew closer to the other end of the room, we could hear Sandra's voice.

"Get her tracker synced and pull up what she's seeing, right now. I want her found." Sandra spoke through gritted teeth. "And what's wrong with Jonas's tracker? Why is his monitor dark?"

I squeezed Jonas's hand. No one answered Sandra's question.

Why did you insert a tracker into your neck? What were you thinking? Jonas was rubbing his thumb back and forth against mine. He didn't sound mad, just worried.

I had to pretend to be Maya. I thought it would buy me some time in here before I had to turn myself over to Sandra. The plan was for Alyson to get control of the trackers, including yours.

I'm in control of my own tracker, Lexi. I don't need your help, or your mother's.

I don't understand. Seth said that your DNA was manipulated all those years ago to heal certain blood conditions and diseases, so we assumed it was you that made Jack and Georgia sick—that Sandra forced you to do it through Maya's mind.

Seth's right. Jonas seemed to hold even tighter to my hand. *But I was in control the whole time.*

What are you saying? I tried pulling my hand from his grasp, but he practically cut off the circulation in my fingers. *You did this to him on purpose?* My voice was rising inside my own head as reality began to sink in.

Calm down.

My eyes sprang open. *Jonas, he's dying. Jack and Georgia are dying because of* you. Tears blurred my vision—tears of anger, frustration, and complete betrayal.

I had to do what Sandra instructed me to do, or she would have known that the new tracker wasn't working on me. I couldn't risk what she might do to me if that happened.

So, you risked Jack's life instead? And Georgia's?

They aren't going to die. I'll heal them.

How? They're already dying. Jack could barely stand when I left him. They were both knocking on death's door, according to Seth. I ground my teeth together. *I had to come here alone because he was too sick to come with me.*

Why didn't you *heal them?* Jonas asked.

I stared at him like he was a three-eyed monster. *I couldn't even figure out what was wrong with Jack. I can't heal just anything.*

Yes, you can. Jonas sighed. *We just haven't had time to explore all that you're capable of. But it's time you accept the truth you've fought so hard against. You are the ultimate healer. Your DNA was mapped with every type of healing. You can heal brain injuries, deep open wounds and cuts, broken bones, torn muscles, ruptured appendices, and even cancer.*

You're crazy. I pulled on his hand again with no success. Was Jonas right? Could I have cured Jack all along? I didn't need Sandra's help?

I told you not to come here. That's why Sandra needs you. The rest of us have some abilities, but you have them all. That's why everyone wanted your father's journals. They thought he documented all of this, but he didn't. Well, he did, but not in an easy-to-read format. It's all coded.

You said you figured out his coded writing?

Yes. The key to making more healers like you is hidden within your DNA, in the way your brain's neurons fire. It's more than just getting a blood sample from you.

Sandra wants to study my DNA—my everything. She plans to recreate my brain patterns inside other humans by using a manufactured tracker. I had known this to be true, but with everything that had happened, I hadn't had enough time to imagine the full possibilities.

I began prying Jonas's fingers away from mine. *And thanks to you, now she'll get to. I have no way of getting back to Jack. I have to trust that Sandra will do what she promised and heal him.*

What are you planning to do?

I'm handing myself over. If I don't do something soon, it'll be too late.

Jonas pulled me closer. *I can't let you do that. This is not what Jack would want. He'd never let you sacrifice yourself for him.*

Jack isn't capable of knowing what he wants right now. Look at us. I have no choice.

So, what? We're just supposed to let Sandra win? Let her keep cloning humans in this evil government factory?

I laughed inside his head—a hysterical, hopeless chuckle. *Why do you think the Nature Conservancy is coming here?*

That was you? You told them what was going on here? Why would you do that?

I told them some *of what was going on here. Enough for them and the president of the United States to know that this is not the kind of publicity our country needs.*

Sandra has no idea.

Exactly. And I need her to heal Jack—or to let me or you heal Jack—before government officials arrive. If she freaks out and we don't get to Jack in time...

I'm still not letting you turn yourself over to her. Just wait until they leave. Let's at least get the trackers transferred over first.

There isn't time, now. That can be your job. I tried yanking my arm away from him, which only resulted in pain in my hand, elbow, and shoulder. *Let go of my hand, Jonas, or I'll scream. And then we'll both be caught.*

When Jonas's grip wouldn't loosen, I raised my knee and used my escalating adrenaline to nail him in a spot that I knew would make him let go of me.

He released me and crumbled to the ground. His face turned crimson red as he suppressed a scream. I had to hope the constant sound of the cooling system would mask the sound of his fall.

I moved farther down the row of servers. When I reached the end, I glanced around the machines at Sandra, Maya, and Addison.

"Why can't we connect with her tracker?" Sandra asked Maya.

"I'm not sure. It's here. I can see it, but the system's not connecting with it."

"Can you see if the Omega Directive is programmed into the tracker already?"

Maya cast a glance over her shoulder. She shifted in her seat before she typed again on the computer. "It's there."

"Is she on the satellite system? Did Alyson get it set up before the three of you left?" Sandra placed a fisted hand on her hip as she stood over both girls.

"No." Addison's voice was quiet. "But Lexi's first job when she got here was supposed to be to make sure all the tracker communications were transferred from the cell tower to the satellite system."

A lighting storm of rage fired through my body. I couldn't believe Addison had so easily revealed my plan.

"Is that right?" Sandra sighed. She suddenly about-faced, and I jumped backward and out of sight. My hand flew to my heart as I tried to catch my breath. Sandra walked to the only doors that led out of the room. If she turned in my direction even a little, I was caught. I held my breath as she approached a glass cabinet containing a fire extinguisher and a fire axe. She grabbed the axe and marched back to the computers.

"Can you see where she is?" Sandra asked Addison. She white-knuckled the axe like she was about to chop down the largest coconut tree on the island.

I slipped inside Addison's brain but found no tracker there. She was *willingly* helping Sandra. "No." She squinted her eyes. "That's so strange. I've never had trouble finding her before."

I glanced backward at Jonas. He was on his hands and knees. He reached up and grabbed the edge of one of the machines and began pulling himself to his feet. *Are we even now?* he asked. *I hit you when I didn't know it was you. In return, you've made sure I'll never have children? Can we please work together on getting you out of here now?*

I walked back to him. He was bent over at the waist, his hands on his knees. *Why is Addison having trouble tracking me?*

You're suppressing your mind from others more and more every day, especially when you're angry. You think I've been staying out of your mind because I'm nice? I don't do nice. You've been blocking me.

What is the Omega Directive?

Jonas bowed his head and shook it slowly from side to side. *Oh, Lexi. Why did you have to go and let that tracker burrow itself into your neck?*

What is it?

After a long, heavy sigh, he mindspoke again. *There are two features of the tracker that I can't block or bypass: Sandra's ability to terminate me with the push of a few buttons, and the Omega Directive. I'm only guessing you'll be in the same boat.*

What does it do?

It's not what it does. It's what it prevents you from doing.

And what is that?

The Omega Directive prevents anyone with a tracker from harming Sandra. Now that you have a tracker, you'll be unable to do anything that goes against Sandra, including defending yourself. Nor will you be able to direct someone else to harm Sandra. That tracker completely prevents any one of us from hurting Sandra in any way. Period.

But you said you had complete control of your tracker. What makes this feature different?

No idea. I just know that Sandra has a team of specialists improving these trackers every day. So even if we're able to get the trackers switched over to satellite, she may already know a workaround.

The situation was becoming more and more hopeless. And I had no idea how much time Jack had left. Especially now that Sandra knew I had deceived her by pretending to be Maya.

I grabbed Jonas's chin and directed his face toward mine. I wished his eyes were open so he could see my eyes. *If Jack dies, I will never forgive you. And everything that I've been working to save will be nothing to me. I'll give you one last chance to help me get the trackers transferred over to the satellite, but if we can't make that happen soon, I'm going to turn myself over to Sandra, and whatever happens, happens.* Even if this mission failed, I craved that communication with *La Luna y el Sol*, if only to make sure that Jack was all right before I sacrificed myself. I hoped I wasn't already too late.

Jonas lifted his chest. His eyes remained closed. I hadn't been able to see his eyes during any part of our conversation. If Maya and Sandra were able to activate my tracker, they'd see I was standing less than a hundred feet from them, and with Jonas. And then Sandra would know that Jonas had command over his own tracker and was betraying her. Again. She'd have me cornered, and Jonas would no longer be able to help me. I didn't even want to think about what she would do to Jonas if that were to happen.

I'm sorry about Jack and Georgia. I did what I thought I had to. They'll understand.

I turned away from Jonas and paced. Nothing but the large machines separated me from the person who wanted to poke and prod me like a giant lab rat. But if Sandra was telling the truth, the same large machines separated me from the cure for Jack.

I eased toward the end of the row again. *I'm letting you inside my head so that you can see what's going on over there.*

Jonas slipped inside my head and watched as Sandra continued to hold the deadly axe in her hand. *What's she going to do with that?*

Maya punched a key and looked up. "I found Lexi's tracker. It's now synced with the system. You can communicate with her."

"Why can't we see what she's seeing?" Sandra asked. I stared at the snowy monitor above Maya's head.

Maya pushed away from the computers in frustration. "I don't know. I can't seem to tap into the feed. Maybe her tracker was damaged. She carried it around for several weeks. And there's no telling what Alyson did to it."

Finally, a break. If I could just continue to control my own actions when Sandra got inside my head, the tracker would be useless to her. Unless she decided to terminate me, of course. I shuddered.

Sandra growled in exactly the way I imagined an angry mother bear would, and lifted the axe. For a brief moment, I thought she might split it over Maya's head. My entire body tensed. I was about to scream out when Sandra ran past the chairs where Maya and Addison sat. Past the computers and monitors.

She raised the axe over her head and let it come down. Metal crunched on metal. Sparks flew. A direct hit.

My breath was knocked out of me. I closed my eyes tight, trying to unsee what she had done. The distinct smell of burning electricity reached my nose.

When I reopened my eyes, Sandra breathed heavily and dropped the axe to the floor. She had just taken out the switches that would allow me—or anyone—to switch the trackers to satellite communication. There was no way Alyson could hack in now. I was further than ever from communicating with Alyson, Jack, or anyone on *La Luna y el Sol*.

~~~~~

Jonas never had the slightest chance of stopping what happened next.

I need you to do me a favor, I mindspoke to Jonas as I backed away from him toward the edge of the row of servers.

Anything.

Don't try to be a hero right now, and don't, under any circumstances, open your eyes. I'll let you into my head, but don't open your eyes.

I took a deep breath, rounded the corner, and faced the group. "Well, well, well," I said. "Look at what we have here. I've been looking for you everywhere, Addison."

After the initial surprise, Addison looked down at her plaid canvas Toms. Maya stood up from her seat, glancing from Sandra to me and back to Sandra. And Sandra just stared
~~~~~

open-mouthed. Her usual confident grin was missing in action. Instead, rage still colored her face red from her fire-axe tirade, when she'd shattered my hopes of connecting with Alyson and Jack.

"What? You're surprised to see me?" I rotated my shoulders back and stood tall, trying to be the largest one in the room, which proved to be difficult given that three of us were identical heights. "I told you I would come."

"And here you are." Sandra crossed her arms across her chest and jutted a hip out. "Maya, call Security."

Maya pulled a phone from her pocket and began tapping it with her thumb. I held a hand up. "That won't be necessary."

Maya looked to Sandra for direction.

"Tell Security to come to the tracker room, now!" Sandra ordered.

I slipped inside Maya's head, allowing equal parts anger and fear to fuel what I needed to do. *Drop your phone on the floor.* She lowered her arm to her side and let the phone slide from her fingers. It fell with a clank to the tile floor. *Pick up that axe and smash the phone.*

Maya did exactly as I ordered, cracking the phone's screen into a thousand pieces and splitting the phone in half like a piece of firewood.

Now, my dear twin, I want you to grab your friend Addison in a headlock, and place the blade of the axe to her throat.

As the blade made light contact with Addison's skin, the eight-year-old gasped. Her chest rose and fell in quick repetitions.

Sandra just stood back and watched as I took control of Maya's mind. She cocked her head, studying me. "You know I'll only kill them both, right?" Her grin resurfaced. Maya's brows pulled inward, forming a vertical line in the middle of her forehead. Addison's face paled.

"Whatever," I said. "They're nothing to me."

Maya's scowl deepened. Did they really think I was without a breaking point? If I'd learned nothing else from my evil DNA donator... Sandra killed people whether I wanted her to or not. Sometimes, especially if I didn't want her to.

"However, I'll only come willingly under one condition."

Sandra smirked. "You think you're in a position to bargain with me?"

I smiled back, trying to look more confident than I felt. "Do you really want a fight? I escaped once. I can do it again. Either way, I'll leave a nasty path of destruction. Do you even have any idea what I've been doing since I arrived on Palmyra?"

Sandra narrowed her eyes. "What's your condition?"

"I want proof that Jack and Georgia have been completely healed."

Before Sandra could respond, the doors behind me opened, and in walked three people: Dr. John DeWeese; Dr. Mendez, the doctor from The Farm who took blood from me and hooked me up to machines at Sandra's orders; and an armed security guard dressed in a khaki uniform.

Sandra smiled. "Apparently, Maya's a fast dialer." She nodded toward Dr. Mendez and Dr. DeWeese.

Before I could react, Dr. Mendez stuck me in the arm with a needle and syringe. The room tilted and the people in it went fuzzy.

And I collapsed into the arms of my boyfriend's father.

THIRTY

I woke to the sights and sounds of various medical machines. The heart monitor to my right beeped at a constant rate. An oxygen tube led from my nose to some unidentified source behind me, but did nothing to block out the smells of sterilization.

I turned my head left and right. Leather straps bound my wrists and ankles. I was dressed in gray hospital scrubs.

After several seconds, Dr. Mendez came into view. "This would have been much easier if you had simply complied with Dr. Whitmeyer's wishes from the beginning."

I opened my mouth to speak, but nothing came out. I couldn't form words. I opened my eyes wider, pleaded with Dr. Mendez.

"Oh, honey. Don't bother trying to talk. Dr. Whitmeyer thought it necessary to simply—how should we say—*turn off* the area of your brain that would allow you to speak. It will wear off shortly. In time for the tests."

I heard what she said. Understood it even. But I struggled to process what it meant.

Dr. Mendez leaned over me, lifting one perfectly sculpted eyebrow as she spoke. "Here's what's going to happen. We need to get a complete picture of what happens inside your brain. We're going to measure the changes in blood flow to the different areas of your brain, and we're going to take readings of your neuronal activity."

As her words sank further and further into my thoughts, they began to make sense. I wanted to ask how she planned to take these pictures, but then the reality of my situation began to rear its ugly head.

I had turned myself over to Sandra. Strapped to a gurney and hooked up to various machines, I was living my worst nightmare. I stretched out my fingers, curling them into fists, while trying to slip them from the straps that held me there.

My pulse sped up. I could feel it against the table where my wrist was bound too tightly. An alarm sounded on one of the machines.

"Sarah, you need to calm down. Your heart rate is too fast." Dr. Mendez placed her small hands on my shoulders and stared into my eyes. "Breathe, Sarah."

I bucked, but Dr. Mendez quickly placed a strap across my hips, keeping me immobile. She backed away, then turned and sprinted to an intercom on the wall. "Dr. Whitmeyer, come quickly."

I willed myself to slow my respiration. Deep breath in, deep breath out. I could do this. If I was the ultimate healer Sandra believed me to be—and what my father had created me to be—then I should possess abilities that would get me out of this predicament.

Sandra raced into the room, followed by Dr. DeWeese, who limped in with the help of a cane. The image of me shooting him in the leg at The Farm flashed through my mind.

I should have aimed higher.

They both stood over me and regarded me like a caged animal. Dr. DeWeese looked so much like Jack...

Jack. What had happened to him? How long had I been out? I searched Sandra's eyes for any sign that she had held up her end of the bargain and made him better. My heart constricted. The pain of missing him overwhelmed me.

I opened my mouth to speak, but couldn't.

Sandra smiled. "Oh, look, John. It wants to speak."

Dr. DeWeese leaned toward me, using his cane as support. A sneer touched the corners of his lips.

"Dr. Mendez, I would like for you to do the fMRI immediately," Sandra said. "We don't have a lot of time. It has to be complete before our guests arrive. Then I want her sedated and locked up. This lab needs to be running a completely normal operation before the Nature Conservancy arrives. They need to believe we're studying the effects of tropical plants on the treatment of chronic illness. Or some such shit."

If the Nature Conservancy would be here soon, it was already the next morning. I'd been out the entire night.

"Right away, ma'am. But we'll need her brain fully functional while I run the fMRI." When Sandra looked at her questioningly, she continued. "A functional MRI can only be done when the brain is in use. In order to measure the cerebral blood flow, I'll have to—"

Sandra held up a hand, effectively silencing Dr. Mendez. "Just do it."

I narrowed my gaze at Dr. DeWeese. Did he know how sick his son was? Would he care? I lowered my eyes to look at the area of his leg that I had injured with the rubber bullet. I saw through his khaki pants, his skin, and zeroed in on the healing kneecap. The muscles, ligaments, and bone structure surrounding the knee were surrounded by significant inflammation. The doctors in the room continued to speak about the tests and computer mapping of my DNA and neuronal activity while I used my mind to wrap a hand around Dr. DeWeese's patella. Then with a surge of mind power, I squeezed it with every ounce of strength I possessed.

Dr. DeWeese screamed out in agonizing pain. My eyes popped wider in surprise at what I had just done. He reached for his leg as he crumpled to the floor. I squeezed even harder, making him yell out louder.

Both Dr. Mendez and Sandra knelt beside him. After I let go of his knee and Dr. DeWeese stopped screaming, Sandra's head popped to attention. "We have to do this quickly. She's figuring out how to use more of her abilities."

I suppressed the smile of satisfaction that threatened to lift my lips. Instead, I leaned my head back and mentally brought up an image of my own brain for examination. My neurons fired in many shades of purple. Some neurons fired with a dark indigo hue, some glowed lavender, while others flashed almost a bright white, like a streak of lightning with purple edges.

I immediately saw the darkness in my frontal lobe. That same darkness ran in a straight line from the frontal lobe all the way to the tracker at the base of my skull. I was seeing the effect of the tracker, seeing precisely where it was suppressing my ability to speak. But Jonas had told me that he was able to control every aspect of his tracker—perhaps I could do the same. I found the spot on the tracker where the darkness was the greatest. With my mind, I closed off that part of the tracker's function, shutting down the message the tracker was sending to my frontal lobe. I knew instantly that I was able to speak again.

Jonas, where are you?

Nothing.

Jonas! Jack! Even if Jack hadn't been dying, he wouldn't have been able to hear me on a boat out in the middle of the ocean—but I had to try.

Dr. Mendez strapped my head down on the table. I wanted to slip inside her head and control her actions, but I decided to let her run her tests for now. At this point they were just taking pictures of my brain. I'd give them what they wanted, pretend to be helpless, and wait for my opportunity.

The fMRI machine was loud, and the vibrations practically caused a migraine. But I didn't fight them; I remained perfectly still. While the machine did its scan, I concentrated my focus on the straps across my ankles and wrists. I started with my wrists, slowly using my mind to undo the straps. I was surprised at how easily I loosened both straps; I had apparently gotten better and better at using telekinesis to move inanimate objects.

Since my legs stuck out of the machine, and I couldn't be sure that no one was watching, I left my ankle straps alone. And although I could slip my hands free, I left them loosely inside the straps.

Thirty minutes later, my body was brought back out of the cylinder. All three doctors were still in the room and staring at the images of my brain on the monitors.

"It'll take time to analyze these images," Sandra said.

"Are we going to keep her sedated forever while we finally get the answers we need?" Dr. DeWeese asked. He sat on the edge of a table, keeping most of his weight on his non-injured leg.

I could answer that question for him: absolutely not.

"If we have to." Sandra turned to Dr. Mendez. "How many more tests do we need?"

Dr. Mendez had admitted that my brain needed to be fully functioning in order to do the fMRI, yet they looked at me now like they thought I was a vegetable. I wanted to prove them wrong, but it was three against one, and since Sandra had injected herself with the mind-altering DNA matter, she'd been able to reject a clone's attempt to control her actions. Besides which, she was now protected from me by the Omega Directive. "We may already have all that we need. I got a lot done while she slept. I only needed her fully awake and functioning for the fMRI. I'd love to study her brain activity while she's in the process of healing another human, but otherwise I think we're all set."

It was almost fun to watch them decide what to do next—speaking as if I couldn't possibly comprehend the lengths they were going to extract information from me.

"Agreed. Sedate her," Dr. DeWeese said. "I don't need to constantly worry that she's getting inside my head while we convince the Nature Conservancy that we're a legitimate research lab."

Dr. Mendez pulled a syringe out of her pocket. My heart rate skyrocketed again, as noted by the annoying monitor beside me. I was just preparing to pull my hands free and stop her when there was a knock at the door. They all turned, and I took the opportunity to concentrate on loosening the strap across my hips and the ankle straps.

A security guard entered. "Dr. Whitmeyer, a boat is approaching. No one is answering our calls. What would you like us to do?"

"Could it be representatives from the Nature Conservancy or from the U.S. Fish and Wildlife?"

"I don't know, ma'am. I would think the feds would announce themselves."

"Well, take a dinghy out to the boat and see who's on board. Take several officers with you, but keep your weapons hidden unless necessary. Then report back to me immediately."

When Sandra and Dr. DeWeese turned back to me, I had successfully loosened all of the straps, but they didn't notice, and I remained perfectly still. I quickly slipped inside Dr. Mendez's head. *Dr. Mendez, please stick that needle into your own neck and sedate yourself.*

She did as I commanded, then collapsed to the floor.

Sandra rolled her eyes and pulled her smartphone out of her pocket. "Sarah, you don't want to play this game with us."

Dr. DeWeese backed up. He held his hands out, as if to tell me he wasn't armed, though I could see a Glock holstered at his hip.

I sat up and pushed off the hospital bed. "Oh, I assure you, this is no game." I would find a way to watch this woman suffer slowly.

"We still haven't healed Jack. You need us."

At this point, I was pretty sure that Sandra had no power to heal Jack. It was up to Jonas and me to do that. "You promised if I turned myself over, you'd reverse whatever it was you did to him."

She cocked her head and clucked her tongue against the roof of her mouth. "And you believed me. That's so sweet."

I slipped inside her head. *Sandra, please get the gun from Dr. DeWeese and point it at your head.*

"Your mind tricks don't work on me, Sarah. Remember?"

It was worth a try.

Dr. DeWeese had retreated and was now sitting at Dr. Mendez's computer, scrolling through images of my brain. Sandra began pushing buttons on her phone. "John? Do we have what we need?"

"I'm analyzing it now. The images look clear."

"I'm going to need you to analyze faster."

"I think I'm done. I'm uploading the information to you now."

Sandra smiled at me. "You and I both know that you were never going to become a part of my team. Such a shame, but you've become a liability to me." Her shoulders lifted and lowered in a lazy shrug.

She was going to terminate me. "Dr. Mendez said you didn't have everything." My panicked voice betrayed me.

"Dr. Mendez has a flair for the dramatics. Between the information we got from you at The Farm, and the information we've compiled here overnight, we no longer need you. Or any of the originals, for that matter."

Dr. DeWeese, I want you to stand and point your gun at Sandra.

He immediately did as I instructed.

Sandra laughed. "You can't make him hurt me."

"Oh no? Are you sure about that?" *Dr. DeWeese, I want you to shoot Sandra in the shoulder.* We'd find out if I could harm Sandra. I'd managed to break through other limitations on my abilities. And with each power I worked on, often with the help of Jonas, I became stronger.

Dr. DeWeese's hand shook. Droplets of sweat formed along his forehead and across his nose. But he did not shoot.

Sandra's smile grew. "As I was saying… Well, this has been fun, but now that I have the information I needed—"

"You think murdering us will solve all your problems?" I had been so naïve to ever think that Sandra wouldn't do away with all of us. Jack. Georgia. Me. The others would be next.

"Murder? I'm not planning on *killing* you." She laughed. "Now that I have the map of your brain, I can undo everything your father did to you when you were just a young child. You haven't wanted these healing abilities anyway, right? For the most part, you refuse to use them. And without your supernatural powers, you're not a threat. So don't worry: I'll probably let you live. You're still an intelligent person. You're me, for crying out loud. And with the proper tracker, you'll be another Maya. She's proven to be quite useful."

I reached out a hand to balance myself on the edge of the hospital bed as I took in that possibility. Could I part with my medical abilities? She was right, I hadn't wanted them. It seemed wrong that we could do things that had been meant for a higher power. But there was no way I would let Sandra control me like she did Maya.

"Now, let's see how your tracker is working before we wipe your brain clean." Sandra began typing something on her phone, while I considered the future this woman held in the palm of her hands. I was one stupid phone app away from being the normal teen I had always wished to be, back when I first discovered I was different.

If Sandra stole my healing abilities, maybe the rest of my mind powers would go, too. If I could escape from this place and remove the tracker, I'd finally be free to live a normal life, away from all of this mess that came with being a living science experiment. No one would ever want to get inside my head or kill me, because I would no longer have the special powers they coveted.

And I had the money to do whatever I wanted. I could help people—with or without the supernatural healing abilities.

My mind shifted to memories of the little boy in the emergency room at the University of Kentucky Hospital. He had lost so much blood, and I had been able to do a simple procedure to help him. It wasn't a life-threatening injury, but my abilities had helped him and his father.

And Jonas and Jack were both convinced that without the threat of the IIA and Sandra, we'd find our powers to be useful—life-changing, even. That, without the darkness, we'd bask in the light. We'd find beauty in something created by evil. With my money, we could turn Wellington into a school of future medical geniuses.

But what about Jack? What if he was gone from my life forever? Could I do anything without him? I swallowed hard as I stared down the cliff into despair.

I had risked everything by leaving Jack and coming to Palmyra. I could have healed him all along, and hadn't realized it. This was all my own fault for not accepting the reality of my destiny sooner. I wouldn't let the chance I took be for nothing. I wouldn't let Jack's sacrifice be in vain.

Now, I seemed to have enough knowledge and money to control my own destiny, and I could help others find theirs. I would find a way to make Jack proud of me.

I would fight back. If I could change a life—heal someone of a horrible disease or injury—I would do it. These supernatural abilities were a gift. They may have come from corrupt intentions, but I would find a way to use them for good.

I would not let Sandra take away any part of me. I was not hers to control or manipulate.

A strange sensation erupted at the back of my neck. My tracker had come to life. *Sarah, I would like for you to put Dr. Mendez on the bed there. It's bad manners to leave her on the dirty floor.*

The orders came through loud and clear. I knew it was a test. Yet I immediately realized that I didn't feel the least bit compelled to do as Sandra had ordered. My mind was stronger than anything she could manufacture.

Still, I couldn't let Sandra know that she didn't control me. Not yet. So I proceeded to do as Sandra directed. I lifted the good doctor from the floor, struggling with her since she was at least twenty pounds heavier than me.

"Help her, John," Sandra ordered. "Show Sarah that we can be a team if she cooperates."

Dr. DeWeese limped over. Keeping his injured leg straight, he bent at the waist and grabbed Dr. Mendez's feet while I slid my hands under her armpits. Together we lifted her to the bed. "You really are her pawn," I said with disgust.

Dr. DeWeese looked up, and the corners of his lips lifted in an evil grin. "You might think that." He stepped to Sandra and yanked the phone from her hands.

"John, what the hell are you doing?"

"I'm tired of you playing around with these clones. It's time to end this. The original clones have been nothing but pains in our asses. Do you really think that Jonas hasn't been helping her since she arrived on Palmyra?"

"I found no proof of that." Sandra actually sounded panicked. "Believe me, I searched. Besides, if he was helping her, she wouldn't be standing here."

She had a point.

"Now hand me the phone," she demanded with an outstretched hand.

Thank goodness Jonas had been smart enough to keep his eyes closed in the server room. Where the hell was he?

"Hand me the phone, John. What are you going to do, kill them all?" Sandra asked. She suddenly lunged at Dr. DeWeese, grabbing at the phone, but he easily held it out of her reach. To my surprise, she actually looked concerned.

"Like you murdered my father?" I added, my eyes fixed on Dr. DeWeese.

His grin grew. "Yes. Exactly like that. Except no fiery car bomb this time."

I clenched my fingers into fists, and mentally prepared to take John DeWeese out at the knees. But another knock at the door stopped me.

Two men in scrubs entered. "We have problems."

THIRTY-ONE

The island is surrounded. Military, it would seem. Navy. Ten ships in various locations off shore."

My mouth hung open as two IIA agents, disguised as lab techs, explained the situation to Jack's father and Sandra. There had to be some mistake. The military was not supposed to get involved.

"What do they want?" Sandra asked.

"They're not saying, but if it's the U.S. military, there are enough of them that they could take this entire island off the map if they wanted to."

While Sandra discussed the situation with the two agents, Dr. DeWeese continued to type on Sandra's phone. Was he killing the original clones? Removing my medical abilities? I had to do something. I wasn't ready to part with my medical powers. Not when it wasn't my choice. And I certainly wasn't going to let him hurt more of my friends.

Stop typing, Dr. DeWeese, I commanded, and he complied. I slipped into his brain and began diverting some of the blood flow from his frontal lobe, hopefully disrupting his problem-solving ability. Two could play at this frontal lobe game, and apparently the Omega Directive didn't prevent me from harming him.

I searched through his brain until I found the nerves connecting the prefrontal cortex with the thalamus, then used my mind to clamp down on the nerves, partially severing the connection and thereby inflicting a near lobotomy on Dr. DeWeese. *Put the phone away.*

He slid the phone in his pocket, and I directed my attention back to the conversation before me, looking for any hint that someone other than the military had come to help. I knew that if it came down to it, the military would take out this island if they even suspected that the clones being created or the trackers produced here were designed as weapons.

Sandra was still talking with the agents, oblivious to what had been going on between me and Dr. DeWeese. "You're IIA," she snapped, lifting her hands in frustration. "Surely there's something you can do!"

The man who appeared to be the spokesperson of the two took a deep breath. "Dr. Whitmeyer, our orders are to not get caught covering up what's going on at this facility. As far as we're concerned, the IIA has nothing to do with what's happening here."

"Well, isn't that just perfect. And what about the other boat approaching the island?"

"They were just members of your staff." The man's brows knitted together. He was confused about something. "They said they didn't hear us when we radioed them."

Strange, I thought.

"My staff? Who?"

Both men shrugged.

"Any sign of members of the Nature Conservancy?"

"None."

"I want to know if those boats get any closer or if you see anything strange from them. And I want men watching each and every boat. Something moves, I expect to hear about it."

"Yes, ma'am." The men left.

Only one thing comforted me in that exchange. I was pretty sure that if the military had intentions of coming on this island or of destroying the labs here, they would have done so already. Act first, take names later.

Sandra turned to face me again. "*You* did this. They're here because of you."

I smiled. "It doesn't matter what you do now. We're in the middle of the Pacific Ocean. There's no escape."

"Hand me the phone." She held out a hand to Dr. DeWeese, who just stared at her. His face had paled, and his eyes were unfocused and glazed over. Sandra didn't appear to realize that I was the reason for his silence—that thanks to me, his brain was barely functioning.

"What's wrong with you?" She pulled the phone from Dr. DeWeese's pocket, dialed a number, then raised it to her ear. "Seal up the main incubator lab. No one gets in." She hung up, typed something else, then turned again to me.

"Now, my dear Sarah, it's time for you to say goodbye to your supernatural gifts forever. Control is mine. You will be my puppet."

As she punched buttons on her phone, I took in a breath and prepared to tackle her. The Omega Directive had stopped me before, but maybe—maybe if I used every ounce of my mind power, I could overcome the Omega Directive and take her out. I had to try.

I lowered my shoulder and leaned forward. Just as I made the decision to launch myself at her, a loud boom broke through the quiet. The ground shook. Small vials on a nearby shelf clinked together like chimes.

Both Sandra and I turned our heads in the direction of the only window in the room. She darted to it and raised the blinds, giving us full view of a fiery explosion on the south side of the building.

I took in another breath as I waited for something more to happen. Was it the military? Were they obliterating Palmyra? Was I going to die right here, right now, along with everyone else on the island?

Sandra spun around and shoved me hard. I fell backward against the bed. A growl erupted from somewhere deep inside her chest, and she returned to punching buttons on her phone. After several seconds, she raised her head and just stared at me.

Was that it? Had she just wiped my DNA and my mind of all its special abilities?

I slipped inside Dr. DeWeese's brain. I could still see the damage I had inflicted. Would I be able to see his brain if I no longer had abilities? No. Whatever Sandra had just done, my mind, and my abilities, were still my own.

Just to be sure, I proceeded to change how the blood was flowing in Dr. DeWeese's brain. Not enough to do any damage, just to give him a slight headache—while maintaining the lobotomy already in place.

Dr. DeWeese touched a gentle hand to his head, and his brow remained crinkled in confusion.

Sandra looked from me to Dr. DeWeese and back. "What's happening?"

Suddenly a familiar presence slipped in and around my head like silk, and I welcomed it like I never had before.

Jack!

The door to the exam room burst open, and Jack, Jonas, and Briana bolted inside. Jonas marched straight up to Sandra and stopped in front of her. "Take one for the team, mommy dearest."

Jonas raised his rifle, and as the butt of the gun made contact with Sandra's face, she gasped, and her eyes bulged in a look of shock and disbelief I'd never seen.

She bent forward, cupping her injured cheekbone. "How did you do that?"

Jonas shoved her into a chair and proceeded to tie her to it. But I knew that what he had just accomplished was much more than an injury to the woman who'd delivered and raised him, but a direct annihilation of the Omega Directive.

Dr. DeWeese collapsed into a chair across from her, his eyes empty, lost.

I flew at Jack, jumping into his arms.

"Whoa." He stumbled backward, then leaned his face into my hair. "Miss me?"

My body began to shake as I cried into his neck. "I thought you were dead. I've been going out of my mind."

"You're not getting rid of me that easily. I'm here. As are several very influential people from the president's staff. Apparently you made quite an impression on his deputy chief of staff." He pulled his head away and glanced toward Jonas, whose lips tugged downward. Jack's head fell forward.

"What's wrong?" I searched their faces.

"I couldn't heal him." Regret filled Jonas's voice. "He's unconscious."

"What?" I clutched Jack's cheeks. "I don't understand."

Jack smiled weakly. "I'm sorry." He leaned his forehead against mine. "Kyle's got control of me. The yacht is close. But he can't keep it up much longer. He's losing his hold on me, and... Lexi, I'm fading."

Tears blurred my vision. "You tried everything?" I asked Jonas.

He nodded, looking away. "I was able to help Georgia, but Jack's condition is far worse. I... I'm sorry."

I searched Jack's eyes. *What do I do? I can't lose you.*

He stroked my hair. Our eyes were locked. *It's okay.*

Jack was giving me permission to let go, but I couldn't. I wouldn't. I shook my head. *It's not okay. Nothing about this would ever be okay.* If Jonas couldn't heal Jack, how was I supposed to?

"Lexi," Jonas said behind me. "You can do this. You have all the tools you need to heal him. You're the strongest of any of us."

Slipping my hand into Jack's, I pulled him over to the gurney. I eased him onto the bed, laid him flat on his back, and leaned over him. "I'm going to need Kyle to let go of you."

His eyes struggled to focus on mine. Reaching a hand to my cheek, he wiped the falling tears from my face. "I love you. I want the very best for you. Don't stop searching for the good in what we were created to do."

More tears streamed down my cheek and landed on his arm. "Never goodbye."

"Never goodbye. I'll see you soon." His head relaxed into the pillow, and his eyes closed.

~~~~~
~~~~~

The neurons inside Jack's head were firing, but at a sluggish rate. They were the color of a dull, smoky blue, unlike anything I had seen in his head in the past. Still, nothing looked out of place. I continued my scan down his neck and spine, checking carefully, vertebra by vertebra.

My heart pounded at an alarming pace, but all tears were gone. If I had any hope of Jack surviving, I had to get it together.

Jonas entered my mind. He was watching how I searched through Jack's body. *You can do this. I know you've got the power to help him, Lex.*

When you inflicted him with this illness, what exactly did you do?

She had me play with the bacteria that are produced naturally in our bodies. I moved it around as she directed. Through his organs, along his spine, and even into his legs.

I turned my attention back to Jack's body. His brain looked normal other than the fading neurons and low activity. I examined his other organs—heart, lungs, kidneys, stomach, spleen, liver. Everything looked normal. Nothing looked diseased, but his white blood cell count was overwhelming.

Lexi. Kyle's voice eased inside my head. *Seth says that Jack's body is acting like it has late-stage leukemia, even though it doesn't have any cancer at all. His immune system and his body's ability to fight infection are failing.*

What do I do? I worked hard to keep my voice even and calm.

He says you need to do a stem cell transplant.

A what? How was I supposed to do that? That would require a perfect match. I didn't have time—

My head snapped to attention. I turned to Jonas. "Bring John DeWeese back."

While I'd been examining Jack, Secret Service agents had arrived with a member of the president's staff and had taken Dr. DeWeese and Sandra into their custody. Now, Jonas and a man I didn't recognize led Dr. DeWeese back into the room and sat him in a chair beside Jack. The expression on DeWeese's face still screamed of confusion.

"Miss Matthews?" the man with Jonas said. "The deputy chief of staff is waiting to meet with you."

"Well she'll just have to be patient," I snapped. I wasn't meeting with anyone until I had Jack back.

~~~~~

Seth, through Kyle's mindspeaking, had explained everything I needed to know to move the stem cells from Dr. DeWeese's bone marrow into Jack's bloodstream. Briana searched the medical cabinets for supplies we needed while I stared at Jack's lifeless body, searching for the inspiration I needed to believe I could heal him and not do more damage. His eyes were closed, his face pale, but he was void of any stress or pain, thanks to Jonas.

Lexi, Kyle mindspoke, a warning in his voice. *As you do this, you'll need to monitor his organs. Watch for any damage to his heart, lungs, kidney, and liver.*

No pressure, right?

You need to get started. You're running out of time.
~~~~~

Jonas placed a hand on my shoulder. "I'll watch his organs for any damage while managing his pain. You concentrate on the transplant."

I played with the blond hair that lay across Jack's forehead, moist from a fever that broke and spiked intermittently. Leaning over, I brushed a kiss across his lips, chapped and dry from exposure to sun and tropical breezes. *I won't let you go, Jack. But I can't do this alone. You have to fight.* I kissed him again. "Never goodbye," I whispered against his mouth.

Briana stood patiently beside me with a tray of instruments we might need.

I took a deep breath. "Let's do this."

I began by administering a bag of IV fluids into one of Jack's arms to prevent dehydration during the process. Briana did the same to Dr. DeWeese.

Next, I took another needle and inserted it into Dr. DeWeese's opposite arm, then did the same to Jack's, attaching a tube between them.

Now it was time to see what kind of healing I was capable of—a true test of my creation. With my mind, I searched through Dr. DeWeese's body and located the stem cells that Seth had described to me—stem cells that were capable of fighting infection, capable of multiplying into the healthy cells that Jack's body needed in order to take over and fight the disease.

I directed the stem cells into the plastic tube and slid them into Jack's blood. I massaged and finessed the cells Jack needed in hopes that they would travel to the parts of the body that needed them most. Luckily, Dr. DeWeese—the person Jack had been cloned from—couldn't have been a more perfect match.

What I was doing was so much more advanced than anything I had ever done before. Sweat formed on my brow and dripped down into my eyes. I blinked it away. But despite the effort, the mental strain, the intense concentration, it felt right. It felt... natural. Like I had been meant to help people. And I supposed I had.

I knew I couldn't cure *all* the ills of the world, but I could cure *this* one. I could save this one person. I could save Jack.

Jonas looked up. "Lexi, his heart is slowing. The blood isn't getting to his brain quickly enough."

I looked from Jonas to Jack. "C'mon, Jack. Don't do this to me." I redirected my attention to his heart, massaging it with my mind to keep it pumping.

Jack gasped, his breathing becoming labored.

"We're losing him," Jonas said.

"No we're not!" I pumped Jack's heart for him, urging the blood to enter and leave and travel on toward the brain. *I've got you, Jack. Don't you leave me.*

And then I felt his heart kick on its own. Even though my hand wasn't literally touching Jack's heart, I could sense it taking over, doing the job it was meant to do.

"Good job, Lexi. He's stabilizing."

I let out a sigh of relief.

I returned my attention to the stem cells. They, too, were doing their job, moving to the infected cells and squeezing them out of existence, cleaning his bloodstream and freeing it of all disease.

I had done all that I could do.

But would it be enough? During the process I had felt confident, powerful, but now the reality of Jack's situation hit me.

Even with everything I had done, even with Jonas's help and Seth's expertise... Jack's body was weak. Had I acted quickly enough? Would the stem cells be able to reverse the damage he had already suffered? Had his brain received enough oxygen throughout the procedure? Could Jack summon the strength he would need to recover?

I was afraid I might need a miracle for Jack to wake up normal again.

But whatever happened next... it simply wasn't up to me anymore.

~~~~~

A procedure that would have taken infinitely more preparation and much longer to perform in a typical hospital setting was completed in less than an hour.

"Now what?" Briana asked. She appeared tired and disheveled.

Jonas leaned against the far wall. His shoulders drooped forward.

"Now we wait." I slid my hand under Jack's, and sitting in a chair beside his bed, laid my head on his stomach. I couldn't imagine my life if this didn't work. I didn't want to. But I wouldn't let him down.

I don't know how long it took before I drifted off to sleep.

~~~~~

Something woke me. I glanced around the room, looking for movement or a sound that could have disturbed my restless sleep. Jonas sat against a wall. Briana lay across his lap.

Jonas raised his head. His eyes were bloodshot.

The room was silent except for the blowing sound of the air conditioning.

Then it happened again—the smallest squeeze to my hand. I jumped to my feet, knocking the chair over behind me, but not removing my hand from Jack's. I searched his face. The coloring in his cheeks had transformed from a dull gray to a nice tropical suntan. His nose was tinted pink from recent sun exposure.

Come back to me, I whispered with my mind.

He squeezed my hand harder, but still a bit feebly. *Where am I?*

Palmyra. Do you remember anything?

His closed eyes tightened. *I remember blowing something up.*

A happy sob escaped my lips. *Boys. That's what you* would *remember.*

Hey! I blew up a cell tower to save you from Sandra's wrath.

Thank you. I laughed. *What about the satellite connection?*

We couldn't fix it. Your mom is going nuts.

He lifted a hand then, reaching out until he found my cheek, brushing at the moisture. His eyes fluttered open.

"Hi." I leaned into his touch.

"Told you I would see you later."

I laughed through another sob. "That you did." I swallowed hard. "You scared me."

"Ditto." He leaned back and stared up at the ceiling. "That's some healing power you've got there. I'm feeling much better, I think."

I laughed again, out of relief. "Georgia?"

"She's doing okay; Jonas saved her. She's back on the boat, recovering. Fred's with her."

Jonas and Briana stood and made their way over to us. "Welcome back, man," Jonas said. "I'm so sorry."

Jack reached out and grasped his friend's hand. "You kept my girl safe. And you did what you had to. You're forgiven."

"How did you find me?" I asked.

He tugged on my braid. "The ribbon, remember? I'm considering permanently implanting GPS into your hair."

"Sandra was going to strip me of my abilities." I shuddered. "I couldn't get the tracker communications routed to the satellite. I was so scared, Jack. I don't even know why she didn't simply terminate me along with the rest of the clones with trackers."

"We took out the cell tower."

I grinned. "I saw the big boom. I'm glad you managed to have a little fun while I was being treated like a monkey in a cage."

A pensive expression shadowed his face. "Did you know there are more than a hundred cloned humans living in the building behind us?"

"I knew there were a lot. Which reminds me. Now that you're awake, I need to meet with the people who came to see what was happening on this atoll. The president could have already launched a missile to take us all out for all I know." I stood and kissed Jack on the forehead. "I'll see you in a few minutes."

He nodded. *Never goodbye.*

Before I left the room, I turned to Jonas. "What's going to happen to Sandra and Dr. DeWeese?"

"A plane landed thirty minutes ago. I was told they'll be moved to a special high-security facility in Hawaii for now." Jonas smiled. "Their days of experimenting on humans are over."

THIRTY-TWO

"Hi, Ms. Meyers." I shook the hand of the president's deputy chief of staff. "So nice of you to come to Palmyra." She and I stood inside a meeting room at the end of a hallway of laboratories.

"Well, Miss Matthews, this is quite a facility."

"Yes, ma'am. And it sounds like you have an impressive military fleet awaiting orders from the president on what to do about this place."

She waved her hand. "Oh, them? That's nothing. Just a few vessels that didn't mind sitting around this island for a day or two. They don't even know why they're here."

I smiled. "What about the Conservancy?"

"We have convinced the Conservancy that private ownership of the atoll is a good idea. They, of course, will continue to own their portion of the island and protect it as a nature preserve, but at the direction of the president, they understand that the new owners are a nonprofit organization created for the protection of 'animal life.' The members that are here now have toured the island and have seen exactly what we needed them to see. There's a slew of paperwork that will iron out the details, but as far as the president is concerned, this island will run privately—although still under U.S. law, you understand. As long as you obey the laws of your country, Ms. Matthews, this island is yours."

"What about Dr. DeWeese and Sandra Whitmeyer?"

"They have been taken into custody and charged with multiple federal crimes. I doubt they'll ever see the outside of a prison again."

"Thank you, Ms. Meyers."

"Don't thank me. I'm not sure what you're getting yourself into by purchasing this island, but I wish you the best of luck. I can see that you're a smart young woman, and you seem to have a great team behind you."

"That I do."

~~~~~

"Are you saying that no one beyond the deputy chief of staff knows exactly what's happening here on Palmyra?"

Jonas sat on a log at the edge of the tree line facing the ocean. His eyes were hidden behind a pair of dark Prada sunglasses.

I knew Jonas was hiding more than exhaustion from the events of the past twenty-four hours. He'd been fighting pangs of guilt for what had almost happened to Jack and for what Sandra had put me through.

"That's right." I leaned backward against Jack. His arms were circled around me, and he drew figure eights on my arm. "I've been assured that the president understands just enough to know that any mention of the goings-on here needs to be buried deep in classified documents. And the FBI agents Coach called to Wellington were his trusted friends. Even so, we were careful about what we actually told them."

"Do you trust them?"

"As much as I trust anyone." I tried to laugh.
~~~~~

Jack came around beside me and faced the ocean.

You okay? I asked. I inhaled the salty air. The soothing sound of the waves wasn't enough to cut through the tension that surrounded the four of us.

Better than okay. I'm alive, thanks to you.

"So what happens now?" Jack asked aloud. "The IIA agents will be taken to a Secret Service field office and questioned. But what about the doctors and lab techs that are still here?" I noticed that Jack had avoided asking the questions we all were afraid to talk about: What happens to the clones here on Palmyra? Do we take them to Wellington? And what about the ones in incubators who have yet to be born?

Jonas drew shapes in the sand with a long stick. "I've been inside every one of their heads over the last few weeks while Sandra thought I was under her control. The ones who are loyal to Sandra and John will be taken into custody as well. The ones I think I can trust are staying."

The tropical breeze blew hair across my face. I tucked the loose strands behind my ears. "Bree? You're awfully quiet."

Briana had been sitting quietly, several feet away from Jonas. At my words, she seemed to come back to our conversation from some faraway place, but still didn't say anything. She, too, hid behind a pair of oversized sunglasses.

Jonas reached a hand out to her, urging her to move closer. She did, but didn't take his hand. Instead, he put an arm around her shoulders, tucked her beside him, and kissed her temple. When he looked up, he met Jack's eyes, then mine, and said, "I've decided to stay here on Palmyra."

That explained Briana's melancholy. She swiped her fingers across her cheek and under her sunglasses, appearing to clear tears from beneath her eyes.

"Are you sure you want to do that?" I asked.

"Who else is going to do it?"

I glanced back toward the ocean. I didn't know how to answer him, so I walked over and knelt before him. I wrapped my arms around his neck. "Thank you." It was what I'd hoped would happen, but I couldn't possibly have asked him to do it.

When I stood back up, Jack pulled me into his arms again, and I let him. Anything to be close. "Jonas, I'll stay until we know why the Delta clones are dying. I'll do what I can to heal them."

"*We'll* stay," Jack corrected, giving me a squeeze.

Briana looked up, holding a hand in front of her face to shield her eyes from the sun. "Where do I fit into all of this?"

I smiled. "You're one of us, Bree. Where do you want to fit in?"

The sound of running footsteps stopped Bree from answering. An out-of-breath agent stopped when he saw us. "Where did she go?"

Briana and Jonas stood, and Jack and I walked closer to the agent. The muscles in my shoulders tightened in dread. "Where did *who* go?" I asked, my heart rate already at a steep climb.

"Sandra Whitmeyer. One minute I had her, the next minute she was gone."

"Shit. Addison." I shrugged out of Jack's hold.

We ran toward the airstrip where a plane was supposed to be taking off any minute with Sandra, Dr. DeWeese, Maya,

Addison, and Sandra's followers. Jonas and Bree followed the fed closely. Jack and I brought up the rear; Jack was still weakened by his illness.

Suddenly, I stopped. "Jack, I know where she's gone. I've got to stop her."

I turned and took off running in the other direction.

"Lexi, wait!" I heard Jack yell.

I knew he would eventually catch up to me, but I didn't have time to wait. I entered the main building from the side entrance and sprinted up the stairs and down the long hallway. When I arrived at the tracker room, the door was ajar.

Sandra sat at one of the computers, typing furiously, looking up every so often at the monitor in front of her.

"Move away from the computers, Sandra."

She looked up, but didn't stop typing. "Oh, good, you're here. How wonderful to see you again, Sarah."

I examined her face. The area around her right cheekbone was swollen and starting to bruise. "Looks like Jonas nailed you pretty good. I'm afraid you're going to have a nice shiner to go with that swollen cheek by tomorrow."

"He should never have been able to hurt me like that."

She was speaking of the Omega Directive, of course. Jonas had explained how he'd been able to use his mind to get past that constraint. Our minds had been overcoming obstacles left and right recently.

Sandra stopped typing and turned to face me. "Do you have any idea how long I've worked to create the perfect healer, Sarah?"

Surely Jonas and the agents would find us here any second. I decided to stall, to keep distracting her from whatever it was she was doing on the computer. "No. A long time, I guess."

"I was going to be the one who saved the world from disease and life-threatening injuries."

"That's very noble of you." I eased closer. "Why couldn't you have worked toward that goal without killing innocent people?"

"Innocent people? I haven't killed any innocent people. Everyone I've terminated was guilty of something."

"Oh really? And what was my dad guilty of?"

"He kept things from me. You, and the other clones he knew about. And when I discovered Wellington, he planned to hide you and the rest of the clones again." She started to turn back to the computer.

I held out both hands. "And what about my friend Dani? What did *she* ever do to you?"

Sandra's lips thinned into a tight line. "Danielle Gray. Daughter of Victoria and Samuel Gray. Her spinal cord was severed when she was ten years old when a drunk driver struck her mom's car. She would never walk or use her arms again."

"What?" I had never heard any such story. "That is a one-hundred-percent lie." I balled my fingers into fists.

"I beg your pardon. One-hundred-percent *truth*. Your father knew about it. He let the Grays hide their daughter at Wellington after I healed her injury. They told everyone that their daughter died from her injuries so that they could keep what I did a secret."

"Why would they keep it a secret?" The blood in my veins coursed like turbulent rapids. I walked slowly toward Sandra.

"Because what I did was very controversial. Genius, an amazing medical miracle, but 'morally questionable,' whatever that means." She shrugged. "I took stem cells from a clone that was a compatible match to your best friend. The clone died after the surgery, but your friend lived. In fact, not only did she live, she thrived." Sandra sneered. "And then they hid my miracle-working ability from the world. I didn't know she had survived until I found you both at Wellington. You can imagine my surprise."

At that moment, all I wanted to do was wrap my hands around Sandra's neck. The feeling was so intense that I actually imagined doing it. And as I did so, Sandra suddenly struggled to breathe. My mind was smashing through the barriers she had constructed.

"So, you see," she said between gasps. "She was most certainly not innocent. And her parents deserved to suffer."

I reached up and pulled a ruby clip from my hair. I could paralyze Sandra for a long time with the liquid from this pin. I stared down at it while keeping my telekinetic hold around Sandra's neck.

She stared wide-eyed. "What are you doing?" she asked with a shocked voice, refusing to accept that she wasn't invincible.

I cocked my head. Could I kill her? I could probably justify it. I glanced up at the video screens and nodded toward them. "What were you planning to do?"

"I've switched all the trackers over to satellite. I'm going to pull the plug on you and the rest of the clones." She started to turn toward the keyboard again, and I tightened the grip my mind had around her neck, stopping her.

I looked down at the pitiful hairpin in my hand and tossed it aside. Instead, I slipped inside Sandra's head and weaved in and around the various sections of her brain. Her neural activity was like nothing I'd ever seen. Hot orange, like a raging bonfire, swirled throughout her frontal lobe, the part of the brain tied to acts of violence and aggression. It was like peeking into the depths of hell. I had fully accepted my ability to fix injuries and diseases, but it had never occurred to me to cure *this*. Could it ever be possible to cure evil?

Images of Sandra's terrible acts washed over me. I was overwhelmed by conflicting emotions, and then a mental picture came into focus—and I knew in that instant that she would never stop trying to inflict evil.

In my mind's eye, I pictured firefighters hosing down a burning building. With a surge of power from my own mind, I transformed the orange flame-like flashes of Sandra's neurons to red, then green, and then black.

Completely entranced by dousing the evil fire of Sandra's soul, I lost track of my surroundings. Suddenly, I was tackled to the floor from behind. I screamed as I hit the hard tile.

"I won't let you hurt her!" Addison had me pinned. Sandra slumped out of her chair, and Addison left me to scramble over to her. She gathered Sandra's head into her lap. "What did you *do* to her?" She stroked Sandra's hair. "I'll fix it. I promise."

I stood up and backed away, confused by Addison's intense reaction. I heard footsteps behind me, and turned to see Jonas, Jack and several agents enter the room, staring at Addison, who rocked Sandra's limp body back and forth.

The agents approached Sandra and Addison with slow, calculated steps. I could have predicted what would happen next.

The agents reached down and started to reach for Addison—and she disappeared. The agents turned in frantic circles, looking for her, but I knew she was gone.

One of the agents spoke into his two-way radio. "We're going to need a stretcher in the large upstairs lab."

Jonas and Jack stared at me open-mouthed for a brief eternity before I turned and exited the server room. Neither questioned what I had done to Sandra.

THIRTY-THREE

Two weeks later...

The Wednesday before Thanksgiving was chilly but bearable. The seasons were changing, and the cold November air had left bare the many trees lining the Roslin Farm's roads and fences. Though the trees appeared naked and vulnerable, the seasons that came before winter prepared them for a time of rest.

The Roslin Farm was my home now, I supposed, as I walked along the drive from the house to the fence line. Jack and I, along with Briana and Kyle, had decided to return to Kentucky to finish our senior year of high school at Wellington, but a long weekend away from school was certainly in order. We figured we deserved a day off from class, and who was going to stop us? I owned the school, after all.

Alyson and Seth stayed behind at Palmyra to help Jonas right Sandra's moral and ethical medical atrocities, so we had the house to ourselves. Separate bedrooms, though, at Alyson's insistence.

I gripped my down jacket tighter. The gold scarf around my neck protected my skin from the brisk late autumn air.

Jack rode along the fence line on the back of Cheriana. She whinnied as they approached, and when he pulled back on the reins and stopped Cheriana in front of me, she snorted and pawed at the ground in her version of "Hello." I climbed up on the fence. After giving Jack a quick kiss, I climbed on Cheriana in front of him.

"Briana, Kyle, Georgia, and Fred are coming over Thursday," I said. "I'm thinking I'll make a turkey."

Jack chuckled. "You don't 'make' a turkey. You roast a turkey."

"You're in charge of mashed potatoes." I smiled. "I hate peeling potatoes. And I don't want to know how much butter you put in them."

"You've spent a lot of time with Briana since we got back. How does she seem? Has she spoken to Jonas?"

I nodded. "She'll be okay. She knows she needs to finish school. And she wants to learn more about her abilities. Jonas isn't going anywhere."

Jonas was fighting his own demons on Palmyra. He was still working through his feelings of guilt for hurting Jack and Georgia, and like the rest of us, he was trying to figure out what role he should play in our advanced world of medical research and what he truly wanted out of life. For now, he was determined to do what he could for Sandra's clones—humans who knew no other life than what she had taught them inside her cold, sterile laboratories.

Jack's arms circled around me. He clucked his tongue to the roof of his mouth and led Cheriana away from the fence. "You think the Delta clones have a chance?"

"I think a lot of them will survive." My eyes watered as Jack picked up speed and the cool air hit my face. With Seth's and Alyson's help, we'd done the best we could. We'd discovered a lot of mutated cells, a terrible byproduct of Sandra's flawed attempt to recreate what she, Dr. DeWeese, Alyson, and my dad had produced all those years ago. I still struggled with the number of viable embryos and live humans who had died at

Sandra's hands. "There's just so much that can go wrong when we try to duplicate something that's a miracle in the first place."

"And when you add a heavy dose of crazy to the science..."

"Sandra Whitmeyer was something beyond insane. She was..." I shuddered. *Evil.* I snuggled into Jack's embrace. We rode around the farm and explored the entire property, getting to know the land my father had left me.

"It's amazing: your mom has more security on this farm than all of Wellington." He pointed to the double-wired electric fence in addition to the plank fencing on the back of the property. "She's got video cameras with motion detector sensors installed for every possible angle. No one is getting on this farm without her knowing about it."

"I guess we should feel safe, then." I leaned back into his chest.

"*Do* you feel safe?" The warmth of his breath feathered against my cheek.

"When you're with me, I do." I was still having nightmares almost every night, replaying the many ways Sandra had manipulated and tormented the human clones she'd created. And worse, I was still haunted by memories of her power to destroy any one of us whenever the whim struck.

"She can't hurt us anymore." Jack squeezed his thighs against mine and held me tighter as Cheriana walked along a stream that ran through the property. "The best way to get back at everyone who wreaked so much havoc on our lives is to go out and *live.*"

"Which is why I have something to tell you."

"Oh, yeah?" I felt his body go rigid against mine.

I shifted my body so that I could look him in the eyes. "I've been accepted into Brown University's pre-med program for next fall."

Jack's face remained expressionless. "You have, have you?"

I turned back around. A wind picked up and bit at my cheeks.

"Brown, huh," Jack said as if he were trying it out on his tongue. "You know it gets cold in Rhode Island."

We rode in silence for a bit longer before Jack directed Cheriana back to the barn. He dismounted, then helped me down, letting me slide down the length of his body.

I backed up and sat on a bench while he took care of the equipment. "You didn't ask if I was planning on going."

Eyeing me briefly, Jack tossed some grain in Cheriana's food container. "I'm trying to decide how I feel about it, first." He held out his hand to me. Brown wasn't a school Jack had applied to.

We held hands as we walked up toward the back of the house. As we neared, I noticed that someone had lit the large fire pit on the stone patio. I looked up at Jack, and he winked at me. "Thought a cozy evening outside might be nice. But first, I have a gift for you."

"You know I hate surprises."

"Not a surprise. A lost treasure."

I quirked an eyebrow. "Well, when you put it that way."

Jack disappeared inside the house for a moment and returned with a long skinny package wrapped in white paper with a pretty green ribbon. "It's a belated birthday present." He tilted his head from side to side. "Partly."

I smiled, then held the present to my ear and gave it a little shake. It made a nice rattle.

"Go ahead, open it."

I tore through the wrapping, then slowly removed the lid from the silver box. "My necklace!" My hand went instinctively to my neck where my starfish necklace used to hang. "But it's different."

Jack reached in the box and took out the silver chain that now held not just one, but three charms. "I searched the yacht for your necklace after you left—tore the boat apart, to be honest." He grinned. "I finally found it under the dresser in your cabin. The clasp was broken, and it had found its way behind one of the dresser legs. Then, during the week we spent on Palmyra, I found this piece of sea glass."

I studied the frosted green piece of glass—smooth and uniquely shaped. "A gem of the sea," I whispered. "My father taught me about sea glass years ago. He was a lover of all things from the ocean."

"I had the jeweler add the pearl."

"Another treasure of the ocean."

He nodded. I turned around and let Jack put the necklace on me, then faced him again. "Thank you," I whispered. "I love it."

We snuggled into the large chaise lounge under an oversized comforter. I lay across his body, my cheek pressed against his fleece pullover. "So, have you decided?" he asked at last.

"Yes."

When he said nothing else, I strained my neck to look up at him. His head was propped up by a bent arm. He leaned forward and placed a kiss gently across my lips.

"Fine." I sat up. He kept a hand on my leg and drew nervous circles on my thigh. "Here's what I'm thinking," I began. "I know I'm supposed to be this strong, independent girl."

"Woman," he corrected. I quirked a brow at him, and he shrugged. "It sounds better. More mature."

"Okay, a strong, independent *woman*. And most high school students are eager to go off to college—to study and experience and figure out what we want to do with the rest of our lives. We're supposed to be just reckless enough to learn who we really are."

"Let me guess... You've decided to give up your life of recklessness?"

I poked him in the ribs, and he flinched. "Ha ha." I grabbed his hand. "I know I'm not supposed to follow a boy off to college—"

"Man."

"Stop." I laughed. "And I'm not supposed to want a *man* to follow *me*. And then there's Wellington to consider. Like, what are my responsibilities where the school's concerned?"

"Seth has already agreed to travel back and forth between Palmyra and Wellington. And you've got Dean Fisher and Coach Williams. And your mom."

"Right. I know." It was a foreign feeling to have so many people around me who cared and wanted what was best for me. "But none of them share our abilities. Think about how much easier it will be for the clones at Wellington to learn what powers they have with us to guide them. Think about the months and years of confusion they could skip with our help."

"Why can't you just say it?" he asked.

I pulled in a deep breath and let it out slowly. "I think I have to stay near Wellington. And attend the University of Kentucky." I fidgeted with the corner of the blanket. "I don't expect you to stay with me. We've been through so much, and you deserve to go out into the world and find your own way. You need to—"

He raised up and cut off my words by covering my lips with his. When he pulled back, his eyes captured mine. "I need you to listen to me now. And I don't want you to say anything."

I nodded.

"I've watched you practically die several times. And now you've seen me on the brink of death."

Moisture pooled in my eyes.

"You saved my life." He cupped my face as the tears spilled over. "I don't think two people can look death and evil in the face the way we have and not come out of it with a renewed sense of purpose."

I leaned into his touch. "Just spit it out, will ya?"

The flames of the fire reflected off the blue of his eyes as he pinned me with his intense gaze. "I go where you go."

I waited several beats while his words sank in. "Are you sure?"

He leaned his head back and laughed. "Of course I'm sure. I've always been sure. I knew the moment I saw you standing outside the Wellington swimming pool, dripping with chlorine and water. I knew the moment you tried to get out of showing me around that first day. I knew the first time I heard your voice inside my head. I've always known."

"Okay, then it's settled." I lay back down and stared up at the sky. And as Jack held me in his arms, I dreamed of a future—a future where darkness is silenced by science and love.

A Note From the Author

There is more *Mindspeak* coming...

Thank you for joining Lexi and Jack on this journey of self-discovery. Though Lexi's trilogy concludes with *Mindsurge*, the characters of the *Mindspeak* world have more adventures ahead of them, beginning with Kyle's story coming spring 2015.

Be sure to sign up for my free newsletter—A Piece of My Mind—at http://heathersunseri.com/newsletter to hear about this and future releases. I only send out newsletters when I have important news to share. I respect your privacy and would never share your information.

Now that you've finished reading the *Mindspeak* trilogy, please consider recommending it to a friend or leaving a review on any of the bookseller sites. Word-of-mouth and reviews are the greatest ways to help other readers discover new books. I would truly appreciate it. If you do review any of my books, please send me an email at heather@heathersunseri.com so that I can personally thank you.

Happy Reading!
Heather

ACKNOWLEDGEMENTS

John 3:16. My son's favorite Bible verse.

Many people helped me on the journey to bring *Mindsurge* to life.

Mike. You never cease to amaze me with your selflessness in putting others first. I seriously couldn't do what I do without you. Thank you for always being my first reader. For always helping me with cover design and photographic marketing needs. For everything. I love you.

Jessica Patch and Laura Pauling. You see my writing before you and other angels step in and raise it from despair.

David Gatewood. I'm blessed to call you my editor. You are my lead angel.

To my early readers who are willing to search and destroy all pesky typos. To Jenny Kays, Connie Boyce, Toni Congleton, Elizabeth Nelson, and Joy Soper.

To Dawn Duncan. You are my rock. Your near daily texts always give me the lift I need. Thank you for knowing a Samoan Navy officer who could tell me how long it would take to get from Hawaii to Palmyra Atoll in the middle of the Pacific Ocean by boat.

To Heather Plunkett. For cover design. Mike and I know how hard it was to deal with Lexi's hair on that cover. We appreciate your hard work.

Last but certainly not least. To the Kentucky Indie Writers. Every single one of you is simply amazing. The support and encouragement that you offer me is incredible. You are my water cooler.

ABOUT THE AUTHOR

Heather Sunseri was raised on a tiny farm in one of the smallest towns in thoroughbred horse country near Lexington, Kentucky. After high school, she attended Furman University in Greenville, South Carolina, and later graduated from the University of Kentucky with a degree in accounting. Always torn between a passion for fantasy and a mind for the rational, it only made sense to combine her career in accounting with a novel-writing dream.

Heather now lives in a different small town on the other side of Lexington with her two children and her husband, Mike, the biggest Oregon Duck fan in the universe. She is a recovering CPA, and when she's not writing, she spends her time tormenting her daughter's cat, Olivia, and loving on her son's Golden Retriever, Jenny.

Heather loves to hear from readers. Please sign up for her newsletter—*A Piece of My Mind*—to hear when future novels are released by following this link: http://heathersunseri.com/newsletter. You can also connect with her in several other ways:

Heather Sunseri
P.O. Box 1264
Versailles, KY 40383

Web site: http://heathersunseri.com
Blog: http://heathersunseri.com/blog/
Email: heather@heathersunseri.com
Facebook: http://www.facebook.com/heathersunseri.writer
Twitter: @HeatherSunseri

Photo by Candace Sword

CPSIA information can be obtained
at www.ICGtesting.com
Printed in the USA
BVOW03s0717090717
488883BV00001B/50/P